D0405102

BIAP Interview No. 12
Host Name: Paul Pelizzarro
BIAP Name: Frank Juskit
Length of Interview: fifty-seven minutes
Interpretation: None. See video.
Comments/Personal Reactions/Other: I am, as usual, both saddened by the death and repelled by the patient's actions, by my dutiful response; in fact, by the nature of the work: the tricks we play and the patients themselves, comic in their weakness, horrible in their desire for life and the flash of ardor that ends them. . . . Green fireballs lodged in their eye sockets, their minds going nova with the joy of a lifetime crammed into a few minutes. Still, I find that the patients in their compressed, excited states are far more interesting than any of my acquaintances, and I believe that even relative failures such as Mr. Juskit would—had they lived a full span at this accelerated pace—have accomplished a great deal more than they have related. Their repellent aspects, in my opinion, are outweighed by the intensity of their expression. For this reason I wish to withdraw my resignation tendered yesterday, October 24, 1986.

Therapist's Signature: *Jocundra Verret*

Staff Evaluation: *Let's assign Verret to a slow-burner as soon as possible, but not just the first one that comes along. I'd like to see a photograph and data sheet on each new slow-burner, and from that material I'll make an appropriate selection.*
                                        A. Edman

GREEN EYES
LUCIUS SHEPARD

ACE SCIENCE FICTION BOOKS
NEW YORK

All characters in the book are fictional and any resemblance between any person living or dead is entirely coincidental; all names are either products of the author's imagination or are used fictionally, and have no correspondence with any actual person, event, or place.

GREEN EYES

An Ace Science Fiction Book / published by arrangement with the author

PRINTING HISTORY
Ace Original / May 1984

All rights reserved.
Copyright © 1984 by Lucius Shepard
Introduction copyright © 1984 by Terry Carr
Cover art by Katheryn Holt
This book may not be reproduced in whole or in part,
by mimeograph or any other means, without permission.
For information address: The Berkley Publishing Group,
200 Madison Avenue, New York, N.Y. 10016

ISBN: 0-441-30274-2

Ace Science Fiction Books are published by The Berkley Publishing Group,
200 Madison Avenue, New York, New York 10016.
PRINTED IN THE UNITED STATES OF AMERICA

This book is for my Mother
For all the usual and well-deserved reasons,
And for Kim,
for reasons not so usual.

Acknowledgments: Thanks to Marta Randall for shelter, to Mary Steedly for fast fingers, to Laura Scroggins for the bacteria, to James Wolf for lots of stuff, and especially to Terry for the opportunity.

I have no more desire to express
The old relationships of love fulfilled
Or stultified, capacity for pain,
Nor to say gracefully all that poets have said
Of one or other of the old compulsions.
For now the times are gathered for confession.

Alun Lewis

INTRODUCTION

by Terry Carr

If you're getting a little tired of reading science fiction novels that are just like the ones you read last month or last year, this book is for you. It's published under the label "An Ace Science Fiction Special" because it's just that, something fresh and different and, we believe, a novel superior to most of those you'll find today.

I'll tell you why I think so a little later; first, though, I should say a little about the Ace Science Fiction Specials series.

The SF Specials program is specifically designed to present new novels of high quality and imagination, books that are as exciting as any tale of adventures in the stars and as convincing as the most careful extrapolation of the day after tomorrow's science. Add to that a rigorous insistence on literary quality—lucid and evocative writing, fully rounded characterization, and strong underlying themes (but not Messages)—and you have a good description of the stories you'll see in this series.

The publishers of Ace Books believe that there are many readers today who are looking for such books, at a time when so many science fiction novels are simply skilled (or not so skilled) rehashings of plots and ideas that have been popular in the past. Science fiction by its very nature ought to tell stories that are new and unusual, but too many of the science fiction books published recently have been short on real imagination—they are, in fact, timid and literarily defensive. The Ace SF Specials are neither.

The SF Specials began more than fifteen years ago, when the science fiction field was in a period of creative doldrums similar to the present: science fiction novels then were mostly of the traditional sort, often hackneyed and familiar stories that relied on fast action and obvious ideas. Ace began the first series of SF Specials with the idea that science fiction readers would welcome something more than that, novels that would expand the boundaries of imagination, and that notion proved to be correct: the books published in that original series sold well, collected numerous awards, and many of them are now considered classics in the field.

Beginning in 1968 and continuing into 1971, the Ace SF Specials included such novels as *Past Master* by R. A. Lafferty, *Rite of Passage* by Alexei Panshin, *Synthajoy* by D. G. Compton, *The Left Hand of Darkness* by Ursula K. Le Guin, *Picnic on Paradise* and *And Chaos Died* by Joanna Russ, *Pavane* by Keith Roberts, *The Isle of the Dead* by Roger Zelazny, *The Warlord of the Air* by Michael Moorcock, *The Year of the Quiet Sun* by Wilson Tucker, *Mechasm* by John Sladek, *The Two-Timers* by Bob Shaw, and *The Phoenix and the Mirror* by Avram Davidson . . . among many others that could be mentioned, but the list is already long.

Most of those books were nominated for awards. *Rite of Passage* won the Nebula Award; *The Left Hand of Darkness* won both the Nebula and the Hugo; *The Year of the Quiet Sun* won the John W. Campbell Award. Other books in the series won more specialized awards. Most of the novels have remained in print over the years since they were first published.

That original series ended when I left Ace Books and moved to California in 1971, but its successes hadn't gone unnoticed. Both writers and publishers saw that a more "adult" sort of science fiction could attract a large readership, and during the seventies more venturesome sf novels were published than ever before.

A number of critics have credited the Ace Science Fiction Specials with bringing about a revolution in sf publishing, and I like to think this is at least partly true. But nothing would have changed if there hadn't been editors and publishers who *wanted* to upgrade the product; and in particular, it required science fiction writers who could produce superior novels. Fortunately, such writers were there; some of them had contributed to the SF Specials series, some had been writing quality sf novels already (Samuel R. Delany, Philip K. Dick, and Robert Silverberg are examples), and many writers of talent entered the science fiction field during this period who didn't feel constrained by the thud-and-blunder traditions of earlier sf.

So in the early seventies science fiction was an exciting field: quality sf novels appeared from many publishers, they sold very well, and science fiction moved toward the front of literary achievement. It was reviewed in *The New York Times* and analyzed by academic critics; major universities offered courses studying science fiction. It seemed that science fiction had finally become respectable.

But other trends began to be felt, and although they brought many new readers to science fiction, for the most part they caused sf to look back instead of forward. The television series *Star Trek* attracted an enormous following, as did the *Star Wars* movies, *Alien*, *Close Encounters of the Third Kind*, *E.T.*, and others; these products of the visual media introduced millions of people to science fiction, but though many were enthusiastic enough to buy sf books too, what they wanted were stories as simple and familiar as the films they had enjoyed. When they found science fiction books that were like the television and movie productions, they bought them in great numbers; when the books were more complex or unusual, sales were much lower.

So in recent years sf publishers have catered to this vast new market. The result has been that most of the science fiction published today is no more advanced and imaginative than the sf stories of the fifties, or even the forties: basic ideas and plots are reworked time and again, and when a novel proves to be popular, a sequel or a series will come along soon.

There's nothing wrong with such books; when they're well written they can be very good. But when authors are constrained to writing nothing but variations on the plots and styles of the past, much of the excitement of science fiction disappears. Science fiction is a literature of change; more than any other kind of writing, sf needs to keep moving forward if it's to be exciting.

The novels in this new series of Ace SF Specials do look forward rather than back. They're grounded in the traditions of science fiction but they all have something new to add in ideas or literary development. And they are all written by authors who are comparatively new to science fiction, because it's usually the new writers who have the freshest ideas. (Most of those novels in the original series that came to be called classics were written by authors who were then at the beginnings of their careers.)

Ace Books asked me to edit this new SF Specials series because they believe the time is right for such adventurous books. The new readers who swelled the science fiction market in the last several years are by now familiar with the basic ideas and plots, and many of them will want something more. This new SF Specials series offers stories that explore more imaginative territory.

Lucius Shepard's *Green Eyes* is a very different and exciting science fiction novel, and will introduce most readers to a strong new talent; it is his first novel, though he's published short stories and novelettes in *Universe* and *The Magazine of Fantasy and Science Fiction*. This is a novel about "zombies," but it's not a fantasy novel; it considers and explains how such beings might come to be, scientifically, much as James Blish once treated werewolves in "There Shall Be No Darkness" and Suzy McKee Charnas dealt with vampires in *The Vampire Tapestry*. Shepard's speculations are startling, but the story that grows from them is even more so.

It's a tale of intrigue, adventure, and characters both warm and sinister, set against a richly depicted near-future background in the southern U.S., where experiments with life-after-death inevitably attract the devotees of older, darker cults. You may think, at one point or another, that you can see where the plot is leading—but don't be too sure. Shepard's imagination is unfailingly daring; there are wonders here for which I couldn't prepare you if I tried.

There will be more Ace Science Fiction Specials coming soon, and each will be as different from the usual science fiction fare as this one is. I hope you'll watch for them.

CHAPTER I

**From Conjure Men: My Work With Ezawa at Tulane
by Anthony Edman, M.D., Ph.D.**

...I did not see my first "zombie" until my second day at
Tulane when Ezawa permitted me to witness an interview.
He ushered me into a cubicle occupied by several folding
chairs and switched on a two-way mirror. The room beyond
the mirror was decorated in the style of a turn-of-the-century
bordello: red velvet chairs and sofa perched on clawed feet,
their walnut frames carved into filigree; brass urns holding
peacock plumes; burgundy drapes and maroon-striped wallpaper; a branching chandelier upheld by a spider of black
iron. The light was as bright as a photographer's stage.
Though "zombies"—at least the short-termers—do not see
clearly until the end, they react to the color and the glare,
and ultimately the decor serves to amplify the therapist's
persuasive powers.

In passing, I should mention that I considered the lack
of a suitable chair within the observation cubicle a personal
affront. Being a compactly built man himself, it might be
assumed Ezawa had simply committed an oversight and not
taken my girth into account; but I cannot accept the proposal
that this meticulous and polite gentleman would overlook
any detail unless by design. He had exerted all his influence
to block my approval as psychiatric chief of the project,
considering my approach too radical, and I believe he enjoyed watching me perch with one ham on, the other off,
for the better part of an hour. Truthfully, though, what I
was to see beyond the mirror banished all thought of my
discomfort, and had it been necessary to balance on a shooting stick and peer between the shoulders of a crowd, I would
still have felt myself privileged.

The therapist, Jocundra Verret, sat on the edge of the

1

sofa, her hands folded in her lap. She was a shade under six feet tall, slender, impassively beautiful (therapists are chosen, in part, on the basis of physical attractiveness), and dressed in a nurse's white tunic and slacks. She looked younger than her twenty-five years, long-limbed, solemn and large-eyed. Dark brown hair wound through by strands of gold fell to her shoulders, and her skin had the pale olive cast of a Renaissance figure. The most notable feature of her appearance, though, was the extent of her makeup. Lipstick, eyeliner and mascara had been applied so as to transform her face into an exotic mask, one which evoked the symmetry of design upon a butterfly's wing. This gilding the lily was an essential part of the therapist's visual presentation, and similar makeup was utilized during the early stages of a slow-burner's existence, gradually being minimized as their perceptions sharpened.

Jocundra's movements were graceful and unhurried, and her expressions developed slowly into distant smiles and contemplative frowns, giving the impression of a calm and controlled personality. I later learned in my work with her that this impression was half a lie. Indeed, she viewed the world as a system of orderly processes through which one must maneuver by reducing experience to its logical minimum and analyzing it; but her logical bias, her sense of orderliness, her passivity in engaging life—these traits were counterbalanced by a deep romantic strain which caused her to be high-strung and, as has been publicized, occasioned her to acts of recklessness.

I asked Ezawa whether it was difficult to recruit therapists, and he replied that though the combination of physical beauty, lack of squeamishness, and a scientific background was uncommon, the turnover rate was low and there was a waiting list of applicants. I further asked if he had observed a general similarity of history or personality among the therapists, and he said with a trace of embarrassment that many had a history of checkered academic careers and interest in the occult. Jocundra was fairly typical in this regard. She had done undergraduate work in physics, switched to anthropology in graduate school, and had been involved in a study of voodoo cults before joining the project. Ezawa, for whom the truth appeared to consist of microbiological data, exhibited little interest in the psychological puzzles posed by our subjects, none whatsoever in the therapists, and constantly sought to downplay the mysterious aspects of the project. In light of this, I found curious his use of the term "zombie" rather than the official "Bacterially Induced Artificial Personality" or its acronym: it signaled some backsliding from his position of scientific rigor.

"I must admit," he said, "the process has elements in common with a voodoo recipe. We *do* isolate the bacteria from dirt taken from the old slave graveyards, but that's simply because of the biodegradable coffins. . . . They permit the decomposing tissues to interact with micro-organisms in the soil."

Once the bacteria was isolated, Ezawa explained, a DNA extract from goat's rue was introduced into the growth medium and the bacteria was then induced to take up chromosomes and DNA fragments from the goat's rue, thereby mediating recombination between the two types of DNA. The resultant strain was injected via a heart pump into the cerebellum and temporal lobes of a corpse less than an hour dead, whereupon the bacteria began pretranscriptional processing of the corpse's genetic complement, bringing the body sufficiently alive so it could begin the post-transcriptional processing. Twenty-four hours after injection the "zombie" was ready for the therapist.

An orderly entered the room beyond the mirror, pushing a pale, heavy-set man in a wheelchair: jowly, middle-aged, with receding brown hair and a five o'clock shadow. He wore a green hospital gown. The orderly assisted him onto the sofa, and the man struggled feebly to rise, kicking aside the coffee table. His name, I saw from Ezawa's clipboard, had been Paul Pelizzarro, a vagrant, though he would soon begin to recall a different name, a different history. Random fragments of the transforming DNA in the recombinant bacteria coded for an entirely new personality, or so Ezawa expressed it. When I suggested that the personality might not be entirely new, that we might be observing wish-fulfillment on the cellular level, he gave me a startled look, as if suddenly suspecting I was addled——or so I characterized it at the time, though in retrospect it is clear he knew far more than I about the nature of our subjects and could not possibly have been surprised by my obvious interpretation. Perhaps he was simply reacting to my perspicacity.

Pelizzarro sat unmoving, head resting on his shoulder, eyes dull, mouth open. On being revivified they are all intractable and lax, blank slates, much like the zombies of folklore. They are told by the orderly that they have died and been brought back to life by means of an experimental process, and that he is taking them to someone who will help. It is the therapist's job to make the "zombie" want to please her—or him—by stimulating a sexual response, initiating a dependency.

"Naturally," said Ezawa, "the sexual response has the side effect of increasing acetylcholine and norepenephrin production at the neuromuscular junctions . . . improves the motor control." He switched on the audio. The orderly had left, and the interview had already begun.

Jocundra stood in front of the "zombie," swaying her hips like a starlet tempting a producer.

"Why won't you talk?" she asked.

He rolled his head from side to side, pushed at the cushions, still too weak to stand. When his head impacted with the plush of the sofa, his breath came out in a soft grunt.

Jocundra stepped behind him and trailed her fingers along his neck, stimulating the spinal nerves. He froze, his head cocked as if listening to an ominous whisper; his eyes flicked back and forth. He seemed terrified. Jocundra moved around the sofa and posed before him once again.

"Do you remember your death?" she asked coldly. "Or anything afterwards?"

The "zombie" floundered, flailed his arms; his lips drew back, revealing rows of perfect white teeth, small and feminine-looking in contrast to his fleshiness. "No!" His voice was choked. "No! God, I . . . I don't!"

"Maybe I should just leave. You don't seem to want to talk."

"Please . . . don't." He lifted his hand, then let it fall onto the cushion.

I was to learn that each therapist employed a distinctive method of relating to the "zombies," but—perhaps only because Jocundra was the first therapist I observed—I have never found another style more compelling, more illustrative of the essential myth-construct at the heart of the therapist-"zombie" relationship. I have mentioned that her movements were graceful and unhurried under normal conditions; when working, however, they grew elegant and mesmerizing, as if she were displaying invisible veils, and I was reminded of the gestures of a Balinese dancer. The "zombie," then, would perceive her initially as a blurred silhouette, a shadowy figure at the center of a dim candleflame, an unknown goddess weaving a spell to attract his eye until, at last, his vision cleared and he saw her there before him, taken human form. Jocundra utilized the classic feminine tactic of approach and avoidance to augment her visual and tactile presentation, and, in this particular interview, once the "zombie" had begged her not to leave, she sat beside him on the sofa and took his hand.

"What's your name?" she asked.

He appeared to be stunned by the question, but after several seconds he answered, "Frank. Frank Juskit." He peered at her, searching for her reaction, and managed a smile. "I was a . . . a salesman."

"What sort of salesman? My uncle's a salesman, too."

"Oh, I was just an old horse trader," he said, assuming a character at once pompous and self-deprecating. A midwestern accent nagged at his vowels, becoming more acute as he grew more involved in telling his story. "At the end, there, I didn't do much selling. Just kept an eye on the books. But I've sold franchises and factories, swampland and sea coasts. I've worked land contracts and mortgages and tract developments. Hell, I've sold everything every which way and backwards!"

"Real estate?"

"Yes, ma'am! Both real and surreal!" He clapped his hands together and attempted a wink which, due to his lack of muscle control, came off as a grotesque leer. "And if I couldn't sell it, I bought it! I turned landfills into shopping malls, tree-lined suburbs into neon wastes. I swallowed quiet suburbs and shat out industrial parks. I was the evil genius of the board room! I sharked through the world with blood on my teeth and a notary's seal for a left eye! And when I get down to Hell, I'll sell the devil two bedrooms and a bath overlooking the Promised Land and take over the goddamned place myself...."

Ezawa has labeled these outbursts "ecstatic confessions," but I find the term inexact and prefer "life story." Because the "zombie's" senses are dim, his motor control limited, he must compress the variety of his synthesized experience into a communicative package in order fully to realize himself. The result is a compact symbolic structure, one summing up a lifetime of creative impulse: a life story.

"This is typical," said Ezawa. "I doubt we'll learn anything of value. Do you see the eyes?"

I looked. There were flickers of phosphorescent green in the irises, visible to me at a distance of ten feet; they were faint at first, but quickly increased in frequency and brilliance.

"It's the impingement of the bacteria on the optic nerve," said Ezawa. "They're bioluminescent. When you see it you know the end's near. Except in the case of the slow-burners, of course. Their brains retard the entire process. We have one out at Shadows who's been showing green for two months."

At Jocundra's questioning, Mr. Juskit—I came to think of him by his assumed name, convinced by the assurance of his memories—detailed a final illness which led to a death he had previously failed to remember. The flickerings in his eyes intensified, glowing like swampfire, blossoming into green stars, and he made the fisted gestures of a company president exhorting his sales force. As he gained control of his muscles, he seemed more and more the salesman, the Napoleon of the board room, the glib, nattering little man born of the union between a vagrant and the bacterial DNA. When I had first seen him in the room beyond the mirror, dazed, dull, barely conscious, I had been struck by the perversity of the situation: an unprepossessing, half-dead man was being danced for by a lovely woman in a nurse's uniform, all within a gaudy room which might have been the private salon in a high class whorehouse. The scene embodied a hallucinated sexuality. But now there was a natural air to the proceedings, a rightness; I could not imagine any room being made unnatural by Mr. Juskit's presence. He dominated his surroundings, commanding my attention, and I saw that Jocundra, too, was no longer weaving her web of elegant motion, no longer the temptress; she leaned toward him, intent upon his words, hands folded in her lap, attentive as would be a dutiful wife or mistress.

Mr. Juskit began to address her as "babe," touching her often, and, eventually, asked her to remove her tunic. "Take it off, babe," he said with contagious jollity, "and lemme see them puppies." So convinced was I of his right to ask this of her, of its propriety in terms of their relationship, I was not taken aback when she stood, undid her buttons and let the tunic drop onto her arms. She lowered her eyes in a submissive pose. Mr. Juskit pushed himself off the sofa, his hospital gown giving evidence of his extreme arousal, and staggered toward her, a step, arms outstretched and rigid, eyes burning a cometary green. Jocundra leaped aside as he fell to the floor, face downward. Tremors shook him for nearly half a minute, but he was dead long before they ceased.

Ezawa opaqued the mirror. I had been leaning forward, gripping the edge of the mirror, and I believe I stared wildly at him. Seeing my agitation, no doubt thinking it the product of disgust or some allied emotion, he said, "It frequently ends that way. The initial sexual response governs them, and during the final burst of vitality they commonly attempt to embrace the therapist or . . . ask favors." He shrugged. "Since it's their last request, the therapists usually comply."

But I was not disgusted, not horrified; instead I was stunned by the sudden extinction of what had seemed a dynamic imperative for the last half hour or thereabouts: Mr. Juskit's existence. It was unthinkable that he had so abruptly ceased to be. And then, as I gained a more speculative distance from the events, I began to understand what I had witnessed, its mythic proportions. A beautiful woman, both Eve and Delilah, had called a man back from the dead, lured him into vivid expression, coaxed him to strive for her and tell his secrets, to live in a furious rush of moments and die one breath short of reward, reaching out to her. The "zombie"-therapist relationship, I realized, made possible a new depth of scrutiny into the complete range of male-female interactions; I was eager to take up residence at Shadows and begin my investigations of the slow-burners. *They* were the heart of the project! The scene I had just witnessed—the birth, life and death of Frank Juskit while in the company of Jocundra Verret—had transmitted an archetypal potency, like the illustration on a Tarot trump come to life; and though I had not yet met Hilmer Magnusson or Donnell Harrison, I believe at that moment I anticipated their miraculous advent.

CHAPTER II

BIAP Interview No. 1251
Host Name: Paul Pelizzarro
BIAP Name: Frank Juskit
Length of Interview: fifty-seven minutes
Interpretation: None. See video.
Comments/Personal Reactions/Other: I am, as usual, both saddened by the death and repelled by the patient's actions, by my dutiful response; in fact, by the nature of the work: the tricks we play and the patients themselves, comic in their weakness, horrible in their desire for life and the flash of ardor that ends them. . . . Green fireballs lodged in their eye sockets, their minds going nova with the joy of a lifetime crammed into a few minutes (that is how I imagine it, though I'm certain Dr. Ezawa will quarrel with such an unscientific appraisal). I have long since become accustomed to the slight difference in body temperature and the

other salient differences between the patients and the ordinary run of humanity, but I doubt I will ever grow callous enough to be unaffected by those final moments.

At times like these I realize how much my work has distanced me from friends and family. Still, I find that the patients in their compressed, excited states are far more interesting than any of my acquaintances, and I believe that even relative failures such as Mr. Juskit would—had they lived a full span at this accelerated pace—have accomplished a great deal more than they have related. Their repellent aspects, in my opinion, are outweighed by the intensity of their expression. For this reason I wish to withdraw my resignation tendered yesterday, October 24, 1986.

Therapist's Signature: *Jocundra Verret*

Staff Evaluation: *Let's assign Verret to a slow-burner as soon as possible, but not just the first one that comes along. I'd like to see a photograph and data sheet on each new slow-burner, and from that material I'll make an appropriate selection.*

A. Edman

CHAPTER III

February 10, 1987

The road to Shadows was unmarked, or rather the marker—an old metal Grapette sign—had been overgrown by a crepe myrtle, and a live oak branch, its bark flecked with blue-green scale, had cracked off the trunk and fallen across the bush, veiling it in leaf spray and hanks of Spanish moss. But Jocundra caught a glint of metal as she passed and slammed on the brakes. The van fishtailed and slewed onto the shoulder, and the man beside her was thrown forward against the safety harness. His head bounced on the back of the seat, then he let it loll toward her and frowned.

"I'm sorry," she said. "These brakes are awful. Are you all right?" She touched his leg in sympathy and felt the muscles jump.

The silence between them sang with tension. Crickets sawed, a jay screamed, the thickets seethed and hissed in a sudden breeze, and all the sharp sounds of life seemed to be registering the process of his hostility toward her. His frown softened to a reproving gaze and he turned away, staring out at the clouds of white dust settling around the van.

"We should be there in another half hour," she said. "And then I'll fix us some lunch."

He sighed but didn't comment.

Heat rippled off the tops of the bushes, and every surface Jocundra touched was slippery with her sweat. A mosquito whined in her ear; peevish, she slapped at it and blew a strand of hair from her eyes. She backed up, setting his head bouncing again, and headed down a gravel track whose entrance was so choked with vegetation that vines trailed across the windshield, and twigs bearing clusters of yellow-tipped leaves tattered at the side vent and swatted her elbow. Rows of live oaks arched overhead and the road was in deep shade, bridged by irregular patches of sunlight falling through rents in the canopy. Once it had been a grand concourse traveled by gleaming carriages, fine ladies and fancy gentlemen, but now it was potholed, ferns grew in the wheel ruts, and the anonymous blue vans of the project were its sole traffic.

The potholes forced her to drive slowly, but she could hardly wait to reach Shadows and hand him over to the orderlies. Maybe an hour or so of being alone would make him more amiable. She leaned forward, plucking her dress away from her damp skin, and glanced at him. He just stared out the window, his fingers twitching in his lap. The brown suit they had issued him at Tulane was too short in the arms, exposing knobbly wrists, and when she had first seen him wearing it she had thought of the teenage boys from her home town dressed in their ill-fitting Sunday best, waiting for the army bus to carry them off to no good future. He was much older, nearly thirty, but he had the witchy look that bayou men often presented: hollow-cheeked, long-nosed, sharp-chinned, with lank black hair hanging ragged over his collar. Not handsome, but not ugly either. Large hazel eyes acted to plane down his features and gave him a sad, ardent look such as you might find in an Old Master's rendering of a saint about to die of wounds gotten for the love of Christ. His irises were not yet showing a trace of green.

"You know, I was born about forty miles from here," she said, embarrassed by the artificial sunniness in her voice. "Over on Bayou Teche. It's beautiful there. Herons and cypresses and old plantation homes like Shadows..."

"I don't want to talk." His voice was weak but full of venom; he kept his eyes turned toward the window.

"Why are you so angry?" She put her hand on his arm, probing the hollow of his elbow. "I'm just trying to be friendly."

He looked at her, eyes wide, confused, and she wondered how it would be, her own flesh cool and numb, and the fingers of a more vital creature firing the nerves, sending charges into the midnight places of the brain. She pictured mental lightnings striking down in a landscape of eroded thoughts, sparking new life, new memories; but it would be nothing so dramatic. Things dawned slowly upon them. Every sensation, it seemed, held for them a clue to their essential wrongness, their lack of true relation to the world, and they struggled to arrange the murky shapes and unfamiliar smells and ringing voices into structures which would support them.

Breath whistled in his throat, but he didn't speak; he leaned back and closed his eyes.

His name—his "zombie" name—was Donnell Harrison, though the body had once hosted the dreams and memories of Steven Mears, a carnival worker dead of alcohol poisoning at the age of twenty-nine. He did not remember Mears' life, however; he remembered having been a poet and living with his wife Jean in a mountain cabin. "The air was clarity," he had said. "The rain fell like peace." Almost singing the phrases, he had told her how his wife had died, crushed beneath a roofbeam during a storm. His hand had clawed at the armrest of the sofa as he strained to express the emotion swelling in him, and Jocundra had imagined that his skin contained not flesh and blood, but was tightly stretched over a cool darkness lit by a tendril of green fog, the magical analogue of a tungsten filament at the center of a light bulb. She had listened to the tapes so often since the initial interview that she had memorized his final outburst.

"Old men, old liars drowsy with supper and the hearth, their minds grazing on some slope downward of illusion into death, they'll tell you that the wild north king visits the high country disguised as a wind, blowing up spectacles of lightning-flash and hosannas of cloud. But this storm was animal, a wave of black animal breath bigger than the beginning. All its elements infected the land, making it writhe like the skin of a flea-infested dog, setting St. Elmo's fire to glimmer in the pinetops, decaying the stones into thunder, rotting the principles of ordinary day until the light caught fire and roared. . . ."

Then, at the realization of loss, understanding the magnitude of the tragedy he had invented for himself, he had broken off his life story and sunk into a depression. Jocundra had not been able to rouse him. "Slow-burners always go through a fugue," Edman had told her. "It's as if they realize they're in for the long haul and better get their act together, slow their pace, reduce their intensity. Don't worry. Sooner or later he'll come around." But Jocundra was not sure she believed Edman; all his advice to her reeked of bedside manner, benign assurances.

The potholes became so wide she had to ease down into them and use the four-wheel drive to climb out. The live oaks thinned and swamp country began. Stretches of black, earth-steeped water were ranked by gaunt cypresses, their moss-bearded top branches resembling the rotted crosstrees of a pirate fleet mouldering in the shallows. Gnats blurred the air above a scaly log; a scum of rust-colored bubbles clung to the shoreline reeds. It was dead-still, desolate, but it was home ground to Jocundra, and its stillness awakened in her a compatible stillness, acting upon her tension like a cold compress applied to a fevered brow. She pointed out the landmark sights to Donnell: a wrinkle in the water signaling the presence of a snake, dark nests in the cypress tops, a hawk circling over a thicketed island. Prodded by her touch, he lifted his head and stared, using—she knew—some vague shape or color of what he saw to flesh out his life story, adding hawks or a pattern of cloud to the sky above his mountain cabin.

The swamp gave out into palmetto glades and acacia, stands of bamboo, insects whirling in shafts of sunlight, and they came to an ironwork gate set into a masonry wall. A tar paper shack stood beside it. The security guard logged their arrival on his clipboard. "Y'all have a nice day," he said, winking at Jocundra as if he knew nice days were not in the cards.

The grounds were gloomy and gently rolling. A flagstone path bordered with ferns and azalea meandered among enchanted-looking oaks, which fountained up at regular intervals. They overspread the lawn, casting a dark green shade upon the stone benches beneath them; thin beams of sun penetrated to the grass as a scatter of gold coins. And at the center of the gloom, glowing softly like the source of the enchantment, was a two-story house of rose-colored brick with white trim and fluted columns across the front. A faceted glass dome bulged from the midpoint of its gabled roof. Two orderlies hustled down the steps as Jocundra pulled up and helped Donnell into his wheelchair.

"If you'll take Mr. Harrison to the suite," she said, "I'll see he gets checked in." And paying no attention to Donnell's alarmed reaction, she walked out along the drive.

From the bench nearest the gate, the brightness of the brick and trim made the house appear to be rippling against the gloom, as if while she had been walking it had reverted to its true form—a black castle, a gingerbread house—and in turning back, she had caught it unawares. It was an unlikely place for scientific work, though its gothic atmosphere bolstered the image Edman had fostered; he had suggested that Shadows would be an Experience, spoken about it in terms suited to the promotion of a human potential group rather than de-mystifying it as he usually did any hint of the occult. She had talked to other therapists who had been at Shadows, but most had seemed traumatized, unwilling to discuss it. Even the microbiologists had been hazy at her briefing, saying they knew little about the new strain of bacteria with which Donnell had been injected. "He'll be longer lived," Ezawa had said. "Better motor control, sharper senses. Watch his visual development especially, and keep in mind he won't be easy to fool. He's no short-termer."

No doubt about that, she thought, as she began strolling back to the house. Before lapsing into his depression, Donnell had displayed a subtle good humor, a joyful appreciation of life apparently grounded in a realistic assessment of its pleasures and pains, this far different from the short-termers: cloudy, grotesque creatures who clutched and stared until you feared you would burn up under the kindling glare of their eyes. They had many of the qualities of the zombies in her father's lurid bedtime stories: dazed, ragged men and women stumbling through plantation fields at midnight, penned in windowless cabins fifty or more to a room, stinking, shuffling, afraid to touch each other, sustained on water and unsalted bread. "They ever get a taste of salt," her father had said, "they'll head straight for the buryin' ground and try to claw their way back into Hell." Sometimes the straw boss would send them after runaway slaves, and the slave would scramble through the swamp, eyes rolling and heart near to bursting, hearing the splash of the zombie's footsteps behind him or seeing its shadow rear up from the weird fogs wreathing the cypress, reaching for him with rotting fingers and arms rigid as gibbets. Let the slave escape, however, and the zombie would wander on, single-mindedly searching until years later—because a zombie lives as long as the binding magic holds; even if its flesh disintegrates the particles still incorporate the spirit—maybe a hundred years later, the image of its quarry grown so amorphous that it would react to any vaguely human form, the zombie spots a lighted window in a house on the bayou and is drawn by the scent of blood. . . . Her father had banged the bottom of the bed, jumped up in mock terror, and she had lain awake for hours, shivering, seeing the tortured faces of zombies in the grain of the ceiling boards.

But there was no such witchery involved with Donnell, she thought; or if there was, then it was witchery of an intensely human sort.

She had a moment of nervousness at the door; her stomach grew fluttery, as if crossing the threshold constituted a spiritual commitment, but she laughed at herself and pushed on in. No one was in sight. The foyer faced large cream-colored double doors and opened onto a hallway; the walls were painted pale peach, and the doorways ranging them were framed with intricate molding. Ferns splashed from squat brass urns set between them. Church quiet, with the pious, sedated air common to sickrooms and funeral homes.

"Jocundra!" A lazy, honeysuckle voice.

From the opposite end of the hall, a slim, ash blond girl in hospital whites came toward her, giving a cutesy wave. Laura Petit. She had been an anomaly among the therapists at Tulane, constantly encouraging group activities, parties, dinners, whereas most of them had been wholly involved with the patients. Laura punctuated her sentences with breathy gasps; she batted her eyes and fluttered her hands when she laughed. The entire repertoire of her mannerisms was testimony to filmic generations of inept actresses playing Southern belles as shallow, bubbly nymphs with no head for anything other than fried chicken recipes and lace tatting. But despite this, despite the fact she considered the patients "gross," she was an excellent therapist. She seemed to be one of those people to whom emotional attachment is an alien concept, and who learn to extract a surrogate emotionality from manipulating friends and colleagues, and—in this case—her patients.

"That must have been yours they just wheeled in," she said, embracing Jocundra.

"Yes." Jocundra accepted a peck on the cheek and disengaged.

"Better watch yourself, hon! He's not too bad lookin' for a corpse." Laura flashed her Most Popular smile. "How you doin'?"

"I should check in. . . ."

"Oh, you can see Edman when he makes his rounds. We're real informal here. Come on, now." She tugged at Jocundra's arm. "I'll introduce you to Magnusson."

Jocundra hung back. "Is it all right?"

"Don't be shy, hon! You want to see how your boy's goin' to turn out, don't you?"

As they walked, Laura filled her in about Magnusson, pretending genuine interest in his work, but that was camouflage, a framework allowing her to boast of her own triumph, to explain how she had midwifed the miracle. Dr. Hilmer Magnusson had been their initial success with the new strain: the body of a John Doe derelict now hosting the personality of a medical researcher who, less than a month after his injection, had casually handed them a cure for muscular dystrophy: a cure which had proved ninety-five percent effective in limited testing.

"One day," said Laura, her voice rising at the end of each phrase, turning them into expressions of incredulity, "he asked me for his Johns Hopkins paper, the one he remembered first presentin' the process in. Well, I didn't know *what* he was talkin' about, but I played along and told him I'd send for it. Anyway, he finally got impatient and started workin' without it, complainin' that his memory wasn't what it used to be. It was incredible!"

Things, Jocundra observed, had a way of falling into place for Laura. Doors opened for her professionally, attractive men ditched their girlfriends and came in pursuit, and now Magnusson had produced a miracle cure. It was as if she were connected by fine wires to everything in her environment, and when she yanked everything toppled, permitting her passage toward some goal. The question was: were her manipulative skills intellectually founded, or had she simply been gifted with dumb luck as compensation for her lack of emotionality? It was hard to believe that anyone of intelligence could erect such a false front and not know it was transparent.

Slashes of sunlight fell from louvred shutters onto the carpet, but otherwise Magnusson's room was dark, suffused by an odor of bay rum and urine. At first Jocundra could see nothing; then a pair of glowing eyes blinked open against the far wall. His pupils had shrunk to pinpricks; his irises flared green and were laced with striations of more brilliant green, which brightened and faded. The glow illuminated a portion of his face, seamed cheeks tattooed with broken veins and a bony beak of a nose. His wheelchair hissed on the carpet, coming close, and she saw that he was an old, old man, his facial muscles so withered that his skull looked melted and misshapen.

Laura introduced them.

"Jocundra. Such a charming name." Magnusson's voice was weak and hoarse and expressed little of his mood. Each syllable creaked in his throat like an ancient seal being pried up.

"It's Creole, sir." She sat on the bed facing him. There were food stains on his bathrobe. "My mother was part Creole."

"Was?"

"Both my parents died several years ago. A fire. The police suspected my father had sct it."

Laura shot her a look of surprise, and Jocundra was surprised at herself. She never told anyone about the police report, and yet she had told Magnusson without the slightest hesitation.

He reached out and took her hand. His flesh was cool, dry, almost weightless, but his pulse surged. "I commiserate," he said. "I know what it is to be alone." He withdrew his hand and nodded absently. "Rigmor, my great-grandmother, used to tell me that America was a land where no one ever need be alone. Said she'd had that realization when she stepped off the boat from Sweden and saw the mob thronging the docks. Of course she had no idea to what ends the Twentieth Century would come, the kinds of shallow relationships that would evolve as the family was annihilated by television, automobiles, the entire technological epidemic. She had her vision of families perched on packing crates. Irish, Poles, Italians, Arabs. Plump girls with dark-eyed babies, apple-cheeked young men in short-brimmed hats carrying their heritage in a sack. Strangers mingling, becoming lovers and companions. She never noticed that it all had changed." Magnusson attempted an emphatic gesture, but the effect was of a palsied tremor. "It's terrible! The petty alliances between people nowadays. Worse than loneliness. There's no trust, no commitment, no love. I'm so fortunate to have Laura."

Laura beamed and clasped her hands at her waist, a pose both virtuous and triumphant. Magnusson studied the backs of his hands, as if considering their sad plight. Several of his fingers had been broken and left unset; the nail of his right thumb was missing, exposing a contused bulge of flesh. Jocundra was suddenly ashamed of her presence in the room.

"Perhaps it's just my damned Swedish morbidity," said Magnusson out of the blue. "I tried to kill myself once, you know. Slit my wrists. Damned fool youngster! I was discouraged by the rain and the state of the economy. Not much reason, you might think, for self-destruction, but I found it thoroughly oppressing at the time."

"Well," said Laura after an uncomfortable silence. "We'll let you rest, Hilmer." She laid her hand on the doorknob, but the old man spoke again.

"He'll find you out, Jocundra."

"Sir?" She turned back to him.

"You operate on a paler principle than he, and he will find you out. But you're a healthy girl, even if a bit transparent. I can see it by your yellows and your blues." He laughed, a hideous rasp which set him choking, and as he choked, he managed to say, "Got your health, yes. . . ." When he regained control, his tone was one of amusement. "I wish I could offer medical advice. Stay off the fried foods, take cold showers, or some such. But as far as I can see, and that's farther than most, you're in the pink. Awful image! If you were in the pink, you'd be quite ill."

"What in the world are you talkin' about, Hilmer?" Laura's voice held a note of frustration.

"Oh, no!" Magnusson's bony orbits seemed to be crumbling away under the green glow of his eyes, as if they were nuggets of a rare element implanted in his skull, ravaging him. "You're not going to pick my brain anymore. An old man needs his secrets, his little edge on the world as it recedes."

* * *

"Ezawa thinks he might be seein' bioenergy . . . auras."
Laura closed the door behind them and flexed the lacquered
nails of her left hand as if they were blood-tipped claws.
"I'll get it out of him! He's becoming more and more aroused.
If his body hadn't been so enervated to begin with, he'd
already be chasin' me around the bed."

Laura went down to the commissary to prepare Magnusson's lunch, and Jocundra, in no hurry to rejoin Donnell,
wandered the hallway. Half of the rooms were untenanted,
all furnished with mahogany antiques and the walls covered
with the same pattern of wallpaper: an infancy of rosebud
cottages and grapevines. Cards were set into brass mounts
on the doors of the occupied rooms, and she read them as
she idled along. Clarice Monroe. That would be the black
girl, the one who believed herself to be a dancer and had
taught herself to walk after only a few weeks. Marilyn
Ramsburgh, Kline Lee French, Jack Richmond. Beneath
each name was a coded entry revealing the specifics of
treatment and the prognosis. There were two green dots
after Magnusson's name, signifying the new strain; his current prognosis was for three months plus or minus a week.
That meant Donnell would have eight or nine months unless
his youthfulness further retarded the bacterial action. A long
time to spend with anyone, longer than her marriage. The
Thirty Weeks War, or so Charlie had called it. She had seen
him a month before. He had cut his hair and trimmed his
beard, was deeply tanned and dressed in an expensive jacket,
gold chains around his neck, a gold watch, gold rings . . . the
petered-out claim of his body salted with gold. She smiled
at her cattiness. He wasn't so terrible. Now that he had
become just another figment of the French Quarter, working
around the clock at his restaurant, clinking wineglasses with
sagging divorcees and posing a sexual Everest for disillu-
sioned housewives to scale, he bore little resemblance to
the man she had married, and this was doubtless the reason
she could now tolerate him: it had been the original she
disliked.

She had been standing beside Magnusson's door for less
than a minute when she noticed her right side—that nearest

the door—was prickly with...not cold exactly, more an animal chill that raised gooseflesh on her arm. She assumed it was nerves, fatigue; but on touching the door she discovered that it, too, was cold, and a vibration tingled her fingertips as if a charge had passed through the wood from an X-ray machine briefly in operation. Nerves, she thought again. And, indeed, the cold dissipated the instant she cracked the door. Still, she was curious. What would the old man be like apart from Laura's influence? She cracked the door wider, and his scent of bay rum and corruption leaked out. White hallway light spilled across shelves lined with gilt and leather medical texts, sweeping back the darkness, compacting it. She leaned on the doorknob, peering inside, and the sharp shadows angled from beneath the desk and chair quivered, poised—she imagined—to snick through the blood and bone of her ankles if she trespassed. Feeling foolish at her apprehension, she pushed the door wide open. He sat in his wheelchair facing the far wall, a dim green oval of his reflected stare puddled head-high on the wallpaper. The uncanny sight gave her pause, and she was uncertain whether or not to call his name.

"Go away," he whispered without turning.

A thrill ran across the muscles of her abdomen. His head wobbled and his hand fell off the arm of the chair, half a gesture of dismissal, half collapse. He whispered once more, "Go away." She jumped back, pulling the door shut behind her, and she leaned against the doorframe trembling, unable to stop trembling no matter how insistently she told herself that her fright was the product of stress alone. His voice had terrified her. Though it had been the same decrepit wheeze he had spoken in earlier, this time it had been full of potent menace, the voice of a spirit speaking through a cobwebbed throat, its whisper created by the straining and snapping of spider silk stretched apart by dessicated muscles. And yet, for all its implicit power, it had been wavering and faint, as if a wind and a world lay between them.

CHAPTER IV

February 11 – March 24, 1987

Every morning at nine-thirty or thereabouts an astringent odor of aftershave stung Donnell's nostrils, and the enormous shadow of Dr. Edman hove into view. Sometimes, though not this morning, the less imposing shadow of Dr. Brauer slunk by his side, his smell a mingling of stale tobacco and sweat, his voice holding an edge of mean condescension. Edman's voice, however, gave Donnell a feeling of superiority; it was the mellifluous croon of a cartoon owl to whom the forest animals would come for sage but unreliable advice.

"Lungs clear, heart rate... gooood." Edman thumped Donnell's chest and chuckled. "Now, if we can just get your head on straight."

Irritated by the attempt to jolly him, Donnell maintained a frosty silence. Edman finished the examination and went to sit on the bed; the bedsprings squealed, giving up the ghost.

"Had a recurrence of that shift in focus?" he asked.

"Not lately."

"Donnell!" said Jocundra chidingly; he heard the whisk of her stockings as she uncrossed her legs behind him.

He gripped the arms of the wheelchair so his vertigo would not be apparent and concentrated on Edman's bloated gray shape; then he blinked, strained, and shifted his field of focus forward. A patch of lab coat swooped toward him from the shadow, swelling to completely dominate his vision: several pens clipped to a sagging pocket. By tracking his sight like a searchlight across Edman's frame, he assembled the image of a grossly fat, middle-aged man with slicked-back brown hair and a flourishing mustache, the ends of which were waxed and curled. Hectic spots of color dappled his cheeks, and his eyes were startling bits of blue china. Donnell fixed on the left eye, noticing the pink gullies of flesh in the corners, the road map of capillaries: Edman hadn't been sleeping.

"Actually"—Donnell thought how best to exploit Edman's lack of sleep—"actually, I had one just when you came in, but it was different. . . ." He pretended to be struggling with a difficult concept.

"How so?" Papers rustled on Edman's clipboard, his ballpoint clicked. His eyelid drooped, and the blue eye rolled wetly down.

"The light was spraying out the pores of your hand, intense light, like the kind you find in an all-night restaurant, but even brighter, and deep in the light something moved, something pale and multiform," Donnell whispered melodramatically. "Something I soon realized was a sea of ghastly, tormented faces. . . ."

"My God, Donnell!" Edman smacked the bed with his clipboard.

"Right!" said Donnell with mock enthusiasm. "I can't be sure, but it may have been . . ."

"Donnell!" Edman sighed, a forlorn lover's sigh. "Will you please consider what our process means to other terminal patients? At least do that, if you don't care about yourself."

"Oh, yeah. There must be thousands of less fortunate stiffs just begging for the chance." Donnell laughed. "It really changes your perspective on the goddamn afterlife. Groping, bashing your head on the sink when you go to spit."

"You know that's going to improve, damn it!" The blue eye blinked rapidly. "You're retarding your own progress with this childish attitude."

"What'll you give me?" Jocundra stroked his shoulder, soothing, but Donnell shrugged off her hand. "How much if I spill the secrets of my vital signs?"

"What would you like?"

"Another whore." Donnell jerked his head toward Jocundra. "I'm bored with this one."

"Would you really prefer another therapist?"

"Christ, yes! Dozens! Orientals, Watusis, cheerleaders in sweatsocks for my old age. I'll screw my way to mental health."

"I see." Edman scribbled furiously, his eye downcast.

What gruesome things eyes were! Glistening, rolling, bulging, popping. Little congealed shudders in their bony nests. Donnell wished he had never mentioned the visual shift because they hadn't stopped nagging him since, and he had begun to develop a phobia about eyes. But on first experiencing it, he had feared it might signal a relapse, and he had told Jocundra.

Edman cleared his throat. "It's time we got to the root of this anger, Donnell." Note-taking had restored his poise, and his tone implied an end to games. "It must be distressing," he said, "not to recall what Jean looked like beyond a few hazy details."

"Shut up, Edman," said Donnell. As always, mere mention of his flawed memory made him unreasonably angry. His teeth clenched, his muscles bunched, yet part of his mind remained calm and watchful, helpless against the onset of rage.

"Tall, dark-haired, quiet," enumerated Edman. "A weaver...or was she a photographer? No, I remember. Both." The eye widened, the eyebrow arched. "A talented woman."

"Leave it alone," said Donnell ominously, wishing he could refine his patch of clear sight into a needle beam and prick Edman's humor, send the fluid jetting out, dribbling down his cheek, then watch him go squealing around the room, a flabby balloon losing flotation.

"It's odd," mused Edman, "that your most coherent memories of the woman concern her death."

Donnell tried to hurl himself out of the wheelchair, but pain lanced through his shoulder joints and he fell back. "Bastard!" he shouted.

Jocundra helped him resettle and asked Edman if they could have a consultation, and they went into the hall.

Alone, his anger ebbing, Donnell normalized his sight. The bedroom walls raised a ghostly gray mist, unbroken except for a golden fog at the window, and the furniture rippled as if with a gentle current. It occurred to him that things might so appear to a king who had been magicked into a deathlike trance and enthroned upon a shadowy lake bottom among streamers of kelp and shattered hulls. He preferred this gloom to clear sight: it suited his interior gloom and induced a comforting thoughtlessness.

". . . don't think you should force him," Jocundra was saying in the hall, angry.

Edman's reply was muffled. ". . . another week . . . his reaction to Richmond . . ."

A mirror hung beside the door to Jocundra's bedroom, offering the reflection of a spidery writing desk wobbling on pipestem legs. Donnell wheeled over to it and pressed his nose against the cold glass. He saw a dead-gray oval with drowned hair waving up and smudges for eyes. Now and again a fiery green flicker crossed one or the other of the smudges.

"You shouldn't worry so about your eyes," said Jocundra from the door.

He started to wheel away from her, upset at being caught off guard, but she moved behind his chair, hemming him in. Her mirror image lifted an ill-defined hand and made as if to touch him, but held back, and for an instant he felt the good weight of her consolation.

"I'd be afraid, too," she said. "But there's really nothing to worry about. They'll get brighter and brighter for a while and then they'll fade."

One of the orderlies sang old blues songs when he cleaned up Donnell's room, and his favorite tune contained the oft-repeated line: "Minutes seem like hours, hours seem like days. . . ."

Donnell thought the line should have continued the metaphorical progression and sought a comparative for weeks, but he would not have chosen months or years. Weeks like vats of sluggish sameness, three of them, at the bottom of which he sat and stewed and tried to remember. Jocundra urged him to write, and he refused on the grounds that she had asked. He purely resented her. She wore too damn much perfume, she touched him too often, and she stirred up his memories of Jean because she was also tall and dark-haired. He especially resented her for that. Sometimes he took refuge from her in his memories, displaying them against the field of his suffering, his sense of loss, the way an archeologist might spread the fragments of an ancient medallion on a velvet cloth, hoping to assure himself of the larger form whose wreckage they comprised: a life having unity and purpose, sad depths and joyous heights. But not remembering Jean's face made all the bits of memory insubstantial. The hooked rugs on the cabin floor, the photograph above their bed of a spiderweb fettering a windowpane stained blue with frost, a day at a county fair. So few. Without her to center them they lacked consistency, and it seemed his grief was less a consequence of loss than a blackness welling up from some negative place inside him. From time to time he *did* write, thinking the act would manifest a proof, evoke a new memory; the poems were frauds, elegant and empty, and this led him to a sense of his own fraudulence. Something was wrong. Put that baldly it sounded stupid, but it was the most essential truth he could isolate. Something was *very* wrong. Some dread thing was keeping just out of sight behind him. He became leery of unfamiliar noises, suspicious of changes in routine, convinced he was about to be ambushed by a sinister fate masquerading as one of the shadows that surrounded him. There was no reasonable basis for the conviction, yet nonetheless his fear intensified. The fear drove him to seek out Jocundra, she in turn drove him to thoughts of Jean, round and round and round, and that's why the weeks seemed like goddamn centuries, and the month—when it came to be a month and a little more—like a geologic stratification of slow, sad time.

One summerlike afternoon Jocundra wheeled him out to the stone bench nearest the gate and tried to interest him with stories of duels and courtship, of the fine ladies and gentlemen who had long ago strolled the grounds. He affected disinterest but he listened. Her features were animated, her voice vibrant, and he felt she was disclosing a fundamental attitude, exposing a side of herself she kept hidden from others. Eventually his show of boredom diminished her enthusiasm, and she opened a magazine.

High above, the oak crowns were dark green domes fogged by gassy golden suns, but when he shifted his field of focus he could see up through the dizzying separations of the leaves to the birds perched on the top branches. His vision was improving every day, and he had discovered that it functioned best under the sun. Colors were truer and shapes more recognizable, though they still wavered with a seasick motion, and though the brightness produced its own effects: scrollworks of golden light flashing in the corners of his eyes; transparent eddies flowing around the azalea leaves; a faint bluish mist accumulating around Jocundra's shoulders. He tracked across the glossy cover of her *Cosmopolitan* and focused on her mouth. It was wide and lipsticked and full like the cover girl's; the hollow above her lips was deep and sculptural.

"How do I look?" The lips smiled.

Being at such an apparently intimate distance from her mouth was eerie, voyeuristic; he covered his embarrassment with sarcasm. "What's up in the world of bust enhancement these days?"

The smile disappeared. "You don't expect me to read anything worthwhile with you glowering at me, do you?"

"I didn't expect you could read at all." Flecks of topaz light glimmered in her irises; a scatter of fine dark hairs rose from her eyebrow and merged with the hairline. "But if you could I assumed it would be crap like that. Makeup Secrets of the Stars."

"I suffer no sense of devaluation by using makeup," she said crisply. "It cheers me up to look nice, and God knows it's hard enough to be cheerful around you."

He turned, blinking away the patch of clear sight, considering the blurs of distant foliage. It was becoming increasingly difficult for him to maintain anger against her. Almost without his notice, as subtly as the spinning of a web, threads of his anger had been drawn loose and woven into another emotion. Its significance escaped him, but he thought that if he attempted to understand it, he would become more deeply ensnared.

"I have a confession," she said. "I read through your notebook this morning. Some of the fragments were lovely. . . ."

"Why don't you just look in the toilet after I go . . ."

". . . and I think you should finish them!"

". . . and see if my shit's spelling out secret messages!"

"I'm not trying to pry out your secrets!" She threw down her magazine. "I thought if you had some encouragement, some criticism, you might finish them."

Halting footsteps scraped on the path behind him, and a scruffy, gassed voice asked, "What's happenin', man?"

"Good morning, Mr. Richmond," said Jocundra with professional sweetness. "Donnell? Have you met Mr. Richmond?"

Richmond's head and torso swam into bleared focus. He had a hard-bitten, emaciated face framed in shoulder-length brown hair. Prominent cheekbones, a missing lower tooth. He was leaning on a cane, grinning; his pupils showed against his irises like planets eclipsing green suns.

"That's Jack to you, man," he said, extending his hand.

The hairs on Donnell's neck prickled, and he was tongue-tied, unable to tear his eyes off Richmond. A chill articulated his spine.

"Another hopeless burn-out," said Richmond, his grin growing toothier. "What's the matter, squeeze? You wet yourself?"

A busty, brown-haired woman came up beside him and murmured, "Jack," but he continued to glare at Donnell, whose apprehension was turning into panic. His muscles had gone flaccid, and unable to run, he shrank within himself.

The brown-haired woman touched Richmond's arm. "Why don't we finish our walk, Jack?"

Richmond mimicked her in a quavery falsetto. " 'Why don't we finish our walk, Jack!' Shit! Here they go and stock this place with these fine bitches, and they won't do nothin' for you 'cept be polite!" He bent down, his left eye inches from Donnell's face, and winked; even when closed, a hint of luminous green penetrated his eyelid. "Or don't you go for the ladies, squeeze? Maybe I'm makin' you all squirmy inside." He hobbled off, laughing, and called back over his shoulder. "Keep your fingers crossed, sweetheart. Maybe I'll come over some night and let you make my eagle big!"

As Richmond receded, his therapist in tow, Donnell's tension eased. He flicked his eyes to Jocundra, who looked quickly away and thumbed through her magazine. He found her lack of comment on his behavior peculiar and asked her about it.

"I assumed you were put off by his manner," she said.

"Who the hell is he?"

"A patient. He belongs to some motorcycle club." Her brow knitted. "The Hellhounds, I think."

"Didn't you feel . . ." He broke off, not wanting to admit the extent of his fright.

"Feel what?"

"Nothing."

Richmond's voice drifted back from the porch, outraged, and he slashed his cane through the air. The rose-colored bricks shimmered in the background, the faceted dome atop the roof flashed as if its energies were building to the discharge of a lethal ray, and Donnell had a resurgence of crawly animal fear.

After the encounter with Richmond, Donnell stayed closeted in his room for nearly two weeks. Jocundra lambasted him, comparing him to a child who had pulled a sheet over his head, but nothing she said would sway him. His reaction to Richmond must have been due, he decided, to a side effect of the bacterial process, but side effect or not, he wanted no repetition of that stricken and helpless feeling: like a rabbit frozen by oncoming headlights. He lay around so much he developed a bedsore, and at this Jocundra threw up her hands.

"I'm not going to sit here and watch you moulder," she said.

"Then get the fuck out!" he said; and as she stuffed wallet and compact into a leather purse, he told her that her skin looked like pink paint, that twenty dollars a night was probably too high but she should try for it, and—as she slammed the door—that she could go straight to Hell and give her goddamn disease to the Devil. He wished she would stay gone, but he knew she'd be harassing him again before lunchtime.

His lunch tray, however, was brought by the orderly who sang, and when Donnell asked about Jocundra, he said, "Beats me, Jim. I can't keep track of my own woman."

Donnell was puzzled but unconcerned. Coldly, he dismissed her. He spent the afternoon exploring the new boundaries of his vision, charting minuscule dents in the wallpaper, composing mosaic landscapes from the reflections glazing the lens of the camera mounted above the door, and— something of a breakthrough—following the flight of a hawk circling the middle distance, bringing it so close he managed to see a scaly patch on its wing and an awful eye the color of dried blood and half filmed over with a crackled white membrane. An old, sick, mad king of the air. The hawk kept soaring out of his range, and he could never obtain a view of its entire body; his control still lacked discretion. It was a pity, he thought, that the visual effects were only temporary, though they did not suffice of themselves to make life interesting. Their novelty quickly wore off.

The orderly who brought his dinner tray was tanned, fortyish, with razor-cut hair combed over a bald spot and silken black hairs matting the backs of his hands. Though he was no more talkative than the singing orderly, Donnell suspected he could be drawn into a conversation. He flounced pillows, preened before the mirror, and took inordinate pleasure in rubbing out Donnell's neck cramp. Gentle, lissome fingers. On his pinky he wore a diamond ring, an exceptionally large one for a person earning orderly's wages, and Donnell, seeking to ingratiate himself, to learn about Jocundra, spoke admiringly of it.

"It belonged to my grandmother," said the orderly. "The stone, not the setting. I've been offered eighteen thousand for it, but I held onto it because you never know when hard times might snap you up." He illustrated the snapping of hard times by pinching Donnell's leg, then launched into an interminable story about his grandmother. "She had lovers 'til she was sixty-seven, the old dear. Heaven knows what she did after that!" Titter. He put on a dismal face. "But it was no picnic being raised by a dirty old woman, let me tell you." And he did.

Donnell had been hoping to weasel information about Jocundra during the course of the conversation, but the orderly showed no sign of allowing a conversation, and he was forced to interrupt. The orderly acted betrayed, said he had no idea where she was, and swept from the room with a display of injured dignity that evoked the angry rustle of taffeta.

Then it dawned on Donnell. She wasn't coming back. She had deserted him. How could she just go without telling him, without arranging a replacement? Panicked, he wheeled out into the hall. As he headed for the foyer, hoping to find Edman, a ripple in the carpet snagged his wheels and canted him into one of the potted ferns; the brass urn toppled and bonged against the floor. The door beside it opened, and a thin blond woman poked out her head. "Shh!" she commanded. She knelt by the fern, her nose wrinkling at having to touch the dirt. She had the kind of brittle prettiness that hardens easily into middle-aged bitchdom, and as if in anticipation of this, her hair was done up into a no-nonsense bun and tied with a dark blue ribbon.

"Have you seen Jocundra?" asked Donnell.

"Jocundra?" The woman did not look up, packing down the dirt around the fern. "Hasn't she left?"

"She's left?" Donnell refused to accept it. "When's she coming back?"

"No, now wait. I saw her on the grounds after supper. Maybe she hasn't gone yet."

"Laura!" A querulous voice leaked out the open door; the woman wiggled all five fingers in a wave, a smile nicked the corners of her mouth, and she closed the door behind her.

It had been easy to tell Jocundra to leave when he had not believed it possible, but now he was adrift in the possibility, all solid ground melted away. He skidded down the ramp into the parking lot. The lanterns above the stone benches were lit, bubbles of yellow light picking out the blackness, and fireflies swarmed under the oaks. Toads

ratcheted, crickets sizzled. She would be—if she hadn't
left—at the bench near the gate. The flagstones jolted the
wheels, his chest labored, his arms ached, a sheen of sweat
covered his face. Something flew into his eye, batted its
wings, clung for a second and fluttered off. A moth. He
crested a rise and spotted Jocundra on the bench. She wasn't
wearing makeup, or was wearing very little, and she looked
hardly more than a girl. He had always assigned her the
characteristic of sophistication, albeit of a callow sort, and
so her youthfulness surprised him. Her melancholy expression did not change when she saw him.

"I don't want you to leave," he said, scraping to a halt
a couple of feet away.

She laughed palely. "I've already left. I just went into
New Orleans for the day." She regarded him with mild
approval. "You made it out here by yourself. That's pretty
good."

"I thought you'd gone," he said, choosing his words
carefully, not wanting to appear too relieved. "I didn't much
like the idea."

"Oh?" She raised an eyebrow.

"Listen." He balked at apology, but gave in to the need
for it. "I'm sorry. I know I've been an asshole."

"You've had good reason to be upset." She smoothed
her skirt down over her knees, then smiled. "But you *have*
been an asshole."

"Could be it's my nature," he said, rankled.

"No, you're not like that," she said thoughtfully. She
slung her purse over her shoulder. "Let's go on in."

As she wheeled him toward the house, Donnell felt
strangely satisfied, as if some plaguing question had been
put to rest. The fireflies pricking the dark, the scrape of
Jocundra's shoes, the insect noises, everything formed an
intricate complement to his thoughts, a relationship he could
not grasp but wanted to make graspable, to write down.
Near the house another moth fluttered into his face, and he
wondered—his wonder tinged with revulsion—if they were
being attracted by the flickers in his eyes. He pinched its
wings together and held it up for Jocundra's inspection.

"It's a luna moth," she said. "There was this old man

back home, a real Cajun looney. He's blind now, or partially blind, but he used to keep thousands of luna moths in his back room and study their wing patterns. He claimed they revealed the natural truth." She shook her head, regretful, and added in a less enthusiastic voice, "Clarence Brisbeau."

"What's wrong?" Donnell loosed the moth and it skittered off, vanishing against the coal-black crowns of the oaks.

"I was just remembering. He scared me once. He got drunk and tried to kiss me. I was only thirteen, and he must have been almost sixty." She stared after the moth as if she could still see it. "It was spooky. Stripes of light were shining between the boards of the cabin, dead moths on the floor, thousands clinging to the walls. Every time he gestured they fluttered off his arms. I remember him walking toward me, dripping moths, talking." She adopted an accent, like French, but with harsher rhythms. "'I'm tellin' you, me,' he said. 'This worl' she's full of supernatural creatures whose magic we deny.'"

CHAPTER V

March 25–April 17, 1987

"Now don't laugh, but I've been thinking about our patients in terms of spirit possession." Dr. Edman folded his hands across his stomach and leaned back; the leather chair wheezed.

Jocundra was sitting across a mahogany desk from Edman in his office: a curious round room whose roof was the glass dome. Shafts of the declining sun struck through the faceted panes, and dust motes swirled idly like the thoughts of a crystal-skulled giant. Recessed bookshelves ringed the room—you entered by means of a stair leading up through a trapdoor—and the volumes were mired in shadow; though now and then the light brightened, crept lower on the walls, and the odd gilt word melted up from the dimness: Witchcraft, Psychologica, Pathology. A chart of the brain was tacked up over a portion of the shelves, and Edman had scribbled crabbed notes along arrows pointing to various of the fissures. The shelf behind his head held an array of dusty, yellowed human crania, suggesting to Jocundra that he was the latest in a succession of psychologist-kings, and that his own brain case would someday join those of his predecessors.

"During a voodoo ritual," Edman continued, "the celebrants experience tremors, convulsions, and begin to exhibit a different class of behaviors than previously They may, for example, show a fondness for gazing into mirrors or eating a particular food, and the *houngan* then identifies these behaviors as aspects belonging to one of the gods."

"There *is* a rough analogue..." Jocundra began.

"Bear with me a moment!" Edman waggled a finger, summoning a thought. "I prefer to regard this so-called spirit possession as the emergence of the deep consciousness. A rather imprecise term, easily confused with Jungian terminology, but generally indicative of what I'm after: the raw force of the identity to which all the socialized and otherwise learned behaviors adhere, barnacling it with fears and logical process and so forth, gradually masking it from the light and relegating it to a murky existence in the..." He smacked his head, as if to dislodge an idea. "Ah! In the abyss of forethought." He scribbled on his notepad, beaming at Jocundra. "That ought to wake up the back rows at the next convention." He leaned back again. "My thesis is that we're simulating spirit possession by microbiological means rather than hypnogogic ones, elevating the deep consciousness to fill the void created by the dissipation of learned behaviors. But instead of allowing this new and unfocused identity to wander about at will for a few hours, we educate and guide it. And instead of a *houngan* or a *mama loi* to simply proclaim the manifestation, we utilize trained personnel to maximize their potential, to influence their growth. Of course if we had a *mama loi* on the staff, she'd say we had conjured up a god." He chuckled. "See what I'm after?"

"It's hardly a scholarly viewpoint." Jocundra found the idea of playing voodoo priestess to Donnell's elemental spirit appealing in the manner of a comic book illustration.

"Not as such! Still, a case might be made for it. And wouldn't it be a surprise package if we learned there were exact correlations between personality types and the voodoo pantheon!" Edman pursed his lips and tapped them with his forefinger. "You must be familiar with anthropological studies in this area. . . . Any input?"

"Well," said Jocundra, unhappy at having to supply grist for Edman's mill, "the voodoo concept of the soul has some resonance with your thesis. According to doctrine all human beings have two souls. The *ti bon ange,* which is more or less the conscience, the socialized part of the mind, and the *gros bon ange,* which is the undying part, the immortal twin. It's been described as the image of a man reflected by a dark mirror. You might want to read Deren or Metraux."

"Hmm." Edman bent to his notepad. "Tell me, Ms. Verret. Do you like Donnell?" He cocked an eye toward her, continuing to write. "You must have some personal reaction."

Jocundra was startled by the question. "I think he's brilliant," she said. "You've seen his work."

"It seems quite competent, but that's not what I'm driving at. Suppose Donnell wasn't your patient, would you be attracted to him?"

"I don't believe that's relevant," she said defensively. "Not to the project or . . ."

"You're right, of course. Sorry." Edman took another note and favored her with a paternal smile. "I'm just an old snoop."

"I'm *concerned* for him, I'm not happy he's going to die."

"Please! Your private concerns are just that. Sorry."

Edman opened a file drawer and rummaged through it, leaving Jocundra a little flustered. The sun was going down, staining the faceted panes to ruby, empurpling the shadows along the wall, and these decaying colors—augmented by the glutinous sound of Edman's breath as he bent over the file, taxed by even this slight exertion—congealed into a perverse atmosphere. She felt soiled. His question had not been idle curiosity; he was constantly prying, hinting, insinuating. Her opinion of him had always been low, but never so low as now. She pictured him alone in the office, entertaining fantasies about the therapists, fondling himself while watching videos of the patients, feeding upon the potential for sickness which the project incorporated.

At last he unbent, his pale face mooning above the desk. "The microbiology people think Magnusson's the key...." He paused, his attention commanded by a clipping in a manila folder; he clucked to himself and closed it. "Did you know they've been letting him work on material related to the bacterial process?"

"Yes, Laura told me."

"Ah! Well, he *is* important. But because of Donnell's youth, his human focus, it's possible he's going to give us a clearer look into the basis of consciousness than even Magnusson. Now that he's in harness it's time to lay off the whip and break out the sugar, although"—Edman fussed with papers—"although I wonder if it isn't time for another forced interaction."

"He's working so smoothly now, I'd hate to disrupt him... and besides, he didn't react well to Richmond."

"None of them react well to Richmond!" Edman laughed. "But I keep thinking if we could override this fear reaction of theirs, we might proceed by leaps and bounds. Even Richmond seems reluctant for intimate confrontation. He enjoys facing down his own fear, but his contacts are kept on the level of ritual aggression."

Edman rambled off onto other matters, talking mainly to himself as he dealt with his files; he admitted to using his sessions with the therapists as a means to order his thoughts, and Jocundra knew her active participation was not required. She wondered how he would wed his latest theory to his previous one: that of cellular wish-fulfillment. He considered Richmond weighty evidence in support of the latter because, unlike the rest of the slow-burners—all of whom had murky backgrounds—the body had a thoroughly doc-

umented past. Richmond, born Eliot Vuillemont, had been
the heir of a prominent New Orleans family, disinherited
for reasons of drug abuse. This young man, Edman argued,
who had lived a life of ineffectual rebellion, whose college
psychiatric records reflected a history of cowardice and re-
pressed violence, had chosen as his posthumous role the
antihero, the apocalyptic lone wolf; the new personality was
a triumphant expression of the feebly manifested drives
which had led to his death by overdose. Edman posited that
the workings of memory chemically changed portions of
the RNA—those portions containing the bioform of our
most secret and complex wish, "the deepest reason we have
made for being"—and intensified their capacity for survival.
It was, Jocundra thought, a more viable theory than his
latest, but she had no doubt both would soon appear in
published form, welded together into a rickety construct
studded with bits of glitter: a Rube Goldberg theory of the
personality.

"I believe I'll bring it up in staff tonight." Edman reached
inside his lab coat and pulled forth a red memorandum book.
"The seventeenth looks free."

Jocundra looked at him questioningly, realizing she must
have missed something. Edman smiled; he slipped the book
back into his pocket, and it seemed to her he had reached
deep within his body and fed his heart a piece of red candy.

"I won't take any more of your time, Ms. Verret. I was
saying that I thought this fear reaction needed to be examined under group conditions, and I proposed we have a
party for our green-eyed friends. Invite the staff from Tulane, arrange for some sort of music, and just see if we
can't get the patients to pass off their fear as another side
effect of the process. At the very least it should be a memorable social occasion."

The main hall was thronged with doctors, technicians,
students and administration people wearing sport jackets and
summer dresses, most gathered around the groupings of
sofas which roughly divided the room into thirds; and scattered throughout the crowd were the five patients—Richmond had not yet arrived. A three piece band played cocktail
jazz on the patio, and several couples were dancing. The

room was huge. Carved angels flowed from the molding, spreading their wings in the corners of the ceiling, and the space whose sanctity they guaranteed was the size of a country church, filled with the relics of bygone years. Gilt chairs and statuettes and filigreed tables occupied every spare nook, and every flat surface was cluttered with *objets d'art,* the emphasis being upon ceramic figurines of be-wigged lords and ladies. The French doors were flanked by curio cabinets, except for those beside which stood a grand piano, its finish holding a blaze of sunlight. Paintings and prints and photographs hung in rows to the ceiling, pre-senting scenes of the countryside, historical personages, hunts, groups of shabbily dressed blacks. One print depicted a masque whose participants were costumed as demons, beasts, and fanciful birds. Passing it on the way to the punch bowl, Jocundra decided that this masque had much in com-mon with Edman's party: though the mix of music and conversation suggested a trivial assemblage, most eyes were fixed on the patients and most talk concerned them, and there was an underlying air of anticipation, as if the par-tygoers were awaiting a moment of unmasking so they could determine which of them was not masked, which was truly a demon, a beast, or a fanciful bird.

Knots of people were clumped along the refreshment table, and Jocundra eavesdropped as she ladled punch.

". . . the greater their verbal capacity, the more credibly they fabricate a past reality." A fruity male voice.

Jocundra moved down the table, examining the sandwich trays, hoping for some less Edmanesque commentary.

". . . and Monroe looked like the devil had asked her to tango!" Laughter, a babble of voices.

"Listen to this!" The click and whir of a tape recorder, and then the tiny, cornpone-accented voice of Kline French: ". . . Ah'm quite an afficionado of the dance, though of course Ah've only been exposed to its regional privations."

Clarice Monroe had been sketching scenes for a ballet on one of the sofas, and French had been maneuvered into approach by his therapist and had asked to see her sketch.

FRENCH: "This appears to be an illumination of an Af-
           rican myth. . . . Am Ah correct?"

MONROE *(tremulously)*:   "It's the Anansi, the Ashanti god of lies and deceit."

FRENCH: "And this young lady has fallen into his clutches?"

MONROE: "She's the sorceress Luweji. She's traveled through the gates of fire. . . ."

FRENCH: "Represented by these red curtains, I presume?"

MONROE: "Yes." *(Silence)*

FRENCH: "Well, it seems quite wonderful. Ah hope Ah'll have the privilege of attendin' its triumphant celebration."

Jocundra spotted French through the press of bodies. He was being wheeled along, nodding his massive head in response to something his therapist was saying. His shoulders were wide as a wrestler's; his eyes sparked emerald in a heavy-jawed, impassive face, and made Jocundra think of an idol ruling over a deserted temple or—perhaps closer to the truth—one of those James Bond villains whose smile only appears when he hears the crunching of a backbone. The doctors said they had rarely had a patient with such muscle tone, dead or alive, and there had been a rumor at Tulane that his body had been introduced to the project via a government agency. But whatever his origins, he now believed himself to be a financial consultant; the administration followed his market analyses with strict attention.

"There goes French," said someone beside her. "I bet he's chasing Monroe again." Giggles.

"He's out of luck. I think she had to go potty after the last time." Laughter unrestrained.

Balancing the punch, slipping between couples, Jocundra threaded her way toward Donnell. He was sitting across the room from the punch bowl, scowling; he had gotten some tan lately, his hollows were filling in, but his social attitudes had not changed much. He had rejected every advance so far, and no one was bothering to talk to him anymore. Jocundra was beginning to feel like the loser in a garden show, watching the crowd encircle the winners, sitting alone with her despirited, green-eyed plant.

"I know, I know," she said, handing him the punch. "Where have I been?"

"Where the hell *have* you been?" He sipped the punch. "God, this is awful! Let's get out of here."

"We have to stay until Edman comes. He should be here soon." A lie. Edman was monitoring the video, overseeing the big picture.

Marilyn Ramsburgh's therapist signaled to Jocundra, and she signaled him back No. Donnell was not ready for Ramsburgh. She was, as far as Jocundra was concerned, the most physically alarming of the patients. Frail, white hair so thin you could see the veined scalp beneath, hunched in her chair, hands enwebbed with yarn, her pupils shrunk to almost nothing. She was due to be "discharged" soon, taken back to Tulane for "a few final tests," and lately she had been chirping about hugging her grandchildren again, promising to write everyone, and had presented Edman with a beautiful hand-woven coverlet worked into a design of knights battling in a forest illuminated by violet will o' the wisps: a token of her gratitude.

Squabbling noises on the patio, a woman's squeal, and Richmond came into view, swinging his cane to clear a path; his therapist, Audrey, trailed behind him. He limped along the refreshment table, picked up a sandwich, had a bite, and tossed the remainder on the floor; he dipped a ladleful of punch, slurped, and spewed it back into the bowl. "Fuckin' fruit juice! Jesus!" Punch dribbled off his chin onto a torn T shirt emblazoned with a crudely painted swastika and letters spelling out Hellhounds M.C. Greasy strands of hair fell down over his eyes, and he glared between them at the crowd like a drunken Indian.

The crowd retreated from the refreshment table, from Richmond, but three men and an overweight girl in a yellow sun dress bravely held their positions. Noticing them, Richmond hooked his cane over an arm, limped forward and grabbed the girl's breast, slipping his free arm around her waist and pulling her close. She shrieked and lifted her hand to slap him.

"Go ahead, bitch," said Richmond, nonchalant. "Lessee what you got."

The girl's mouth puckered, opened and shut, and she let her hand fall. Richmond cupped her breast at different angles, squeezing it cruelly. "Damn, mama!" he said. "I bet you give Grade A."

"Let her go, Jack." Audrey tried to pull his hand loose, but he shook her off. "C'mon back to the room."

"Cool. How 'bout all three of us go and we play a little ring-around-the-rosy?" He tightened his hold on the girl's waist and flicked her nipple with his thumb. Her eyelids lowered, her head drooped to one side, as if she were experiencing a sweet wave of passion.

One of the men, a skinny guy in a madras jacket, did a shuffle forward and said, "Uh, Mr. Richmond..."

"Hey, little savage!" said Richmond good-naturedly. "Guess you wonder what's gonna happen to your squeeze."

The girl spun free. Richmond made no effort to hold her, but as she staggered back, he clawed at the top of her dress. He was too weak to rip the material, but his fingers hooked one of the straps, and in her struggle it came away in Richmond's hand—a little yellow serpent. Her right breast bounded out, pale and pendulous, the imprint of his fingers already darkening to bruises. Richmond sniffed at the strap. "Warthog," he said, identifying the odor. The skinny guy covered the girl with his jacket, and she flung her arms around him, sobbing.

Richmond grinned at the crowd, nodded; then he whirled about and brought his cane down on the punch bowl, shattering it. The punch gushed out, floating cookies off the trays, puddling in the paper plates. He swung again and again, snake-killing strokes, his hair flying, red droplets spraying from the tablecloth, until a sugary dust of pulverized glass lay around his feet. No one spoke. Jocundra could hear the punch dripping onto the carpet.

"Why you citizens just stand there and let me fuck with your women?" asked Richmond, hobbling away from the table. The crowd parted before him, reforming at the rear. "I mean this *is* the real world, ain't it?" He spotted Donnell and headed toward him. "Hey, sweets! You lookin' gorgeous today. How come you think these chickenshits is lettin' me crow?"

Donnell gripped the arms of his wheelchair, but didn't freeze up. "Keep your mouth off me, asshole," he said.

"Hostility!" Richmond was delighted. "Now I can relate to some hostility." He moved closer, tapping the crook of his cane on his palm.

Jocundra set down her punch, preparing to help Audrey restrain him; it was certain no one else would help. The crowd had packed in around them, penning the four of them against the wall, and their faces were the faces of intent observers. Tape recorders whirred, clipboards were in evidence. Jocundra saw that all the patients had pushed into the front rank, and each was exhibiting extreme tension. Magnusson sucked his gums, Ramsburgh plucked feverishly at her knitting, French's fingers drummed on his leg, and the pretty dark face of Clarice Monroe peeked over a shoulder, blinking and stunned. It was, thought Jocundra, one of Ramsburgh's tapestries come to life: a mysterious forest, a myriad faces peering between the branches, the spirits of trees, goblins, ghostly men and women, and a few whose glowing eyes served as the structural focus of the design.

Magnusson rolled a foot forward. "They're observing us, sonny. That's why they're letting you foul the air."

Forgetting about Donnell, Richmond spread his arms in a gesture of false heartiness. "Damn if it ain't Doctor Demento!"

"And they've good reason to observe." Magnusson glanced from one patient to another. "Feel around inside yourselves! Find anything solid, anything real? We're not who we were!"

For a moment, silence; then French spoke. "Ah don't believe I see what you're drivin' at, Doctor." He kneaded his leg with the heel of his palm.

"Don't listen to that old maniac," creaked Ramsburgh. "He was 'round the other day trying to poison me with his ravings." She frowned at Magnusson; his eyes blazed out from the mottled ruin of his face, and they stared at each other like hellish grandparents gloating over an evil thought.

"Your mind's poisoned, Hilmer!" Ramsburgh's hands danced among her needles and yarn. "Your arteries are hard, and your brain's a dried-out sponge! Time you came to grips with the fact and left the rest of us in peace."

"Old woman," said Magnusson gravely. "Don't you feel the winnowing of your days?"

Edman eased through the crowd and seized the handles of his wheelchair. "I think you've had too much excitement, Doctor," he said with professional cheer. He started to wheel him away, but the old man locked his hands onto the wheels and the chair wouldn't budge.

"Don't you see it's a hoax?" Again he glanced at the other patients. "By God, you'll see!" he said to Donnell. "You'll have a glimpse over the edge before you fall."

Laura knelt beside him, prying at his fingers. "Stop this, Hilmer!" she said. "Stop this right now."

Gasping, reddening with the effort, Edman wrangled the chair sideways, and for a split second Jocundra found herself looking into Magnusson's eyes, except it was not merely looking: it was falling down luminous green tunnels so bright they seemed to be spinning, whirlpools sucking her under, and the pattern of gristle and discoloration surrounding them made no sense at all.

"It's so clear." Magnusson shook his head in wonder, then he gazed sternly at Jocundra. "No sorrow is too great to bear," he said, "and this one cannot be averted."

Jocundra thought she understood him, but her understanding fled the instant he turned away and she felt disoriented.

Edman gave way to two black orderlies, who lifted Magnusson's wheelchair, bearing him aloft like a king on a palanquin.

"Hey, niggers!" shouted Richmond, and swung his cane at the nearest orderly; but Audrey wrapped her arms around him from behind and his swing went awry. They swayed together, struggling.

"No hope for you, sonny." Magnusson beamed at Richmond from on high. "You're a dead man."

"Out!" bawled Edman; he waved his fist, abandoning control. "Everybody out! Staff in my office!"

As the orderlies carried Magnusson off, he called back. "Two years, Edman! Three at the most! They'll probe your every hollow, but they'll never find it!"

A babble arose, cries of alarm, milling, and Jocundra was later to reflect that when psychiatrists lost their cool they did not stoop to half measures. She had intended to wait until the crowd thinned, but Dr. Brauer rushed up, poked his face into Donnell's, bleated "Harrison!" then shouted at Jocundra to move it. There were more shouts of "Move it!" and "Let her through!" A hefty red-haired woman tried to get out of her path, snapped a high heel and tumbled head first over the arm of a sofa; her skirt slid down around her hips, exposing thighs dimpled by cellulite. A doctor and an orderly tugged at Clarice Monroe, contending for the right to escort her; French's wheelchair sideswiped Ramsburgh's, and she jabbed at his therapist with a plastic needle. Dodging, swerving, Jocundra pushed Donnell along a tunnel of consternated faces and into the hall. Three doctors had backed the girl whom Richmond had assaulted against the wall; she was straddling a fern, holding the madras jacket together. Tears streaked her face. She nodded in response to a question, but the nod may have had no significance because she continued to bob her head while they scribbled on their clipboards.

Donnell's room was sunny, a breeze shifted the curtains, leaf shadow jittered on the carpet. Jocundra could not think what to say, what lie would soothe him, so she left him at the writing desk and collected the laundry, watching him out of the corner of her eye. He straightened a stack of paper, picked up a pen, doodled, laid it down.

"He's really . . ." He picked up the pen again.

"Pardon?" She tossed his bathrobe into the hamper.

"What's the matter with him? Is he just naturally crazy or is it something to do with the process?" He kept fidgeting, his hands moving aimlessly from pen to paper to notebook.

"He's very, very old." Jocundra knelt beside him, happy for the opportunity to comfort him. "He was probably senile before the process was applied, and it wasn't able to restore him fully." She rubbed the bunched muscles in his shoulder.

He bent his head, allowing her easier access to his neck. "I can't wait to get out of this place," he said.

"It'll be sooner than you think," she said, wishing it weren't so harshly true. She had begun to hate herself for lying, but she had no better thing to tell him. "Please don't let it depress you. I want you to get well."

A poignant sadness rose in her, as if the words "I want you to get well" had been a splash of cold water on the hot stones of her emotions. But the sadness didn't seem attached to his dying. It seemed instead a product of the way the light slanted down, the temperature, the shadows and sounds: a kind of general sadness attaching to every human involvement, one you only felt when the conditions were just right but was there all the time. She thought the feeling must be showing on her face, and to hide it she pretended to cough.

"God," he said, "I wish I was well now." He looked over at her, eyes wide, mouth downturned, the same expression he had worn during the drive from Tulane. "Ah, Hell. I guess there's some virtue to having died. . . ." He trailed off.

She knew he had been about to refer to her as that virtue, to make a joke of it, to address lightly his attraction for her, but he left the punchline unsaid and the last words he *had* said hung in the air between them, taking on the coloration of all the fear and sickness in the room. Shortly afterward she excused herself and went into the bathroom. She sat on the edge of the sink for almost fifteen minutes, expecting to cry, on the verge of crying, tears brimming, but the sob never built to critical in her chest, just hung there and decayed.

CHAPTER VI

**From *Conjure Men: My Work With Ezawa at Tulane*
by Anthony Edman, M.D., Ph.D.**

. . . It was as close as I have ever come to striking a colleague, but Brauer—in his capacity of ambitious underling, thirsting for authority—seemed determined to make a case for my bungling the interaction, allowing the patients too much leeway, and my temper frayed. I forced myself to calm, however, and reminded him that we had achieved exactly the desired result: despite Magnusson's unexpected outburst, or because of it, we had brought the patients' fear of one another into the open where it could be treated with and analyzed.

"Within a week they'll be forming associations," I told him. "Monroe and French are obvious, Harrison and Richmond. . . . Now that Richmond's found someone who'll face up to him, someone more or less his own age, he's bound to make friendly overtures. It's inevitable. Perhaps we've suffered a few flesh wounds, but now they'll have to accept their fear as a side effect of the process and deal with it."

My show of unruffled confidence bolstered staff morale, and, in effect, dismasted Brauer who continued his outraged sputterings, but to no avail. I explained to staff that our loss of control only added authenticity to the proceedings. Had we not, I asked them, reacted in the manner of concerned medical personnel, of doctors responsible for the welfare of patients making a difficult mental adjustment? We had shown them our humanity, our imperfect compassion. I admitted my own loss of control was, like theirs, a response to the possibility that the patients might understand their true natures; still, I felt that any damage caused by our actions or by Magnusson's could be turned to our advantage if we did not attempt a cover-up, if we allowed Magnusson to remain at Shadows, and not—as Brauer suggested—hide him from the world in a cell at Tulane. Let him say what he will, I advised, and we will simply put on a sad face and express pity over his senility, his general deterioration. *We* will be believed.

Of course, it did not prove necessary to debunk Magnusson; just as Ramsburgh had defended herself, so the patients—in defense of their threatened identities—arrived at this conclusion on their own, separately and unanimously.

We had taken a vast step forward as a result of the group interaction. The patients began to speak openly of their fearful reaction to one another, and we analyzed their reports, gaining further insights into the extent of their perceptual abnormalities. For example, it was during the period immediately following the interaction that Harrison revealed the fact he was seeing bioenergy: "... Raw mists of a single color sheathing the upper body, showing patches and glints of secondary colors, all fading in a matter of seconds." His perceptions, in particular, gave me cause to ponder Magnusson's pronouncement concerning my own illness, though at the time I assumed his diagnosis to be a vindictive rather than an accurate one. But while such insights provided clues to the developmental processes of these phenomenal strangers who were the BIAP patients, they shed no direct light upon the essential mystery of their existence; and the illumination of this mystery must be, I felt, the primary goal of the project. So, instead of pursuing a hands-off policy in the wake of Magnusson's revelations to the group, I continued as planned to set up problematic situations which would, I hoped, stimulate the patients to more profound depths of self-discovery.

Throughout the hullabaloo which eventuated after the media's disclosure of the project, my detractors have labeled me a manipulator, and while I do not accept the term with its overtones of maleficence, I submit that all psychotherapy is manipulation; that as psychiatrists we do not heal people, but manipulate their neuroses into functional modes. Any psychiatrist worth his salt is at heart a sophist who understands he is lost in a great darkness and who utilizes theories not as doctrinal cant, but as guideposts to mark the places he has illumined in his dealings with specific patients. Thus, also, did ancient alchemists incise their alembics with arcane symbols representing the known elements. I have been accused of ruthlessly swaying the courses of lives to satisfy my academic whimsies. This charge I deny. I maneuvered both patients and therapists as would a man lost in a forest strike flint and steel together to make a light. And we *were* lost. Before my arrival the project had an unblemished record of failure in every area, especially as regards the unraveling of the patients' intrinsic natures. This memoir is not the proper framework in which to detail all we *did* unravel after my arrival, but I must point out the various papers and monographs of my detractors as evidence of my successes (the more scholarly reader may wish to avail himself of my own soon-to-be-published *The Second Death* and its speculative companion, *Departed Souls: A Psychoanalytic Reassessment of Animist Beliefs*).

My detractors have addressed with especial venom what one of them has termed my "unprofessional obsession with Jocundra Verret," and have laid the blame for all consequent tragedy at my feet. In this I admit to some complicity, yet if I am to shoulder the blame, then surely I must take credit for all that has been gained. While I do not discount my colleagues' responsibility, and while Ms. Verret herself has testified that she acted for reasons of her own, if they are insistent I will accept full blame and credit, and leave history to confer final judgment on the worth of my contribution. Yes, I took chances! I flew by the seat of my pants. I was willing for all hell to break loose in order to learn the patients' secrets, and perhaps a measure of hell was necessary for the truth to emerge. We were cartographers, not healers; it was our duty to explore the wilderness of this new human preserve, and I could not accept, as Brauer seemingly could, my role as being merely that of babysitter to the undead.

Though my case study of the relationship between Harrison and Verret—and never has a courtship been so thoroughly documented as theirs, recorded on videotape and footnoted by in-depth interviews of the participants—though this study revealed much of value, as the weeks passed I came to regard the relationship primarily as a star by which I navigated, one whose unwavering light signaled the rightness of my course. This may seem an overly romantic attitude for a member of my profession to hold, and perhaps it was, but I believe I can justify having held it in terms of my own emotional needs. The pressures on me were enormous, and I was only able to cope with them by commuting to and from New Orleans on the weekends and spending the nights in my own home. Project officials screamed for results, my colleagues continually questioned my concern for the patients' well-being. *My* concern? Because I refused to indulge in banal Freudian dissections and quasi-metaphysical coffee klatches with these second-rate theoreticians, did I lack concern? I stimulated the patients, encouraged them, tried to provide them with a pride in their occupations. Should I, instead, have pampered them, patted them on the head and admired the fact that they actually breathed? This was Ezawa's attitude: having made them, he was well pleased, looking upon them as mere monuments to his cleverness.

But, of course, the greatest pressure was that exerted by the patients themselves. Imagine, if you will, indwelling with a group of brilliant and charismatic individuals, thoroughly dominant, whose vivid character suppresses and dulls your own. It was a constant strain to be around them; I cannot think of a single person who did not suffer a severe depression at some time or another as a result. They were mesmeric figures: green-eyed monsters with the capacities of angels. Harrison's poems, Monroe's ballet, even Richmond's howled dirge . . . these were powerful expressions, dispiriting to those of us incapable of emulating them, especially dispiriting because of the wan light their productions appeared to shed on the nature of creativity, demystifying it, relegating it to something on the order of a technological twitch, like the galvanic response of a dissected frog. And yet neither could we totally disabuse ourselves of mystical notions concerning the patients. At times it seemed to me that we were a strange monastic order committed to the care and feeding of crippled, green-eyed saints whose least pronouncement sent us running to examine the entrails for proof of their prophetic insight. All the therapists stood in awe of them, or—as did Laura Petit—maintained an artificial distance; all, that is, except Jocundra Verret.

Watching Verret and Harrison, observing the relaxed attitude they had adopted with each other, their responses increasingly warm and genuine, I felt I was witnessing the emergence of some integral shape from the chaotic sphere of Shadows: a sweet, frail truth which—despite its frailty—underlies our humanity. Always a beautiful woman, Verret grew ever more beautiful; her skin glowed, her hair shone and her walk—previously somnolent, head down, arms barely aswing—grew sprightly and girlish. I often pointed out to her during our sessions that she——every bit as much as the residual RNA—was a determining factor in Harrison's personality, that just as the *mama loi* identifies the possessing spirit in a voodoo rite, so she was "identifying" Harrison, evoking the particular complex of his behaviors to conform with her own needs. He was, after all, trying to please her, molding himself to suit her requirements as a man. Given Harrison's perceptual abilities, his concentrated focus upon her, it is likely he was being influenced by her on levels we can only begin to guess at, and the extent of her influence is equally unfathomable. She preferred, however, to downplay her role of creatrix, insisting he was something more mysterious and self-determining. I am certain she did not know what was happening, not at first, hiding her feelings behind the pose of duty.

Although I had detected this potential in Verret at our initial meeting, still it dazzled me that love could arise between two such ill-matched individuals and under such intimidating circumstances. Their relationship provided a breath of normalcy amidst the abnormal atmosphere of Shadows, one which I inhaled deeply, rising to it as a miner trapped in a gas-filled tunnel would lift his head at the scent of fresh air. I became more and more interested to learn how far this affair might progress, interested to the point of adding my own thread to the tapestry they were weaving.

Manipulate? Yes, I manipulated. And despite the ensuing events, I would do so again, for it is the function of psychiatry to encourage the living to live, and thus did I encourage Harrison and Verret.

One day, while lunching in the commissary, I was joined by Laura Petit and Audrey Beamon. Petit had with her a Tarot deck and proceeded to tell Beamon's fortune, and, thereafter, insisted on telling mine. I chose the Hierophant as my significator, cut the cards and listened as Laura interpreted their meanings. I could see the cards were ordinary, showing no pattern; I had not concentrated during the shuffle or the cut. Laura was not aware of my familiarity with the Tarot and therefore did not realize I learned more of her character from the reading than of my fate. Punctuating her delivery with "Oh dears" and "Now, wait a minutes," she twisted the meanings of the cards, telling me a glittering tale of my future—fame after struggle—and told me also by the flattering, insinuating nature of her interpretation that here was a clever ally whom I could entrust with any mission, no matter how underhanded. Afterwards, she laid a card face up on the table: the Devil, a great, shaggy, horned figure crouched on a black stone to which a naked man and woman were chained. "I *really* think you should have chosen this as your significator, Dr. Edman," she said, fluttering her lashes and giggling. Despite the apparent triviality of the comment, her identification of me with this awesome masculine figure, this cruel master, signaled her willingness to enlist in my cause, to submit, and, as well, displayed her sly delight in what she presumed we were really doing: all the subterfuge and nastiness of the project. All right, I thought, if I am to be Satan, then Laura will be my imp. I would put her simpering guile to use. And I did, though I am certain my manipulation was not the sole causal agent of the affair.

The character and climate of Shadows, no doubt, exerted an influence on my actions. This great manor house glooming on the edge of the swamp amid sentinel oaks and penitential moss, inhabited by dead men come to life again . . . here were both magical setting and characters, the stuff from which great drama arises, and perhaps, unconsciously, I was trying to spark such a drama, obeying the commands of some inner theatricality which the house had stirred in my depths, my "deep consciousness." Perhaps, were I to be injected with the Ezawa bacterium after death, I might well reincarnate as a playwright. But each morning before rounds as I took my constitutional, I would look back at the house and experience a thrill of excitement and fear. From a distance its windows appeared dead black as if it contained not furniture and walls and lives, but only a ripe and contaminating darkness. We inhabited that darkness, and I alone of all the project dared strike matches and dispel the gloom. Most of my colleagues, I believe, feared what would be revealed and satisfied themselves with behavioral studies. But this was an experiment, not a behavioral clinic; we were there to learn, not to footnote extant knowledge.

And what did we learn? We uncovered new forces, we took a step along what may be an endless path toward divinity, we redirected the entire thrust of psychoanalytic theory, and, as with all knowledge, we found that deeper and more compelling mysteries yet lay beyond those we had reduced to the security of fact.

CHAPTER VII

April 18–May 3, 1987

"You should come on a run with me sometime," said Richmond; he lay back, arms behind his head, and pondered the passing clouds. "Cruisin' through some half-ass town, pullin' up to the fountain in the park or whatever they got for a public eyesore. 'Bout forty or fifty of you. The cops ain't to be found, man. You know, they got sudden problems out on the highway, and you are in *control* of the situation. That's when the ladies will do some flockin' around. The ladies dig on a Harley, man! They wanna run their fingers 'long your gas tank, you understand?"

"Uh huh," said Donnell, too exhausted to do more than listen to Richmond. He had managed to walk almost a hundred yards, and as a result his legs trembled, his chest hammered, and sweat was trickling into his eyes; but the accomplishment gave him a feeling of serenity.

"Dig it, man. After we blow outta here, we'll head on down to the Gulf, place I know, do some money trips, and then get the fuck outta Dodge City! Put our shit nationwide!" He held out his hand to be slapped five.

Donnell propped himself up on an elbow and accommodated him, amused by Richmond's adoption of him as a sidekick. His function, it seemed, was to agree, to share Richmond's enthusiasm for drugs, violence, and sleazy sex — those things he considered the joys of life — and to confirm

Richmond's wisdom in all areas except that of intellectual wisdom, dominion over which he accorded to Donnell. He did not particularly like Richmond, and he still had a nervous reaction to him, but the vivid stories shored up his confidence in his own memories.

"There's a feelin', man," said Richmond, solemn as a priest, "and don't nothin' else feel like it. That goddamn four-stroke's howlin' like a jet, and your ol' lady's got her tits squashed against your leathers, playin' with your throttle. Whoo! Sex and death and sound effects!"

Audrey and Jocundra were sitting on a bench about thirty feet from where they were lying, and Donnell concentrated on Jocundra. He lowered his head, looked up at her through his brows, and brought her aura into focus: an insubstantial shawl of blue light, frail as the thinnest of mists, glimmering with pinpricks of ruby and gold and emerald-green.

"Takes a commitment, though," said Richmond soberly. "If you gonna ride with the 'hounds, you gotta kill a cop."

"You killed a cop?" Donnell was surprised to learn that Richmond was capable of mortal violence; he had sensed an underlying innocence, a playfulness, and had assumed most of the bloody tales to be lies or exaggeration.

"Naw, I was just runnin' probate, but the day's gonna come, man." Richmond plucked a handful of grass and tossed it up into the breeze, watched it drift. "My ol' lady says I ain't got what it takes to be a one-percenter, but what the hell's she know? She works in a goddamn massage parlor, punchin' ol' farts' hornbuttons for fifty bucks a pop. That don't make her no damn expert on my *po*tential!"

Donnell let the aura fade and studied Jocundra. He constantly was finding new features to examine—a nuance of expression, the glide of a muscle—and it was beginning to frustrate him to the point of physical discomfort. Through an unbuttoned fold of her blouse he saw the curve of her breast molded into a swell of beige silk, and he imagined it was as near to him as it appeared, warm and perfumed, a soft weight nudging his cheek. He suspected she was aware of his frustrated desire, and he did not think she was put off by the fact he wanted her.

Wheels crunched on the flagstones, footsteps, and Magnusson rolled up, his therapist beside him. "Go have a talk with your friends, Laura," he said. She started to object, then tossed her head in exasperation and stalked off.

"Fine ass," said Richmond. "But no tits. Ain't none of 'em got tits like ol' Audrey."

"Gentlemen!" Magnusson's lips pursed spasmodically as if he were trying to kiss his nose. "I've given up attempting to enlist your support, but I've made a decision of which you should be aware." He glared at them, squeezing the arms of his chair: a feeble old king judging his unworthy subjects. "May the third, gentlemen. I want you to mark that date."

"Why's that, Doc?" asked Richmond. "You havin' a party?"

"In a manner of speaking, yes. Mr. Harrison! I'm determined you'll listen to me this time."

Donnell avoided the old man's eyes. His nervous reaction was becoming more pronounced, and as often happened around Magnusson, his vision was playing tricks, shifting involuntarily.

"As I told you last week, it's obvious to me that the life span of the bacteria within the host should be on the order of a day or thereabouts. No more. Well, I believe I've deduced the reason for our longevity, though to be sure I'd have to take a look inside an infested brain."

Richmond's back humped with silent laughter.

"Your brain would do nicely, Mr. Richmond. Dissection may well prove its optimal employment." Magnusson cackled. "Initially, they wouldn't give me brain data. Said all the patients had recovered, and there was no such data. But I succeeded in convincing Brauer to assist me. Surely, I said, there must have been early failures, animal experiments. If I could see those files, I told him, no telling what insights they might elicit."

Out of the corner of his eye, Donnell saw Magnusson embedded in a veil of red light, an aural color so deep that the old man's head showed as featureless and distorted as the darkness at the heart of a flawed ruby.

"There's too much data to relate it all," said Magnusson, "so let me take a tuck in my argument. Each of us has

experienced perceptual abnormalities, abilities the uninformed would categorize as 'psychic.' It's clear that some
feature of our brain allied with these abilities is retarding
the bacterial process. Three of the case studies Brauer loaned
me revealed extensive infestation of the dopamine and norepenephrine systems. I didn't dare ask him about them, but
I believe they were like us, and that the seat of the retarding
factor, and therefore of 'psychic' potential..."

"Doc, you borin' the shit outta me!" Richmond stood,
only a little awkwardly, and Donnell envied his ease of
mobility.

"You won't have to put up with me much longer, Mr.
Richmond." A loose cough racked Magnusson's chest. "I'm
being discharged on May the fourth. Ezawa himself will be
on hand to oversee my ... my liberation." He sucked at his
teeth. "Mr. Harrison. I want you to promise me that on
May the third you'll look closely at your bedroom walls.
A simple duty, but your assumption of it will both guarantee
my peace of mind and substantially prove my point."

Donnell nodded, wishing Magnusson away.

"Your nod's your bond, I suppose. Very well. Look
closely, Mr. Harrison. As closely as only you can look."
He wheeled off, calling for his therapist.

"Senile old bastard," said Richmond.

"Every time he's around," said Donnell, "it's like something's crawling up my spine. But he doesn't sound senile
to me."

"So what. I get weird vibes off you, and you ain't senile,"
said Richmond with his usual eccentric logic. "Just 'cause
you get weird vibes off a dude don't mean they gotta be
one way or another...." He lost the flow of his argument.
" 'Course maybe I'm just used to weirdness," he continued
moodily. "Where I grew up there was a cemetery right
across the street, and all kinds of weird shit was goin' on.
Funerals and shit. Especially on Thursdays. How come you
think Thursdays is such a big day for funerals, man?"

"Probably a slow business day." Donnell picked up his
cane.

"I'm gonna head on back with the cooze. Who knows!"
Richmond waggled his tongue in a parody of lust. "Tonight

might be the night me and ol' Audrey get down and do the low yo-yo!"

As Richmond sauntered off, his limp barely evident, Donnell levered himself up with his cane. His first step sent pains shooting from his feet into his knees.

"Hi." Jocundra came up beside him. "Should I bring the chair?"

"I can deal with it." He linked arms with her, and they walked toward the house at a ceremonial pace. His skin was irritated to a glow each time her hip brushed him.

"Was Dr. Magnusson bothering you again?"

"Yeah. He says he's being discharged May the fourth."

"That's right."

Donnell stepped on a pebble, teetered, but she steadied him. "Where's he going to end up?" he asked. "He can't take care of himself."

"A home for the elderly, I suppose," she said. "I'll find out from Laura if you like."

Her smile was sweet, open, and he smiled back. "It doesn't matter." He started to tell her of his promise to Magnusson, but thought better of it, and told her instead about Richmond having to kill a cop.

Toward the end of April, Jocundra dreamed that Donnell came into her room one night while she was asleep. Within the logic of the dream, a very vivid dream, she was not surprised to see him because she knew—just as in reality—that he often waked before her and would sometimes become lonely and ask her to fix breakfast. This time, however, he did not wake her, merely sat beside the bed. The moon was down, and he was visible by the flickers in his eyes: jagged bursts of green lightning sharply incised upon the darkness, yet so tiny and short-lived they seemed far away, as if she were watching a storm at the extreme edge of her horizon. After a minute he reached out and rested his fingers briefly on the inside of her elbow, jerking them back when a static charge crackled between them. He sat motionless for a few seconds, and she thought he was holding his breath, expecting her to wake; at last he stretched out his hand again and brushed his fingertips across the nipple of her left breast, teasing it erect beneath her nightgown, sending shivery electricities down into the flesh as if he were conducting the charges within his eyes. Then he cupped her breast, a treasuring touch, and the weight of his hand set a pulse throbbing between her legs.

She had another dream immediately afterward, something about clowns and chasing around a subdivision, but she most remembered the one about Donnell. It disturbed her because she was not certain it had been a dream, and because it brought to mind a talk she had had with Laura Petit several days before. Donnell had requested a morning alone to begin a new project—a story, he said—and so Jocundra had picked out a magazine and gone onto the grounds. Laura had accosted her in the parking lot, saying she needed a friendly ear, and they had walked down to the stone bench near the gatehouse.

"I'm losin' touch with Hilmer," said Laura. "He wants to be alone all the time." Strands of hair escaped from her barrette, there were shadows around her eyes, and her lipstick was smeary.

Jocundra was inclined to sympathy, but she couldn't help being somewhat pleased to learn that Laura was not impervious to human affliction. "He's just involved with his work," she advised. "At this stage you have to expect it."

"He's not workin'," said Laura bitterly. "He wanders! All day long. I can't keep track of him. Edman says to let him have the run of the house, but I just don't feel right about it, especially with the cameras breakin' down so much." She gave Jocundra a dewy, piteous look and said, "I should be with him! He's only got a week, and I know there's somethin' he's hidin'."

Appalled by the depth of Laura's self-interest, her lack of concern for Magnusson, Jocundra opened her magazine and made no reply.

Suddenly animated, Laura pulled out a file from her pocket and began doing her nails. "Well," she said prissily, "I may not have *totally* succeeded with Hilmer, but I've done my job properly . . . not like that Audrey Beamon."

Jocundra was irritated. Audrey, though dull, was at least no aggravation. "What's your problem with Audrey?" she asked coldly.

"It's not *my* problem." Registering Jocundra's displeasure, Laura assumed a haughty pose, head high, gazing toward the house: a proud belle watching the plantation burn. "If you don't want to hear it, that's fine! But I just think you should know who you're associatin' with."

"I know Audrey quite well."

"Really!" Laura hmmphed in disbelief. "Well, then I'm sure you know she's been doin' it with Jack Richmond."

"Doing it?" Jocundra laughed. "Do you mean sex?"

"Yes," said Laura primly. "Can you imagine?"

"No. One of the orderlies is telling you stories to get you excited."

"It wasn't any orderly!" squawked Laura. "It was Edman!"

Jocundra looked up from her magazine, startled.

"You can march right up there and ask him if you don't believe me!" Laura stood, hands on hips, frowning. "You remember when the cameras went out a whole day last week? Well, they didn't go out...not for the whole day. Edman wanted to see what might happen if people didn't know they were bein' observed, and he got an eyeful of Audrey and Richmond!"

After Laura flounced off, Jocundra whimsically considered the prospect of green-eyed babies and thought about Laura's capacity for lying—no doubt, vast; but she decided it was perfectly in keeping with Edman's methods to have done what Laura said. She tried to imagine Audrey and Richmond making love. It was not as difficult to imagine as she had expected, in fact, given Audrey's undergraduate reputation at Tulane—the sorority girl run amok—she probably would find Richmond fascinating. Further, Jocundra recognized that her own fascination with Donnell had allowed her to relax the role of therapist and become his friend; and if you could become the friend of a man such as Donnell, if you could put aside the facts of his life and see the person he really was—something which had been no chore to do because he *was* both fascinating and talented—well, then it might even be less of a chore to become his lover.

The dream, however, shone a new light on all this. Jocundra realized the boundaries of her friendship for Donnell were fraying, and she was glad of the realization. Now that it was out in the open she could deal with it, and dealing with it was important. There certainly was no future in letting it develop. The more she thought about the dream, the more convinced she was that Donnell had actually entered her room, that she had convinced herself she was asleep, observing him from the cover of sleep, from a dreamlike perspective. Self-deception was a particular talent of hers, and had already led her to a terrible marriage. Charlie had not wanted to be married, but she had persuaded him. He had been her first lover, and after the rite of passage was unsatisfactorily concluded, feeling sullied, ruined, the ghost of her Catholic girlhood rearing up like a dead queen out of a sarcophagus, she had seduced herself into believing she could love him. From a painfully ordinary and unattractive present she had manufactured the vision of a blissful future, and had coached herself to think of Charlie foremost, to please him, thinking these submissions would consolidate her vision, yet knowing all the while that he was not only her first lover, but also her first serious mistake. And now, it seemed, this same self-deception was operating along a contrary principle: disguising the growth of strong emotion as symptoms of friendship and responsibility.

To deal with it Jocundra let the routines of Shadows carry her away from Donnell. She attended staff meetings religiously and took every opportunity to join the other therapists for conversation and coffee; but when forced to be alone with Donnell she found these measures were not sufficient to counter the development of an attachment. She began to lie awake nights, brooding over his death, counting the days left him, wishing they would pass quickly, wishing they would pass slowly, experiencing guilt at her part in the proceedings. But despite her worries, she was satisfied that she could eventually cultivate a distance between herself and Donnell by maintaining an awareness of the problem, by adherence to the routines, and she continued to be thus satisfied until May the third arrived and all routines were shattered.

"I was born in Rented Rooms Five Dollars
Down on Adjacent Boulevard,

You know that funky place got no fire escape,
No vacancies, and a dirt front yard.
My mama was Nobody's fool,
He left her for a masseuse down in New Orleans,
Take the cash and flush the credit cards
Was the best advice he ever gave to me...."

Four doctors were holding conference in the main hall, but Richmond's raucous voice and discordant piano stylings flushed them from the sofa, set them to buttoning their lab coats and clipping their pens in a stiff-necked bustle toward the door. "Turkeys!" snarled Richmond. He hammered out the chords, screaming the words after them, elbowing Donnell, urging him to join in the chorus.

"Early one mornin' with a light rain fallin'
I rode off upon my iron horse,
You seen my poster and you read my rap sheet:
Armed and dangerous, no distinguishin' marks,
Wanted for all the unnatural crimes
And for havin' too much fun,
He leads a pack of one-eyed Jacks,
He's known as Harley David's son!
Aw, they say hell hath no fury
Like a woman scorned,
But all them scornful women catch their hell
From Harley David's son!"

The door slammed; Richmond quit pounding and noodled the keys, a musical texture more appropriate to the peaceful morning air. Sunlight laid a diagram of golden light and shadow over the carpet, the lowest ranks of the paintings were masked in reflected glare, and ceramic figurines glistened on end tables beside the French doors. Jocundra and Audrey were sitting on a sofa, talking, at ease, and their voices were a gentle, refined constant like the chatter of pet birds. The old house seemed to be full of its original atmosphere, its gilt and marble and lacquer breathing a graciousness which not even Richmond's song could disrupt. And yet Donnell detected an ominous disturbance in the air, fading now, as if a gong had been struck and the rippling note had sunk below the audible threshold. He felt it dooming through his flesh, insisting that the peace and quiet was an illusion, that today was May the third, Magnusson's May the third, and thereafter nothing would be the same. He was being foolish, he told himself, foolish and suggestible. He did not understand half of what Magnusson spouted, and the other half was unbelievable, but when he tried to finalize his disbelief, to forget about Magnusson, he could not. The old man's arguments—though they sounded insane—were neither disassociative nor rambling, not senile.

"Hey!" Richmond nudged him and handed him a piece of paper. "Check it out."

Donnell was glad for the distraction. He read the lines, then used the piano bench as a table on which to scrawl changes. "Try this." He passed the paper back to Richmond, who frowned and fingered the chords:

> "Cold iron doesn't stop me
> And you ain't got no silver gun. . . ."

Richmond clucked his tongue. "Lemme see how it works together." He sang the song under his breath, filling with the chords.

The song was Richmond's sole creation, and Donnell approved of it; it was, like Richmond, erratic and repetitive and formless. The choruses—there were dozens, detailing the persona of a cosmic outlaw who wore a three-horned helmet—were sung over a major chord progression; Richmond talked the verses in a minor blues key, telling disconnected stories about cheap crooks and whores and perverts he had known.

The slow vibration in the air ended, sheared off, as if a circuitbreaker had engaged, and Donnell suddenly believed it *had* been in the air, a tangible evidence of Magnusson's proof, and was not a product of suggestion or sensory feedback from his own body.

"This here's the best goddamn one yet!" Richmond poised his hands above the keyboard. "Dig it!"

"I think Magnusson's done something," said Donnell.

Richmond snorted. "You hearin' voices or something, man? Shit! Listen up."

"If you hear a rumblin',
It's too late to run,
Cold iron doesn't stop me
And you ain't got no silver gun,
Then your girlfriend's breast starts tremblin'
And she screams, 'Oh God! Here he comes!'
Half beast, half man, half Master Plan,
It's Harley David's son!
Aw, I'll kiss your one-eyed sister,
Hell, I'll lick her socket with my tongue!
I'm Christ-come-down-and-fucked-around,
I'm Harley David's son!"

"Now that..." said Richmond proudly. "That's got it. What'd you say about the last one?"

"The archetypal power of good graffiti."

"Yeah." Richmond plinked the keys. "Archetypal!"

The main doors swung open and Laura Petit wandered in, stopped, and trailed her fingers across the gilt filigree of a table. The same slow, rippling vibration filled the room, more forcibly than before, as if it hadn't died but had merely grown too weak to pass through walls and now could enter. Audrey waved, and Laura walked toward the sofa, hesitant, looking nervously behind her. She asked something of Jocundra, who shook her head: No. "Please!" shrilled Laura. Audrey stood, beckoned to Jocundra, and they all went into the hallway, closing the door after them. The vibration was cut off.

"Squeeze, you might have a point about the Doc." Richmond shut the piano lid and swiveled around to face the door. "There was some strange bullshit walked in with that little lady!"

"What is it?" Audrey shut the door to the main hall.

Laura was very pale; her Adam's apple worked. "Hilmer," she said, her voice tight and small; she looked up to the glass eye of the camera mounted above the door and was transfixed.

Jocundra sprinted ahead, knowing it must be bad.

Magnusson's door stood ajar; it was dark inside. Sunlight through the louvered shutters striped a heraldic pattern of gold diagonals across the legs of the shadowy figure on the bed. She leaned in. "Dr. Magnusson?" Her words stirred a little something within the darkness, a shiver, a vibration, and then she saw a flicker of fiery green near the headboard, another, and another yet, as if he were sneaking a peek between his slitted eyelids. "Are you all right, Doctor?" she asked, relieved, thinking Laura had overreacted and nothing was seriously wrong. She turned on the ceiling light.

It was as if she had been watching someone's vacation slides, the projectionist clicking from scene to scene, narrating, "Here's grandpa asleep in his room . . . kinda pretty the way the light's falling through the shutters there," click, the screen goes black, and the next slide is the obscene one which the neighbor's teenage kid slipped in as a prank. Click. Magnusson's room was an obscenity. So much blood was puddled in the depression made by his head and shoulders, streaked over the headboard and floor, that at first she could not bring her eye to bear on the body, tracking instead the chaotic sprays of red. A mild heated odor rose from the glistening surfaces. She clutched the doorknob for support, tucking her chin onto her chest, dizzy and nauseated.

"Oh, Jesus!" said Audrey behind her. "I'll get Edman." Laura snuffled.

Jocundra swallowed, gathering herself. Magnusson lay on his side, his right arm upflung across his face and wedged against the headboard, concealing all except his forehead and the corner of his right eye. She switched off the lights, and the green flickers were again visible. God, she thought, what if somehow he's alive. She switched the lights back on. It was becoming easier to bear, but not much. She stepped around the bloody streaks and stopped a foot from the bed. His chest was unmoving. She knelt beside him and was craning her neck, trying to locate the wound, when his arm came unwedged and dangled against her knee. The shock caused her to overbalance. She tipped forward and planted her hand on the bed to stabilize. Blood mired between her fingers, and her face bobbed to within inches of a neat slice in his throat. Its lips were crusted with a froth of pink bubbles. One of them popped, and a clear fluid seeped from the wound.

Laura screamed—an abandoned, throat-tearing scream—

and Jocundra threw herself back and sat down hard on the carpet, face to face with Magnusson. Folds of waxy skin sagged from his cheeks, and the bacteria were in flux within his eyes. Spidery blobs of luminescence spanned the sockets, their edges eroding, gradually revealing sections of his liverish whites and glazed blue irises. Jocundra was spellbound. Then she felt something soaking her slacks and realized that the horrid paste sticking them to her thighs was a spill of Magnusson's blood. She scrambled up and started for the door. And stopped. Laura had fallen to her knees, sobbing, and behind her stood Richmond and Donnell.

"There's been an accident," Jocundra said, obeying the stupid reflex of lies. She pushed them away and tried to shut the door, but Richmond knocked her hand aside and jammed the door open with his foot.

"No shit!" he said, peering into the room. "Ol' Doc musta tripped or somethin', huh?"

Jocundra decided she couldn't worry about Richmond; she took Donnell's arm and propelled him along the hall. "I think he killed himself. It's going to be a madhouse in a minute. You wait in the room and I'll find out what I can."

"But why would he kill himself?" he asked, as she forced him through the door. "He was getting out."

"I don't know." She helped him lower into the wheelchair. "Let me go now. I've got to make my report." A flash of memory showed her the old man's eyes, his throat, something still alive after all that blood, and she shuddered.

Donnell blinked, looking at the wall above his writing desk. "Yeah, go ahead," he said distractedly. He wheeled over to the desk and picked up a pen.

"What's the matter?"

"Nothing." He opened a notebook. "I'll figure it out."

She knew he was holding something back, but she was in no mood to pry and no shape to field his questions. She reassured him that she would return quickly and went into the hall. Agitated voices lifted from Magnusson's room; Laura was still sitting outside the door, collapsed against the ornate molding like a beggar girl beneath a temple arch. Jocundra leaned against the wall. From the moment she had seen Magnusson, she had been operating on automatic, afraid for either herself or for Donnell, and now, relieved of pressure, she began to tremble. She put her hand up to cover her eyes and saw the brown bloodstains webbing the palm; she wiped it on her hip. She did not want to think anymore, about Magnusson, about herself or Donnell, and so, to occupy her mind and because no one else would be likely to bother, concerned only with their experiment gone awry, she hurried down the hall to find if anything could be done for Laura.

DON'T TELL JOCUNDRA was written on the wall in crudely printed letters about the size of a fist; the letters were not of a color but were indented into the wallpaper, and it had taken only a slight shift in focus to bring them clear. Beneath the first line was a second message: THE INSTANT YOU ARE ALONE, LOOK UNDER YOUR MATTRESS.

Donnell didn't hesitate. He felt around under the mattress, touched something hard and thin, and pulled out a red account ledger from which an envelope protruded; the words READ THIS NOW! were printed on the envelope, and inside were five typewritten pages and a simple plan of the first floor and basement. There were only a few lines on the first page.

> I am dying early for your benefit, Mr. Harrison, and I hope you will therefore give my rationality the benefit of the doubt and act at once upon my instructions. If you have learned of my death shortly after its event, then these instructions apply; if more than twenty minutes have elapsed, you must use your own judgment. Leave your room immediately. Do not worry about the cameras: they are currently malfunctioning. Follow the diagram and enter the room marked X. All personnel will be doubtless involved in frantic inessentials, but if you happen to be observed, I am certain you can supply an adequate excuse. The ledger and the letter will clarify all else.

Donnell cracked the bedroom door. An orderly rushed past and into Magnusson's room; Jocundra was hunkered next to Laura outside the room, but she had her back to him and was blocking Laura's view. No one else was in the hall. He eased out the door and wheeled toward the foyer, expecting her to call out at any second; he passed the foyer, continued along the hall and turned the corner. The door leading to the basement was the first on his left. He stood, wobbly on his cane, and shoved the wheelchair back into the front hall so they could not tell where he had gone. The stairs were steep, and each step jolted loose pains in his hips and spine. A dimly lit corridor led off the stair; he entered the second door and twisted the latch. Gray-painted walls, two folding chairs facing a large mirror, and a speaker and switches mounted beside the mirror. Breathing hard, he sat and fumbled out the remainder of Magnusson's letter.

In the event it is Dr. Edman who reads this: sir, you are a great ass! If, however, it has reached your hands, Mr. Harrison, you have my congratulations and my thanks.

The ledger contains my notes on the bacterial process which enlivens us and an appendix which attempts a description of certain psychophysical abilities you will soon enjoy, if you do not already. Whereas the medical notes might be digested best at a time affording you a degree of leisure, I suggest you look over the appendix after concluding this letter.

I am not sure what has compelled me to give my posthumous counsel, but I have been so compelled. Perhaps it is because we are microbiologically akin, or because I believe that *we* should have a voice in determining the course of these mayfly existences. Perhaps an arc of destiny is involved. But most assuredly it is because I have seen (mark the verb!) in you a future of greater purpose than my past has proved. There is a thing you must do, Mr. Harrison. I cannot tell you what it is, but I wish you its accomplishment.

I have chosen this precise time to die because I knew Dr. Ezawa would be in residence and would—being a good research man—wish to perform the autopsy at once. The laboratory next to this room is the only place suitable for such work. If you will turn on the wall switches beside the mirror, in due course you will see and hear all the proceedings. . . .

Donnell hit the switches. A light bloomed within the mirror, and a wide room dominated by two long counters became visible; a lamp burned on the nearest counter, illuminating beakers, microscopes and a variety of glass tubing. No one was in sight. He turned back to the letter.

. . . though it is likely your view will be impaired as the doctors crowd around, shoving each other aside in their desire for intimacy with my liver and lights. I doubt you will be disturbed; the basement will be off-limits to all but those involved in my dissection, and the room you occupy has no video camera. It was, I suspect, designed as an observation post from which to observe the initial recovery phase of creatures like ourselves, but apparently they chose to sequester that portion of the project at Tulane. In any case, it will take some hours at least to restore the video, and if you exercise caution you should be able to return upstairs unnoticed.

Enough of preamble. Hereafter I will depend a list of those things I have learned which may be pertinent to your immediate situation.

1) If you concentrate your gaze upon the cameras, you will sooner or later begin to see bright white flashes in the air around them: cometary incidences of light which will gradually manifest as networks or cages of light constantly shifting in structure. I am convinced these are a visual translation of the actions of electromagnetic fields. When they appear, extend your hand toward them and you will feel a gentle tugging in the various directions of their flow. The ledger will further explore this phenomenon, but for now it will suffice you to know that you can disrupt the system by waggling your fingers contrary to the flow, disrupting their patterns. . . .

The laboratory door swung open, a black arm reached in and switched on the overhead fluorescents; two orderlies entered wheeling Magnusson's corpse on a dolly. Then a group of lab-coated doctors squeezed through the door, led by Dr. Brauer and an elderly Japanese man whose diminished voice came over the wall speaker. "...matter who gave him the scalpel, but I want to know where it has vanished to." He stalked to the dolly and pinched a pallid fold of flesh from Magnusson's ribs. "The extent of desanguination is remarkable! There can't be more than two or three pints left in his body. The bacteria must have maintained the heart action far longer than would be normal."

"No wonder Petit's so freaked," ventured a youngish doctor. "He must have gone off like a lawn sprinkler."

Ezawa cast a cold eye his way, and he quailed.

Seeing his creator filled Donnell with grim anger, righteous anger, anger based upon the lies he'd been told and funded by the sort of natural anger one feels when one meets the wealthy or the powerful, and senses they are mortals who have escaped our fate. Ezawa had an elegant thatch of silky white hair and eyebrows to match; his eyes were heavy-lidded and his lips full, pursed in an expression of disapproval. Moles sprinkled his yellow cheek. He had a look of well-fed eminence, of corporate Shintoism, of tailor-made pomposity and meticulous habits and delicate sensibilities; but with a burst of insight Donnell knew him for a pampered soul, a sexual gourmandizer of eccentric appetites, a man whose fulfilled ambitions had seeded an indulgent nature. The complexity of the impression confused Donnell and lessened his anger.

"Actually," said Ezawa, "it's quite an opportunity being able to get inside the brain before termination of the cycle."

"I don't suppose," said the youngish doctor, obviously seeking to re-establish himself, "that there's any chance he's still alive?"

"Anyone connected with this project should realize that the clinical boundary for death may never be established." Ezawa smiled. "But I doubt he will have any discomfort."

The two orderlies lifted Magnusson onto the counter and began cutting away his pyjamas and robe; one held his shoulders down while the other pulled the soaked cloth from beneath him, laying bare his emaciated chest. Troubled by the sight, Donnell went back to the letter.

> ...I must admit I had misgivings as to my sanity on first learning this was the case. I am, be it illusion or

not, a scientist, and thus the parameters of my natural expectation were exceeded. But each time I have done as I described, the result has been the same. I cannot rationalize this as being the result of miraculous coincidence.

2) You possess, as do we all, a commanding presence. I realize you are prone to deep anxieties, insecurities, but nevertheless you can exert a profound influence on our nursemaids. Argue forcefully and you will achieve much. This may sound simplistic, but in this way did I convince Brauer to bring me files, various materials, and, eventually, to allow me access to the laboratory where I secured my means of exit from this world.

3) Trust your intuitions, especially as regards your judgments of people. I have discovered I can discern much of a person's general character and intent by simply looking at his or her face. It may be there is a language written in the wrinkles and muscular movements and so forth. But I have no clear idea of the process. The knowledge simply comes unbidden to my brain. It is my contention that when we stumble across someone we cannot read—our fellow patients, for example—it causes us nervousness, trepidation. I have only been able to read the other patients on one occasion: during Edman's social. And then it was as if a light shone upon all of us, perhaps engendered by our group presence. This particular ability is extremely erratic, but I would trust it when it occurs.

There is more, much more, all sounding equally mad. The ledger contains all the proof of which I have been capable.

I am not overborne by the prospect of my imminent death. This body is vile and stinks in my nostrils, and the condition of death seems far more mutable to me than it did when I began these investigations. That is what most astounds me about the project personnel: they have raised the dead and see nothing miraculous about it, treating it as merely an example of technological prestidigitation. Ah, well, perhaps they are correct and I am totally deluded.

Use this information as you see fit, Mr. Harrison. I will not instruct you further, though I will tell you that had I the strength I would have long ago left Shadows. I believe that outside these walls I might have been capable of vital action, but within them I could not see in what direction I might act.

Goodbye. Good luck.

Donnell folded the letter. The exhilaration of his race down the hall had worn off, and his muscles were cramping from the exertion. His mind was fogged with gloomy, half-formed thoughts. The doctors blocked his view of the body, ringing the counter, leaning forward, peering downward and inward like gamblers around a dice table, and over the wall speaker came the tinny reproduction of a splintering whine as Ezawa broke into Magnusson's skull.

CHAPTER VIII

May 3–May 17, 1987

"Looking onto the top of the brain," said Ezawa, "I find the usual heavy infestation of the visual cortex.... Is the recorder on?"

Dr. Brauer assured him it was; some of the doctors whispered and exchanged knowing glances. Between their shoulders Donnell saw a halation of green radiance, but then they crowded together and blocked his view entirely.

"In addition," Ezawa continued, "I see threadlike striations of bioluminescence shining up through the tissues of the cerebral cortex. All right." He brushed a lock of hair from his eyes with the back of his hand, which contained a scalpel. "I'm now going to sever the cranial adhesions and lift out the brain."

The doctors attended Ezawa with the silent watchfulness of acolytes, bending as he bent to his labor, straightening when he straightened, bending again to see what he had removed. "Let's get some shots of this," he said. The doctors moved back, enabling one of the orderlies to obtain good camera angles, and Donnell had a glimpse of the brain. It was resting on Magnusson's chest, a gray convulsed blossom with bloody frills and streaks of unearthly green curving up its sides, like talons gripping it from beneath. He looked away. There was no need to watch any more, no need to puzzle or worry. Form had been given to the formless suspicions which had nagged him all these weeks, and he was surprised to discover that he had already accepted a death sentence, that this crystallization of his worst fears was less frightening than uncertainty. Veils of emotion were blowing through him: anger and revulsion and loathing for the glowing nastiness inside his own skull, and—strangely enough—hope. An intimation of promise. Perhaps, he thought, riffling the pages of the ledger, the intimation was simply an instance of the knowledge springing—as it had to old Magnusson—unbidden to his brain.

Flashcubes popped. He wondered if they would pose with their bloody marvel, link arms and smile, get a nice group shot of Ezawa and the gang to show at parties.

Ezawa cleared his throat. "On the ventral and lower sides I find a high concentration of bacteria in those areas traversed by the catecholamine pathways. Patches of varying brightness spreading from the hind brain to the frontal cortex. Now I'm going to cut along the dorsal-ventral axis, separating the upper and lower brain."

The doctors huddled close.

"God! The entorhinal system!" Brauer blurted it out like a hallelujah, and the other doctors joined in an awed litany: "I told Kinski I suspected . . ." "Brain reward and memory consolidation . . ." "Incredible!" The babble of pilgrims who, through miraculous witness, had been brought hard upon their central mystery.

"Doctors!" Ezawa waved his scalpel. "Let's get an anatomical picture down on tape before we speculate." He addressed himself to the recorder. "Extremely high concentrations of bacteria in the medial and sulcral regions of the frontal cortex, the substantia regia, the entorhinal complex of the temporal lobe. It appears that the dopamine and norepenephrine systems are the main loci of the bacterial activity." He began to slice little sections here and there, dropping them into baggies, and Magnusson's chest soon became a waste table. He held up a baggie containing a glowing bit of greenery to the ceiling lights. "Remarkable changes in the ventral tegumentum. Be interesting to run this through the centrifuge."

Donnell switched off the speaker. A wave of self-loathing swept over him; he felt less than animal, a puppet manipulated by luminous green claws which squeezed his ventral tegumentum into alien conformations. The feathery ticklings inside his head were, he hoped, his imagination. Magnusson was right: logic dictated escape. He could not see what was best for himself unless he left behind this charnel house where crafty witch doctors chased him through mazes and charted his consciousness and waited to mince him up and whirl his bits in a centrifuge. But he was going to need Jocundra's help to escape, and he was not sure he could trust her. He believed that her lies had been in the interests of compassion, but it would be necessary to test the depth of her compassion, the quality of the feelings that ruled it. Having thought of her for weeks in heavy emotional contexts, it amazed him he could think so calculatingly of her now, that—without any change in his basic attitude, without the least diminution of desire—he could so easily shift from needing her to using her.

With Brauer assisting, Ezawa opened Magnusson's chest and they examined the organs. Bastards! Donnell switched off the mirror. He flipped through the ledger, skimming paragraphs. It was a peculiar record, a compendium of scientific data, erratic humor, guesswork, metaphysical speculations, and he drew from it a picture of Magnusson not as the cackling old madman he had appeared, but as he had perceived himself: a powerful soul imprisoned in a web of wrinkled flesh and brittle struts of bone. One of the last entries spoke directly to this self-perception:

> . . . Over the past months I have had contact with thirteen fellow patients, half of them now deceased, and in each

case, as in my own, I have noticed we exhibit—manifest both in our work and our behavior—an obsession with nobility, with regal imagery; it seems to comprise part of our innate self-image. I suspect a psychiatrist might countenance this a result of the death trauma, suggesting we had linked the myth of Christ arisen to our deep insecurity at having died and been reborn so changed and incomplete. But I sense in myself and the others nothing that reflects the gentle Christian fabrication; rather the imagery is of a pagan sort and the feeling of nobility is one of a great brooding spirit, half-animal, his perceptions darkening the trivial light of day. When I feel this spirit moving within me, I cannot believe otherwise than that all my illusory dry-as-dust memories of sorting test tubes and sniffing after some crumb of scientific legend have been foisted on me by the process of my life at Shadows, and that they are a veneer covering a reservoir of more potent memories.

All of us now alive embody this spirit in individualistic fashion: Richmond, who poses as the hoodlum warrior; Monroe, with her alter ego the sorceress Luweji; French, the corporate duke; Harrison, the bleak poetic prince; Ramsburgh, the mad dowager who knits coverlets and shawls which depict Druidic scenes of haunted woods and graven altars. I believe that this common tendency is of extreme importance, though I am not certain in what way; but lately I have experienced a refinement of these feelings.

One night, a splendid windy night, I went unaccompanied onto the grounds and sat in my wheelchair atop a rise close to the house. Everything, it seemed, was streaming away from me. The wind poured in a cold, unbroken rhythm off the Gulf, the oaks tossed their shadowy crowns, and silver-edged clouds raced just beneath the moon, which was itself a disc of silver, almost full. I was the single fixed point in that night's flowing substance. Black leaves skittered across silvery falls of moonlight, and my clothes tugged and snapped as if they wished to be rid of me. Time was going on without me, I thought, and I was becoming timeless once again. That was all the rectitude of life and death, then, this process of becoming timeless. My whole attention was focused

outward upon the flow of night and wind, and I felt
myself grown stern and intractable in relation to the petty
scatterings of these inessential things, felt my little rise
swell into a lofty prominence, and felt my flesh to be
the sounding of a music, fading now, but soon to sound
anew after the indrawing of an ancient breath. Dreams,
you might say, fantasies, an old man's maunderings on
mystery as his second death approaches. But it is dreams
which make us live, and mystery, and who is to say they
will not carry us away when life is done.

They took Laura back to Tulane under sedation. "'Bye,"
she said at the door, weakly, staring into Jocundra's eyes
with puzzled intensity, as if wondering at their strange color,
and then repeated, "'Bye," looking down to the floor, saying
it the way you might say a word you had just learned, trying
out its odd shape in your mouth.

Like everyone else, Jocundra assumed Laura had been
in the room when Magnusson slit his throat—if such was
the case: the missing scalpel permitted the possibility of
alternate scenarios, though it was generally held that Laura,
in her distracted state, had picked it up and mislaid it. But
unlike everyone, Jocundra did not believe the violence of
the death was wholly responsible for Laura's condition. That
alone could not have transformed her into this pale doll
creature who was led by the elbow and helped to sit in
Ezawa's gray Cadillac, who pressed her face against the
smoked glass window and gazed wanly back at the house.
Her apparent callousness toward Magnusson must, Jocundra
thought, have masked real feelings of attachment, and it
was the damage done these feelings which had most contributed to her breakdown.

"She'll be fine," said Edman at the staff meeting later
in the day. "You knew there'd be some trauma."

But Jocundra had not known there was a potential for
collapse, for derangement, and she was outraged. "The end
will be difficult," a vastly paternal Edman had told her at
the briefing before she left Tulane. "But you'll take from
it something very human and strengthening." And she had
swallowed it! She wanted nothing more to do with lies or

with Edman, who was the father of lies; she would prepare as best she could for the inevitable crash of Donnell's ending, and afterward she would wash her hands of the project.

For the next two weeks she intensified her commitment toward cultivating a distance between herself and Donnell, and attempted as well to create distance between herself and the project, though this did not prove easy. The atmosphere of Shadows had grown more muted and clandestine than ever. It was as if there had been a unity in the house, some league now dissolved by Magnusson's death, and no one could be certain of the new alignments which might emerge. The therapists passed each other in the hall with averted eyes; French and Monroe hid behind their bedroom doors, and Richmond wandered by himself. The doctors broke off whispered conferences whenever anyone of lesser authority came near and withdrew to the upstairs offices. Even the ubiquitous ferns in their brass pots seemed instruments of subterfuge, their feathery fronds capable of concealing sensitive antennae. Yet despite this divisiveness, or because of it, everyone pried and eavesdropped and agitated. Once Dr. Brauer pulled Jocundra aside and heaped invective upon Edman who, he said, spent most of his time on the telephone to Tulane, begging the administration to keep hands off, not to disrupt the process.

"But don't you think a disruption is necessary? Haven't the patients been exposed to enough of Edman's incompetence?" When she shrugged, unwilling to join in any power struggle, he drew his sour, thin features into a measly smile and asked, "How's Harrison doing?"

"Frankly," she said, furious at his false concern, "I don't care who runs this damned place, and as for Harrison, he's dying!"

For several days Jocundra worried that Donnell had learned something about his own situation from Magnusson's death. She picked up a change in him, a change too slippery and circumstantial to classify. On the surface it appeared to have affected him in a positive way: he redoubled his efforts at walking; his social attitudes improved, and he went poking about the house, striking up conversations with the orderlies; he finished his story and started a new one. But when they talked—and they talked far less often than before—the exchanges were oddly weighted. One afternoon he sat her down and had her read his story. It was a violent and involuted fantasy set upon a world with a purple sun, specifically within a village bounded by a great forest, and it dealt with the miserable trials of an arthritic old tradesman, his vengeance against an evil queen and her black-clad retinue, eerie magic, grim conclusions for all. The circuitous plot and grisly horrors unsettled Jocundra. It was as if a curl of purple smoke had leaked out of the manila folder and brought her a whiff of some ornate Persian hell.

"It's beautifully written," she said, "but there's too much blood for my taste."

"Yeah, but will it sell?" He laughed. "Got to make a living somehow when I get out of here. Right?"

"I prefer your poetry." She shut the folder and studied a fray in her skirt.

"No money in poetry." He walked to the desk and stood over her, forcing her to look at him. "Seriously, I'd like to have your opinion. I want to live in the city for a change, travel, and that takes money. Do you think I can earn it this way?"

She could only manage a puny, "Yes, I suppose," but he appeared satisfied by her answer.

Donnell's new independence allowed Jocundra to cultivate her distance. Though the cameras continued to break down—"Like some damn bug's in the wires," said the maintenance man—the orderlies kept track of his comings and goings, and each morning she put on shorts and a T-shirt, took a blanket and found a sunny spot in which to pass the day. She pored over graduate school catalogs, thinking she might go after her doctorate at Michigan or Chicago, or maybe Berkeley. Within a couple of years she could be doing her field work. Africa. Thatched huts on a dusty plain, baobab trees and secretary birds, oracular sacrifices and tattooing rituals, great fireball sunrises, the green mountains still full of gorillas and orchids and secret kingdoms. Each noon she could almost believe that Shadows was the seat of a lost African empire or some empty Eden; the grounds were deserted, the only sounds were those of insects and birds, and the sunlight hung in gauzy shafts straight down through the canopy, as if huge golden angels were beaming down from their orbiting ark to seed civilization. She drowsed; she read ethnography, the French theorists, rediscovering an old enmity for the incomprehensible Jacques Lacan, reacclimating her mind to the rigorous ingrown language of academics. But after a while, after a shorter while each day, it grew boring in the sun and Donnell would stray into her thoughts. Drowsy, nonspecific thoughts, images of him, things he had said, as if he were brushing against her and leaving bits of memory clinging.

May the 18th was her mother's birthday. She had forgotten it until an orderly in the commissary asked her for the date, but all through dinner she thought about what her family might have done to celebrate. Probably nothing. Her father might have given her mother a present, mumbled a tepid endearment and gone out onto the porch to twang his guitar and sing his sad, complaining songs. Her mother would have tidied the kitchen, put on her frumpy hat and scurried off to church for a quick telling of the beads, for fifteen minutes of perfumed darkness at the chipped gilt feet of the Virgin. The Church had been her one stab at individualism, her single act of rebellion against her husband, who had been an atheist. Not that he had tried to dominate her. She had slipped into his shadow like a fearful mouse who had been searching her whole life for such a shelter and would be happy to scuttle around his feet forever. It annoyed Jocundra when she noticed incidences of her mother's character in herself.

After dinner she had intended to go to the staff meeting — the big showdown, it was rumored, between Brauer and Edman — but Donnell asked her to stay and talk. He had her sit on the bed and himself leaned against the window ledge, his cane propped beside him. For a long time he was silent, merely staring at her, but finally he said, "We're having a private conversation. The cameras quit working."

His stare unnerved Jocundra; it was calm and inquisitive and not the usual way he looked at her. "How do you know?"

"It doesn't matter." He gave a sniff of amusement. "They have enough data on my psychological adjustment, and besides, my adjustment's complete. I'm ready to leave right now."

She laughed edgily; though his tone was casual, everything he said had the weight of a pronouncement. "You're not strong enough, not yet."

"I want to tell you something about yourself." The curtain belled inward, eerily swathing his face in lace; he brushed it away. The ceiling lights diminished the green in his eyes to infrequent refractions. "You're not totally aware of it, because you try to constrain it, but I don't think you can totally deny it either. You feel something for me, something like love, though maybe that's too extreme a word for what you feel because you have been somewhat successful in denying it."

He paused to let her respond, but she was at first too confused to answer, then annoyed that he would assume so much, then curious because he exhibited such assurance.

"Of course I'm in love with you." He mumbled it as if it were hardly worth mentioning. "I know it's part of the program for me to love you, that you've..." He ran his cane back and forth through his hands. "I don't guess that's important." He stared at her, his mouth thinned, his eyebrows arched, as if what he saw offered a prospect both mildewed and glorious. "Do you want to deny anything?" he asked.

"No," she said, and was surprised at the buoyancy she felt on saying it.

"The day Magnusson died," he said, "I went down to a little room next to the lab and watched them chop him up."

"You couldn't have," she said, coming to her feet.

"The usual heavy infestation of the visual cortex," he said. "Remarkable changes in the ventral tegumentum."

She started to go to him, but then she thought how he must despise her for lying, and she sat back down, heavy with guilt.

He picked up a paper sack from the windowledge and walked to the bed. "I'm going to do something about it. It's all right."

"I'm sorry." The foolish sound of the words caused her to laugh, and the bitter laugh dynamited the stoniness of her guilt and left her shaky.

"Magnusson gave me his notes before he died," he said. "I think there's a chance I can use them to prolong my life. I'm not sure, but I'll never find out here. I'm going to leave."

"You can't!"

"Sure I can." He plucked a set of keys out of the paper sack: she recognized them as the standard set issued to orderlies, keys to the vans and the pantry and various other rooms. "The staff is in conference," he said. "The orderlies are playing poker in the lab. None of the phones or cameras are working. And the gate." He smiled. "It's taken care of, too."

His arguments were smooth, logical, insistent. He had, he said, a right to go where he chose, to spend his time as he wished. What was the future in remaining here to be probed and tested and eventually dissected? He needed her help. Where did her true responsibilities lie? To herself, to him, or to the project? She had no contrary argument, but the thought of being cast adrift with him made her afraid.

"If you're worried about my loss to the scientific community," he said, "I can assure you I'm not going to co-operate anymore."

"It's not that," she said, hurt. "I'm just not sure what's right, and I don't think you are either."

"Right? Christ!" He lifted a small tape recorder out of the sack; the cassette within it bore Edman's handwriting on the label. "Listen to this."

"Where'd you get that?"

"Edman's office. I told him I wanted to see how life looked from inside a crystal ball. It thrilled his tiny soul to have the beast sniffing round his pantry. These were lying about like party favors on the shelves, so I collected a few." He punched down the play switch, and Edman's voice blatted from the speaker:

"April 27th . . . (a cough) . . . Despite all reason to the contrary, romance blooms between Harrison and Verret.

I expect one morning I will walk onto the grounds and find a valentine containing their initials carved upon an oak. I've today received the package of information concerning Verret's divorce proceeding. In layman's terms, it might be said that Verret seems to have a penchant for losers. Her husband, one Charles Messier, a musician, apparently misused her physically: the divorce was granted on the grounds of physical and mental cruelty. I haven't had time to study it in detail, but there are obvious similarities between the two men. Artistic avocation, both four or five years older than Verret, a general physical resemblance. Of course I am not yet clear how large a part these similarities play in what is now transpiring, but I am convinced we will soon begin to learn. The relationship is, I believe, at a stage of breakthrough . . . (a sigh) . . . I must admit to feelings of paternity toward Harrison and Verret in that I have served as their matchmaker . . . (a laugh) . . . It does not seem wholly improbable that we may one day be treated to the pageant of a nuptial, one of those such as are consummated between prisoners and their loving correspondents—or, more aptly, between terminal patients and their fiancées. I can easily imagine it. Verret, beautiful in white beneath the arching oaks. Harrison, his eyes ablaze, the lustful groom. And the priest intoning sonorously, 'What Ezawa hath joined, let no man put asunder. . . .' "

"Is *that* right?" Donnell smashed down the off switch. "To have this fat vulture perch in his crystal cave and drool over our libidos!"

Jocundra ejected the cassette and read Edman's inscription: "Harrison, Verret—XVII." She turned it over in her hand; it was like holding a jar containing her appendix, a useless organ which once had poisoned her, but was now trivial, powerless. Leaving offered no secure hope, but neither did it offer the hopelessness of Shadows. They had no choice. At the very least, Edman was dangerously unethical, and it was probable he was mad, cunningly mad, passing his madness off as a clever form of sanity, infecting everyone and fooling even himself. It was, she thought, a little dreamlike to be doing something so extreme.

"We'll need money," she said. "I've got credit cards and . . . Why are you looking at me that way?"

"For a minute I thought I'd lost you," he said.

The engine caught, exploded to a roar, then died as Jocundra's foot slipped off the clutch. Overanxious, she failed twice to restart it, but finally succeeded and backed the van until it was facing the drive and headed out. The headlights veered across the grounds, spotlighting a menagerie of leafy shapes, and the side mirror showed the house receding against the darkness, doll-sized, a lantern-lit confection of rose and white topped by a rhinestone bauble. Jocundra's throat was dry. She had almost lost her resolve half a dozen times before they reached the parking lot, and Donnell's plan for the gate—what little he had revealed of it—did nothing to bolster her confidence; her hands and feet, though, honored her commitment, working the gearshift and pedals seemingly without her cooperation. She pulled up close to the gate. Branches of the magnolia bush beside it scraped Donnell's door. He slumped down, pretending unconsciousness. The headlights sprayed between the bars, playing over the glistening tarpaper of the gatehouse, and the guard sidled forth, sleepily scratching his ribs. "What you want?" he called. He yawned and blinked away the glare, settling his holster around his hips: a pudding-faced, pot-bellied man wearing chinos.

"I've got an emergency!" Jocundra called back, hoping to inject an appropriate desperation into her voice. "One of the orderlies! It's his heart!"

"I don't see no doctor with you. Can't let you by without no doctor." He waved her back to the house.

"Get out!" hissed Donnell. "Convince him!"

She climbed out. "Please," she said, pressing against the bars. "He's had a coronary!"

The guard's eyes flicked to her breasts. "I wish they'd get them damn phones straightened out. Awright." He punched a button set into the masonry, and the gate whined open a foot. He slipped inside, and she stepped out of his way, standing at the front of the van while he slapped the magnolia branches aside and shone the flashlight in the

window to check on Donnell. Jocundra heard a rustle from
the bush behind him and saw a pair of blazing green eyes
emerging from the welter of white blossoms and waxy leaves.
"This ol' boy ain't no orderly," said the guard, and something swooshed through the air and struck his neck, then
struck again. Jocundra jumped back, coming up against the
gate, and the guard fell backwards out of sight behind the
van. In a moment Richmond stood, stuffing the guard's gun
into his belt. Jocundra moved out onto the road, putting the
bars between them.

"You better be scared, lady," he said, and laughed. "When
you motherfuckers made me, you created a monster."

He ducked back into the bush, then came around the
front of the van, holding his guitar. Underlit by the headlights, his face was seamed and gruesome; his eyes efflo-
resced. Donnell climbed down, limped to the gate, and
pushed the button. The iron bars swung open. "Pull it on
through," he said to Richmond.

As Richmond drove the van out, the moon sailed from
behind the clouds and everything grew very sharp and bright.
The gate whined shut. Pearly reflections rippled over the
side of the van; the road arrowed off toward the swamp, a
bone-white strip vanishing between dark walls of cypress,
oak and palmetto. Fresh mosquito bites suddenly itched on
Jocundra's arm, as if the moon had broken through her own
cloudiness, her confusion, illuminating her least frailty. She
did not want to be with Richmond. The road was a wild,
unreckonable place crossed by devious slants of shadow.

The guard moaned.

"Hurry up!" yelled Richmond.

Donnell was doing something to the lock mechanism,
molding voluptuous shapes in the air around it with his
hands; he stopped, apparently satisfied, stared at it, then
stepped over to the wall and jabbed the control button several
times.

The gate remained shut.

"Man, I can handle this road at twice the speed," said
Richmond from the back of the van. "She's drivin' like a
fuckin' old lady."

"She's got a license," said Donnell patiently. "You don't."

"Listen, man!" Richmond stuck his head up between the seats. "It was cool you runnin' the show when we was inside 'cause you could deal with the cameras and shit, but I ain't . . ." He nearly toppled into the front as the van hit a pothole, then he fell back. "Look at this shit! She's gonna kill our ass!"

"Quit yelling in her ear, damn it! How the hell can she drive when you're yelling at her!"

Hearing them argue, Jocundra had a moment of hysteria, a happy little trickle of it eeling up from her depths, and all the unhappy particulars of the situation were bathed in a surreal light. There they sat like TV hoodlums planning a spree of Seven-11 stick-ups and high times, fighting over who was boss—to further this impression they were both wearing sunglasses which Richmond had stolen from the orderlies—and there she sat, the mute flunky, the moll. At length they agreed on a compromise: Donnell would serve as the mastermind, while Richmond would take charge in situations calling for swift action and street smarts. Donnell asked her if she knew a place nearby where they could be safe for a couple of days.

"The swamp," she said. "It's full of deserted shanties and cabins. But shouldn't we get as far away as possible?"

"Jesus!" said Richmond, disgusted. He scrunched around on the floor; his guitar banged hollowly. "I'm gonna lay back for a while. You deal with her, man."

"You weren't listening," said Donnell, exasperated.

"I'm sorry. I was concentrating on the road."

"We're going to switch license plates. They'll expect us to run, I think, so we're going to stay nearby, maybe pick up another car. The swamp won't do. We need someplace near a town, within a couple of hours' drive. That's how long the gate and the phones should stay out."

"Well, over on Bayou Lafourche there's a stretch of motels," she said. "Mostly dumps. I doubt they pay much attention to who their customers are."

"Make it some place near a liquor store," said Richmond. "I need to get fucked up!"

When they reached the state highway, Jocundra boosted

the speed to fifty and raised her window. Wind keened in
the side vent. White houses bloomed phosphorescent among
the brush and scrub pine; gas stations with broken windows
and boarded-up restaurants. Near the town of Vernon's Parish they passed a low building with yellow light streaming
from its doors and windows, a neon champagne glass atop
it, surrounded by cars. Black stick figures, armless and
faceless, jostled in the doorway, and their movements made
them seem to be flickering, pulsing to the blare of light
around them like spirits dancing in a fire. Then they were
gone, the moon was occluded, and a wave of unrelieved
darkness rolled over the van. Richmond chorded his guitar.

> "Past the road to Vernon's Parish,
> Our tailpipe was sprayin' sparks.
> The preacher in the Calvary Church
> Felt cold fingers 'round his heart...."

The song and the air of stale, forced confinement in the
van reminded Jocundra of traveling with Charlie's band.
When he had described it to her, it had sounded romantic,
but in reality it had been greasy food and never enough
sleep and being groped by Quaaluded roadies. The only
good part had been the music, which served to mythologize
the experience. She glanced at Donnell; he rested his head
wearily against the window as Richmond's cawing voice
wove into the rush of the highway.

> "Now if you see a fiery fall
> Of comets in the East,
> Or the shadow slinkin' 'cross the moon
> Of some wiry, haggard beast,
> If you feel your blood congeal
> And you've the urge to call a priest,
> Never fear, it'll disappear,
> You can rest tonight in peace.
>
> "Well, you might want to run outside
> And fall down on your face,
> You might scream or you might pray
> Or you might vacillate,

You might give the United Way,
But no matter what you done,
I tell you, straight,
You can't escape the fate
Of Harley David's son!
Oh, the days they've swept away from me
Like fires through a slum.
But when I die I'll roam the night,
The Ghost of Harley David's son!

"Bullshit song," said Richmond, dejected. He leaned between the seats. "But what the hell, squeeze! It sure feels good to be hittin' the highway again." He punched Donnell's arm and grunted laughter. "Even if we never did feel it before."

CHAPTER IX

May 17–May 19, 1987

A stand of stunted oaks hemmed in Sealey's Motel-Restaurant against the highway. Bats wheeled in the parking lot lights, and toads hopped over the gravel drive and croaked under the cabins, which were tiny, shingle-roofed, with peeling white paint and ripped screen doors. Mr. Sealey— Hank Jr. according to the fishing trophy on the office desk— was squat and glum as a toad himself, fiftyish, jowly, wearing a sweat-stained work shirt and jeans. He hunched in a swivel chair, showing them the back of his seamed neck and gray crewcut hair, and when they asked for a room he spun slowly around; he closed his right eye, squinted at Jocundra through the trembling, lowered lid of his left, clucked his tongue, then tossed them a key and resumed tying a fishing fly large and gaudy enough to be a voodoo fetish. Donnell pictured him clad in scarlet robes, dangling said fly into a fiery pit from which scaly, clawed hands were reaching.

"Don't want no screechin' or bangin' after midnight," grumbled Sealey. "Take Cabin Six."

The cabin, twelve dollars for two singles and a cot ("You got to tote the cot yourself") was no bargain, being the home of moths and crickets and spiders. "All things small and horrible," said Donnell, trying to cheer Jocundra, who sat eyeing with disfavor a patch of mattress, one of several visible through holes in the sheet, dotting it like striped islands in a gray sea. For light there was a naked light bulb hung from the ceiling, fragments of moth wings stuck to its sides; between the beds stood an unfinished night table whose drawer contained no Bible but a palmetto bug; the walls were papered in a faded design of flesh-colored orchids and jungle leaves, and mounted cockeyed above the bathroom sink was a flyspecked Kodachrome of Lake Superior.

Though it was poor and pestilent, Richmond made Cabin Six his castle. He cracked the twelve-pack he had bought from Sealey, chugged the first can, belched, and threw himself on the bed to chord his guitar and drink. After three beers he suggested they go for a ride, after five he insisted upon it, but Jocundra told him they were low on gas. Disgruntled, he paced the cabin, interrupting his pacing to urinate out the door and serenade the other cabins with choruses of his song. But when Donnell reminded him that rest was necessary, he grumpily agreed, saying yeah, he had to fix up some stuff anyway. Sitting on the bed, he shook his guitar until a rolled-up piece of plastic fell out; he unrolled it, removing a scalpel. Then he emptied the security guard's gun and began to notch the tips of the bullets. At this Jocundra turned to face the wall, drawing her legs into a tight curl.

"Sleep?" Donnell perched on the edge of her mattress.

"Yes," she murmured. "You should, too."

"I want to go over Magnusson's notes awhile."

Dark hairs were fanned across her cheek. He started to

brush them away, a tender response to her vulnerability, but he suddenly felt monstrous next to her, like a creature about to touch the cheek of a swooning maiden, and he drew back his hand. He had a sensation of delicate motion inside his head, something feathery-light and flowing in all directions. His breath quickened, he grasped the bedframe to steady himself, and he wished, as he always did at such moments, that he had not witnessed the autopsy or read Magnusson's morbid self-descriptions. He stayed beside Jocundra until the sensation abated, then stood, his breath still ragged.

"You wanna kill the light, squeeze," said Richmond. "I'm gonna fade." He poured the bullets into an ashtray.

Donnell did as he was told, went into the bathroom and switched on the light. Gray dirt-streaked linoleum peeled and tattered like eucalyptus bark, shower stall leaning drunkenly, chipped porcelain, the mirror stippled with paint drippings, applying a plague to whomever gazed upon it. The doorframe was swollen with dampness, and the door would not close all the way, leaving a foot-wide gap. He hooked his cane over the doorknob, lowered the toilet lid, sat and tried to concentrate on the ledger. According to Magnusson the bacterial cycle was in essence a migration into the norepenephrine and dopamine systems; since his "psychic" abilities increased as the migration progressed, he concluded that these systems must be the seat of such abilities. So much Donnell could easily follow, but thereafter he was puzzled by some of Magnusson's terminology.

> . . . each bacterium carries a crystal of magnetite within a membrane that is contiguous with the cytoplasmic membrane, and a chain of these magnetosomes, in effect, creates a biomagnetic compass. The swimming bacteria are passively steered by the torque exerted upon their biomagnetic compass by the geomagnetic field; since in this hemisphere the geomagnetic field points only north and down, the bacteria are north-seeking and tend to migrate downward, thus explaining their presence in the sediment underlying old graveyards. Of course within the brain, though the geomagnetic field still affects them,

the little green bastards are bathed in a nutrient- and temperature-controlled medium so that movement downward is no longer of adaptive significance. They're quite content to breed and breed, eventually to kill me by process of overpopulation.

Richmond's heavy snores ripped the silence, and Donnell heard footsteps padding in the next room. Jocundra eased through the gap in the door; she had changed into jeans and a T shirt. "Can't sleep," she said. She cast about for a clean place to sit, found none, and sat anyway beside the shower stall. She spread the folds of the shower curtain, examining its pattern of hula girls and cigarette burns, and grimaced. "This place is a museum of squalor."

She asked to see the ledger, and as she leafed through it, her expression flowing from puzzlement to comprehension, he reflected on the difference between the way she looked now—a schoolgirl stuck on a problem, barely a teenager, worrying her lower lip, innocent and grave—and earlier when she had entered the cabin; then she had appeared self-possessed, elegant, masking her reaction to the grime beneath a layer of aristocratic reserve. She had one of those faces that changed drastically depending on the angle at which you viewed it, so drastically that Donnell would sometimes fail to recognize her for a split second.

"I didn't believe you . . . about extending your life," she said excitedly, continuing to pore over the ledger. "He doesn't come right out and say it, but the implication—I think— is that you may be able to stabilize the bacterial colony. . . ."

"Magnetic fields," said Donnell. "He was too much in a hurry, too busy understanding it to see the obvious."

"There's a lot here that doesn't make sense. All this about NMR, for example."

"What?"

"Nuclear magnetic resonance." She laughed. "The reason I almost flunked organic chemistry. It's a spectroscopic process for analyzing organic compounds, for measuring the strength of radio waves necessary to change the alignment of nuclei in a magnetic field. But Magnusson's not talking about its analytic function." She turned a page. "Do you know what these are?"

There were three doodles on the page:

Beneath them Magnusson had written:

What the hell are these chicken-scratchings? Been seeing them since day one. They seem part of something larger, but it won't come clear. Odd thought: suppose the entirety of my mental processes is essentially a letter written to my brain by these damned green bugs, and these scribbles are the Rosetta Stone by which I might decipher all.

"I see them, too," said Donnell. "Not the same ones, but similar. Little bright squiggles that flare up and vanish. I thought they were just flaws in my vision until I saw the ledger, and then I noticed this one. . . ." He pointed to the first doodle. "If you turn it on its side it looks exactly like an element of the three-horned man Richmond drew on his guitar."

"They're familiar." She shook her head, unable to remember where she had seen them; she gave him a searching look. "This is going to take time, and Richmond doesn't have much time."

"Neither do I."

"Maybe we should go back to Shadows. With all the resources of the project . . ."

"Richmond knows he's nearly terminal," said Donnell sharply. "He won't go back, and I have my own reasons not to."

For the first time since Magnusson's death, he had an intimate awareness of her unencumbered either by doubts about her motives or by the self-loathing he felt when he was brought up against the fact of his bizarre existence. Her face was impassive, beautiful, but beneath the calm facade he detected fear and confusion. By escaping with him, she had lost herself with him, and being lost, as she had rarely been before, she was at a greater remove from her natural place in the world than was he, to whom all places were unnatural.

"What are you thinking?" she asked.

"This and that," he said. He took back the ledger and read from the appendix. "'Mitochondria research has long put forward the idea that human beings are no more than motile colonies of bacteria, so why do I shudder and think of myself as a disease in a borrowed brain?' That, too."

The subject obviously distressed her. She looked away and ran her eye along the mosaic of dirt and faded pattern spanning the linoleum. "There wasn't anyone at Shadows who'd subscribe to a purely biological definition of the patients," she said. And she sketched out Edman's theories as an example, his fascination with the idea of spirit possession, how he had snapped up the things she had told him about the voodoo concept of the soul, the *gros bon ange* and the *ti bon ange*.

"The part about your influence on me," he said. "Do you buy that?"

A frail pulse stirred the air between them, as if their spirits had grown larger and were overlapping, exchanging urgent information.

"I suppose it's true to an extent," she said. "But I don't think it means anything anymore."

Sleep did not come easily for Donnell. Lying on the cot, he was overwhelmed by the excitement of being away from Shadows, by the strange dissonance everything he saw caused in his memory, at first seeming unfamiliar but then wedding itself to other memories and settling into mental focus. Triggered by his excitement, he experienced a visual shift of an entirely new sort. The moonlight and the lights of the other cabins dimmed, the walls darkened, and every pattern in the room began to glow palely—the grain of the boards, the wallpaper, the spiderwebs, the shapes of the furniture—

as if he were within a black cube upon whose walls a serpentine alphabet of silver smoke had been inlaid. It frightened him. He turned to Jocundra, wanting to tell her. Both she and Richmond were black figures, a deeper black than the backdrop, with fiery prisms darting inside them, merging, breaking apart: like the bodies of sleeping gods containing a speeded-up continuum of galaxies and nebulae. The screen mesh of the door was glowing silver, and the markings of the moths plastered against it gleamed coruscant red and blue. Even when he closed his eyes he saw them, but eventually he slept, mesmerized by their jewel-bright fluttering.

He waked to the sound of running water, someone showering. Richmond was still snoring, and the sun glinted along spiderwebs, glowed molten in the window cracks. Bare feet slapped the linoleum, the floor creaked under a shifted weight. He rolled over, and looked through the gap in the bathroom door. Jocundra was standing at the window, lifting the heft of her hair, squeezing it into a sleek cable. Water droplets glittered on her shoulders, and she was wearing semi-transparent panties which clung to the hollows of her buttocks. She bent and toweled her calves; her small breasts barely quivered. A feeling of warm dissolution spread across Donnell's chest and thighs. Her legs were incredibly long, almost an alien voluptuousness. She straightened and saw him. She said nothing, not moving to cover herself, then she lowered her eyes and stepped out of sight behind the door. A minute later she came out, tucking her blouse into a wraparound skirt. She pretended it had not happened and asked what they were going to do about breakfast.

That day, as her mother would have said, was a judgment upon Jocundra. Not that it began badly. Richmond went out around ten to scout the area for a change of cars, promising to return at noon, and she buried herself in Magnusson's notes, fearful that she had misread them the night before. She had not. The bacteria were passively steered by the geomagnetic field toward the dopamine and norepenephrine systems, and there they starved to death; the two systems were centers of high metabolic activity, and in performing their functions of brain reward and memory consolidation and—at least so said Magnusson—running the psychic machinery, they used up all the available energy. Of course the bacteria bred during their migration, and their breeding rate was so far in excess of their death rate that eventually they put too much of a burden upon the brain's resources. What Magnusson did not say, but what was implicit, was that if the bacteria could be steered more rapidly back and forth between centers of low and high metabolic activity, this by a process of externally applied magnetic fields, then the excess might be killed off and the size of the colony stabilized.

She discussed with Donnell various lines of investigation, how much money they would need—a lot!—and tried again to convince him to return to Shadows.

"I don't expect you to understand," he said. "But I *know* that's not the way." He had just taken a shower, and with his hair sleeked back, his sunglasses, he looked alert and foxy, every jut of his features pointed toward some dangerous enterprise: a small-time hood plotting a big score. "Maybe New Orleans," he said. "Not as much problem getting money there. Libraries, Tulane."

She marveled at the changes in him. There was such an air of purpose and calculation about his actions, it was as if he had thrown off a cloak of insecure behaviors and revealed himself to have been purposeful and calculating all along. He was, she knew, still uncertain about a great many things, but he seemed confident they would work themselves out and she no longer felt it necessary to soothe his doubts and fears. In fact, when Richmond did not return at noon, he undertook to soothe hers by leading her on a tour of the cabin, describing to her the things she could not see: the weird spindly structures fraying at the edges of spiderwebs, insect eggs joined together and buried in a crack like crystals in rock, a fantastic landscape of refracted light which he saw within a single facet of a dead fly's compound eye. Then he led her outdoors and described what Magnusson believed to be the geomagnetic field.

"I can see it better at night," he said. "Then it's not as translucent, more milky white, like the coil of a huge snake lying across the sky, fading, then reappearing in a new configuration." He scuffed his foot against the cabin steps. "I can always tell how it'll look before I look. Magnusson says that's because the bacteria are interpreting its movements, conveying the knowledge as intuition." He took off his sunglasses and looked at her with narrowed eyes. "Human fields are different. Cages of white fire flickering in and out. Each bar a fiery arc. When I first saw one, I thought of it as a jail to keep the soul in check."

Two o'clock, three, four, and Richmond did not return. He had been preparing for violence, and Jocundra was certain he had met with it. Even Donnell's confidence was sapped. He brooded over the ledger while Jocundra kept watch. A few cars passed, several stopping at Sealy's Restaurant: a building of white concrete block just up the road. Once Sealey himself crossed from the office to the restaurant, pausing to spit on a clump of diseased agave that grew on an island at the center of the parking lot. Palmetto bugs frolicked over the floor, the cabin stank of mildew, and Jocundra's thoughts eddied in dark, defeated circles. When Richmond finally did return, drunk, at dusk, he announced that he had not only found a car—it would be safe to pick up in the early morning—but he had also arranged a date for the movies with Sealey's day-shift waitress.

"Good ol' country girls," he said, rubbing his groin, grinning a tomcat grin; then he looked pointedly at Jocundra and said, "Ain't like them downtown bitches think their ass is solid silver."

Both Jocundra and Donnell argued vehemently against it, but Richmond was unshakable. "I ain't got my cooze with me like you, man," he said to Donnell. "Now you can come with me if you want, but you sure as shit ain't gonna stop me!" He put on his Hellhounds T-shirt and a windbreaker, slicked back his hair and tied it into a pony-tail.

The neon sign above the restaurant—a blue script Sealey's—hummed and sputtered, attracting clouds of moths which fluttered in and out of its nimbus like splotches in a reel of silent film. Jocundra pulled up to the side entrance, and a rawboned blond girl wearing a tube top and cut-offs skipped out and hopped in the back of the van with Richmond. "Couldn't get but a six-pack," she said breathily; she leaned up between the seats. "Hi! I'm Marie." Her face was long-jawed and dopey, heavy on the lipstick and mascara. Introductions all around, Jocundra eased out onto the highway, and then Marie poked Donnell's arm and said, "Sure was a weird wreck you guys had, y'know. The light hurt your eyes, too?"

Donnell tensed and said, "Uh, yeah," but Marie talked right through his answer. "Jack here says he don't never take his glasses off, even when he gets, y'know . . ." She giggled. "Friendly."

The Buccaneer Drive-In was playing TRIPLE XXX LADIES NO CHARGE, and the lot was three-quarters full of vans and pickups and family cars, most honking and whooping, demanding the show begin at once. The first feature was *Martial Arts Mistress;* it detailed the fistic and amorous exploits of a melon-breasted, bisexual Chinese girl named Chen Li, who slept her way up the ladder of the emperor's court so she ultimately could assassinate the evil prime minister, he who had seduced and killed her sister. The film's highlight was a kung fu love battle between Chen Li and the minister, culminating with them both vaulting impossibly high and achieving midair penetration, after which Chen Li disposed of her nemesis by means of a secret grip bestowing unendurable pleasure.

Jocundra might have found it amusing, but Richmond's performance eliminated any possibility of enjoyment. As he and Marie scrunched between the seats, he snorted into her neck and grabbed her breasts, causing giggles and playful slaps, and as the middle of the film approached, he drew her down under a blanket. Rummaging, whispers, a sharply indrawn breath. The van shuddered. Then the unmistakable sounds of passionate involvement, topped off by hoarse exclamations and suppressed squeals. Jocundra sat stiffly, staring at the writhing Oriental shapes, doing for technicolor sex what Busby Berkley had done for the Hollywood musical. Marie made a mewling noise; Richmond popped a beer, glugged, and belched. Feeling imperiled, isolated, Jocundra glanced at Donnell, seeking the comfort of shared misery. He had flipped up his sunglasses and was holding Magnusson's ledger close to his face, illuminating the page with the green flashes from his eyes.

At intermission, the theater lights blazed up, cartoon crows bore fizzing soft drinks to save a family of pink elephants stranded in a desert, and people straggled toward the refreshment stand. Marie declared she had to visit the ladies' room and asked Jocundra to come along; her tone was light but insistent. Some teenagers hassled them outside the bathroom and beat on the door after they entered. The speaker over the mirror squawked, "Five minutes until showtime," and blared distorted circus music. Bugs fried on the fluorescent tubes; the paper towels soaking on the floor looked like mummy wrappings, brown and ravelled; and a lengthy testimonial to the joys of lesbianism occupied most of the wall beside the mirror.

Marie removed lipstick, eyeliner and mascara from her purse, and began to repair the damage done her face by Richmond. "Did they really shoot them boys fulla snake poison?" she asked abruptly. "That why Jack's, y'know, a little cooler than average?"

Jocundra restrained a laugh. "Uh huh," she said, and splashed water on her face.

"I heard about 'em changing people's blood," said Marie. "But I never did hear about 'em replacin' it with snake poison. Is yours the same way?"

"It's only temporary." Jocundra affected nonchalance, patting her face dry.

Two women banged the door open, jabbering, and disappeared into grimy stalls.

Marie tugged at her cut-offs, turned sideways to judge the effect. "Well, it don't bother me none. I just thought ol' Jack was shittin' me. He's one crazy dude." She winked at Jocundra and wiggled her hips. "Anyway, I like 'em crazy! Guess you do, too."

Jocundra was noncommittal.

Marie adjusted her tube top. "He asked me to come along with y'all." Then, seeing Jocundra's stricken expression, she hastened to add, "But don't worry, I'm not. It ain't Jack, y'understand. He's just fine." She headed for the door, pausing for a final look into the mirror; she had, by dint of painstaking brushwork, transformed her eyes into cadaverous pits. "I just know there'd be trouble between you and me," she shot back over her shoulder, tossing her hair and switching her rear end. "I can tell we ain't got nothin' in common."

Marie said she had better be gettin' on home, it had been fun but her mother was sick and would worry—a lie, thought Donnell; her mood had changed markedly since visiting the ladies' room, and she was not as tolerant of Richmond's affections. They left during the credits of the second feature and dropped her at a white stucco house a mile from the motel. The front yard was lined with lawn decorations for sale: stone frogs, plastic flamingos, mirrored balls on pedestals, arranged in curved rows facing the road, like the graduation grouping of an extraterrestrial high school. Richmond stole one of the mirrored balls and stared gloomily at his reflection in it as they drove toward the motel. Donnell suggested they try for the car, and Richmond said that he was hungry.

"I'd like to go back to the room," said Jocundra firmly.

Richmond hurled the ball against the side of the van. Silvery pieces flew into the front seat, and Jocundra swerved.

"Be fuckin' reasonable!" yelled Richmond. "You been stickin' to the room so damn much, Sealey's gonna think we kidnapped you! I ain't boostin' no car 'less I eat."

Sealey's was frigid with air conditioning, poorly lit by lights shining through perforations in the ceiling board. A plate glass window provided a view of highway and scrub. The kitchen was laid out along the rear wall, partitioned off from two rows of black vinyl booths, interrupted by the entrance on one side, a waitress station and cash register on the other. A long-nosed, saw-toothed fish was mounted above the grill, and there were photographs stapled beneath the health classification, all yellowed, several of children, one portraying a younger, less bulbous Sealey in Marine blues. At the end of the aisle a juke box sparkled red and purple, clicking to itself like a devilish robot. They took the booth beside it. Sealey remained behind the register, indifferent to their presence until Richmond called for service; then he stumped over to them. Donnell asked to see a menu.

"Ain't got no menus," said Sealey. "I got burgers and fries, egg salad. I got fish, beer, Pepsi, milk."

He clanged his spatula on the grill as he cooked, clattered their plates on the table, and dumped their silverware in a pile. He folded his arms and glowered at them.

"You folks leavin' tomorrow?"

"Yeah," said Donnell, and Jocundra chipped in with, "We'll be getting an early start."

"Well, I don't mind," said Sealey, regarding them with a mix of superiority and distaste.

"What kind of fish is that?" asked Donnell, pointing to the trophy above the grill, meaning to placate, to charm.

Sealey pitied him with a stare. "Gar." He scuffed the floor in apparent frustration. "Damn," he said; he scratched the back of his neck and refolded his arms. "It ain't that I don't need the business, and I don't give a damn what you do to each other. . . ."

"We ain't doin' shit, man," said Richmond.

"But," Sealey continued, "that don't mean I got to like what's goin' on."

"I think you've got the wrong idea," said Jocundra meekly.

Sealey sucked on a tooth. "If you was my daughter and I seen you with these two in some motel . . ." He shook his head slowly, staggered by the prospect of what he might do were such the case, and stumped back to the register, muttering.

His professed hunger notwithstanding, Richmond did not eat. He fed quarters to the jukebox, syrupy country and western music welled forth, and he danced in the aisle with an imaginary woman. "Broken dreams and heartsick mem-o-rees," he howled, mocking the sappy lyrics as he dry-humped his invisible partner. He ordered beer after beer, taking pleasure in stirring Sealey off his stool, and each time the man brought him a fresh bottle, Richmond would weave threats and insults into his rap. "Some people you can just fuck with their minds and they'll leave your ass alone," he said, squinting up at Sealey. "But some people's

so dumb and ugly you gotta terrorize them motherfuckers."
Sealey either ignored him or did not catch his drift; he retook
his seat behind the register and thumbed through a magazine
whose cover showed soldiers of different eras marching
beneath a tattered American flag.

It would soon be necessary, thought Donnell, to part
company with Richmond; he was becoming uncontrollable.
Richmond would not mind them deserting, he only wanted
to flame out somewhere, but the idea bothered Donnell; he
felt no loyalty whatsoever to Richmond, and this lack reflected on his inhumanity. They should share a loyalty
founded on common trials, the loyalty of prisoners and
victims, yet they did not; the bonds of their association were
disintegrating, proving to be as meager as those between
strangers traveling on a bus. Perhaps loyalty was merely a
chemical waiting to be released, a little vat of sparkling
fluid hidden away in some area of his brain as yet uninfested
by bacteria, and when the bacteria spread to it, he would
light up inside with human virtues.

"Some people you gotta waste," said Richmond, deep
into his rap. "You gotta go to war with 'em, otherwise they
won't let you be." He had untied his pony tail, and his hair
spilled down over his sunglasses; his skin was drawn so
tightly across his bones that whenever he smiled you could
see complex knots of muscle at the ends of his lips. "War,"
he said, savoring the word, and drank a toast to it with the
last of his beer.

Jocundra nudged Donnell's leg; her lips were pressed
together, and she entreated him silently to leave. Donnell
glanced at the wall clock; it was after one. "Let's go, Jack,"
he said. "We want to hit New Orleans before dawn."

They were halfway along the aisle, slowed by Donnell's
halting pace, when a grumbling roar came from the highway
and a motorcycle cop pulled up in front. "Just keep goin',"
said Richmond. "Dude's just comin' off shift. He was in
this afternoon." He laughed. "Looks like a damn nigger
bike . . . all them bullshit fenders and boxes stuck all over."

The cop dismounted and removed his helmet. He was
young with close-cropped dark hair and rabbity features; his
riding jacket was agleam with blue highlights from the neon

sign. The record ended, the selector arm chattered along the rack, stopped, and began clicking.

"Couple of burgers?" asked Sealey as the cop pushed on in, and the cop said, "Yeah, coffee." He gave them a brief onceover and sat at the booth beside the entrance.

They waited at the cash register while Sealey tossed two patties on the grill and brought the cop his coffee; he sipped and made a sour face. "I can't get used to this chicory," he said. "Can't a man get a regular cup of coffee 'round here?"

"Most of my customers are dumb coon-ass Cajuns," said Sealey by way of apology. "They can't live without it." He moseyed back to the register and took Jocundra's money.

Donnell glued his eyes to the countertop.

"Hey, Officer," said Richmond. "What kinda piston ratio you runnin' on that beast?"

The cop blew on his coffee, disinterested. "Hell, I don't know diddley 'bout the damn thing. I'm on temporary with the highway division."

"Yeah?" Richmond was aggravated. "Man don't know what he's ridin' don't belong on the road."

Surprised, the cop glared at Richmond over the edge of his cup, but let it pass.

"Seems like ever since them sand niggers raised the price of gas," said Richmond nastily, "every cheap son of a bitch in the country is gettin' hisself up on a Harley."

The cop set down his coffee. "Okay, buddy. Show me some ID."

"No problem," said Richmond. He reached for his hip pocket, but instead sneaked his hand up under his windbreaker and snatched out the security guard's gun. He motioned for the cop to raise his hands, and the cop complied. "ID!" Richmond laughed at the idea. "You askin' the wrong dudes for ID, Officer. Hell, we ain't even got no birth certificates."

Looking at the gun made Donnell lightheaded. "What are you going to do?" he asked. Jocundra backed away from the register, and he backed with her.

"Ain't but one thing *to* do, man," said Richmond. He moved behind the cop, jammed the gun in his ear, and fumbled inside the leather jacket; he ripped off the cop's badge and stuffed it into his jeans. Then he stepped out into the aisle, keeping the gun trained head-high. "If we don't want the occifer here to start oinkin' on his radio, I'm gonna have to violate his civil rights."

"You could break the radio," said the cop, talking fast. "You could rip out the phone. Hey, listen, nobody drives this road at night. . . ."

Richmond flipped up his sunglasses. "No," he said. "That ain't how it's gonna be, Porky."

The cop paled, the dusting of freckles on his cheeks stood out sharply.

"Them's just contact lenses," said Sealey with what seemed to Donnell foolhardy belligerence. "These people's in some damn cult."

"That's us," said Richmond, edging along the aisle toward the register. "The Angels of Doom, the Disciples of Death. We'll do anything to please the Master."

"Watch it!" said Donnell, seeing a craftiness in Sealey's face, a coming together of violent purpose and opportunity.

As Richmond crossed in front of the register, the partition beneath it exploded with a roar. Blood sprayed from his hip, and he spun toward the door, falling; but as he fell, he swung the gun in a tight arc and shot Sealey in the chest. The bullet drove Sealey back onto the grill, and he wedged between the bubbling metal and the fan, his head forced downward as if he were sitting on a fence and leaning forward to spit. A silvered automatic was clutched in his hand.

The explosiveness of the gunshot sent Donnell reeling against Jocundra, and she screamed. The cop jumped up, unsnapping his holster, peering to see where Richmond had fallen. A second shot took him in the face, and he flew backward along the aisle, ending up curled beneath a booth. His hand scrabbled the floor, but that was all reflex. And then, with the awful, ponderous grace of a python uncoiling from a branch, Sealey slumped off the grill; the grease clinging to his trousers hissed and spattered on the tiles. Everything was quiet. The jukebox clicked, the air conditioner hummed. The cop's hamburgers started to burn on the grill, pale flames leaping merrily.

Jocundra dropped to her knees and began peeling shreds of cloth from Richmond's wound. "Oh, God," she said. "His whole hip's shot away."

Donnell knelt beside her. Richmond's head was propped against the rear of a booth; his eyelids fluttered when Donnell touched his arm and his eyebrows arched in clownish curves with the effort of speech. "Oh..." he said; it didn't have the sound of a groan but of a word he was straining to speak. "...ooh," he finished. His eyes snapped open. The bacteria had flooded the membrane surfaces, and only thready sections of the whites were visible, like cracks spreading across glowing green Easter eggs. "Oh..." he said again.

"What?" Donnell put his ear to Richmond's mouth. "Jack!"

"He's dead," said Jocundra listlessly.

Richmond's mouth stayed pursed in an O shape, but he was not through dying. The same slow reverberation shuddered Donnell as had when Magnusson had died, stronger though, and whether as a result of the reverberation or because of stress, Donnell's visual field fluctuated. White tracers of Richmond's magnetic field stitched back and forth between the edges of his wound, and flashes erupted from every part of his body. Donnell got to his feet. Jocundra remained kneeling, shivering, blood smeared on her arms. The night was shutting down around them, erecting solid black barriers against the windows, sealing them in with the three dead men.

A car whizzed past on the highway.

The light switches were behind the register, and Donnell's cane pocked the silence as he moved to them. He had a glimpse of Sealey open-mouthed on the floor, his chest red and ragged, and he quickly hit the switches. Moonlight slid through the windows and shellacked the formica tables, defining tucks and pleats in the vinyl. The cash drawer was open. He crumpled the bills into his pocket, turned, and was brought up short by the sight of Richmond's corpse.

Richmond was still propped against the booth, his legs asprawl. He should have been a shadow in the entranceway, half his face illuminated by the moonlight, but he was not.

A scum of violent color coated his body, a solarized oil slick of day-glo reds and yellows and blues, roiling, blending, separating, so bright he looked to be floating above the floor: the blazing afterimage of a man. Even the spills of his blood were pools of these colors, glowing islands lying apart from him. Black cracks appeared veining the figure, widening, as if a mold were breaking away from a homunculus within, and prisms were flitting through the blackness like jeweled bees. The reverberation was stronger than ever; each pulse skewed Donnell's vision. Something was emerging, being freed. Something inimical. The colors thickened, hardening into a bright sludge sloughing off the corpse. Donnell's skin crawled, and the tickling sensation reawakened in his head.

He took Jocundra by the arm; her skin was cold, and she flinched at his touch. "Come on," he said, pulling her toward the door. He stepped over the writhe of color that was Richmond and felt dizzy, a chill point of gravity condensing in his stomach, as if he were stepping over a great gulf. He steadied himself on the door and pushed it open. The air was warm, damp, smelling of gasoline.

"We can't go," said Jocundra, a lilt of fear in her voice.

"The hell we can't!" He propelled her across the parking lot. "I'll be damned if I'm going to wait for the police. You get the ledger, the clothes. Clean everything out of the cabin. I'll check the office and see if Sealey wrote anything down."

He was startled by his callousness, his practicality, because he did not recognize them to be his own. The words were someone else's, a fragmentary self giving voice to *its* needs, and he did not have that other's confidence or strength of purpose. An icy fluid shifted along his spine, and he refused to look back at the restaurant for fear he might see a shadow standing in the door.

CHAPTER X

May 20, 1987

According to the map it was eighty-five miles, about two hours' drive, to the town of Salt Harvest, and there they could catch the four-lane to New Orleans; but to Jocundra the miles and the minutes were a timeless, distanceless pour of imaginary cherry tops blinking in the rear view mirror, the wind making spirit noises through the side vent, and memories of the policeman's face: an absurdly neat concavity where his eyes and nose had been, as if a housing had been lifted off to check the working parts. Cypresses glowed grayish-white in the headlights, trees of bone burst from dark flesh. Rabbits ghosted beneath her wheels and vanished without a crunch. And near the turn-off a little girl wearing a lace party dress stepped out onto the blacktop, changing at the last second into a speed limit sign, and Jocundra swerved off the road. The van came to rest amid a thicket of bamboo, and rather than risk another accident, they piled brush around it and slept. But sleep was a thing seamlessly welded to waking, the continuance of a terrible dream, and in the morning, bleary, she saw shards of herself reflected in the fragments of the mirrored ball that Richmond had broken.

They started toward New Orleans, but the engine grated and the temperature indicator hovered near the red. A mile outside Salt Harvest they pulled into Placide's Mobil Service: junked cars resting on a cracked cement apron, old-fashioned globe-top pumps, a rickety, unpainted shack with corroded vending machines and lawn chairs out front. Placide, a frizzy-haired, chubby man chewing an unlit cigar, gazed up at the sky to receive instructions before allowing he would have a look at the van after he finished a rush job. Miserable, they waited. The radio news made no mention of the killings, and the only newspaper they could find was a gossip rag whose headline trumpeted *Teen's Pimples Found To Be Strange Code*.

"Somebody must have seen them by now!" Donnell kicked at a chair in frustration. "We've got to get out of here."

"The police aren't very efficient," she said. "And Sealey didn't even check us in. They may not know there was anyone else."

"What about Marie?"

"I don't know." She stared off across the road at a white wooden house by the bayou. A tireless truck in the front yard; shade trees; children scampering in and out of the sunbeams which penetrated the branches. The scene had an archaic air, as if the backing of a gentle past were showing through the threadbare tapestry of the present.

"Don't you care?" he asked. "Aren't you worried about being caught?"

"Yes," she said tonelessly, remembering the yellow dimness and blood-smeared floors of the restaurant. "I . . ."

"What?"

"You just don't seem bothered by what happened."

"Bothered? Guilty, you mean?" He thought it over. "The cop bothers me, but when Sealey pulled the trigger"—he laughed—"oh, he was a happy man. He'd been waiting for this chance a long time. You should have seen his face. All that frustrated desire and obsession blowing up into heaven." He limped a little way across the apron. "It was Sealey's crime. Richmond's maybe. But it's got no moral claim on me."

Around five o'clock a sorrowful Placide delivered his report: a slow leak in the oil pan. Ten or fifteen more miles and the engine would seize up. "I give you fifty dollars, me," he said. Jocundra gave him a doubtful look, and he crossed himself.

They accepted his offer of a ride into town, and he let them off at the Crawfish Cafe where, he said, they could learn the bus schedules. A sign above the door depicted a green lobsterlike creature wearing a bib, and inside the lighting was hellishly bright, the booths packed with senior citizens—tonight, Sunday, being the occasion of the cafe's Golden Ager All-U-Can-Eat Frog Legs and Gumbo Creole Special $2.99. The smell of grease was filmy in Jocundra's nostrils. The waitress told them that a bus left around midnight for Silver Meadow ("Now you be careful! The shrimp fleet's in, and that's one wild town at night.") and there they could catch a Greyhound for New Orleans where she had a sister, Minette by name, who favored Jocundra some though she wasn't near as tall, and oh how she worried about the poor woman living with her madman husband and his brothers on Beaubien Street like a saint among wolves. . . . Try the shrimp salad. You can't go wrong with shrimp this time of year.

The senior citizens, every liver spot and blotch evident under the bright lights, lifted silvery spoons full of dripping red gumbo to their lips, and the sight brought back the memory of Magnusson's death. Jocundra's stomach did a queasy roll. An old man blinked at her and slipped a piece of frog into his mouth, leaving the fork inserted. The tinkle of silverware was a sharp, dangerous sound at the edge of a silence hollowed around her, and she ate without speaking.

"Do you want to go back?" Donnell asked. "I can't, but if you think it's better for you there, I won't stop you."

"I don't see how I can," she said, thinking that she would have to go back to before Shadows, before the project began.

He toyed with a french fry, drawing circles in the grease on his plate. "I need a more isolated place than New Orleans," he said. "I don't want to lose it in public like Richmond."

"You're nothing like Richmond." Jocundra was too exhausted to be wholeheartedly reassuring.

"Sure I am. According to Edman, and it seems to me he's at least partially right, Richmond's life was the enactment of a myth he created for himself." The waitress refilled Jocundra's coffee, and he waited until she finished. "He had to kill someone to satisfy the myth, and by God he did. And there's something I have to do as well."

She looked up at him. "What do you mean?"

"Magnusson told me I had something special to do, and ever since I've felt a compulsion to do it. I have no idea what it is, but the compulsion is growing stronger and I'm convinced it's not a good deed."

White gleams of the overheads slashed diagonally across the lenses of his sunglasses. For the first time she was somewhat afraid of him.

"A quiet place," he said. "One without too many innocent bystanders."

More senior citizens crammed into the cafe. They huddled at the front waiting for a seat, and the waitress became hostile as Donnell and Jocundra lingered over their empty plates. Jocundra wedged Magnusson's ledger into her purse; they tipped the waitress generously, leaving the overnight bag in her keeping, and walked out into the town.

The main street of Salt Harvest was lined with two-story buildings of dark friated brick, vintage 1930, their walls covered by weathered illustrations of defunct brands of sewing machines and pouch tobacco, now home to Cadieux Drugs, Beutel Hardware, and the Creole Theater, whose ticket taker—isolate in her hotly lit booth—looked like one of those frowsy, bewigged dummies passing for gypsy women that you find inside fortune-telling machines, the yellowed paint of their skin peeling away, their hands making mechanical passes over a dusty crystal ball. The neons spelled out mysterious red and blue and green words— HRIMP, SUNOC, OOD—and these seemed the source of all the heat and humidity. Cars were parked diagonally along the street, most dinged and patched with bondo, windshields polka-dotted by NRA and S.W. Louisiana Ragin' Cajun decals. Half of the streetlights hummed and fizzled, the other half were shattered. Dusk was thickening to night, and heat lightning flashed in the southern sky.

Groups of people were moving purposefully toward the edge of town, and so as not to appear conspicuous, they fell in at the rear of three gabbling old ladies who were cooling themselves with fans bearing pictures of Christ A-risen. Behind them came a clutch of laughing teenage girls. Before they had gone a hundred yards, Donnell's legs began to cramp, but he preferred to continue rather than go contrary to the crowd now following them. Their pace slowed, and a family bustled past: mom, kids, dad, dressed in their Sunday finery and having the prim, contented look of the well-insured. Some drunken farmers passed them, too, and one—a middle-aged man whose T-shirt read *When Farm-boys Do It They Fertilize 'Er*—said "Howdy" to Jocundra and offered her a swig from his paper sack. He whispered in his buddy's ear. Sodden laughter. The crowd swept around them, chattering, in a holiday mood, and Jocundra and Donnell walked in their midst, tense, heads down, hoping to go unnoticed but noticeable by their secretive manner: Jews among Nazis.

The night deepened, gurgling and croaking from the bayou grew louder as they cleared the city limits, and they heard a distorted amplified voice saying, "CHILDREN, CHIL-DREN, CHIL..." The speaker squealed. A brown circus tent was pitched in a pasture beside the bayou, ringed by parked cars and strung with colored bulbs; a banner above the entrance proclaimed What Jesus Promised, Papa Salvatino Delivers. The speaker crackled, and the voice blatted out again: a cheery, sleazy voice, the voice of a carnival barker informing of forbidden delights.

"CHILDREN, CHILDREN, CHILDREN! COME TO PAPA SALVATINO! COME BEFORE THE NIGHT CREEPERS AND THE GHOST WORMS SNIFF YOU OUT, COME BEFORE THE DEVIL GETS BEHIND YOU WITH HIS SHINBONE CLUB AND SMACKS YOU LOW. YEAH, THAT'S RIGHT! YOU KNOW YOU GONNA COME, CHILDREN! YOU GOTTA COME! 'CAUSE MY VOICE GONNA SNEAK LIKE SMOKE THROUGH THE CRACK IN YOUR WINDOW, CURL UP YOUR STAIR AND IN YOUR EAR, AND HOOK YOU, CROOK YOU, BEND YOU ON YOUR KNEE TO JEEESUS! YES, CHIL-DREN, YES..."

A furious, thumping music compounded of sax, organs and drums built up under the voice, which continued to cajole and jolly the crowd; they streamed into the entrance, and the tent glowed richly brown against the blackness of field and sky. As Donnell and Jocundra hesitated, a police car pulled up next to the field and flashed its spotlight over the rows of parked cars; they joined the stragglers walking toward the tent.

At the entrance a mousy girl asked them for three dollars each admission, and when Jocundra balked, she smacked her gum and said, "We used to do with just love offerin's, but Papa fills folks so brimful of Jesus' love that sometimes they forgets all about givin'."

Inside, radiating outward from a plywood stage, were rows of folding chairs occupied by shadowy figures, most standing, hooting and clapping to the music. The mingled odors of sweat and liquor and perfume, the press of bodies, the slugging music, everything served to disorient Donnell. He squeezed Jocundra's hand, fending off a visual shift.

"And lo!" a voice shouted in his ear. "The blind and the halt shall be first annointed." A gray-haired man, tall and lean, his hair cut short above the ears and left thick on top, giving him a stretched look, beamed at Donnell. "We'll get you a seat down front, brother," he said, steering him toward the stage. Jocundra objected, and he said, "No trouble at all, sister. No trouble at all." His smile seemed the product of a wise and benign overview.

As he led them along, people staggered out of their chairs and into the aisle. Deranged squawks, angry shouts, and scuffles, a few cries of religious fervor. A Saturday-night-in-the-sticks-and-ain't-nothin'-else-to-do level of drunkenness. Hardly sanctified. Donnell was grateful when the usher shooed two teenagers off the first row and sat him down beside a fat lady. "Ain't it hot?" she cried, nudging him with a dimpled arm the size of a ham. "'Bout hot enough to melt candles!" The edges of the crimson hibiscus patterning her dress were bleeding from her sweat, and each crease and fold of her exuded its own special sourness. "Oh, Jesus yes!" she screeched as the saxophonist shrilled a high note. She quivered all over, and her eyelids slid down, false lashes stitching them to her cheeks.

The music ebbed, the organist stamped out a plodding beat on the bass pedals, and the saxophonist played a gospel fanfare. The lights cut to a single spot, and a paunchy, balding man, well over six feet tall, slouched onto stage. His walk was an invitation to buy drugs, to slip him twenty and meet the little lady upstairs; his face was yellow-tinged, puffy, framed by a hippie-length fringe of brown hair. He wore a powder-blue suit, a microphone dangled from his hand, and his eyes threw back glitters of the spotlight.

"CHILDREN, CHILDREN, CHILDREN," he rasped. "ARE YOU READY FOR PAPA'S LOVE?"

There were hysterical Yesses in response, a scatter of Nos, and one "Fuck you, Papa!"

He laughed. "WELL, THEM THAT SAY YEA, I AIN'T WORRIED 'BOUT THEM. AND AS FOR THE REST, YOU GONNA LEARN THAT OL' PAPA'S JUST LIKE POTATO CHIPS AND LOVIN'. YOU CAN'T DO WITH JUST ONE HELPIN'!" He bowed his head and walked along the edge of the stage, deep in thought. "I'M HERE TO TELL YOU I'M A SINNER. DON'T YOU NEVER LET NO PREACHER TELL YOU HE AIN'T! HELL, THEY'S THE WORST KIND." He shook his head, rueful; then, suddenly animated, he dropped into a crouch, and his delivery became rapid-fire. "BUT IN HIS INFINITE COMPASSION THE LORD JESUS HAS FILLED ME WITH THE SPIRIT, AND I AIN'T TALKIN' 'BOUT THE IMMATERIAL, PIE-IN-THE-SKY, SOMETHIN'-YOU-GOTTA-HAVE-FAITH-IN SPIRIT! NOSIR! I'M TALKIN' 'BOUT THE REACHABLE, TOUCHABLE, GRAB-AHOLD-OF-YOU-AND-MAKE-YOU-FEEL-AGREE-ABLE POWER OF GOD'S LOVE!"

Faint Praise Gods and Hallelujahs; the crowd rustled; the fat lady raised her hands overhead, palms up, praying silently.

"I'M TALKIN' 'BOUT THE SAME SPIRIT THAT SOON ONE MORNIN'S GONNA LIFT US ON ANGELS' WINGS INTO THE LIGHT OF THE RAPTURE WHERE WE WILL LIVE IN ECSTASY 'TIL HIS EARTHLY KINGDOM IS SECURE HALLELUJAH!"

"Hallelujah!" chorused the crowd. Donnell was beginning to relax, his senses settling; he stretched out his legs, preparing to be bored. Papa Salvatino paced the stage: a downcast, troubled man. The organ rippled out an icy trill.

"OH, CHILDREN, CHILDREN, CHILDREN! I SEE THE PATHS BY WHICH YOU'VE TRAVELED GLEAMIN' IN MY MIND'S EYE. SLIMY SERPENT

TRACKS! YOU BEEN DOWN IN THE MUCK OF SHAL-LOW LIVIN' AND FALSE EMOTION SO LONG YOU'RE TOO SICK FOR PREACHIN'!" He pointed to the fat lady beside Donnell. "YOU THERE, SISTER RITA! I SEE YOUR SIN SHININ' LIKE PHOSPHOR ON A STUMP!" He pointed to others of the crowd, accusing them, and as his gaze swept over Donnell, his yellow face, gemmed with those glittering eyes, was as malevolent as a troll's.

"BUT IT AIN'T TOO LATE, SINNERS! THE LORD'S GIVIN' YOU ONE LAST CHANCE. HE'LL EVEN GET DOWN IN SATAN'S DIRT AND TEMPT YOU. HE'S OFFERIN' YOU A ONE-TIME-ONLY-GUARANTEED-YOUR-SOUL-BACK-IF-YOU-AIN'T-SATISFIED TASTE OF SALVATION! AND I'M HERE TO GIVE YOU THAT TASTE! THAT SOUL-STIRRIN' TASTE OF HOSAN-NAH-IN-THE-HIGHEST AMBROSIA! 'CAUSE EVEN IF HE CAN'T SAVE YOU, THE LORD JESUS HIMSELF WANTS YOU TO HAVE BIG FUN TONIGHT DOWN ON THE BAYOU!"

The crowd was on its feet, waving its arms, shouting.

"YOU WANT THAT TASTE, CHILDREN?"

"Yes!"

"WHAT'S THAT YOU WANT?"

"A taste!" called the organist, prompting the crowd, and they hissed raggedly, "A taste!" The saxophone brayed, the drummer bashed out a shuffle beat, and the organist un-leashed a wash of chords. Papa Salvatino shed his jacket. "AMEN!" he shouted.

"Amen!"

Donnell turned and saw open-mouthed, flushed faces, rolling eyes; people were shouldering each other aside, pois-ing to rush the stage.

"THY WILL BE DONE!" Papa leaped high and came down in a split, gradually humping himself upright, and did a little shimmy like a snake standing on its tail. "I WANT THE SICK ONES FIRST AND THE WHOLE ONES LAST! ALL RIGHT, CHILDREN! COME TO PAPA!"

The crowd boiled toward the stage, bumping Donnell's chair, and once again the gray-haired usher loomed before him. He helped Donnell up. Jocundra pried at his grip, protesting, and Donnell struggled; but the usher held firm and said, "You come with him if you want, sister. But I ain't lettin' you stand in the path of this boy's salvation."

After much shoving, many Biblically phrased remonstrations directed at people who would not move aside, the usher secured a choice spot in line for Donnell, fourth behind Sister Rita and a thin, drab woman with her arm draped around a teenage boy, a hydrocephalic. He grinned stuporously at Donnell. His hair was slicked down, pomaded, a mother's idea of good grooming; but the effect was of a grotesque face painted on a balloon. He let his head roll around, his grin broadening, enjoying the dizzy sensation. A pearl of saliva formed at the corner of his mouth.

"Jody!" The thin woman turned him away from Donnell, and by way of apology smiled and said, "Praise the Lord!" Her hair was piled up in a bouffant style, which accentuated her scrawniness, and her gray dress hung loosely and looked to be full of sticks and air.

"Praise the Lord," muttered Donnell, struck by the woman's sincerity, her lack of pose, especially in relation to the fraudulence of Papa Salvatino; his face was a road map of creepy delights and indulgences, and masked an unaspiring soul who had discovered a trick by which he might prosper. The nature of the trick was beyond Donnell's power to discern, but no doubt it was the cause of the anticipation he read from the shadowy faces bobbing in the aisle below.

The music lapsed into a suspenseful noodling on the organ, and Jocundra leaned close, her face drawn and worried. "Don't let him touch your glasses," she whispered. She pointed to the rear flap of the tent, which was lashed partway open behind the drum kit, and he nodded.

"What's ailin' you tonight, Sister Rita?" Papa clipped the microphone to a stand and approached. "You look healthier than me!"

"Oh, Papa!" Sister Rita wiggled her hips seductively. "You know I got the worst kind of heart trouble."

Papa laughed. "No need to get specific, sister," he said. "Jesus understands full well the problems of a widow woman." He placed his hands palms inward above her head and began to knead the air, hooking his fingers, shaping an invisible substance.

Astounded, Donnell recognized the motions to be the same he had used to disrupt the lock on the gate at Shadows. He brought Sister Rita's magnetic field into focus, and saw that Papa was inducing the fiery arcs to flow inward toward a point at the top of her head; and as they flowed, they ceased flickering in and out, brightened and thickened into a cage of incandescent wires. Her back arched. Her arms stiffened, her fingers splayed. The rolls of fat rippled beneath her dress. And then, as all the arcs flowed inward, a brilliant flash enveloped her body, as if the gate to a burning white heaven had opened and shut inside her. In Donnell's eyes she existed momentarily as a pillar of pale shimmering energy. He felt the discharge on every inch of his skin, a tingling which faded with the same rapidity as the flash

Sister Rita wailed and staggered to one side. His smile unflagging, the gray haired usher led her toward the stairs, and the band launched into a triumphant blare. Fervent shouts erupted from the crowd.

"PRAISE JESUS!" Papa bawled into the mike. "I'M STOKED FULL OF GOD'S LOVE TONIGHT!"

But if Papa were truly a conduit for the Holy Spirit, then the Spirit must consist of a jolt of electro-magnetism channeled into the brain reward centers. That, thought Donnell, would be how Magnusson would have interpreted the event. Papa Salvatino must be psychically gifted, and in effect was serving his flock as a prostitute, bestowing powerful orgasms and passing them off as divine visitations. Donnell glanced down at Sister Rita. She was sprawled in her chair, gasping, her legs spread and her skirt ridden up over swollen knees; an elderly woman leaned over her from the row behind and was fanning her with a newspaper.

The music lapsed once more, the crowd stilled, and Papa began working on the hydrocephalic. The thin woman closed her eyes and lifted her arms overhead, praying silently, the ligature of her neck standing out in cables with the ferocity of her devotion. Things were not going as well as they had for Sister Rita. Papa's eyes were nearly crossed with the strain, sweat beaded his forehead, and the hydrocephalic's head was sunk grimacing on his chest. His field was more complex than Sister Rita's, hundreds of arcs, all of them fine and frayed, woven erratically in a pattern similar to a spiderweb. Instead of slowly fading and rematerializing, they popped in and out with magical quickness. Whenever Papa touched them, they flared and sputtered like rotten fuses. The thing to do, thought Donnell, would be to meld the arcs together, to simplify the pattern; but Papa was doggedly trying to guide them inward, and by doing so he was causing them to fray and divide further. A bubble of spittle burst on the boy's lips, and he moaned. The crowd was growing murmurous, and the organist was running out of fills, unable to build to a climax.

Papa withdrew his hands, spread his arms, and addressed the darkness at the tent top, his lips moving, apparently praying; but his gaze darted back and forth between the crowd and the thin woman.

A feeling of revulsion had been building inside Donnell, a feeling bred by the stink of the tent, the raucous music, the slack-jawed faces, but most of all by Papa Salvatino: this big yellow rat standing on its hind legs and mocking the puny idea which sustained his followers in their fear. With a rush of animosity, and with only a trace of amazement at his own incaution, Donnell stepped forward, hooked his cane onto his elbow, and placed his hands above the boy's head. The fiery arcs tugged at his fingers, and he let them guide his movements. Two of the arcs materialized close together, and he urged them to merge into a single bright stream, setting it coursing inward toward the boy's scalp, a spot to which it seemed to gravitate naturally. As more and more of the arcs were joined, the boy's great head wobbled up. He smiled dazedly and lifted his arms and waggled his fingers, as if in parody of the thin woman's charismatic salute. Dimly, Donnell was aware of Jocundra beside him, of marveling shouts from the crowd. And then a heavy hand fell on his shoulder, spinning him around.

"Blasphemer!" shouted Papa, clutching a fistful of Donnell's shirt; his cheeks were mottled with rage. He drove his fist into Donnell's forehead.

Donnell fell against the drum kit, cracking his head on

the cymbal stand. His sunglasses had snapped in the middle, and one piece dangled from his ear. He did not lose consciousness, but everything had gone black and he was afraid he had been blinded. Footsteps pounded the boards, screams, and a man's voice nearby said, "Oh God, lookit his eyes!" He groped for his cane, feeling terribly exposed and helpless, and then he saw his cane outlined in glowing silver a few feet away, lying across a silver sketch of planks and nails. He looked up. The tent had been magicked into a cavernous black drape ornamented with silver arabesques and folds, furnished with silver-limned chairs, and congregated by ebony demons. Prisms whirled inside the bodies of most, masked the faces of others with glittering analogues of human features; and in the case of two, no, three, one standing where Papa Salvatino had been, the prisms flowed through an intricate circuitry, seeming to illuminate the patterns of their nerves and muscles, forming into molten droplets at their fingertips and detonating in needle-thin beams of iridescent light, which spat throughout the crowd. Yet for all their fearsome appearance, the majority of them edged away from the stage, huddling together, afraid. Curious, Donnell held up his hand to his face, but saw nothing, not even the outline of his fingers.

Jocundra, a gemmy mask overlaying her features, knelt beside him and pressed the cane into his hand. The instant she touched him, his vision normalized and his head began to throb. She pulled him upright. The band had fled, and Papa Salvatino was halfway down the steps of the stage.

"Abomination!" he said, but his voice quavered, and the crowd did not respond. They crushed back against the tent walls, on the verge of panicked flight. Most were hidden by the darkness, but Donnell could see those in the front rank and was fascinated by what he saw.

They were more alien to him now than their previous appearance of ebony flesh and jeweled expressions had been. Lumpy and malformed; protruding bellies, gaping mouths, drooping breasts; clad in all manner of dull cloth; they might have been a faded mural commemorating the mediocrity and impermanence of their lives. Wizened faces topped by frumpy hats; dewy, pubescent faces waxed to a hard gloss with makeup; plump, choleric faces. And each of these faces was puckered or puffed up around a black seed of fear. As he looked them over one by one, bits of intelligence lodged in his thoughts, and he knew them for bad-tempered old men, vapid old women, thankless children, shrewish wives, brutal husbands. But the complications of their lives were only a facade erected to conceal the black ground which bubbled them up. He took a step forward. Jocundra tried to drag him toward the rear flap of the tent, but he shook her off and limped to the front of the stage. Papa backed along the aisle.

"Why are you so afraid?" Donnell asked the crowd. "It's not just my eyes. That's not what drives you to seek salvation." He spotted a portly, sport-jacketed man trying to push through to the entrance. "You!" he called, pointing, and knew the substance of the man's life as if it had rushed up his finger: pompous, gluttonous, every dependency founded on fear and concealing a diseased sexuality, a compendium of voyeurism and the desire to inflict pain. "Don't be afraid," he said derisively, the way a murderer might taunt his victim, and was amazed to see the man swallow and inch toward the stage, his fear lessening. "Come closer," said Donnell. "Tonight, verily, you will bear miraculous witness."

He singled out others of the crowd, coaxing them nearer, and as he did, he felt a distance between his voice and his cautious soul, one identical to that he had experienced when he persuaded Jocundra to leave the scene of the murders at Sealey's. But in this instance the distance was more profound. The element of his consciousness which spoke dominated him totally, and his own fear was swept away by the emotional charge of the words. Disgust, pity and anger met in his mind and pronounced judgment on the crowd, on the culture that had produced it, comparing it unfavorably to a sterner culture existing beneath the flood of his memory like a submerged shoal, unseen, undefined, known only by the divergence of waves around it; but he did not question its reality, rather acted as its spokesman. He could, he thought, tell the crowd anything and they would listen. They were not really listening, they were reacting to the pitch and timbre of his voice, his glowing eyes. Their fear had taken on a lewd, exultant character, as if they had been eagerly awaiting him.

"Lo," he said, spreading his arms in imitation of Papa Salvatino, "the Lord God has raised me up from the ramshackle kingdom of the dead and sent me to warn you. Not of Kingdom Come but of Kingdom Overthrown, of Satan's imminent victory!"

Hesitant, they shuffled forward, some coming halfway along the aisle, soothed by the familiar Biblical cadences, but not yet ready to embrace him fully. The ease with which they could be swayed delighted him; he imagined an army carrying a green-eyed banner through the world, converting millions to his cause.

"Do you remember the good old days?" he asked with a wistful air, hobbling along the edge of the stage. "Those days that always seem just to have vanished or perhaps never even were. Days when the light was full of roses and lovers, when music played out every window and the kids weren't into drugs, when Granny baked her bread fresh each morning and the city streets were places of excitement and wonder. Whatever happened to those days?"

They didn't know but wanted to be told.

"You began to hear voices," he said. "You began to have visions, to receive reports, all of which conjured against that peaceful world. Radio and newspapers preaching a gospel of doom, a spell binding you to its truth. And then along came Satan's Eye Itself. Television." He laughed, as at some fatal irony. "Don't you hear the evil hum of the word, the knell of Satan? Television! It's the ruling character of your lives, like the moon must have been for Indians. An oracle, a companion, a signal of the changing seasons. But rather than divine illumination, each night it spews forth Satan's imagery. Murders, car crashes, mad policemen, perverted strangers! And you lie there decomposing in its flickering, blue-gray light, absorbing His horrid fantasies."

He stared out over their heads as if he saw a truth they could not see, staring for so long that many followed his gaze.

"You'll go home tonight and look at your sets and say,

'Why, it's a harmless entertainment, a blessing when the kids are sick.' But that logic's Satan's sales pitch, brothers and sisters. What it really is is the transmission of Armageddon's pulse, the rumormonger of the war foretold by Scripture, the power cell of Satan's dream for mankind. Take a closer look. Turn it on, touch the glass and feel the crackle of his force, catch a whiff of his lightning brain. It's the thing you fear most, the thing which has seduced you, which is lifting you to its jaws while you think it's preparing to give you a kiss. Know it, brothers and sisters! Or be consumed. And when you truly know it, save yourself. Break the glass, smash the tubes!"

"Break the glass!" shouted someone, and another shouted, "Break it! Break it!"

"Break the glass," said Donnell softly. "Smash the tubes." And the crowd, though unfamiliar with the litany, tried to repeat it.

"Hallelujah!" said Donnell.

They knew that one and were nearly unanimous in their response. He had them say it again, letting them unite within the sound of the word, and then held out his hands for silence.

"Break the glass, smash the tubes, and..." He made them wait, enjoying the expectancy on their faces. "And...renew the earth! Oh, brothers and sisters, don't you remember when you used to walk to the edge of town and into the woods and fields? What's taken their place?"

They weren't sure. "Evil!" someone suggested, and Donnell nodded his approval.

"Right enough, brother. Gas stations and motels and franchise restaurants. Defoliated zones of sameness! Places that have lost their identity and might be anywhere on God's earth. Why, put a good Christian down in one and he might think he was in Buffalo as like as Albuquerque. But you know where he really is? Those bright little huts tinkling with jingles are the anterooms of Hell-on-earth, an infection of concrete and plastic spreading over the land, reducing everything to the primary colors and simple shapes of Satan's dream. Arby's, Big Boy, McDonald's, Burger King! Those are the new names of the demons, of Beelzebub and

Moloch." He shook his head, disconsolate. "Satan's nearly won, and he would have already except for one thing. God has a plan for Salt Harvest. A master plan, a divinely inspired plan! Do you want to hear it?"

Yes, indeed. The boldest of them were three-quarters of the way down the aisle, waggling their hands overhead, praising God and begging His guidance.

"Salt Harvest! Listen to the name. It's a natural name, an advertising man's dream of organic purity, a name that bespeaks the bounty of the sea and of God, redolent of Christian virtue and tasty gumbos. How many people live here?"

They argued briefly, settling on a consensus figure of between fifteen and eighteen thousand.

"And things aren't going too well, are they? The economy's depressed, the cannery's shut down, the kids are moving away. Am I right?"

They agreed.

"Now bear with me, brothers and sisters. Hear me out, because like every great plan this one's so simple it might sound foolish until you get used to it. But imagine! Eighteen thousand Christian souls united in a common enterprise, all their resources pooled, digging for every last cent, competing with Satan for the consumer dollar and the souls of the diners. You've got everything you need! Cannery, shrimp boats, good men and women, and God on your side. Salt Harvest. Not a town. A chain of franchise restaurants coast to coast. I'm not talking about a dispensary of poisoned meat, a Burger Chef, a Wendy's, a Sambo's. No! We'll stuff them full of Gulf shrimp and lobster, burgers made from the finest Argentine beef. We'll outcook and undersell Satan and his minions, drive them into ruin. Instead of pimply, dope-smoking punks, we'll staff our units with Christian converts, and in no time our logo, the sign of the fish and the cross, will not only be familiar as a symbol of God's love but of gracious dining and quality cuisine. We'll snip a page from Satan's book and have a playland for the kids. They'll enter through the Pearly Gates, ride Ferris wheels with winged clouds for cars, cavort with actors dressed as cute angels and maybe even the Messiah Himself. A chapel in the rear, ordained ministers on duty twenty-four hours a day. Every unit will shine with a holy beacon winking out the diamond light of Jesus Christ, and soon the golden arches will topple, the giant fried chicken buckets will fill with rainwater and burst, and we'll bulldoze them under and build the Heavenly City in their place! Oh, there've been Congregationalists and Baptists and Methodists, but we'll have something new. The first truly franchised religion! That's real salvation, brothers and sisters. Economic and spiritual at the same time. Hallelujah!"

"Hallelujah!" Their chorus was less enthused than before; some of them weren't quite sold on his idea.

"Praise the Lord!"

"Praise the Lord!" They were coming around again, and after a few more repetitions they were held back from the stage by the thinnest of restraints. A man in a seersucker suit stumbled along the aisle, keening, almost a whistling noise like a teakettle about to boil, and fell on all fours, his face agonized, reaching out to Donnell.

Overwhelmed with disgust, Donnell said, "I could sell you sorry fuckers anything, couldn't I?"

They weren't sure they had heard correctly; they looked at each other, puzzled, asking what had been said.

"I could sell you sorry fuckers anything," he repeated, "as long as it had a bright package and was wrapped around a chewy nugget of fear. I could be your green-eyed king. But it would bore me to be the salvation of cattle like you. Take my advice, though. Don't buy the crap that's slung into your faces by two-bit wart-healers!" He jabbed his cane at Papa Salvatino, who stood open-mouthed in the aisle, a litter of paper cups and fans and Bibles spreading out from his feet. "Find your own answers, your own salvation. If you can't do that," said Donnell, "then to Hell with you."

He took a faltering step backward. His fascination with the crowd had dulled, and the arrogant confidence inspired by his voice was ebbing. He became aware again of his tenuous position. The crowd was massing back against the tent walls, once more afraid, in turmoil, a clot of darkness sprouting arms and legs, heaving in all directions. Whispers, then a babble, angry shouts.

"Devil!" someone yelled, and a man countered, "He ain't the Devil! He was curin' Alice Grimeaux's boy!" But someone else, his voice hysterical, screamed, "Jesus please Jeesus!"

"Yea, I have gazed into the burning eye of Satan and been sore affrighted," intoned Papa Salvatino. "But the power of my faith commands me. Pray, brothers and sisters! That's the Devil's poison: Prayer!"

The gray-haired usher came up behind him, grabbed a chair, held it overhead and advanced upon the stage while Papa exhorted the crowd. Dark figures began to trickle forward between the chairs, along the aisle. Jocundra stood by the drum kit, pale, her hand poised above the cymbal stand as if she had meant to use it as a weapon, transfixed by the sight of the Army of Our Lord in Louisiana bearing down on them. Donnell felt his groin shriveling. Ordinary men and women were slinking near, gone grim and wolfish, brandishing chairs and bottles, a susurrus of prayer—of "Save us sweet Jesuses" and "Merciful Saviors"—rising from them like an exhaust, ragged on by Papa Salvatino's blood-and-thunder.

"Pray! Let your prayer crack Satan's crimson hide! Shine the light of prayer on him 'til he splits like old leather and the black juice spews from his heart!"

A meek hope of countering Papa's verbal attack sparked in Donnell, but all he could muster was a feeble "Ah..." An old lady, her cane couched spear-fashion, her crepe throat pulsing with prayer, came right behind the gray-haired usher; a tubby kid, no more than seven or eight, clutching his father's hand and holding a jagged piece of glass, stared at Donnell through slit black eyes; Sister Rita, two hundred pounds of blubbery prayer, cooed to the Savior while she swung her purse around and around like a bolo; the man who had tried to worship Donnell had himself a pocket knife and was talking to the blade, twisting it, practicing the corkscrew thrust he planned to use.

"Let's fry Satan with the Holy Volts of prayer!" squalled Papa Salvatino. "Let's set him dancin' like a rat on a griddle!"

Donnell backed away, his own sermon about fear mocking him, because fear was gobbling him up from the inside, greedy piranha mouths shredding his rationality. He bumped against Jocundra; her nails dug into his arm.

"God, I'm healed!" somebody screeched, and two boys sprinted down the aisle. Teenagers. They darted in and out of the crowd, knocked the gray-haired usher spinning, and reeled up to the stage. One, the tallest, a crop of ripe pimples straggling across his cheeks, raised his arms high. "Holy Green-eyed Jesus!" he shouted. "You done cured my social disease!" The other doubled up laughing.

"Goddamn it, Earl!" A barrel-shaped man in overalls dropped his chair and rushed the boys, but they danced away. He lunged for them again, and they easily evaded him.

"Witness the work of Satan!" cried Papa. "How he turns the child against the father! Child!" He pointed at the tall boy. "Heed not the Anti-Christ or he will bring thee low and set maggots to breed in the jellied meats in thine eyes!"

"Shut up, you big pussy!" The boy avoided his father's backhand by a hair and grinned up at Donnell. "You done made my hot dog whole!" he shouted. "Praise the fuckin' Lord!"

A ripple of laughter from the front of the tent, and a girl yelled, "Git him, Earl!" More laughter as the big man fell, buckling one of the chairs.

The laughter disconcerted the crowd, slowed their advance. Donnell turned to Jocundra, thinking they might be able to hide among the cars; but just then she seized him by both hands and yanked him though the rear flap. He sprawled in the cool grass, shocked by the freshness of the night air after the pollution inside. She hauled him to his feet, her breath shrill, rising to a shriek as somebody jumped down beside them. It was Earl.

"Them Christians get their shit together, man," he said, "and they gonna nail you up. Come on!"

He and Jocundra hoisted Donnell by the elbows and carried him between the rows of parked cars to a van with a flock of silver ducks painted on its side. Earl slid open the door, and Donnell piled in. His hand encountered squidgy flesh; a girl's sulky voice said, "Hey, watch it!" and somebody else laughed. Through the window Donnell had a glimpse of people streaming out of the tent, imps silhouetted against a blaze of white light. Then the engine caught, and the van fishtailed across the field.

"Whooee!" yelled Earl. "Gone but not forgotten!" He banged the flat of his hand on the dash. "Hey, that's Greg and Elaine back there. And I am . . ." He beat a drumroll on the wheel. "The Earl!"

Headlights passing in the opposite direction penetrated the van. Elaine was a chubby girl wriggling into a T-shirt, forcing it down over large breasts, and Greg was a long-haired, muscular kid who regarded Donnell with drugged sullenness. He pointed to his own right eye. "Papa Salvatino do that to you, man?"

Elaine giggled.

"He's been sick," said Jocundra. "Radiation treatments." She refused to look at Donnell.

"Actually it was bad drugs," said Donnell. "The residue of evil companions."

"Yeah?" said Greg, half-questioning, half-challenging. He took a stab at staring Donnell down, but the eyes were too much for him.

"You shoulda seen the dude!" The van veered onto the shoulder as Earl turned to them. "He talked some wild shit to them goddamn Christians! Had ol' Papa's balls clickin' like ice cubes!"

Elaine cupped her hand in front of Donnell's eyes and collected a palmful of reflected glare. "Intense," she said.

Greg lost interest in the whole thing, pulled out a baggie and papers and started rolling a joint. "Let's air this sucker out," he said. "It smells like a goddamn pig's stomach."

"You the one's been rootin' in it." Earl chuckled, down-shifted, and the van shot forward. He slipped a cassette into the tape deck, and a caustic male voice rasped out above the humming tires, backed by atonalities and punchdrunk rhythms.

"... Go to bed at midnight,
Wake at half-past one,
I dial your number,
And let it ring just once,

I wonder if you love me
While I watch TV,
I cheer for Godzilla
Versus the Jap Army,
I think about your sweet lips
And your long, long legs,
I wanna carve my initials
In your boyfriend's face.
I'm gettin' all worked up, worked up about you!"

The singer began to scream "I'm gettin' all worked up" over and over, his words stitched through by a machine-gun bass line. Glass broke in the background, heavy objects were overturned. Earl turned up the volume and sang along.

Jocundra continued to avoid Donnell's gaze, and he couldn't blame her. He had nearly gotten them killed. A manic, sardonic and irrationally confident soul had waked in him and maneuvered him about the stage; and though it had now deserted him, he believed it was hidden somewhere, lurking behind a mist of ordinary thoughts and judgments, as real and ominous as a black mountain in the clouds. Considering what he had done, the bacterial nature of his intelligence, it would be logical to conclude that he was insane. But what logic would there be in living by that conclusion? Whether he was insane or, as Edman's screwball theory proposed, he was the embodiment of the raw stuff of consciousness, the scientific analogue of an elemental spirit, it was a waste of time to speculate. He had too much to accomplish, too little time, and—he laughed inwardly—there was that special something he had to do. A mission. Another hallmark of insanity.

Earl turned down the tape deck. "Where you people headin'?"

Jocundra touched Donnell's arm to draw his attention. "I've thought of a place," she said. "It's not far, and I think we'll be safe. It's on the edge of the swamp, a cabin. Hardly anyone goes there."

"All right," said Donnell, catching at her hand. "I'm sorry. I don't know what happened."

She nodded, tight-lipped. "Can you take us as far as

Bayou Teche?" she asked Earl. "We'll pay for the gas."

"Yeah, I guess so." Earl's mood had soured. "Jesus fuckin'
Christ," he said sorrowfully. "My ol' man's gonna kill my
ass."

CHAPTER XI

May 21–May 23, 1987

A tributary of Bayou Teche curled around the cabin, which
was set on short pilings amid a palmetto grove, and from
the surrounding darkness came a croaking, water gulping
against the marshy banks, and the electric sounds of insects.
Yellow light sprayed from two half-open shutters, leaked
through gaps in the boards, and a single ray shot up out of
a tin chimney angled from the roof slope, all so bright it
seemed a small golden sun must be imprisoned inside. The
tar paper roof was in process of sliding off, and rickety
stairs mounted to the door. Jocundra remembered the story
Mr. Brisbeau had told her, claiming the place had been
grown from the seed of a witch's hat planted at midnight.

"This is the guy who kept the moths? The guy who
molested you?" Donnell had put on a pair of mirrored sunglasses — a gift from Earl — and the lenses held two perfect
reproductions of the cabin. "How the hell can we trust him?"

"He didn't molest me, he just . . ."

Before she could finish, the door flew back, giving her
a start, and a lean old man appeared framed in the light.
"Who's there?" he asked, looking out over Jocundra's head,
then down and focusing on her. Gray streaks in his shoulder-
length white hair, a tanned face seamed with lines of mer-
riment. His trousers and shirt were sewn of flour sacking,
the designs on them worn into dim blue words and vague

trademark animals. He squinted at her. "That you, Florence?"

"It's Jocundra Verret, Mr. Brisbeau," she said. "I've got a friend with me."

"Jocundra?" He was silent, the tiers of wrinkles deepening on his brow. "Well," he said, "better you come in than the damn skeeters."

He had them sit on packing crates beside a wood stove while he boiled coffee and asked Jocundra about herself. The cabin was exactly as she remembered: a jackdaw's nest. Waist-high stacks of yellowed magazines along the walls interspersed by even taller heaps of junk. Dented cookware, broken toys, plastic jugs, boxes, papers. Similar junkpiles occupied the room center, creating a miniature landscape of narrow floorboard valleys meandering between surreal mountains. Beside the door was a clothes-wringer, atop it a battered TV whose screen had been painted over with a beach scene. The wood stove and a cot stood on opposite sides of a door against the rear wall, but they were so buried in clutter they had nearly lost their meaning as objects. The walls themselves were totally obscured by political placards and posters, illustrations out of magazines, torn pages of calendars. Layer upon layer. Thousands of images. Greek statues, naked women, jungle animals, wintry towns, movie stars, world leaders. A lunatic museum of art. Mildew had eaten away large areas of the collage, turning it into gray stratifications of shreds and mucilage stippled with bits of color. The light was provided by hurricane lamps—there must have been a dozen—set on every available flat surface and as a result the room was sweltering.

Mr. Brisbeau handed them their coffee, black and bittersweet with chicory, and pulled up a crate next to Jocundra. "Now I bet you goin' to tell me why you so full of twitch and tremble," he said.

Though she omitted the events at the motel and in Salt Harvest, Jocundra was honest with Mr. Brisbeau. Belief in and acceptance of unlikely probabilities were standard with him, and she thought he might find in Donnell a proof for which he had long been searching. And besides, they needed an ally, someone they could trust completely, and honesty was the only way to insure that trust. When she had done, Mr. Brisbeau asked if he could have a look at Donnell's eyes. Donnell removed his glasses, and the old man bent close, almost rubbing noses.

"What you see wit them eyes, boy?" he asked, settling back on his crate.

"Not much I understand," said Donnell, a suspicious edge to his voice. "Funny lights, halos."

Mr. Brisbeau considered this. "Days when I'm out at the traps, me, even though ever'ting's wavin' dark fingers at me, shadows, when I come to the fork sometimes the wan fork she's shinin' bright bright. Down that fork I know I'm goin' to find the mus'rat." He nudged a bale of coal-black muskrat skins beside the stove. "Maybe you see somethin' lak that?"

"Maybe," said Donnell.

Mr. Brisbeau blew on his coffee and sipped. He laughed. "I jus' tinkin' 'bout my *grand-mère*. She take wan look at you and she say, 'Mon Dieu! The Black Wan!' But I know the Black Wan he don't come round the bayou no more. He's gone long before my time." He squinted at Donnell, as if trying to pierce his disguise, and shook his head in perplexity; then he stood and slapped his hip. "You tired! Help me wit these furs and we fix you some pallets."

The back room was unfurnished, but they arranged two piles of furs on the floor, and to Jocundra, who was suddenly exhausted, they looked like black pools of sleep in which she could drown.

"In the mornin'," said Mr. Brisbeau, "I got business wit ol' man Bivalaqua over in Silver Meadow. But there's food, drink, and me I'll be back tomorrow night."

He glanced quizzically at Jocundra and beckoned her to follow him into the front room. He closed the door behind them.

"Wan time I get crazy wit you," he said, "and twelve years it takes to forgive? Don't you know, me, I'm just drunk. You my *petit zozo*." He held out his arms to her.

His entire attitude expressed regret, but the lines of his face were so accustomed to smiling that even his despondency was touched with good humor. Jocundra had the perception of him she had had as a child, of a tribal spirit come to visit and tell her stories. She entered his embrace, smelling his familiar scent of bourbon and sweat and homemade soap. His shoulder blades were as sharp and hard as cypress knees.

"You was my fav'rite of all the kids," he said. "It lak to break my heart you leavin'. But I reckon that's how a heart gets along from one day to the nex'. By breakin' and breakin'."

Jocundra lay on her side, waking slowly, watching out the window as gray clouds lowered against a picket line of cypresses and scrub pine. At last she got up and smoothed her rumpled blouse, wishing they had not left the overnight bag in Salt Harvest. She heard a rummaging in the front room. Donnell was sitting beside one of the junkpiles, his sunglasses pushed up onto his head.

"Morning," she mumbled, and went out back to the pump. A few raindrops hollowed conical depressions in the sandy yard, and the sweet odors of rot, myrtle and water hyacinth mixed with the smell of rain. The roof of an old boathouse stuck up above the palmetto tops about fifty feet away; a car rattled on the gravel road which passed in front of the cabin, hidden by more palmettos and a honeysuckle thicket.

She had expected Donnell would want to discuss the events in Salt Harvest, but when she re-entered he insisted on showing her the things he had extracted from the junkpiles. An armadillo shell on which someone had painted a mushroom cloud, five-years-back issues of *Madame Sonya's Dream Book,* and a chipped football helmet containing a human skull. "You suppose he found them together?" he asked, deadpan, holding up the helmet. She laughed, picturing the ritual sacrifice of a losing quarterback.

"What's he do with this stuff?" He flipped through one of the issues of the *Dream Book.*

"He collects it." Jocundra lit the stove for coffee. "He's kind of a primitive archaeologist, says he gets a clearer picture of the world from junk than he could any other way. Most people think he's crazy, and I guess he is. He lost his son in the Asian War, and according to my father, that's what started him drinking. He'd pin up photos of the president and target-shoot at them for hours."

"Something funny's happening," said Donnell.

She glanced at him over her shoulder, surprised by his abrupt change of subject. "Last night, you mean?"

"The last few days, but last night especially." He riffled the pages of the book. "When I picked this up earlier, I had no idea what it was, but then I had a whole raft of associations and memories. Stuff about palmists, seances, fortune-tellers. That's how my memory has always worked. But lately I've been comparing everything I see to something else, something I can't quite put my finger on. It won't come clear." Discouraged, he tossed the book onto a junkpile, dislodging a toy truck. "I guess I should tell you about last night."

His account took the better part of two cups of coffee, and after mulling it over, Jocundra said, "You have to consider this in light of the fact that your thrust has been to supply yourself with a past, and that your old memories have been proved false. You remember my telling you about the *gros bon ange?* Back at the motel?"

"Yeah. The soul."

"Well, you began to see the black figures almost immediately after I told you about them. It's possible you've started to construct another past from materials I've exposed you to. But," she added, seeing his distress, "you're right. It's not important to speculate about the reality of what you see. Obviously some of it's real, and we have to get busy understanding it. I'll ask Mr. Brisbeau to pick up some physics texts." She plucked at her blouse. "And some clothes."

"Oh, yeah. Here." He reached behind his packing crate. "It might not fit, but it's clean." He pulled forth a dress, a very old, dowdy dress of blue rayon with a design of white camellias. "Try it on," he suggested.

In the back room, Jocundra removed her jeans and blouse, and then, because it was so sweaty, her bra. The dress had been the property of someone shorter and more buxom. It was flimsy and musty-smelling, and she linked the mustiness with all the women she had known who had been habituated to such dresses. Her mother, musty aunts and neighbor ladies sporting hats adorned with plastic berries, looking as if they had dropped in from the 1930s. The skirt ended above her knees, the bodice hung slack, and the worn, silky material irritated her nipples.

"I must look awful," she said, coming out of the back room, embarrassed by Donnell's stare.

He cleared his throat. "No," he said. "It's fine."

To cover her embarrassment, she pretended interest in the camellia pattern. Striations of blue showed through the white of the petals: misprintings. But they had the effect of veins showing through pale, lustrous skin. The blossoms had been rendered with exaggerated voluptuousness, each curve and convolution implying the depth and softness of flesh, as if she were gazing at the throat of a seductively beautiful animal.

Throughout the morning and into the afternoon, they puzzled over the ledger. According to Magnusson, if the Ezawa bacterium existed in the southern hemisphere it would tend to be south-seeking, following the direction of the geomagnetic field in those regions; but it would—like its northern counterpart—migrate downward. However, if a south-seeking bacterium could be transported to the north, then it would migrate upward. It seemed evident to her that a north-seeking bacterium could be induced to become south-seeking by exposure to brief, intense pulses of a magnetic field directed opposite to the ambient field, thereby reversing the magnetic dipolar movement of the magnetosome chain. If necessary the bacterium's north-seeking orientation could be restored by a second pulse delivered anti-parallel to the first. Thus the colony could be steered back and forth between areas of stimulus and deprivation in the brain and its size controlled. Of course the engineering would be a problem, but given the accuracy of Magnusson's data, the basic scenario made sense.

The rain sprinkled intermittently, but by midafternoon the sun was beginning to break through. They walked down to the tributary in back of the cabin, a narrow serpent of lily-pad-choked water that wriggled off into the swamp. Droplets showered from the palmetto fronds when they brushed against them. The sun made everything steamy, and to escape the heat they went into the boathouse, a skeletal old ruin with half its roof missing. Spiders scuttling, beetles, empty wasp nests. The grain of the gray boards was as sharply etched as printed circuits. A single oar lay along one wall, its blade sheathed in spiderweb, and Mr. Brisbeau's *pirogue* drifted among the lily pads at the end of a rotting rope. They sat on the edge of the planking and dangled their feet, talking idly, skirting sensitive topics. He had rarely been so open with her; he seemed happy, swinging his legs, telling her about dreams he'd had, about the new story he had begun before leaving Shadows.

"It had the same setting as the first. Purple sun, brooding forest. But I needed a castle so I invented this immense bramble, sort of a briar patch thousands of feet high growing from the side of a mountain, with the tips of the highest branches carved into turrets." He flipped up a lily pad with the end of his cane; long green tendrils trailed from the underside, thickening into white tubules. "I never had a chance to work out the plot."

A tin-colored heron landed with a slosh in the lily pads about thirty feet away, took a stately step forward and stopped, one foot poised above the surface.

"You should finish it," said Jocundra; she smiled. "You're going to have to do something for a living."

"Do you really think I can?" he asked. "Survive?"

"Yes." She flicked a chip of rotten wood onto the lily pads and watched a water strider scuttle away from the ripples. "You were right to leave Shadows. Here there won't be so much pressure, and it'll be easier to work things out. And they *can* be worked out." She hesitated.

"But what?"

"Given the ledger, everything you're seeing, everything you can do, I'm convinced a solution is possible. In fact, I'm surprised one of the geniuses at Tulane hasn't stumbled on it. If you have the data at hand, it's hardly more than a matter of common sense and engineering. But equipment and materials will be expensive. And the only way I can see of getting the money is to find a bargaining position and force the project to fund us."

"A bargaining position." He stirred the water with his

cane. "What say we sell Edman a new diet plan? Harrison's Magnetotactic Slimming Program. Reorients your fat molecules to be south-seeking and sends them down to Latin America where they're really needed."

"It's Ezawa you'd have to sell."

"Even easier. One jolt of Papa Salvatino's Love Rub and he'd be putty in our hands."

Rainclouds passed up from the south. Big drops splatted on the lily pads, and the sun ducked in and out of cover. Donnell complained of leg cramps, and Jocundra supported his arm as they walked to the cabin. She stopped at the pump to wash off the grime of the boathouse, and as she bent to the gush of water, he rested his hand on her waist. She turned, thinking he had lost his balance. He put his other hand on her waist, holding her, not pulling her to him. His expression was stoic, prepared for rejection. The light pressure of his hands kindled a warmth in her abdomen, and it seemed to her she was building toward him the way the edges of a cloud build, boiling across the space between them. When he kissed her, she closed her eyes and opened her mouth to him as if it were the most natural thing in the world. Then she drew back, dizzy and a little afraid. A pine branch behind his head flared and was tipped with gold, the sun breaking through again.

Tentatively, he fingered the top button of her dress. "It's all right," she said, trying to gloss over his awkwardness. Still tentative, he began undoing the buttons. Static charges crackled wherever he touched the cloth, delicate stings. She wondered how the material could have accumulated such a charge, and then, recalling other occasions when he had touched her, other instances of static, she wondered if he might be their cause. It didn't bother her. All his strangeness was common to her now, a final accommodation had been reached. As if a pool of electricity were draining around her, the dress slid from her shoulders, popping and clinging to her skin as it fell away.

Twilight gathered in the back room. Jocundra lay with her face turned to the ceiling, her arm flung across Donnell's hip. The fur tickled, and as she shifted position, he absently

caressed her leg. Through narrowed eyes she watched the
gaps between the boards empurple, imagining the cabin
adrift in an unfeatured element of purple, a limbo where
time had decayed matter to this one color. The intensity of
her response to him perplexed her. She had not known how
much she had wanted him. The desire had been buried in
some anthracitic fold of herself, and she had seen but a
single facet of it, unaware that it would take only the miner's
pick of opportunity to expose a significant lode. Sex for her
had always involved a token abandonment, a minimal im-
mersion in the act, and she was beginning to realize that
she had been programmed to expect no more. Her mother's
attitude toward sex had been neatly summarized the day
before Jocundra's wedding; she had called Jocundra aside,
thinking her still a virgin, and presented her with a gift-
wrapped plastic sheet. "Sometimes," she had whispered,
peering around to be sure no one would overhear, baring a
horrible secret, "sometimes there's an awful mess."

A moonless dark embedded the cabin, the wind blew
warm and damp through the cracks, and as Donnell's hand
smoothed down the curve of her belly, the easy rise of her
passion made her feel fragile and temporary, a creature of
heat and blackness stirred from shapelessness by the wind
and left to fade. Her arms went around his back, her consciousness frayed. Some childish part of her, a part schooled
to caution by the dictates of a timorous mother, was unwilling to be swept away, fearful of committing to an uncertain future. But she banished it. Exulting in the loss of
control, she cried out when he entered her.

Mr. Brisbeau returned shortly before noon the next day,
earlier than planned and in a surly mood. He unloaded
provisions from a burlap sack, tossing canned goods into a
wooden storage chest, making an unnecessary racket, and
then, with bad grace, thrust two parcels into their hands.
Shirts and jeans for Donnell, blouses and jeans for Jocundra.
Their appreciation did not lighten his surliness. He stood
by the wood stove, squinting angrily at them, and finally
said, "That ol' man Bivalaqua he's nothin' but talk-talk,
tellin' me 'bout the holy show over in Salt Harvest."

Jocundra opened her mouth to say something, but Mr. Brisbeau cut her off. "Why you takin' my hospitality and don't offer to cure me lak that Grimeaux boy?"

"I didn't cure him," said Donnell, nettled by the accusatory tone of his voice. "Nobody could cure him."

A frown carved the lines deeper on the old man's face.

"Look." Donnell sat up from the cot, where he had been going over the ledger. "I'm not even sure what I did. Last night was the first time I've ever done anything like that."

"It can't hurt to try," said Jocundra, coming over to him. "Can it? We might learn something that'll help."

Mr. Brisbeau's magnetic field was distinguished by a misty patch about the size of a walnut behind his right temple, floating amid the fiery arcs like a cloud permanently in place. When Donnell mentioned it, Jocundra dug among the junk and located a pencil and suggested she take notes while he described the process. Each time one of the arcs materialized near the misty patch, it would bend away to avoid contact. On impulse, Donnell began inducing arcs to enter the patch, but they resisted his guidance and tore away from his grip. Rather than the gentle tugging he had expected, they exerted a powerful pull, and the harder he strained at them, the more inelastic they became. After perhaps a half hour of experiment, he tried to direct two of the arcs to enter the patch from opposite sides, and to his amazement they entered easily. The patch glowed a pale whitish-gold, and the arcs held steady and bright, flowing inward toward each other.

"Damn!" said Mr. Brisbeau, clapping his hand to his head. "Feel lak you plug me in or somethin'."

Within a few minutes the arcs began to fade, and this time Donnell introduced four pairs of them into the patch, setting it to glowing like a little gold spider. But for all his success at manipulating the field, Mr. Brisbeau's sight did not improve. He said, though, he felt better than he had in months, and whether due to the treatment or to his satisfaction with Donnell's effort, his mood did brighten. He withdrew a bottle of bourbon and a jar of cherry juice from the storage chest, mixed and added sugar to taste, humming and chuckling to himself. "Cherry flips," he said, handing them each a glass. It tasted awful, bad medicine and melted lollypops, but he downed half a dozen while Donnell and Jocundra nursed their drinks.

His eyes red-veined from the liquor, he launched into the tale of Bayou Vert, the legendary course of green water appearing now and again to those lost in the swamp, which—if they had the courage to follow—would lead them to the Swamp King's palace and an eternity of sexual delights among his beautiful, gray-haired daughters.

"Long gray hair lak the moss, skin white lak the lily," he said, kissing his fingertips. He scooted his crate next to Jocundra and put his arm around her waist. "But can't none of 'em shine lak Jo' here, can they?" His fingers strayed near her breast, and her smile froze. "One time," he went on, "fool me, I'm sick with the fever, and the hurricane she's shreddin' the swamp and I'm out at the traps. That's when I see Bayou Vert. Jus' a trickle runnin' through the flood. But I tink it's the fever, and I'm too scared to follow."

It had been drizzling, but now the sun broke through and slanted into the cabin, heating the air, shining off the veins of glue between the pictures on the walls, melting the images of dead presidents and centerfolds and famous buildings into an abstract of color and glare. Mr. Brisbeau took to staring at Jocundra, madly doting; his narrative grew disconnected, lapsing in midsentence, and his hand wandered onto her thigh. Donnell was on the verge of interrupting, hoping to spare her further molestation, when the old man jumped up and staggered toward the door, sending avalanches of fragments slithering down the junkpiles.

"Le Bon Dieu!" he shouted; he teetered on the top step and fell with a thump in the sand.

By the time they reached the door, he had climbed to his feet and was gazing off at the treeline. Tears slithered down the creases of his cheeks.

"Look there," he said. "Goddamn and son of a bitch! Look there!" He pointed. "I ain't seen that chinaberry for tree-four years. Oh, goddamn, jus' look at that!" He went a step forward, stumbled, and fell again, but crawled on all fours to the edge of the palmettos and pitched face downward beside a stubby, bluish-green shrub. "Indigo," he said wonderingly. "I tink she's gone from here."

"You can see?" Jocundra turned to Donnell, and mixed with the excitement, he thought he detected a new apprehension in her face. He looked down at his hands, shaken by the realization that he had done something material to Mr. Brisbeau.

"Firs' I tink it's the drinkin' and mem'ries givin' me sight of you, girl." The old man wiped his eyes. "But I mus' be seein', 'cause I lose my good-time feelin' when I fall." He pulled himself up and brushed the crust of mucky sand off his shirt; then, struck by a thought, he said, "Me, I'm goin' to bring ol' man Bivalaqua so you can touch his migraine."

"We can't have people coming here," said Jocundra. "We'll have the police..."

"The Cajun he's not goin' to give you away," said Mr. Brisbeau adamantly. "You know better'n that, girl. And besides, the boy he jus' wither up if he try to hide his gift." He walked over to the steps and stared up at Donnell; his eyes were still brimming. "I thank you, boy, but how'm I goin' to thank you for true?" Then he grinned. "Come on! We ask *Le Bon Dieu!* I'm takin' you to see Him." He started toward the boathouse, staggered, and fetched up against the cabin; he turned and went back to the bluish-green shrub. He plucked off a leaf.

"Goddamn," he said, holding it up to the sun so the veins showed. "Indigo."

Mr. Brisbeau poled the *pirogue* into a channel barely wider than the boat. Clouds of mosquitoes descended upon them, and thickly leaved bushes arched overhead, forming a buzzing green tunnel. The branches scratched their arms. They passed along the channel for what seemed to Donnell an inordinate length of time, and bent double to avoid the branches, breathing shallowly, he lost his sense of perspective. Up and down were no longer consistent with the colors of earth and sky. Whenever they passed beneath an opening in the brush, the water reflected a ragged oval of blue and the sun dazzled the droplets tipping the leaves; it was as if they were gliding through a mirrored abyss, one original likeness hidden among the myriad counterfeits. Fragments of dried wasp nest fell on his neck and stuck in the sweat; purplish-veined egg masses clung to holes in the bank, and the dark, web-spanned gaps between the roots of the bushes bristled with secretive movement. Just below the surface at the edge of the bank were fantastic turrets of slime tunneled by black beetles.

Then they were gliding out into a vaulted chamber canopied by live oaks, pillared by an occasional cypress. Here the water forked in every direction, diverging around islands from which the oaks arose, their branches bridging between the islands, laden with stalactites of Spanish moss, some longer than a man, trailing into the water. The sun's beams withdrew, leaving them in a phantom world of grays and gray-greens so ill-defined that the branches appeared to be black veins of solidity wending through a mist of half-materialized forms. An egret flapped up, shrinking to a point of white space. Its flight was too swift to be a spirit's, too slow for a shooting star's, yet had the quality of both. Mr. Brisbeau's pole sloshed, but otherwise there was a thick silence. The place seemed to have been grown from the silence, and the silence seemed the central attribute of the gray.

Mr. Brisbeau beached the *pirogue* upon the bank of an island where three small crosses had been erected; a muskrat skin was nailed to each one. He climbed out and knelt before them. Kneeling, he was a head taller than the crosses: a giant come to his private Calvary. The skins were mouldering, scabbed with larval deposits, but the sight of him praying to this diseased trinity did not strike Donnell as being in any way grotesque. The silence and the great arching limbs abolished the idea of imperfection, and the decomposing skins were in keeping with the grand decomposition of the swamp.

Now and then Mr. Brisbeau's voice carried to Donnell, and he realized it was more of a conversation than a prayer, a recounting of the day's events salted with personal reaction.

". . . You remember the time Roger Hebert smack me wit the oar, sparks shootin' through my head. Well, that's the way it was 'cept there wasn't no pain. . . ."

Sitting in the boat for so long had caused Donnell's hip to ache, and to take his mind off the discomfort he played tricks with his vision. He discovered that if he brought the magnetic fields into view and shifted his field of focus forward until it was dominated by the white brilliance of a single arc, then the world around him darkened and the *gros bon ange* became visible. He looked out beyond the prow and glimpsed a glowing tendril of green among the silvery eddies. He turned his head, blinking the sight away. He did not want to verify or acknowledge it. It dismayed him to think Jocundra might be right, that he might be able to see anything he wished. Anything as ridiculous as Bayou Vert. Still, he was curious.

"What's off there?" he asked, pointing out the direction of the green current to Jocundra.

"Marshlands," she said. "A couple of towns, and then, past that, Bayou Rigaud."

"Rigaud." The word had a sleek feel, an important sound.

He steadied the boat for Jocundra as she moved forward to sit beside him. "Why do you want to know?" she asked. But the old man's voice lifted from the shore and distracted his attention.

"If I was you, me," he said contentiously, talking to the centermost cross, "I'd end this boy's confusion. You let him see wit the eyes of angels, so what harm it goin' to do to let him know your plan?"

CHAPTER XII

May 30–July 26, 1987

One night after patients had begun to arrive in numbers, Donnell and Jocundra were lying on their bed in the back room surrounded by open textbooks and pieces of paper.

The bed, an antique with a mahogany headboard, and all the furniture—bureau, night table, chairs—had been the gifts of patients, as were the flowers which sprouted from vases on the windowsills. Sometimes, resting between sessions, Donnell would crack the door and listen to the patients talking in the front room, associating their voices with the different flowers. They never discussed their ailments, merely gossiped or exchanged recipes.

"Now how much lemon juice you addin' to the meal," Mrs. Dubray (irises) would ask; and old Mrs. Alidore (a bouquet of Queen Anne's lace and roses) would hem and haw and finally answer, "Seem lak my forget-list gets longer ever' week."

Their conversations, their gifts and their acceptance of him gave Donnell a comforting sense of being part of a tradition, for there had always been healers in the bayou country and the people were accustomed to minor miracles.

"I think I'm right," said Jocundra.

"About what?" Donnell added a flourish to the sketch he had been making. It was a rendering of one of the gold flashes of light he saw from time to time, similar to those Magnusson had drawn in the margins of his ledger; but this one was more complex, a resolution of several fragments he had seen previously into a single figure:

"About you being a better focusing agent for the fields than any device." Jocundra smacked him on the arm with her legal pad. "You aren't listening."

"Yeah I am," he said, preoccupied by the sketch. "Go ahead."

"I'll start over." She settled herself higher on the pillows. "Okay. If you transmit an electrical charge through a magnetic field, you're going to get feedback. The charge will experience a force in some direction, and that would explain the changes in light intensity you see. But you're not just affecting the fields. To cure someone as hopeless as Mr. Robichaux, you have to be affecting the cells, probably on an ionic level. You aren't listening! What are you doing?"

"Doodling." Dissatisfied, Donnell closed his notebook. It did not feel complete. He could not attach the least importance to the gold flashes, yet they kept appearing and it bothered him not to understand them. "I'm listening," he said.

"All right." Jocundra was miffed by his lack of enthusiasm for her explanation. "Now one basic difference between a cancer cell and a normal cell is that the cancer cell produces certain compounds in excess of normal. So, going by Magnusson's notes, one likelihood is that you're reducing the permeability of the nuclear membranes for certain ions, preventing the efflux of the compounds in question."

Donnell rested his head on the pillow beside her. "How's that relate to my being the focusing agent?"

"NMR." She smoothed down his hair. "Magnusson's stuff on it is pretty fragmentary, but he appears to be suggesting that your effect on the cameras was caused by your realigning the atomic magnetic nuclei of the camera's field and transmitting a force which altered the electrical capacitance of the film. I think you're doing more or less the same thing to the patients." She chewed on her pencil. "The fact that you can intuit the movements of the geomagnetic field, and that you're able to do the right things to the patients without any knowledge of the body, it seems to me if you had enough metal to generate a sufficiently powerful field, two or three tons, then you'd be able to orchestrate the movements of the bacteria with finer discretion than any mechanical device."

Donnell had an image of himself standing atop a mountain and hurling lightning bolts. "Just climb upon a chunk of iron and zap myself?"

"Copper," she said. "Better conductivity."

"It sounds like magic," he said. "What about the wind?"

"There's nothing magical about that," she said. "The air becomes ionized under the influence of your field, and the ions are induced to move in the direction imposed on the field. The air moves, more air moves in to replace it." She shrugged. "Wind. But understanding all this and being able to use it are two different things."

"You're saying I should go back to the project?"

"Unless you know how we can buy three tons of copper with a Visa card." She smiled, trying to make light of it.

Something was incomplete about her explanation, just as there had been about his sketch, and he did not believe either would come to completion at Shadows. "Maybe as a last resort," he said. "But not yet."

The majority of the patients were local people, working men and housewives and widows, as faded and worn as the battered sofas they sat upon (Mr. Brisbeau had tossed out the junk and scavenged them from somewhere); though as the weeks passed and word spread, more prosperous-looking people arrived from faraway places like Baton Rouge and Shreveport. Most of their complaints were minor, and there was little to be learned from treating them. But from the difficult cases, in particular that of Herve Robichaux, a middle-aged carpenter afflicted with terminal lung cancer, Jocundra put together her explanation of the healing process.

When medical bills had cost him his home, with the last of his strength Robichaux had built two shacks on a weed-choked piece of land near the Gulf left him by his father, one for his wife and him, the other for his five children. The first time Donnell and Jocundra visited him, driven by Mr. Brisbeau in his new pickup, the children—uniformly filthy and shoeless—ran away and hid among the weeds and whispered. Their whispers blended with the drone of flies and the shifting of wind through the surrounding scrub pine into a sound of peevish agitation. In the center of the weeds was a cleared circle of dirt, and here stood the shacks. The raw color of the unpainted boards, the listless collie mix curled by the steps, the scraps of cellophane blowing across the dirt, everything testified to an exacerbated hopelessness, and the interior of the main shack was the most desolate place of Donnell's experience. A battery-operated TV sat on an orange crate at the foot of the sick man's pallet, its pale picture of gray figures in ghostly rooms flickering soundlessly. Black veins of creosote beaded between the ceiling boards, their acrid odor amplifying rather than dominating the fecal stink of illness. Flies crusted a jelly glass half-full of a pink liquid, another fly buzzed loudly in a web spanning a corner of the window, and hexagrams of mouse turds captioned the floors. Stapled on the door was a poster showing the enormous, misty figure of Jesus gazing sadly down at the UN building.

"Herve," said Mrs. Robichaux in a voice like ashes. "That Mr. Harrison's here from Bayou Teche." She stepped aside to let them pass, a gaunt woman enveloped in a gaily flowered housecoat.

Mr. Robichaux was naked beneath the sheet, bald from chemotherapy. A plastic curtain overhung the window, and the wan light penetrating it pointed up his bleached and shrunken appearance. His mouth and nose were so fleshless they seemed stylized approximations of features, and his face communicated nothing of his personality to Donnell. He looked ageless, a proto-creature of grayish-white material around which the human form was meant to wrap.

"Believe," he whispered. His fingers crawled over Donnell's wrist, delicate as insects' legs. "I believe."

Donnell drew back his hand, both revolted and pitying. A chair scraped behind him: Jocundra settling herself to take notes.

The area of the magnetic field around Robichaux's chest was a chaos of white flashes; the remainder of the field had arranged itself into four thick, bright arcs bowing from his head to his feet. Donnell had never seen anything like it. To experiment he placed his hands over the chest. The attraction was so powerful it locked onto his hands, and the skin of his fingers—as well as the skin of Robichaux's chest—dimpled and bulged, pulled in every direction. He had to wrench his hands loose. They disengaged with a loud static pop, and a tremor passed through the sick man's body.

Donnell described the event to Jocundra, and she suggested he try it again, this time for a longer period. After several minutes he detected a change in the field. The pulls were turning into pushes; it was as if he had thrust his hands into a school of tiny electric fish and they were swimming between his fingers, nudging them. After several minutes more, he found that he could wiggle the top joints of his fingers, and he felt elements of the field cohere and flow in the direction of his wiggle. A half hour went by. The four bright arcs encaging Robichaux began to unravel, sending wispy white streamers inward, and the pyrotechnic display above his chest diminished to a barely perceptible vapor.

Sweat poured off Robichaux, his neck arched and his hands clawed the sheet. Whimpers escaped between his clenched teeth. A spray of broken capillaries appeared on his chest, a webbing of fine purplish lines melting up into view. He rocked his head back and forth, and the whimpers swelled to outright cries. At this, Donnell withdrew his hands and noticed the wind had kicked up outside; the room had grown chilly. Jocundra was shivering, and Mrs. Robichaux knelt by the door. "Holy Jesus please, Holy Jesus please," she babbled.

"What happened?" Jocundra's eyes were fixed upon the sick man, who lay gasping.

Donnell turned back to Robichaux; the field was reverting to its previous state. "I don't know," he said. "Let me try again."

The cure took three days and two nights. Donnell had to work the field an hour at a time to prevent its reversion; then he would break for an hour, trembling and spent. Her husband's torment frightened Mrs. Robichaux, and she fled to the second cabin and would not return. Occasionally the eldest boy—a hollow-cheeked eleven-year-old—poked his head in the window to check on his father, running off the instant Donnell paid him the slightest attention. Mr. Brisbeau brought them food and water, and waited in the pickup, drinking. Donnell could hear him singing along with the radio far into the night.

The first night was eerie.

They left the oil lamp unlit so Donnell could better see the field, and the darkness isolated them in a ritual circum-

stance: the healer performing his magical passes; the sick
man netted in white fire, feverish and groaning; Jocundra
cowled with a blanket against the cold, the sacred witness,
the scribe. Crickets sustained a frenzied sawing, the dog
whined. Debris rustled along the outside walls, driven by
the wind; it kicked up whenever Donnell was working,
swirling slowly about the shack as if a large animal were
patroling in tight circles, its coarse hide rubbing the boards.
Moonlight transformed the plastic curtain into a smeared,
glowing barrier behind which the shadows of the pines held
steady; the wind was localized about the cabin, growing
stronger with each treatment. Though he was too weak to
voice his complaints, Robichaux glared at them, and to
avoid his poisonous looks they took breaks on the steps of
the shack. The dog slunk away every time they came out,
and as if it were Robichaux's proxy, stared at them from
the weeds, chips of moonlight reflected in its eyes.

During their last break before dawn, Jocundra sheltered
under Donnell's arm and said happily, "It's going to work."

"You mean the cure?"

"Not just that," she said. "Everything. I've got a feeling."
And then, worriedly, she asked, "Don't you think so?"

"Yeah," he said, wanting to keep her spirits high. But
as he said it, he had a burst of conviction, and wondered
if like Robichaux's belief, his own belief could make it so.

The second day. Muggy heat in the morning, the slow
wind lifting garbage from the weeds. Weary and aching,
Donnell was on the verge of collapse. Like the rectangle of
yellow light lengthening across the floor, a film was sliding
across his own rough-grained, foul-smelling surface. But to
his amazement he felt stronger as the day wore on, and he
realized he had been moving around without his cane. During the treatments the sick man's body arched until only his
heels and the back of his head were touching the pallet.
Two of the man's teeth shattered in the midst of one con-
vulsion, and they spent most of a rest period picking fragments out of his mouth. The fly in the web had died and
was a motionless black speck suspended in midair, a bullet-
hole shot through the sun-drenched backdrop of pines. The

spider, too, had died and was shriveled on the windowsill. In fact, all the insects in the cabin—palmetto bugs, flying ants, gnats, beetles—had gone belly up and were not even twitching. Around noon the eldest boy knocked and asked could he borrow the TV "so's the babies won't cry." He would not enter the cabin, said that his mama wouldn't let him, and stood mute and sullen watching the heaving of his father's chest.

On the second night, having asked Mr. Brisbeau to keep watch, they walked down to the Gulf, found a spit of solid ground extending from the salt grass, and spread a blanket. Now and again as they made love, Jocundra's eyes blinked open and fastened on Donnell, capturing an image of him to steer by; when she closed them, slits of white remained visible beneath the lids. Passion seemed to have carved her face more finely, planed it down to its ideal form. Lying there afterward, Donnell wondered how his face looked to her, how it displayed passion. Everything about the bond between them intrigued him, but he had long since given up trying to understand it. Love was a shadow that vanished whenever you turned to catch a glimpse of it. The only thing certain was that without it life would be as bereft of flesh as Robichaux's face had been of life: an empty power.

Jocundra rolled onto her stomach and gazed out to sea. An oil fire gleamed red off along the coast; the faint chugging of machinery carried across the water. Wavelets slapped the shore. Sea and sky were the same unshining black, and the moonlit crests of the waves looked as distant as the burning well and the stars, sharing with them a perspective of great depth, as if the spit of land were extending into interstellar space. Donnell ran his hand down her back and gently pushed a finger between her legs, sheathing it in the moist fold. She kissed the knuckles of his other hand, pressed her cheek to it, and snuggled closer. The movement caused his finger to slip partway inside her, and she drew in a sharp breath. She lifted her face to be kissed, and kissing her, he pulled her atop him. Her hair swung witchily in silhouette against the sky, a glint of the oil fire bloomed on her throat, and it seemed to him that the stars winking behind her were chattering with crickets' tongues.

* * *

On the afternoon of the third day, Donnell decided he had done all he should to Mr. Robichaux. Though his field was not yet normal, it appeared to be repairing itself. His entire chest was laced with broken capillaries, but his color had improved and his breathing was deep and regular. Over the next two weeks they visited daily, and he continued to mend. The general aspect of the shacks and their environ improved equally, as if they had suffered the same illness and received the same cure. The dog wagged its tail and snuffled Donnell's hand. The children played happily in the yard; the litter had been cleared away and the weeds cut back. Even Mrs. Robichaux gave a friendly wave as she hung out the wash.

The last time they visited, while sitting on the steps and waiting for Mr. Robichaux to dress, the youngest girl—a grimy-faced toddler, her diaper at half-mast—waddled up to Donnell and offered him a bite of her jelly donut. It was stale, the jelly tasteless, but as he chewed it, Donnell felt content. The eldest boy stepped forward, the other children at his rear, giggling, and formally shook Donnell's hand. "Wanna thank you," he muttered; he cast a defiant look at his brothers and sisters, as if something had been proved. The toddler leaned on Donnell's knee and plucked off his sunglasses. "Ap," she said, pointing at his eyes, chortling. "Ap azoo."

Robichaux was buttoning his shirt when Donnell entered. He frowned and looked away and once again thanked him. But this time his thanks were less fervent and had a contractual ring. "If I'm down to my last dollar," he said sternly, "that dollar she's yours."

Donnell shrugged; he squinted at Robichaux's field. "Have you seen a doctor?"

"Don't need no doctor to tell me I'm cured," said Robichaux. He peered down inside his shirt. The web of broken capillaries rose to the base of his neck. "Don't know why you had to do this mess. Worse than a goddamn tattoo."

"Trial and error," said Donnell without sympathy. It had come as a shock to him that he did not like Mr. Robichaux; that—by gaining ten pounds and a measure of vigor—the characterless thing he had first treated had evolved into a contemptible human being, one capable of viciousness. He suspected the children might have been better off had their father's disease been allowed to run its course.

"It ain't that I ain't grateful, you understand," Robichaux said, fawning, somewhat afraid. "It's just I don't know if all this here's right, you know. I mean you ain't no man of God."

Donnell wondered about that; he was, after all, full of holy purpose. For a while he had thought healing might satisfy his sense of duty unfulfilled, but he had only been distracted by the healing from a deeper preoccupation. He felt distaste for this cringing, devious creature he had saved.

"No, I'm not," he said venomously. "But neither are you, Mr. Robichaux. And that little devil's web on your chest might just be an omen of worse to come."

* * *

"... Since the great looping branches never grew or varied, since the pale purple sun never fully rose or set, the shadow of Moselantja was a proven quantity upon the grassy plain below. Men and beasts lived in the shadow, as well as things which otherwise might not have lived at all, their dull energies supplied, some said, by the same lightless vibrations that had produced this enormous growth, sundered the mountain and sent it bursting forth. From the high turrets one could see the torchlit caravans moving inward along the dark avenues of its shadow toward the main stem, coming to enlist, or to try their luck at enlistment, for of the hundreds arriving each day, less than a handful would survive the rigors of induction...."

"What do you think?" asked Donnell.

Jocundra did not care for it, but saw no reason to tell him. "It's strange," she said, giving a dramatic shudder and grinning. She emptied the vase water out the window, then skipped back across the room and burrowed under the covers with him. Her skin was goose-pimpled. It had been warm and dead-still the night before, but the air had cooled and dark, silver-edged clouds were piling up. Sure signs of a gale. A damp wind rattled the shutters.

"It's just background," said Donnell petulantly. "It has to be strange because the story's very simple. Boy meets

girl, they do what comes naturally, boy joins army, loses
girl. Years later he finds her. She's been in the army, too.
Then they develop a powerful but rather cold relationship,
like a hawk and a tiger."

"Read some more," she said, pleased that he was writing
a love story, even if such an odd one.

"War is the obsession of Moselantja, its sole concern,
its commerce, its religion, its delight. War is generally
held to be the purest natural expression of the soul, an
ecological tool designed to cultivate the species, and the
cadres of the Yoalo, who inhabit the turrets of Moselantja, are considered its prize bloom. Even among those
they savage, they are revered, partially because they are
no less hard on themselves than on those they subjugate.
As their recruits progress upward toward the turrets, the
tests and lessons become more difficult. Combat, am-
bush, the mastery of the black suits of synchronous energy. Failure, no matter how slight, is not tolerated and
has but one punishment. Each day's crop of failures is
taken to the high turret of Ghazes from which long nooses
and ropes are suspended. The nooses are designed not
to choke or snap, but to support the neck and spine. The
young men and women are stripped naked and fitted with
the nooses and lowered into the void. Their arms and
legs are left unbound. And then, from the clotted darkness of the main stem, comes a gabbling, flapping sound,
and the beasts rise up. Their bodies are reminiscent of
a fly's but have the bulk of an eagle's, and indeed their
flights recall a fly's haphazard orbiting of a garbage heap.
Their wings are leathery, long-vaned; their faces var-
iously resemble painted masks, dessicated apes, frogs,
spiders, every sort of vile monstrosity. Their mouths are
all alike, set with needle teeth and fringed with delicate
organelles like the tendrils of a jellyfish. As with any
great evil, study of them will yield a mass of contradic-
tory fact and legend. The folk of the plain and forest
will tell you that they are the final transformation of the
Yoalo slain in battle, and this is their Valhalla: to inhabit
the roots and crevices of Moselantja and feed upon the
unfit. Of course since the higher ranks of the Yoalo model
their energy masks upon the faces of the beasts, this is
no doubt a misapprehension.

"There are watchers upon the battlements of Ghazes, old men and women who stare at the failed recruits through spyglasses. As the beasts clutch and rend their prey, these watchers note every twitch and flinch of the dying, and if their reactions prove too undisciplined, black marks are assigned to the cadres from which they had been expelled. Many of the recruits are native-born to Moselantja, and these are watched with special interest. Should any of them cry out or attempt to defend themselves or use meditative techniques to avoid pain, then his or her parents are asked to appear the next day at Ghazes for similar testing. And should *they* betray the disciplines, then their relatives and battle-friends are sought out and tested until the area of contagion is obliterated. Occasionally a seam of such weakness will be exposed, one which runs throughout the turrets, and entire cadres will be overthrown. Such is the process of revolution in Moselantja. . . ."

As he read, Jocundra tried to force her mind away from the unpleasant details, but she could not help picturing the hanged bodies in stark relief against the purple sun, rivulets of blood streaming from their necks as the beasts idly fed, embracing their victims with sticky insect legs. When he had finished, she was unable to hide her displeasure.

"You don't like it," he said.

She made a noncommittal noise.

"Well," he said, blowing on his fingers as if preparing to crack a safe. "I know what you *do* like."

She laughed as he reached for her.

A knock on the door, and Mr. Brisbeau stuck in his head. "Company," he said. He was hung over, red-eyed from last night's bottle; he scowled, noticing their involvement, and banged the door shut.

Hard slants of rain started drumming against the roof as they dressed. In the front room a broad-beamed man was gazing out the window. Dark green palmetto fronds lashed up behind him, blurred by the downpour. He turned, and Jocundra gasped. It was Papa Salvatino, a smile of Christian fellowship wreathing his features. He wore a white suit of raw silk with cutaway pockets, and the outfit looked as appropriate on him as a lace collar on a mongrel.

"Brother Harrison!" he said with sanctimonious delight and held out his hand. "When I heard you was the wonder-worker down on Bayou Teche, I had to come and offer my apologies."

"Cut the crap," said Donnell. "You've got a message for me."

It took a few seconds for Papa to regain his poise, a time during which his face twisted into a mean, jaundiced knot. "Yes," he said. "'Deed I do." He assessed Donnell coolly. "My employer, Miss Otille Rigaud . . . maybe you heard of her?"

Mr. Brisbeau spat. Jocundra remembered stories from her childhood about someone named Rigaud, but not Otille. Claudine, Claudette. Something like that.

"She's a wealthy woman, is Miss Otille," Papa went on. "A creature of diverse passions, and her rulin' passion at present is the occult. She's mighty intrigued with you, brother."

"How wealthy?" asked Donnell, pouring a cup of coffee.

"Rich or not, them Rigauds they's lower than worms in a pile of shit," said Mr. Brisbeau, enraged. "And me I ain't havin' their help in my kitchen!"

Papa Salvatino beamed, chided him with a waggle of a finger. "Now, brother, you been cockin' your ear to the Devil's back fence and listenin' to his lies."

"Get out!" said Mr. Brisbeau; he picked up a stove lid and menaced Papa with it.

"In good time," said Papa calmly. "Miss Otille would like the pleasure of your company, Brother Harrison, and that of your fair lady. I've been authorized to convey you to Maravillosa at once if it suits. That's her country place over on Bayou Rigaud."

"I don't think so," said Donnell; he sipped his coffee. "But you tell her I'm intrigued as well."

"She'll be tickled to hear it." He half-turned to leave. "You know, I might be able to satisfy your curiosity some-what. Me and Miss Otille have spent many an evenin' to-gether, and I've been privy to a good bit of the family history."

"Don't bullshit me," said Donnell. "You're supposed to tell me all about her. That's part of the message."

Papa perched on the arm of a sofa and stared at Donnell. "As a fellow professional, brother, you mind tellin' me what you see that's givin' me away?"

"Your soul," said Donnell; he stepped to the window and tossed his coffee into the rain. At this point his voice went through a peculiar change, becoming hollow and smooth for half a sentence, reverting to normal, hollowing again; it was not an extreme change, just a slight increase in resonance, the voice of a man talking in an empty room, and it might not have been noticeable in a roomful of voices. "Want to know what it looks like? It's shiny black, and where there used to be a face, a face half spider and half toad, there's a mass of curdled light, only now it's flowing into helical patterns and rushing down your arms."

Papa was shaken; he, too, had heard the change. "Brother," he said, "you wastin' yourself in the bayou country. Take the advice of a man who's been in the business fifteen years. Put your show on the road. You got big talent!" He shook his head in awe. "Well"—he crossed his legs, leaned back and sighed—"I reckon the best way to fill you in on Otille is to start with ol' Valcours Rigaud. He was one of Lafitte's lieutenants, retired about the age of forty from the sea because of a saber cut to his leg, and got himself a fine house outside New Orleans. Privateerin' had made him rich, and since he had time on his hands and a taste for the darker side of earthly pleasures, it wasn't too surprisin' that he fell under the influence of one Lucanor Aime, the leader of the Nanigo sect. You ever hear 'bout Nanigo?"

Mr. Brisbeau threw down the stove lid with a clang, muttered something, and stumped into the back room, slamming the door after him. Papa snorted with amusement.

"Voodoo," he said. "But not for black folks. For whites only. Valcours was a natural, bein' as how he purely hated the black man. Wouldn't have 'em on his ships. Anyway, ol' Lucanor set Valcours high in his service, taught him all the secrets, then next thing you know Lucanor ups and disappears, and Valcours, who's richer than ever by this time, picks up and moves to Bayou Rigaud and builds Maravillosa." Papa chuckled. "You was askin' how rich Miss Otille was. Well, she's ten-twenty times as rich as Valcours, and to show you how well off he was, when his oldest girl got herself engaged, he went and ordered a cargo of spiders from China, special spiders renowned for the intricacy and elegance of their webs, and he set them to weavin' in the pines linin' the avenue to the main house. Then he had his servants sprinkle the webs with silver dust and gold dust, all so that daughter of his could walk down the aisle beneath a canopy of unrivaled splendor."

The wind was blowing more fiercely; rain eeled between the planking and filmed over the pictures and the walls, making them glisten. Jocundra closed and latched the shutters, half-listening to Papa, but listening also for repetitions of the change in Donnell's voice. He didn't appear to notice it himself, though it happened frequently, lasting a few seconds, then lapsing, as if he were passing through a strange adolescence. Probably, she thought, it was just a matter of the bacteria having spread to the speech centers; as they occupied the various centers, they operated the functions with more efficiency than normal. Witness his eyes. Still, she found it disturbing. She remembered sneaking into Magnusson's room and being frightened by his sepulchral tone, and she was beginning to be frightened now. By his voice, the storm, and especially by the story. Fabulous balls and masques had been weekly occurrences at Maravillosa, said Papa; but despite his largesse, Valcours had gained an evil reputation. Tales were borne of sexual perversion and unholy rites; people vanished and were never seen again; zombies were reputed to work his fields, and after his death his body was hacked apart and buried in seven coffins to prevent his return. The story and the storm came to be of a piece in Jocundra's head, the words howling, the wind drawling, nature and legend joined in the telling, and she had a feeling the walls of the cabin were being squeezed together and they would be crushed, their faces added to the collection of pasted-up images.

"Valcours' children spent most of their lives tryin' to repair the family name," said Papa. "They founded orphanages, established charities. Maravillosa became a factory of good works. But ol' Valcours' spirit seemed to have been reborn in his granddaughter Clothilde. Folks told the same stories 'bout her they had 'bout him. And more. Under her stewardship the family fortune grew into an empire, and them-that-knowed said this new money come from gun-runnin', from white slavery and worse. She was rumored to own opium hells in New Orleans and to hang around the waterfront disguised as a man, a cutthroat by the name of Johnny Perla. It's a matter of record that she was partners with Abraham Levine. You know. The Parrot King. The ol' boy who brought in all them Central American birds and set off the epidemic of parrot fever. Thousands of kids dead. But then, right in the prime of life, at the height of her evil doin's, Clothilde disappeared."

Papa heaved another sigh, recrossed his legs, and went on to tell how Clothilde's son, Otille's father, had followed the example of his grandparents and attempted to restore the family honor through his work on behalf of international Jewry during World War II and his establishment of the Rigaud Foundation for scientific research; how Otille's childhood had been scandal after scandal capped by the affair of Senator Millman, a weekend guest at Maravillosa, who had been found in bed with Otille, then twelve years old. Donnell leaned against the stove, unreadable behind his mirrored lenses. The storm was lessening, but Jocundra knew it would be a temporary lull. July storms lingered for days. The damp air chilled her, breaking a film of feverish sweat from her brow.

"The next few years Otille was off at private schools and college, and she don't talk much 'bout them days. But around the time she was twenty, twenty-one, she got bitten by the actin' bug and headed for New York. Wasn't long before she landed what was held to be the choicest role in many a season. Mirielle in the play *Danse Calinda*. 'Course there was talk 'bout *how* she landed the part, seein' as she'd been the playwright's lover. But couldn't nobody else but her play it, 'cause it had been written special for her. The critics were unanimous. They said the play expanded the occult genre, said she incarnated the role. Them damn fools woulda said anything, I expect. Otille probably had 'em all thinkin' slow and nasty 'bout her. She'll do that to a man, I'll guarantee you." He smirked. "But the character, Mirielle, she was a strong, talented woman, good-hearted but doomed to do evil, bound by the ties of a black tradition to a few acres of the dismal truth, and ol' Otille didn't have no trouble relatin' to that. Then, just when it looked like she was gonna be a star, she went after her leadin' man with a piece of broken mirror. Cut him up severe!" Papa snapped his fingers. "She'd gone right over the edge. They shut her away in a sanitarium someplace in upstate New York, and the doctors said it was the strenuousness of the role that had done her. But Otille would tell you it was 'cause she'd arrived at certain conclusions 'bout herself durin' the run of the play, that she'd been tryin' to escape somethin' inescapable. That the shadowy essence of Valcours and Clothilde pervaded her soul. Soon as they let her loose, she beelined for Maravillosa and there she's been for these last twelve or thirteen years." He puffed out his belly, patted it and grinned. "And I been with her for six of them years."

"And is she crazy?" asked Donnell. "Or is she evil?"

"She's a little crazy, brother, but ain't we all." Papa laughed. "I know I am. And as for the evil, naw, she's just foolin' with evil. The way she figures it, whichever she is she can't deny her predilection, so she surrounds herself with oddballs and criminal types. Nothin' heavy duty. Pickpockets, card sharps, dopers, hookers . . ."

"Tent show hucksters," offered Donnell.

"Yeah," said Papa, unruffled. "And freaks. You gonna fit right in." He worried at something between his teeth. "I'll be up front with you, brother. Goin' to Otille's is like joinin' the circus. Three shows daily. Not everybody can deal with it. But gettin' back to her theory, she figures if she insulates herself with this mess of lowlife, she'll muffle her unnatural appetites and won't never do nothin' *real* bad like Valcours and Clothilde." He fingered a card out from his side pocket and handed it to Donnell. "You wanna learn more 'bout it, call that bottom number. She's dyin' to talk with you." He stood, hitched up his trousers. "One more thing and I'll be steppin'. You're bein' watched. Otille's says they on you like white on rice."

Donnell did not react to the news; he was staring at the

card Papa had given him. But Jocundra was stunned. "By who?" she asked.

"Government, most likely," said Papa. "Otille says you wanna check it out, you know that little shanty bar down the road?"

"The Buccaneer Club?"

"Yeah. You go down there tomorrow. 'Bout half a mile past it's a dirt road, and just off the gravel you gonna find a stake out. Two men in a nice shiny unmarked car. They ain't there today, which is why I'm here." Papa twirled his car keys and gave them his most unctuous smile. "Let us hear from you, now." He sprinted out into the rain.

Jocundra turned to Donnell. "Was he telling the truth?"

He was puzzled by the question for a moment, then said, "Oh, yeah. At least he wasn't lying." He looked down at the card. "Wait a second." He went into the back room and returned with a notebook; he laid it open on top of the stove. "This," he said, pointing to a drawing, "is the last sketch I made of the patterns of light I've been seeing. And this"— he pointed to a design at the bottom of the card—"this is what my sketch is a fragment of."

Jocundra recognized the design, and if he had only showed her the fragmentary sketch, she still would have recognized it. She had seen it painted in chicken blood on stucco walls, laid out in colored dust on packed-earth floors, soaped on the windows of storefront temples, printed on handbills. The sight of it made all her explanations of his abilities seem as feckless as charms against evil.

"That's what I want to build with the copper," said Donnell. "I'm sure of it. I've never been . . ." He noticed her fixation on the design. "You've seen it before?"

"It's a *veve,*" said Jocundra with a sinking feeling. "It's a ritual design used in voodoo to designate one of the gods, to act as a gateway through which he can be called. This one belongs to one of the aspects of Ogoun, but I can't remember which one."

"A *veve?*" He picked up the card. "Oh, yeah," he said. "Why not?" He tucked the card into his shirt pocket.

"What are you going to do?"

"I'm going to wait until morning, because I don't want to appear too eager." He laughed. "And then I guess I'll go down to the Buccaneer Inn and give Otille a call."

Donnell dropped in his money and dialed. A flatbed truck passed on the road, showering the booth with spray from its tires, but even when it had cleared he could barely make out the pickup parked in front of the bar. The rain dissolved the pirate's face above the shingle roof into an eyepatch and a crafty smile, smeared the neon letters of the Lone Star Beer sign into a weepy glow.

"Yes, who is it?" The voice on the line was snippish and unaccented, but as soon as he identified himself, it softened and acquired a faint Southern flavor. "I'm pleasantly surprised, Mr. Harrison. I'd no idea you'd be calling so quickly. How can I help you?"

"I'm not sure you can," he said. "I'm just calling to make a few inquiries."

Otille's laugh was sarcastic; even over the wire it conveyed a potent nastiness. "You obviously have pressing problems, or else you wouldn't be calling. Why don't you tell me about them? Then if I'm still interested you can make your inquiries."

Donnell rubbed the phone against his cheek, thinking how best to handle her. Through the rain-washed plastic, he saw an old hound dog with brown and white markings emerge from the bushes beside the booth and step onto the road. Sore-covered, starved-thin, dull-eyed. It put its nose down and began walking toward the bar, sniffing at litter, unmindful of the pelting rain.

"I need three tons of copper," he said. "I want to build something."

"If you're going to be circuitous, Mr. Harrison, we can end this conversation right now."

"I want to build a replica of the *veve* on your calling card."

"Why?" she asked after a pause.

At first, prodded by her questions, he told half-truths, repeating the lies he had been told at the project, sketching out his plan to use the *veve* as a remedy, omitting particulars. But as the conversation progressed, he found he had surprisingly few qualms about revealing himself to her and became more candid. Though some of her questions maintained a sharp tone, others were asked with childlike curiosity, and others yet were phrased almost seductively, teasing out the information. These variances in her character reminded him of his own fluctuations between arrogance and anxiety, and he thought because of this he might be able to understand and exploit her weaknesses.

"I'm still not quite clear why you want to build this precise *veve*," she said.

"It's an intuition on my part," he said. "Jocundra thinks it may be an analogue to some feature of my brain, but all I can say is that I'll know after it's built. Why do you have it on your card?"

"Tradition," she said. "Do you know what a *veve* is, what its function in voodoo is?"

"Yes, generally."

"I'm quite impressed with what I've heard about you," she said. "If anyone else had called me and suggested I build the *veve* of Ogoun Badagris out of three tons of copper, I would have hung up. But before I commit . . . excuse me."

The hound dog had wandered into the parking lot of the bar and stood gazing mournfully at Mr. Brisbeau's tailgate;

it snooted at something under the rear tire and walked around to the other side. Donnell heard Otille speaking angrily to someone, and she was still angry when she addressed him once again.

"Come to Maravillosa, Mr. Harrison. We'll talk. I'll decide then whether or not to be your sponsor. But you had better come soon. The people who're watching you won't allow your freedom much longer."

"How do you know?"

"I'm very well connected," she said tartly.

"What guarantee do I have they won't be watching me there?"

"Maravillosa is my private preserve. No one enters without my permission." Otille made an impatient noise. "If you decide to come, just call this number and talk to Papa. He'll be picking you up. Have that old fool you're staying with take you through the swamp to Caitlett's Store."

"I'll think about it," said Donnell. Gray rain driven by a gust of wind opaqued the booth; the lights of the bar looked faraway, the lights of a fogbound coast.

"Not for too long," said Otille; her voice shifted gears and became husky, enticing. "May I call you Donnell?"

"Let's keep things businesslike between us," he said, irked by her heavy-handedness.

"Oh, Donnell," she said, laughing. "The question was just a formality. I'll call you anything I like."

She hung up.

Someone had drawn a cross in blue ink above the phone, and someone else, a more skillful artist, had added a woman sitting naked atop the vertical piece, wavy lines to indicate that she was moving up and down, and the words "Thank you, Jesus" in a word balloon popping from her lips. As he thought what to do next, he inspected all the graffiti, using them as a background to thought; their uniform obscenity seemed to be seconding an inescapable conclusion. He walked back to the truck, cold rain matting his hair.

After Donnell described the conversation, proposing they see what Maravillosa had to offer, Mr. Brisbeau grunted in dismay. "Me, I'd sooner trust a hawk wit my pet mouse," he said, digging for the car keys in his pocket.

"She sounds awful," said Jocundra. "Shadows can't be any worse. At least we're familiar with the pitfalls."

"She's direct," said Donnell. "You have to give her that. I never knew what was going on at Shadows."

Jocundra picked at an imperfection of bubbled plastic on the dash.

"Besides," said Donnell, "I'm convinced there's more to learn about the *veve,* and Maravillosa's the place to learn it."

Rain drummed on the roof, the windows fogged, and the three of them sat without speaking.

"What's today?" asked Donnell.

"Thursday," said Mr. Brisbeau; "Friday," said Jocundra at the same time. "Friday," she repeated. Mr. Brisbeau shrugged.

Donnell tapped the dash with his fingers. "Is there a back road out of here, one the truck can handle?"

"There's a track down by the saw mill," said Mr. Brisbeau. "She's goin' to be damn wet, but we can do it. Maybe."

"If Edman still spends his weekends at home," said Donnell, "we'll give him a chance to make a counterproposal. We'll leave now. That way we'll catch whoever's watching by surprise, and they won't expect me to show up at Edman's."

"What if he's not home?" Jocundra looked appalled by the prospect, and he realized she had been counting on him to reject Otille's offer.

"Then I'll call Papa, and we'll head for Caitlett's Store. Truthfully, I can't think of anything Edman could say to make me re-enter the project, but I'm willing to be proved wrong."

She nodded, downcast. "Maybe we should just call Papa. It might be a risk at Edman's."

"It's all a risk," he said, as Mr. Brisbeau switched on the engine. "But this way we'll know we did what we had to."

As Mr. Brisbeau backed up, the right front tire jolted over something, then bumped down, and Donnell heard a squeal from beneath. He swung the door open and climbed down and saw the old hound dog. The truck had passed over its neck and shoulders, killing it instantly. It must have given up looking for food and bellied under the wheel for shelter and the warmth of the motor. One of its eyes had been popped halfway out of the socket, exposing the thready structures behind, and the rain laid a glistening film upon the brown iris, spattering, leaking back inside the skull. Bright blood gushed from its mouth, paling to pink and wending off in rivulets across the puddled ground.

Mr. Brisbeau came around the front of the truck, furious. "Goddamn, boy! Don't that tell you somethin'?" he shouted, as if it had been Donnell's fault he had struck the dog. "You keep up wit this Rigaud foolishness, and you goin' against a clear sign!"

But if it was a sign, then what interpretation should be placed upon it? Pink-muzzled, legs splayed, mouth frozen open in a rictus snarl; the grotesque stamp of death had transformed this dull, garbage-eating animal into something far more memorable than it had been in life. Donnell would not have thought such a miserable creature could contain so brilliant a color.

CHAPTER XIII

from *Conjure Men: My Work With Ezawa at Tulane* by Anthony Edman, M.D., Ph.D.

. . . Though Ezawa's funding was private, he had been required by regulation to notify the government of his work with recombinant DNA. Government involvement in the project was minimal, however, until the death of Jack Richmond. The morning after his death—I had not yet learned of it—Douglas Stellings, our liaison with the CIA, visited me without appointment. I was not happy to see him. We had managed to keep news of the escape from the other patients, but Staff was in shock and the general reaction was one of utter despondency, of resignation to failure. Not even Dr. Brauer could bestir himself to muster a sally against me. We had all been expecting a breakthrough, but with the exit of Magnusson, Richmond and Harrison our little stage had been robbed of its leading players, and we of our central focus. And so, when Stellings appeared, I greeted him as the bereaved might greet a member of the wake, with gloomy disinterest, and when he notified me of the deaths, I could only stare at him.

Stellings, a thin, fit man given to punctuating his phrases with sniffs, was wholly contemptuous of me, of Staff, in fact of anyone with less than CIA status. "We've told the locals to back off," he said. Sniff. "The Bureau's taking care of it...under our supervision, thank God!" As he glanced at the display of aboriginal crania behind my head, a tic of a smile disordered his features, which were, to my mind, pathologically inexpressive. "Get your people up here," he commanded. "I want to see videos of Harrison."

Until late in the evening we reviewed Harrison's last four days of tape. After a few initial questions, Stellings withheld comment; then, around midnight, he asked that three particular segments be rerun. The first showed Harrison sitting at his desk; he leaned forward, resting his head in his left hand, propped his right elbow on the desktop and wiggled his fingers. He gave the impression of being deep in thought. Shortly thereafter the image broke up and the screen went blank. The second section was similar, except that Harrison was limping along the downstairs hall, and the third, recorded the night of the escape, was identical to the first.

"Cameras are always screwing up," muttered someone.

Stellings ran the tape back to the beginning of the third segment, then ran it forward again. "He's peeking at the camera," he said. "He's looking up and sideways so you won't notice, masking his eyes behind his fingers. And then he waggles his fingers, we count to ten"—he counted—"and the camera malfunctions. Got it?"

"Just like Magnusson," breathed Dr. Leavitt in tones of awe, tones which sounded false to my ear.

"What about Magnusson?" snapped Stellings.

"He exhibited similar finger-eye behavior prior to video malfunctions," said Leavitt—earnest, deeply respectful Leavitt. "I mentioned it to Dr. Brauer, but he didn't assign it much importance."

"You people ought to be in short pants," said Stellings with disgust.

"Why wasn't I apprised of this?" I asked of Brauer. I was, I admit, delighted to see him squirm, though I realized that the downfall of a Brauer only permits the rise of a Leavitt; and Leavitt, our learning expert, whose primary contribution had thus far been a study of the patients' acquisition of autobiographical detail from their exposure to television, was if anything more of an opportunist than Brauer. Of course I had not noticed Harrison's behavior myself, but there sat Brauer, narrow-eyed, licking his lips, the image of a crook set up to take the rap.

Stellings dismissed everyone excepting myself and called his superiors. He recommended that all measures be taken to remove the FBI from the case, thus beginning the jurisdictional dispute which, in effect, allowed Harrison and Verret to find refuge at the home of Clarence Brisbeau. At the moment Harrison stood upon the stage of the revival in Salt Harvest, not one agent or officer was searching for him. All the hounds had been frozen at point, waiting until their masters could untangle their leashes, and by the time the CIA had won dominance and Harrison had been located, the decision had been made to permit his continued freedom. The idea was, as Stellings put it, to "let him roll and see if he comes up sevens." Harrison would certainly prove uncooperative if captured; therefore it would be more profitable to monitor him. Brisbeau's cabin was not an optimal security situation, but its isolation was a positive factor, and neither Stellings nor his superiors expected Harrison to run. Besides, there would be other slow-burners; the more Harrison inadvertently revealed, the more effectively we would be able to control them. When it was learned that Harrison was practicing a form of faith healing, the CIA, in a master stroke of bureaucratic efficiency, sent him patients from their hospital, all of whom experienced miracle cures; and it was then—awakened by this luridly mystical image of sick spies being made whole by the ministrations of a "zombie" healer—that I came out of the fog which had lowered about me since the escape and began to be afraid.

The surveillance devices planted within Brisbeau's cabin malfunctioned most of the time, but on days when no patients visited and Harrison's electrical activity was at a minimum, we were sometimes able to pick up distorted transmissions; and from them, as well as from our extant knowledge and agents' reports, we pieced together the science underlying Harrison's abilities. Stellings evinced little surprise upon learning of the cures or any other of the marvels; his reactions consisted merely of further schemes and recommendations. Yet I was shaken. Harrison had been alive five months, and he was already capable of miracles. And listening to one particular exchange between him and Verret, we caught a hint of some new evolution of ability.

VERRET: What is it?
HARRISON: Nothing. Just the *gros bon ange*. I'm getting better at controlling it *(laughter)* or vice versa.
VERRET: What do I look like?
HARRISON: You've got a beautiful soul. *(Verret laughs)*. What I was reacting to was that all the bits of fire were swarming about in the black, coalescing at random, and then, whoosh! they all converged to form into your mask. It wasn't the same as usual, though the features were the same. Are the same. But the colors are different. Less blue, more gold and ruby.
VERRET: I wonder. . . .
HARRISON: What?
VERRET: A second ago I was thinking about you . . . very romantically.
HARRISON: Yeah? *(A rustling sound.)*
VERRET: *(laughing)* Do I feel different? *(A silence.)* What's wrong?
HARRISON: Just trying to shift back. It's hard to do sometimes.
VERRET: Why don't you not bother? I don't mind.
HARRISON: *(His voice becoming briefly very resonant, as if the transmission were stabilizing.)* It'd be like

two charred corpses making love. *(A long silence.)*
There. Are you okay?

VERRET: *(shakily)* Yes.

HARRISON: Oh, Christ! I wasn't thinking. I didn't mean
to say that. I'm sorry.

VERRET: You've no reason to be.

Thereafter Harrison's electrical activity increased, and
the transmission distorted into static.

The capacity to manipulate magnetic fields, to affect
matter on the ionic level, and now this mysterious reference
to the voodoo term for the soul. I realized we had no idea
of this man's potential. My imagination was fueled by the
sinister materials of the project, and I was stricken by a
vision of Harrison crumbling cities with a gesture and raising
armies of the dead. I suggested to Stellings that we bring
him in, but he told me the risks were "acceptable." He did
not believe, as I was coming to, that Harrison might be one
of the most dangerous individuals who had ever lived. Of
course Stellings had no knowledge of Otille Rigaud . . . or
did he? Perhaps there was no end to the convolution of this
circumstance. It seemed to unravel by process of its own
laws, otherworldly ones, like a cunning tapestry of black
lace worked with tiny figures, whose depicted actions fore-
shadowed our lives.

And then came the night of July 26, 1987, a night during
which all my fears were brought home to me. I had been
asleep for nearly an hour, not really asleep, drowsing, listening to the rain and the wind against the dormer window,
when I thought I heard a footfall in the corridor. Though
this was hardly likely—my security system being extensive—I sat up in bed, listening more closely. Nothing. The
only movement was the rectangle of white streetlight cast
on the far wall, marred by opaque splotches of rain and
whirling leaf shadow. I settled back. Once again I heard a
sound, the glide of something along the hallway carpet.
This time I switched on the bedside lamp, and there, framed
in the door, was a preposterous old man with shoulder-
length white hair and wearing a loose-fitting shirt decorated,

it seemed to my bleary eyes, with the image of a blue serpent (I later saw this was actually the word *Self-rising*, the imprint of a flour company). "Goddamn, he's a big one, him," said the old man to someone out of sight around the corner. A second figure appeared in the doorway, and a third, and I understood why my burglar alarms had failed. It was Verret, troubled-looking, and beside her, disguised by a pair of mirrored glasses, was Harrison. He had gained weight, especially in the shoulders, but he was still gaunt. His hair had grown long, framing his face, giving him a piratical air.

"Edman," he said.

The word was phrased as an epithet, containing such a wealth of viciousness I almost did not recognize it as my name.

His movements revealing no sign of debility, he picked up a straight-backed chair, carried it to the bed and sat next to me. How can I tell you my feelings at that moment, the effect he had upon me? I have stated that the patients were charismatic in the extreme, but Harrison's personal force was beyond anything of my experience. To put it simply, I was terrified. His *anima* wrapped around me like an electrified fist, immobilizing and vibrant, and I stared helplessly at my agog reflection in his mirrored lenses. The wind rattled the window, branches ticked the glass, as if heralding his presence. I wondered how Verret and the old man could be so at ease with him. Did they not notice, or had they become acclimatized to his aura of power? And what of *his* patients? Were all faith healers equally potent beings? Could it be that the power to heal was in part conferred by the faithful upon the healer, and this exchange of energies immunized the patients against awe? It is, I believe, a testament to the rigorous discipline of my education that, despite my fear, I was able to make a mental note to investigate the subject.

"Any successes lately with the new strain?" he asked.

I am not sure what I expected him to say, a threat perhaps, an insult, but certainly not this. "Two," I managed to gasp.

Expressionless, he absorbed the information. "Edman," he said, "I need money, a place to work unimpeded, and a guaranteed freedom of movement. Can you supply it?"

I wish I had said that I could offer no guarantees, that the CIA was involved and I no longer had substantive control of the project; then he might have accorded me a measure of confidence. But as it was, I obeyed the reflexes of my office and said, "Come back to the project, Donnell. We'll take care of you."

"I bet," he said, and here his voice became resonant for the space of a few syllables, the voice of a ghost rather than a man. "I should be taking care of you. You're quite ill, you know." He turned to the old man and gestured toward the door. "See if there's anything around we can use, okay?" And then to Verret: "He's totally untrustworthy. One second frightened, the next scheming. Do you have any money?" he asked, turning back to me.

I pointed to my trousers hanging on the clothes rack. Verret went over and emptied my wallet of bills. I felt sudden hostility toward her, seeing her as the betrayer of our mutual cause, and I commented on her thievery.

"Thief?" She lashed out at me. "You ghoul! Don't call me names!"

"Don't waste your breath on him." Harrison regarded me with displeasure. "He's just random molecules bound together by the stickum of his education."

Normally I would have been infuriated by such a description, but he said it with kindness, with pity, and for the moment I accepted it as accurate, a sad but true diagnosis. This, and the fact that during our encounter I was prone to fits of depression, a characteristic I had associated with Harrison, led me to wonder whether or not his energies were materially affecting my thought processes.

Verret left to join the old man in his search, and Harrison gazed at me thoughtfully. "Get up," he said. He pushed back his chair and stood.

I was afraid he was about to harm me. My fear may seem to you irrational; I was, after all, a much larger man, and I might well have been able to overpower both him and Verret, though the old man had a wiry, dangerous look. Yet I was very afraid.

"I'm not going to hurt you," he said, thoroughly disgusted. He removed his sunglasses. "I'm going to try to cure you."

As he moved his hands above my head, concentrating his efforts at the base of my skull, I lost track of the storm, the others in the house, and was caught up in the manner of my healing. Mild electric shocks tingled me from head to foot, my ears were filled with oscillating hums. Once in a while violent shocks caused my muscles to spasm, and after each of these I experienced a feeling of—I am hesitant to use the term, but can think of no other—spirituality. Not the warm *bona fides* of Jesus as advertised by the Council of Churches. Hardly. It was a cold immateriality that embraced me, that elevated my thoughts, sent them questing after a higher plane; it was less a palpable cold than a mental rigor, one implying an icy sensibility in whose clutch I foundered. I had an image of myself lying in a gold-green scaly palm, tiny as a charm. Was this the biochemistry of salvation in action, an instance of Harrison's effect releasing spiritual endorphins? Or was it the overlapping of his sensibility with my own? I only know that each sight I had of the flashes within his eyes gave credence to my newfound apprehension of the supernatural.

"Sorry," he said at last. "It's going to take too long. A day or more, I'd guess." He smiled. "Maybe you should have one of the new patients check you over." (And I would have, had not the project been taken from me.) He must have forgotten that Verret had left the room, for he half-turned and spoke over his shoulder, assuming her presence, saying, "If this works out, we should think about setting the others loose. There's no..." Then, realizing she was elsewhere, a puzzled expression crossed his face.

"What is the *gros bon ange?*" I blurted. "What are you intending to do?" I was still frightened, but the character of my fear had changed. It was the unknown quantity he represented that assailed me, and I was desperate to understand.

"The *gros bon ange?*" His voice became resonant and hollow again, gusting at me like a wind from a cave, merging with the howling wind outside. "A dream, a vision, or maybe it's the shadow a dog sees slipping out of an open coffin." Then his voice reverted to normal, and he described what he had seen.

I am not sure why he humored my question. Boredom,

perhaps; or it may have been simply that he had no reason to hide anything from me. There were, he said, three types, the most commonplace a black figure in which prisms of light whirled chaotically. The second most common type seemed to exert a measure of control over its inner fires (his term), able to form of them faces, simple patterns; and the rarest, a type of whom he had seen only three, were capable of wielding extensive control, even to the point of sending bursts of light shooting from their fingers.

"As to what I intend," he said, "I intend to live, Edman. I'm going to build the *veve* of a voodoo god out of copper. Three tons of copper." He laughed. "I don't suppose you know about *veves,* though."

Indeed, I assured him, I did know, having done quite a bit of reading on the subject of *vaudou,* this at the urging of Ms. Verret.

"Oh?" He scratched the back of his neck. "Tell me about Ogoun Badagris."

"One of the aspects of Ogoun," I said, "who is essentially the warrior hero of the pantheon. I believe that Ogoun Badagris is associated with wizardry. A *rada* aspect."

"*Rada?*"

"Yes. *Rada* and *petro* are more or less equivalent to white and black magic. Good and evil."

"And which is *rada?*"

"Good," I said.

"Well," he said softly, more to himself than to me, "I guess I should be thankful for that."

He went on to tell me of a plan he had, hardly a plan, more a vague compulsion to act in some direction, and though the action was as yet unclear, as the days passed the parameters of the deed were defining themselves. Something decisive, he said, something dangerous. It was evident to me that he was evolving past the human, and I was in mortal terror of the vibrant devil he was coming to be. I lay half hypnotized, helpless before him, the tongues of his words tasting me, licking me prior to taking a bite. Finally Verret and the old man returned; he was carrying a brandy bottle and she a coil of rope. Without further ado they gagged me and lashed me to the bed, and afterward Harrison asked me to break free if I could. Ordinarily I would have pretended to struggle, but at his behest I shook the bed in earnest.

And then they were gone, gone to Maravillosa, swallowed up and gone beyond the reach of the CIA, the project, and for all I know beyond the hand of God Himself. We had no word of them until news came of Harrison's actions on Bayou Rigaud.

I may well have met Otille Rigaud; however, from all reports, it is unlikely I would have forgotten the occasion. She was a woman who traveled freely through the various strata of society, and the mention of her name was sufficient to cause highly respected citizens to cough, make their excuses, and leave the room. I wish that I had met her. Though many have tried to explain the events which occurred upon Bayou Rigaud, she alone might have illuminated them. Stacked on my writing table at this moment is page after page of dubious yet accurate explanation. Data sheets, medical records, government documents. For example, here we have the results of an autopsy performed on an unidentified body, citing one hundred and seventy separate fractures caused by the instantaneous degeneration of bone tissue, blood clots, cell damage, crushed spinal ganglia, and so forth. Appended is a telephone-book-sized study exploring the victim's agony, which must have been substantial, and speculating on the nature of the forces that came into play. I will quote from the summary section.

. . . Movements of the Ezawa bacteria within the brains of Subjects One and Two created electrical currents which interacted with the electrical functions of the neurons, thereby enabling them to intuit the direction of the geomagnetic field. The copper device, aside from its function of conductivity, seems to have acted as a topological junction, its design such that all possible formulae of energy manipulation—the vibrational and rotational states of electrons, spin states of magnetic nuclei—were reduced to the choreographed movements of an electrical field (either Subject One or Two) within the geomagnetic field. Together with the device, the subjects became dynamos. They provided the current fed through the device, which in turn fed a magnetic field back through their bodies. Dependent on the exact choreography, the field could attain a potential strength of at least several hundred thousand times that of the geomagnetic field.

The energies redirected through the bodies of both subjects must have been of sufficient strength to disrupt in coherent fashion their atomic structures. Bulman hypothesizes there may have been a particular reaction involved with the hemoglobin. Electrons were raised to higher energy states, unipolar fields were created at the fingertips of the subjects, and photons transmitted along the lines of the fields. The emission of light visible in the tapes resulted from energy loss when the electrons dropped back to lower energy states. Essentially, the physical damage sustained by Subject One occurred when his nuclei absorbed enough radiation to flip their orientation and align with Subject Two's field, this being a structural irony his component particles could not maintain. . . .

All well and good. But none of this speaks to the absolute question: Can the events on Bayou Rigaud be taken at face value, or were more consequential historical actions involved? It may be unanswerable. It may be that when we peer over the extreme edge of human experience, we will find nothing but a mute darkness. Or, and this is my conviction, it may be that there is a process of nature too large for us to perceive, an ultimate conjoining of the physics of coincidence and probability, wherein an infinite number of events, events as minuscule as two people meeting in the street and as grandiose as a resurrection, combine and each take on radiant meanings so as to enact an improbable and magical fate. But my own answer aside, I prefer above the rest that given me by an old Cajun woman whom I interviewed preparatory to beginning this memoir. At the very least, it does not beg the question.

"*Le Bon Dieu* He got riled at all the funny doin's down on Bayou Rigaud," she said. "So He raised up The Green-eyed Man to do battle wit His ancient enemy."

CHAPTER XIV

July 27–July 28, 1987

The oak tree sheltering Caitlett's Store looked as if it had undergone a terrifying transformation: a hollow below its crotch approximating an aghast mouth, swirled patterns in the bark for eyes, thin arms flung up into greenery. Mr. Brisbeau parked the truck beside it, keeping the motor running, while Jocundra and Donnell slid out. Someone cracked the screen door of the store and peeked at them, then let it bang shut, rattling a rusted tin sign advertising nightcrawlers. Nothing moved in the entire landscape. The marshlands shone yellow-green under the late afternoon sun, threaded by glittering meanders of water and pierced by the state highway, which ran straight to the horizon.

"Are you going back to the cabin?" Jocundra asked Mr. Brisbeau.

"The damn gov'ment ain't puttin' me on their trut' machine," he said. "Me, I'm headin' for the swamp."

"Goodbye," said Donnell, sticking out his hand. "Thank you."

Mr. Brisbeau frowned. "You give me back my eyes, boy, and I ain't lettin' you off wit 'goodbye' and 'thank you.'" He handed Donnell a folded square of paper. "That there's my luck, boy. I fin' it in the sand on Gran Calliou."

The paper contained a small gold coin, the raised face upon it worn featureless.

"Pirate gold," said Mr. Brisbeau; he harumphed, embarrassed. "Now, me, I ain't been the luckiest soul, but wit all my drinkin' I figure I cancel it out some."

"Thank you," said Donnell again, turning the coin over in his fingers.

"Jus' give it back nex' time you see me." Mr. Brisbeau

put his hands on the wheel. "I ain't so old I don't need my luck." He glanced sideways at Jocundra. "You wait twelve more years to come around, girl, and you have to whisper to my tombstone."

"I won't." She rested her hand on the window, and he gave it a pat. His fingers were trembling.

"Ain't sayin' goodbye," he said, his face collapsing into a sad frown; he let out the clutch and roared off.

Jocundra watched him out of sight, feeling forlorn, deserted, but Donnell gazed anxiously in the other direction.

"I knew the son of a bitch would be late," he said.

The interior of the store was dark and cluttered. Shelf after shelf of canned goods and sundries, bins of fish hooks and sinkers, racks of rods and reels. The fading light was thronged with particles of dust, and their vibration seemed to register the half-life of some force that radiated from a tin washtub of dried bait shrimp set beneath the window.

"Cain't wait here 'less you buy somethin'," said the woman back of the counter, so they bought sandwiches and went outside to eat on the steps.

"Funny thing happened last night," he said, breaking a long bout of chewing. "I was talking to Edman while you were searching the house, and I felt you behind me. I could've sworn you'd come back in the room, but then I realized I was feeling you walk through the house. It's happened before, I think, but not so strongly."

"It's probably just sexual," she said.

He laughed and hugged her.

"You folks cain't wait here much longer," said the woman from inside the door. "I'm gonna close real soon, and I don't want you hangin' round after dark."

"There must be some kind of feedback system in operation," said Jocundra after the woman had clomped back to the counter. "I mean considering the way your abilities have increased since you began healing. I'd expect more of an increase while you're on the *veve*. Even though you'll be trimming back the colony, you'll be routing them through the systems that control your abilities."

"Hmm." He rubbed her hip, disinterested. "It was really weird last night," he said. "Sort of like the way you could tell the Gulf was beyond the pines at Robichaux's. Something about the air, the light. A thousand micro-changes. I knew where you were every second."

The sun was reddening, ragged strings of birds crossed the horizon, and there were splashes from the marsh. A Paleozoic stillness. The scene touched off a sunset-colored dream in Jocundra's head. How they sailed down one of the channels to the sea, followed the coast to a country of spiral towers and dingy portside bars, where an old man with a talking lizard on a leash and a map tattooed on his chest offered them sage advice. She went with the dream, preferring it to thinking about their actual destination.

"That's him," said Donnell.

A long maroon car was slowing; it pulled over on the shoulder and honked. They walked toward it without speaking. There were bouquet vases in the back windows, a white monogrammed R on the door. Jocundra reached out to open the rear door, but Papa Salvatino, his puffy face warped by a scowl, punched down the lock.

"Get in front!" he snapped. "I ain't your damn chauffeur!"

"You're late," said Donnell as he slid in. Jocundra scrunched close to him, away from Papa.

"Listen, brother. Don't you be tellin' me I'm late!" Papa engaged the gears; the car shot forward. "Right now, right this second, you already at Otille's." He shifted again, and they were pressed together by the acceleration. "We got us a peckin' order at Maravillosa," Papa shouted over the wind. "And it's somethin' you better keep in mind, brother, 'cause you the littlest chicken!"

He lit a cigarette, and the wind showered sparks over the front seat. Jocundra coughed as a plume of smoke enveloped her.

"I just can't sit behind the wheel 'less I got a smoke," said Papa. "Sorry." He winked at Jocundra, then gave her an appraising stare. "My goodness, sister. I been so busy scoutin' out Brother Harrison, I never noticed what a fine, fine-lookin' woman you are. You get tired of sharpenin' his pencil, give ol' Papa a shout."

Jocundra edged farther away; Papa laughed and lead-footed the gas. The light crumbled, the grasses marshaled into ranks of shadows against the leaden dusk. They drove on in silence.

The house was painted black.

On first sight, a brief glimpse through a wild tangle of vines and trees, Donnell hadn't been certain. By the time they arrived at the estate, clouds had swept across the moon and he could not even make out the roofline against the sky. A number of lighted windows hovered unsupported in the night, testifying to the great size of the place, and as they passed along the drive, the headlights revealed a hallucinatory vegetable decay: oleanders with nodding white blooms, shattered trunks enwebbed by vines, violet orchids drooling off a crooked branch, bright spears of bamboo, shrubs towering as high as trees, all crammed and woven together. Peeping between leaves at the end of the drive was the pale androgynous face of a statue. Things crunched underfoot on the flagstone path, and nearing the porch Donnell saw that the boards were a dull black except for four silver-painted symbols which seemed to have fallen at random upon the house, adjusting their shapes to its contours like strange unmelting snowflakes: an Egyptian cross floating sideways on the wall, a *swastika* overlapping the lower half of the door and the floorboards, a crescent moon, a star. He assumed there were others hidden by the darkness.

Papa led them down a foul-smelling, unlit corridor reverberating with loud rock and roll. Several people ran past them, giggling. At the end of the corridor was a small room furnished as an office: metal desk, easy chairs, typewriter, file cabinets. The walls were of unadorned black wood.

"Wait here," he said, switching on the desk lamp. "Don't you go pokin' around 'til Otille gives you the say-so."

The instant he left, Jocundra slumped into a chair. "God," she said; she opened her mouth to say something else, but let it pass.

Shrieks of laughter from the corridor, the tangy smell of cat shit and marijuana. Oppressed by the atmosphere himself, Donnell had no consolation to offer.

"The ends of the earth," she said, and laughed despondently. "My high school yearbook said I'd travel to the ends of the earth to find adventure. This must be it."

"The ends of the earth are but the beginning of another world," someone intoned behind them.

The gray-haired usher from Papa Salvatino's revival stood in the door; neither his beatific smile nor his shabby suit had changed. At his side was a crewcut, hawk-faced young man holding a guitar, and lounging beside him was a teenage girl, whose costume of a curly red wig and beige negligee did not disguise her mousiness.

"This here's Downey and Clea," said the usher. "I'm Simpkins. Delighted to have you back in the congregation."

Downey laughed, whispered in Clea's ear, and she grinned.

Jocundra was speechless, and Donnell, struck by a suspicion, shifted his visual field. Three black figures bloomed in the silver-limned door; the prismatic fires within them columned their legs, delineated the patterns of their musculature and nerves, and glowed at their fingertips. Simpkins and one of the other two, then, along with Papa, must have been the three figures Donnell had seen in Salt Harvest, and he thought he knew what their complex patterns indicated. He shifted back to normal sight and studied their faces. Clea and Downey were toadies and boot-lickers, but each with a secret, a trick, an ounce of distinction. Simpkins was hard to read.

"So you're Otille's little band of mutants," said Donnell, walking over to stand behind Jocundra.

"How'd you know that?" asked Clea, her voice a nasal twang. "I bet Papa told you."

"Lucky guess," said Donnell. "Where's the other one? There's one more besides Papa, isn't there?"

Simpkins maintained his God-conscious smile. "Right on all counts, brother," he said. "But if half what we been hearin's true, we can't hold a candle to you. Now Downey here"—he gave Downey's head a friendly rub—"he can move things around with his mind. Not big things. Ping-pong balls, feathers. And then only when he ain't stoned, which ain't too often. And Sister Clea . . ."

"I sing," said Clea defiantly.

Downey snickered.

"And when I do," she said, and stuck out her tongue at Downey, "strange things happen."

"Sometimes," said Downey. "Most times you just clear the room. Sounds like someone squeezin' a rat."

"It's true," said Simpkins. "Sister Clea's talent is erratic, but wondrous things do happen when she lifts her voice in song. A gentle breeze will blow where none has blown before, insects will drop dead in midflight. . . ."

"She oughta hire out to Orkin," said Downey.

"And," Simpkins continued, "only last week a canary fell from its perch, never more to charm the morning air."

"That was just a coincidence," said Downey sullenly.

"You're just jealous 'cause Otille kicked you outta bed," said Clea.

"Coincidence or not," said Simpkins, "Sister Clea's stock has risen sharply since the death of poor Pavarotti."

"And what's your specialty, Simpkins?" asked Donnell.

"I suppose you'd classify me as a telepath." Simpkins folded his arms, thoughtful. "Though it never seemed I was pickin' up real thoughts, more like dreams behind thoughts. . . ."

"Simpkins once had a rather exotic vision which he said derived from my thoughts," said a musical voice. A diminutive, black-haired woman swept into the room, Papa and a heavy-set black man at her heels. "It was a pretty vision," she said. "I incorporated it into my decorating scheme. But his talent failed him shortly thereafter, and we never did learn what it meant." She walked over to Donnell; she was wearing a cocktail dress of a silky red material that seemed to touch every part of her body when she moved. "I'm Otille Rigaud." She gave her name the full French treatment, as if it were a rare vintage. "I see you've been getting to know my pets." Then she frowned. "Baron!" she snapped. "Where's Dularde?"

"Beats me," said the black man.

"Find him," she said, shooing them off with flicks of her fingers. "All of you. Go on!"

She gestured for Donnell to sit beside Jocundra, and after he had taken a chair, she perched on the desk in front of him. Her dress slid up over her knees, and he found that if he did not meet her stare or turn his head at a drastic angle, he would be looking directly at the shadowy division between her thighs. She was a remarkably beautiful woman, and though according to Papa's story she must be nearly forty, Donnell would have guessed her age at a decade less. Her hair fell to her shoulders in serpentine curls; her upper lip was shorter and fuller than the lower, giving her a permanently dissatisfied expression; her skin was pale, translucent, a tracery of blue veins showing at the throat. Delicate bones, black eyes aswim with lights that did not appear to be reflections. A cameo face, one which bespoke subtle understandings and passions. But her overall delicacy, not any single feature of it, was Otille's most striking aspect. Against the backdrop of her pets, she had seemed fashioned by a more skillful hand, and when she had entered the office, Donnell had felt that an invisible finger had nudged her from the ranks of pawns into an attacking position: the tiny ivory queen of a priceless chess set.

"You have a wonderful presence, Donnell," she said after a long silence. "Wonderful."

"Compared to what?" he said, annoyed at being judged. "The rest of your remaindered freaks?"

"Oh, no. You're quite incomparable. Don't you think so, Ms. Verret? Jocundra." She smiled chummily at Jocundra. "What an awful name to saddle a child with! So large and cumbersome. But you *have* grown into it."

Jocundra registered surprise on being addressed, but she was not caught without a reply. "I'm really not interested in trading insults," she said. She opened her purse and pulled out a manila folder. "These are our cost estimates. Shouldn't we get down to business?"

Otille laughed, but took the folder. She carried it back to the desk, sat, and began to examine it.

A tap on the door, and Papa leaned in. "Otille? They spotted Dularde in the ballroom, but there's so damn many people, we can't catch up with him."

"All right. Don't do anything. I'll be down in a minute." She waved him away. "These don't seem out of line," she said, closing the folder. "And I'm quite impressed with you,

Donnell. But I think we should both sleep on it and see how we feel in the morning. Then we can talk. Agreed?"

"Fine by me," he said. "Jocundra?"

She nodded.

"I apologize for getting off on the wrong foot," said Otille, scraping back her chair and standing. "I have to deal with so much falsity, I end up being false myself. And I suppose my theatrical background has affected me badly." She tipped her head to one side, considering an idea. "Would you like to hear something from my play? *Danse Calinda?*"

Donnell shrugged; Jocundra said nothing.

Otille adopted a distracted pose behind her chair. "I'll do a brief passage," she said, "and then we'll find Dularde." As she spoke the lines, she darted about the room, her hands fidgeting with her dress, papers on the desk, straightening furniture, and all her movements had the electrified inconsistency of someone prone to flashes of otherworldly vision.

"'. . . And then coming back from Brooklyn Heights, the cabbie was talking, looking at me in the rear view mirror, winking. He was very friendly, you know how they are when they think you're from out of town. But anyway as he was talking, the skin started dissolving around his eye, melting, rotting away, until there was just this huge globe surrounded by shreds of green flesh staring at me in the mirror. And I was afraid! Anyone in their right mind would have been, but all down Broadway I was mostly afraid that if he didn't keep his eye on the road we were going to crash. Isn't that peculiar? I'm terribly hot. Are you hot?'" She walked over to the wall and pretended to open a window. "'There. That's better.'" She fanned herself. "'I know you must think I'm foolish running on like this, but I talk to so few people and I have . . . I was going to say I have so many thoughts to express, so many tragic thoughts. So many tragic things have happened. But my thoughts aren't really tragic, or maybe they are, they're just not nobly tragic. The only thing noble I ever saw was a golden anvil shining up in the clouds over Bayou Goula, and that was the day before I came down with chicken pox. No, my thoughts are like the radio playing in the background, pumping out jingles and hit tunes and commercials and the news bulletins. Flash. A tragic thing occurred today, ten thousand people lost their lives, then nervous music, typewriters clicking, and moving right along, on the last leg of her European tour the First Lady presided over a combined luncheon and fashion show for the wives of the foreign press. Ten thousand people! Corpses, agony, death. All that breath and energy flying out of the world. You'd think there'd be a change in the air or something, a sign, maybe a special dark cloud passing overhead. You'd think you would *feel* something. . . .'"

Donnell had been absorbed by the performance, and when Otille relaxed from the manic intensity she had conjured up, he felt cut off from a source of energy. "That was pretty good," he said grudgingly.

"Pretty good!" Otille scoffed. "It was a hell of a play, but the trouble was I tended to lose myself in the part."

Otille's pets and the black man she had called Baron were waiting by the doors of the ballroom. Though the doors were shut, the music was deafening and she had to raise her voice to be heard. "I really hate to interrupt things on account of Dulardc," she said, looking aggrieved.

Downey and Clea and Papa put on expressions of concern, displaying their sympathetic understanding of Otille's position, but Simpkins' smile never wavered, apparently feeling no need to cozy up. The black man stared at Jocundra, who hung back from the group, ducking her eyes, lines of strain bracketing her mouth.

"Is this important?" asked Donnell. "We're tired. We can meet him in the morning."

"I won't be awake in the morning," said Otille angrily; she turned to the others. "Please try to find him once more. I'll wait here." She gestured to the Baron, and he flung open the doors.

Music, smoky air and flashing lights gusted out, and Donnell's immediate impression was that they had pierced the hollow of a black carcass and stumbled onto an infestation of beetles halfway through a transformation into the human. Hundreds of people were dancing, shoving and mauling each other, and they were dressed in what appeared to be the overflow of a flea market: feathered boas, ripped dinner jackets, sequined gowns, high school band uniforms. Orange spotlights swept across them, coils of smoke writhing in the beams. As his eyes adjusted to the alternating brilliance and dimness, he saw that the ceiling had been knocked out and ragged peninsulas of planking left jutting from the walls at the height of about twenty feet; these served as makeshift balconies, each holding half a dozen or more people, and as mounts for the spotlights and speakers, which were angled down beneath them. Ropes trailed off their sides, and at the far end of the room someone was swinging back and forth over the heads of the crowd.

". . . party!" shouted Otille, as her pets infiltrated the dancers, pushing their way through.

"What?" Donnell leaned close.

"It's Downey's party! He just released . . ." Otille pointed to her ear and drew him along the hall to where the din was more bearable. Jocundra followed behind.

"He's just released his first record," said Otille. "We have our own label. That's him playing."

Donnell cocked an ear to listen. Beneath the distortion, the music was slick and heavily synthesized, and Downey's lyrics were surprisingly romantic, his voice strong and melodic.

". . . Just like a queen upon a playin' card,
A little cheatin' never hurt your heart,
You just smile and let the deal go on
'Til the deck's run through. . . .
See how they've fallen for you."

"It's one of the benefits of living here," said Otille. "I enjoy sponsoring creative enterprise." She strolled back down to the doorway, beckoning them to follow.

The shining blades of the spotlights skewed wildly across the bobbing heads, stopping to illuminate an island of ecstatic faces, then slicing away. Some of the dancers—both men and women—were naked to the waist, and others wore rags, yet they gave evidence of being well-to-do. Expensive haircuts, jewelry, and many of the rags were of good material, suggesting they had been ripped just for the occasion.

Five minutes passed, ten. Jocundra stood with her hand to her mouth, pale, and when he asked her what was wrong, she replied, "The smoke," and leaned against the wall. Finally Downey and Papa returned, Simpkins behind them.

"I think I saw him," said Downey. "But I couldn't get close. It's like the goddamn stockyards out there."

"Somebody said he was headed this way," said Papa; he was huffing and puffing, and it was clear to Donnell that he was exaggerating his winded condition, making sure Otille noticed how diligently he had exerted himself on her behalf.

"I guess we'll have to stop the dancing," said Otille. "I'm sorry, Downey."

Downey waved it off as inconsequential.

"Now, hold up," said Papa, earnestly addressing the problem. "I bet if all of us, maybe Brother Harrison here as well, if we all got out there and kinda formed a chain, you know, about five or six feet apart, and went from one end to the other, well, I bet we could flush him that way."

Otille glanced shyly up at Donnell. "Would you mind?"

What he read from Otille's face angered Donnell and convinced him this was to be his induction into petdom, the first move in a petty power play which, if he were nice, would bring him treats, and if he weren't, would earn him abusive treatment. When he had met Otille, her face had held a depth of understanding, intimations of a vivid character, but now it had changed into a porcelain dish beset with candied lips and painted eyes, the face of a precious little girl who would hold her breath forever if thwarted. And as for the rest, they would go on happily all night trying to tree their kennelmate, delighting in this crummy game of hide-and-seek, woofing, wagging their tails, licking her hand. Except for Simpkins; his smile in place, Simpkins was unreadable.

"Christ!" said Donnell, not hiding his disgust. "Let me try."

The ballroom darkened, and the world of the *gros bon ange* came into view. It was laughable to see these black, jeweled phantoms flailing their arms, shaking their hips, flaunting their clumsy eroticism to the accompaniment of

Downey's song. He scanned the crowd, searching for the complex pattern that would single out Dularde; then Otille could loose her hounds, and he and Jocundra could rest. He wondered what Dularde's punishment would be. Banishment? Gruel and water? Perhaps Otille would have him beaten. That would be well within the capacity for cruelty of the spoiled brat who had batted her lashes at him moments before. He swung his gaze up to the makeshift balconies, and there, at the far end of the room, were two figures holding hands and kicking out their legs in unison on the edge of a silver-trimmed platform. Glittering prisms twined in columns around the legs of the taller figure, delineated the musculature of his chest, and fitted a mask to his face.

"There," said Donnell, adding with all the nastiness he could muster, "is that your goddamn stray?"

He pointed.

As he did, his elbow locked sharply into place, and his arm snapped forward with more force than he had intended. The lights inside Dularde's body scattered outward and glowed around him so that he presented the silhouette of a man occulting a rainbow. He wavered, staggered to one side, a misstep, lost his grip on his partner, fought for balance, and then, just as Donnell normalized his sight and drew back his arm, Dularde fell.

Hardly anyone noticed. If there were cries of alarm, they could not be heard. But Otille was screaming, "Turn off the music! Turn it off!" Papa and Simpkins and Downey echoed her, and several of the dancers, seeing it was Otille who shouted, joined in. The outcry swelled, most people not knowing why they were yelling, but yelling in the spirit of fun, urging others to add their voices, until it became a chant. "Turn off the music! Turn off the music!" At last it was switched off, and someone could be heard above the hubbub calling for a doctor.

Otille flashed a perplexed look at Donnell, then pressed into the crowd, Papa Salvatino clearing a path before her. Downey craned his neck, gawking at the spot where Dularde had fallen. Simpkins folded his arms.

"My, my," he said. "We're purely havin' a rash of co-incidences. Ain't we, Brother Downey?"

* * *

Their bedroom was on the second floor, as were those of all the pets, and though the furnishings were ordinary, Jocundra had spent a sleepless night because of the walls. They were paneled with ebony, and from the paneling emerged realistically carved, life-sized arms and legs and faces, also ebony, as if ghosts had been trapped passing through the tarry substance of the boards. Everywhere she rested her eyes a clawed hand reached for her or an angelic face stared back, seeming interested in her predicament. The faces were thickest on the walls of the alcove leading into the hall, and these, unlike the others, were agonized, with bulging eyes and contorted mouths.

Donnell, too, had spent a sleepless night, partly because of her tossing and turning, but also due to his concern over the man who had fallen. She didn't fully understand his concern; he had taken worse violences in stride. She tried, however, to be reassuring, telling him that people commonly survived far greater falls. But Dularde, said Otille, when she came to visit early in the afternoon, had suffered spinal injuries, and it was touch and go. She did not appear at all upset herself and insisted on showing them the grounds, which were fantastic in their ruin.

It had rained during the night, the sky was leaden, and peals of distant thunder rolled from the south. They walked along the avenue of pines where long ago Valcours Rigaud's daughter had wed beneath a canopy of gold and silver spiderwebs. Now the webs spanned even between the trunks, creating filmy veils dotted with the husks of wasps and flies. Otille slashed them down with her umbrella. The entire landscape was so overgrown that Jocundra could only see a few feet in any direction before her eye met with a plaited wall of vines, an impenetrable thicket of oleander, or the hollow shell of a once mighty oak, itself enwrapped by a strangler fig whose sinuous branchings had spread to other trees, weaving its own web around a series of gigantic victims. The world of Maravillosa was a dripping, parasitical garden. Yet underlying this decay was the remnant of artful design. Scattered about the grounds were conical hills fifteen and twenty feet in height, matted with morning glory and ivy, saplings growing from their sides, like the jungle-shrouded tops of Burmese temples. Paths entered the hills, curving between mossy walls, and at the center they would find broken benches, fragments of marble fountains and sundials, and once, a statue covered in moss and vines, its hand outheld in a warding gesture, as if a magician had been struck leafy and inanimate while casting a counterspell.

"Valcours," said Otille bemusedly, rubbing away the moss and clearing a circular patch of marble.

From atop one of the hills, between walls of bamboo and vines, they had a view of the house. Black; bristling with gables; speckled with silver magical symbols; a ramshackle wing leading off behind; it had the look of a strange seed spat from the heart of night and about to burst into a constellation. Beyond the hills lay an oval pool bordered in cracked marble and sheeted with scum, enclosed by bushes whose contours were thrust up into odd shapes. Valcours, Otille explained, had been fascinated with the human form, and the bushes overgrew a group of mechanical devices he had commissioned for his entertainment. She hacked at a bush with her umbrella and uncovered a faceless wooden figure, its head a worm-trailed lump and its torso exhibiting traces of white paint, as well as a red heart on its chest. A rusted *epee* was attached to its hand.

"It still worked when I was a child," she said. "Ants lived inside it, in channels packed with sand, and when their population grew too large, traps were sprung and reservoirs of mercury were opened, flooding the nests. The reservoirs were designed to empty at specific intervals and rates of flow, shifting the weight of the figure, sending it thrusting and lurching about in a parody of swordsmanship. The only ants to survive were those that fled into an iron compartment here"—she tapped the heart—"and then, after it had been cleaned, they were released to start all over." She cocked an eyebrow, as if expecting a reaction.

"What was it for?" asked Jocundra. The apparent uselessness of the thing, its death-powered spurts of life, horrified her.

"Who knows what Valcours had in mind," said Otille, stabbing the dummy with her umbrella. "Some plot, some game. But I hated the thing! Once, I was about eight, it scared me badly, and after it had stopped moving, I took out the iron compartment and dropped it in the bayou." She sauntered off along the rim of the pool, scuffing algae off the marble. "I've ordered the copper," she said over her shoulder. "You can stay if you like."

"How long will it take?" asked Donnell.

"A week to get here, then a few weeks for construction." She started walking toward the house. "You can think about it a few more days if you wish, but if you do stay, I hope you understand that it's a job. You'll have to keep yourself available to me five days a week from noon until eight. For my experiments. Otherwise, you're on your own." She turned and gave Donnell a canny look. "Are you sure you've told me everything about the *veve*, why you're building it?"

"I hardly know myself," he said.

"I wonder how it relates to *Les Invisibles*," she said.

"Les Invisibles?"

"The voodoo gods," said Jocundra. "They're sometimes called *Les Invisibles* or the *loas*."

"Oh," he said derisively. "Voodoo."

"Don't be so quick to mock it," said Otille. "You're about to build the *veve* of Ogoun Badagris out of three tons of copper. That sounds like voodoo to me."

"It's quite possible," said Jocundra, angry at Otille's know-it-all manner, "that the *veve* is an analogue to some mechanism in the brain and can therefore be used by mediums as a concentrative device, one which Donnell—because of his abilities—can use in a more material way."

"Well," Otille began, but Jocundra talked through her.

"If you're a devotee of voodoo, then you certainly know that it's a very social religion. People bring their day to day problems to the temple, their financial difficulties, lovers' quarrels. It's only reasonable to assume they're receiving some benefit, something more than a placebo of hope, that there are valid psychological and even physiological principles embedded in the rituals."

"Oh, my," said Otille, rolling her eyes. "I'd forgotten we were keeping company with an academic. Let me tell you a story, dear. There was a man in Warner's Parish, a

black man, who was on the parish council and who believed
in voodoo, and his colleagues put pressure on him to dis-
avow his beliefs publicly. It was an embarrassment to them,
and they weren't too happy about having a black on the
council in any case. They threatened to block his re-election.
Well, the man thought it was important to have a black on
the council, and he made the disavowal. But that same night
hundreds of men and women came into town all possessed
by Papa Legba, who was the man's patron *loa*. They were
all dressed up as Legba, with moss for gray hair, canes,
tattered coats and pipes, and they went to the man's house
and demanded he give them money. It was a mob of stiff-
legged, entranced people, all calling out for money, and
finally he gave it to them and they left. He said he'd done
it to make them go away, which is true no matter how you
interpret the story. The people of the parish put it off to a
bunch of crazy backwoods niggers getting excited about
nothing, but as a result the man kept his post and satisfied
his god. And of course it hasn't happened since. Why should
it? The necessary had been accomplished. That's the way
Les Invisibles work. Singular, unquantifiable events. Impossible to treat statistically, to define with theory."

Otille smiled at Jocundra, and Jocundra thought of it as
the smile of a poisoner, someone who has seen her victim
sip.

"Hardly anyone notices," said Otille.

Behind the house was a group of eight shotgun cabins,
each having three rooms laid end to end, and here, said Otille,
lived her "friends." Slatternly women peered out the windows
and ducked away; slovenly men stood on the porches,
scratched their bellies and spat. To the west of the cabins
was a graveyard centered by a whitewashed crypt decorated
with *rada* paintings—black figures holding bloody hearts,
sailing in boats over seas of wavy blue lines—this being
home to Valcours' seven coffins. And at the rear of the
graveyard, through a thicket of myrtle, was the bayou, a
grassy bank littered with beer cans and bottles, a creosote-
tarred dock, and moored to it, a black sternwheeler: an
enormous, grim birthday cake of a boat with gingerbread

railings and a smokestack for a candle. It had originally belonged to Clothilde, Otille's grandmother.

"It was to have been her funeral barge," said Otille. "She had planned to have it sailed down to the Gulf carrying her body and a party of friends. My father used to let us play on it, but then he found out that she had boobytrapped it in some way, a surprise for her friends. We never could find out how."

Jocundra was beginning to think of Maravillosa as an evil theme park. First, the Black Castle studded all over with silvery arcana; then the Bacchanal of Lost Souls with a special appearance by the Grim Reaper; the Garden of Unholy Delights; the cabins, an evil Frontierland where back porch demons drooled into their rum bottles and groped their slant-eyed floozies, leaving smoldering handprints on their haunches; and now this stygian riverboat which had the lumbering reality of a Mardi Gras float. Somewhere on the grounds, no doubt, they would find Uncle Death in a skeleton suit passing out tainted candy, black goat rides for the kiddies, robot beheadings. Perhaps, she thought, there had once been a real evil connected with the place, a real moment of brimstone and blood, but all she could currently discern were the workings of a pathetic irrationality: Otille's. Yet, though Maravillosa reeked of an impotent dissolution rather than evil, Otille the actress could bring the past to life. Leaning against the pilot house, her black hair the same shade as the boards, making it seem she was an exotic bloom drooping from them, she told them another story.

"Have you heard of Bayou Vert?" she asked.

Donnell perked up.

"They say it runs nearby. It's extraordinary that a place like this could create a myth of Heaven, even such a miserable one as the Swamp King's palace. Gray-haired swamp girls don't sound very attractive to me." She let her eyes contact Jocundra's, her lips twitching upward. "Clothilde wrote me a letter about Bayou Vert, or partially about it. Of course she died long before I was born, but she addressed it to her grandchild. The lawyer brought it to me when I was sixteen. She said she hoped I would be a girl because girls are so much more adept at pleasure than boys. They have, in her phrase, 'more surfaces with which to touch the world.' She instructed me in the use of . . . my surfaces, and confessed page after page of her misdeeds. Mutilations, murders, perversions." Otille crossed to the railing and gazed out over the water. "She said that she had fertilized the myth of Bayou Vert—it had been old even in Valcours' day— by spreading rumors of sightings, new tales of its wonders, tales about the Swamp King's black sternwheeler that conveyed the lucky souls to his palace. Then she poured barrels of green dye into the water, sending swirls of color down into the marshes, and waited. Almost every time, she said, some fool, a trapper, a fortune hunter, would come paddling up to the boat, and there he'd find Clothilde, naked, gray wig in place, the handmaiden of Paradise." Otille ran her hand over the top of a piling and inspected the flecks of creosote adhering to her palm. "They must have had a moment of glory on seeing her because they could never say anything. They just looked disbelieving. Happy. She'd make love with them until they slept, and they slept deeply, very, very deeply, because she gave them drugged liquor. And after they woke, too groggy yet to feel anything, she said they always had the most puzzled frowns when they looked down and saw what she had done with her knife."

The clouds were breaking up, the sun appearing intermittently, and the beer cans on the bank winked bright and dulled, as if their batteries were running low.

"Come on," said Otille sadly. "There's lots more to see."

CHAPTER XV

July 29—August 14, 1987

Those first weeks at Maravillosa, Jocundra had time on her hands. She wandered the corridors, poking into the cartons and crates that were stacked everywhere, exploring the various rooms. The motif of ebony faces and limbs emerging from the walls was carried out all through the house, but in the downstairs rooms most of the faces had been painted over or disfigured, and it was common to see nylons fitted over a wooden leg, coffee cups hooked to fingers, a black palm holding a soiled condom. The furniture was wreckage. Footless sofas, stained mattresses, cushionless chairs, everything embedded in a litter of beer cans and wine bottles. And here Otille's "friends" could be found at any hour of the day or night. Drinking, making love, arguing. Many of the arguments she overheard involved the virtues of religious cults and gurus; they were uninformed, usually degenerating into shoving matches, and their most frequent resolution was the use of sentences beginning with, "Otille said . . ." It soon became clear that this interest in religion only mirrored Otille's interest, and that the "friends" hoped by arguing to gain some tidbit of knowledge with which to intrigue her.

To further pass the time, Jocundra decided to put together an ethnography of the estate and went about securing an informant. Danní ("It's really Danielle, but there's so many Danielles who's actresses already, so I dropped the endin', you know, just said 'to 'elle with it,' kept the i and accented it. I think it sounds kinda perky, don't you?") was typical of the women. Pretty, though ill-kempt; blond and busty; accustomed to wearing designer T-shirts and jogging shorts; an aspiring actress in her mid-twenties. She had come to

187

Maravillosa in hopes that Otille would "do something" for her career. "You see what she's done for Downey, don't you? I mean he's almost a star!" She identified the other "friends" as gamblers in need of a stake, poets looking for a patroness, coke dealers with a plan, actors, singers, dancers, musicians and con artists. All young and good-looking, all experts on Otille's past and personality, all hopeful of having something done.

"But what do you do for her?" asked Jocundra one day. "I understand you provide her with companionship, an audience, and she gives you room and board...."

"And actin' classes," Danní interrupted. "I wouldn't be here if it wasn't for the classes."

"Yes, but knowing Otille, it seems she'd expect more for her money."

"Sometimes she entertains," said Danní, uncomfortable, "and we help out." When Jocundra pressed her, Danní became angry but finally said, "We sleep with the bigwigs she brings out from New Orleans! Okay?" Ashamed, she refused to meet Jocundra's eyes. "Look," she said after a petulant silence. "Otille's a terrific actress. Bein' taught by her, it's... well, I'd sleep with the Devil himself for the chance. You learn so much just watchin' her! Here." She affected a pose Jocundra recognized as a poor caricature of Otille. "Baron!" she snapped. "Bring Downey to me at once. If he's not here in ten minutes, I'm not going to be responsible!" She relaxed from the pose and grinned perkily. "See?"

The hierarchy of the pets was, according to Danní, the main subject of study among the "friends"; they spent most of their energy trying to associate themselves with whomever they believed was in the ascendancy. Going to bed with Otille's favorite was the next best thing to going to bed with Otille herself: a rare coup for a "friend," so rare it had been elevated to the status of a myth. Clea was currently much in demand, and Papa, because of the reliability of his gift, was always ranked first or second. Simpkins was scarcely more than a "friend" himself, and Downey, due to his star quality, could have his pick regardless of his status in Otille's eyes. Even Clea had a crush on him. And as for the Baron, he was apparently neither "friend" nor pet, and Danní was of the opinion that he had some sort of hold over Otille.

"I used to be Downey's girl," said Danní one day while they were having coffee in Jocundra's room. "I used to live right down the hall. Otille even invited me upstairs a couple of times. Boy, is that gorgeous! But then"—she made a clownishly sad face—"she took a fancy to him again, and I got kicked back down to the cabins." She sipped her coffee. "That could be what happens to you pretty soon, at least the way I hear it."

"I know Otille's after Donnell," said Jocundra. "But I doubt she'll succeed."

"You better not doubt it," said Danní. "Men don't stand a chance with Otille. She'll have him doin' lickety-split before . . ." She gave herself a penitential slap on the cheek. "I'm sorry. I'm just used to dealin' with the others, and you're so nice and all. I shouldn't be talkin' to you like that."

"I'm not offended," said Jocundra. "I admit I worry about it." She sloshed the dregs of her coffee. "We're in a difficult position with Otille."

Danní took her hand and said it would probably be all right, that she understood.

Despite the difference in their backgrounds, Jocundra enjoyed Danní's company. Having a girlfriend made the wormy atmosphere of the house easier to bear, and Danní, too, seemed to enjoy the relationship, taking special pleasure in helping Jocundra search for clues to the estate's history among the crates and cartons. One morning, while digging through a dusty crate in a downstairs closet, they found an old book, a diary, embossed with the gilt letter A and bearing another gilt design on the foreleaf; this last, though worm-trailed beyond recognition, was obviously the remains of a *veve*.

"I bet that's, you know, what's his name . . ." Danní banged the side of her head. "Aime! Lucanor Aime. The one who taught ol' Valcours his tricks."

The initial entry was dated July 9, 1847, and graphically

described a sexual encounter with a woman named Miriam T., which sent Danní into fits of giggles. There followed a series of brief entries, essentially a list of appointments kept, saying that the initiate had arrived and been well received. Then Jocundra's eye was caught by the words *les Invisibles* midway down a page, and she went back and read the entire entry.

Sept. 19, 1847. Today I felt the need for solitude, for meditation, and to that end I closed the temple and betook myself to the levee, there spending the better part of the afternoon in contemplation of the calligraphy of eddies and ripples gliding past on the surface of the river. Yet for all my peaceful reverie, I could not arrive at a decision. Shortly before dark, I returned to the temple and found Valcours R. waiting in the robing room...

"Valcours!" breathed Danní. "I don't know if we should be lookin' at this." She shuddered prettily.

...his noxious pit bull at his feet, salivating on the carpet. Suddenly, my decision had been made. As I met Valcours' imperturbable stare, it seemed I was reading the truth of his spirit from his wrinkled brow and stonily set mouth. Though by all he is accounted a handsome man, at that moment his handsomeness appeared to have been remolded by some subtle and invisible agency, as by a mask of the clearest glass, into a fierce and hideous countenance, thus revealing a foul inner nature. Without a word of greeting, he asked for my decision.

"No," I said. "What you propose is the worst form of *petro*. I will not trifle with *les Invisibles*."

He exhibited no surprise and merely pulled on his gloves, saying, "Next Saturday I will bring three men to the temple. Together we will penetrate the mysteries."

"Keep your damned mysteries to yourself!" I shouted.

"Sunday," he repeated, smiling. Then he inclined his head in one of those effete bows I find so irritating and left me, his accursed dog at his heels.

It is in my mind now that I should work spells against him, though by doing so I would in effect be practicing *petro* of the sort he wishes me to practice. And yet, it would be strictly in the service of the temple, and thus not a violation of my vows, only of my self-esteem. Be that as it may, there is an aura of significant evil about Valcours, such as I have not met with in all my experience, and it is time our association came to an end, one way or another.

Thereafter the diary continued in ordinary fashion, lists of appointments and more sex with Miriam T., until a third of the way through the volume, at which point the entries ceased.

Aime's account only posed new mysteries, and reading it had knotted Jocundra's muscles and set her temples to throbbing, as if it had contained the germ of an old disease. She begged off the rest of the morning, telling Danní she wanted to lie down a while, but Danní insisted on coming along and giving her a massage.

"There ain't nothin' like massage for tension," she said; she winked slyly. "I learned all about it out in Hollywood."

She accompanied Jocundra back to the room, had her remove her blouse and unhook her bra and lie flat on her stomach. At first the massage was relaxing. Danní straddled her, humming, rubbing out the tension with expert hands, but then she slipped a hand under to cup Jocundra's breast, kissed her shoulder and whispered how beautiful she was. Shocked, Jocundra rolled over, inadvertently knocking Danní off the bed.

"I thought you wanted me," sobbed Danní, completely unstrung, her facial muscles working, tears glistening in her eyes. "Don't you like me?"

Jocundra assured her she did, just not that way, but Danní was inconsolable and ran from the room.

Their relationship deteriorated swiftly. Jocundra tried to convince Danní to leave Maravillosa, pointing out that Otille had never given substantial help to any of the "friends," and offered to lend her money; but Danní rejected the offer and told her she didn't understand. She began to avoid Jocundra, to whisper asides to her companions and giggle whenever Jocundra passed by, and a few days later she

made an ineffectual play for Donnell. That, Jocundra realized, had been Danní's objective all along, and she had
been foolish not to anticipate it. The pathos of the "friends,"
of this talentless child-woman and her imitation of Otille,
her Otille-like manipulations, caused Jocundra to wonder if
she had not underestimated the evil influence of the place.
Donnell was becoming moody and withdrawn again, as he
had not been since leaving Shadows, refusing to talk about
what transpired during the days; and one night toward the
end of the second week, waiting for him to return, staring
out their bedroom window, she had a new appreciation of
Maravillosa.

Screams, some of them desperate sounding, arose from
the cabins. Torches flared in the dark thickets behind them.
The half moon sailed high, sharp-winged shadows skimming across it, and the conical hills and the vine-shrouded
trees washed silver-green under the moonlight had the look
of a decaying city millennia after a great catastrophe.

Morning sunlight shafted from the second-story windows, the rays separate and distinct, leaving the lower half
of the ballroom sunk in a cathedral dimness, but revealing
the wallpaper to be peeling and covered with graffiti. Crudely
painted red and green *veves,* including that of Ogoun Badagris, occupied central positions among the limericks and
sexual advertisements. Otille held her acting classes in the
ballroom, and wooden chairs were scattered throughout,
though only five were now taken, those by Otille, Donnell,
and the rest of the pets. Except for Otille and Donnell, they
sat apart, ringed about Clea, who was hunched over a chewed-
up yellow guitar, looking pale and miserable. Without her
wig, she lacked even the pretense of vivacity. She wore a
slip which showed her breasts to be the size of onions, and
passing her in the door, Donnell had caught a faint rancid
odor that reminded him of spoiled milk. Around her feet
were half a dozen cages filled with parakeets and lovebirds.

"What are you going to play for us, dear?" Otille's voice
rang in the emptiness.

"I ain't ready yet," said Clea, pouting.

Simpkins sat with folded arms; Papa leaned forward, his

hands clasped between his knees, affecting intense interest; and Downey sprawled in his chair, bored. The birds hopped and twittered.

"Allrighty," said Clea bravely. "Here goes nothin'."

She plucked a chord, humming to get the pitch, and raised a quavering soprano, souring on the high notes.

> "Beauty, where have you fled tonight,
> In whose avid arms do you conspire..."

"Aw, God!" said Downey, banging his heels on the floor. "Not that. Sing somebody else's song!"

"I wanta sing this," said Clea, glowering at him.

"Let her alone, Downey," said Otille with maternal patience. She put her hand on Donnell's arm. "Downey wrote the song when he thought he was in love with me, but then he entered his narcissistic period and he's ashamed to have written anything so unabashedly.romantic." She turned again to Clea. "Go ahead, dear."

"We're behind you, sister," said Papa. "Don't be bashful."

Donnell wondered if anyone could possibly buy Papa's cheerleading act. His face was brimful of bad wishes, and by course of logic alone it was obvious that Clea's failure would improve his lot. She lifted her reedy voice again, and it seemed to Donnell to be the voice of Maravillosa, the sad, common sound of the dead trees and the "friends" and the ebony faces, of Otille herself, of the sullen and envious relationships between the pets, the whine of a supernatural nervous system which governed them all. Even if no one were there to hear it, he thought, the sound would go on, arising from the wreckage of evil. A futile transmission like the buzz of a half-crushed wasp.

Clea faltered, a high note shrilled. "I can't sing when he's grinnin' at me," she said, gesturing at Downey. "He's makin' me too nervous."

"Oh, hell!" said Downey. "Lemme help her." He stalked over and took the guitar from her.

"If it won't interfere," said Otille. "Will it interfere?"

Clea could not hide her delight. She blushed, casting a furtive glance at Downey. "Maybe not," she said.

He pulled up a chair beside her, picked a fancy introduction of chords, and this time the song had the courtly
feel of a duet between a country girl and a strolling balladeer.

> "... Beauty is everywhere, they say,
> But I can't find a beauty like thine.
> Beauty, I love you so much more
> Than I do truth, which only lasts for a moment,
> While you live forever,
> Eternal and fleeting,
> And without you no truth
> Has any meaning...."

Some of the birds were fluttering up in their cages, chirping, agitated; others perched on the bars, trilling, throats
pulsing in a transport of song. Donnell felt Otille tense
beside him, and he focused on Clea. Her magnetic field
was undifferentiated by arcs, a nimbus of white light en-
compassing her and Downey and sections of all the cages.
Through the glow, she looked like an enraptured saint at
prayer with her accompanying angel. The face of her *gros
bon ange* was ecstatic, a mosaic of cobalt interlaced by fine
gold threads. Nearing its end, the song grew more impas-
sioned and the white glow spread to surround the cages and
every one of the birds was singing.

> "... Beauty, you've come only once to me,
> And now you've gone, you seem so rare and inviting,
> A chalcedon lady,
> Gold glints in your dark eyes,
> Admitting no imperfections,
> Miraculous diamonds
> Clasped round your slim throat,
> Where the pulse beats in the hollow
> And the blue veins are showing
> Their cryptic pattern
> Leading to somewhere,
> An infinite gleaming
> Trapped here forever
> Here in my song,
> Pure paragon."

Otille was disappointed at song's end. She praised Clea's effort, acknowledged the result, but her displeasure was evident.

"Lemme have a crack at them birds, Otille," said Papa. He popped his knuckles, eager to get started.

"We all know what you can do, Papa," said Otille. "It will prove nothing to see it again. I was hoping for something more . . . more out of the ordinary."

Clea hung her head. Downey picked out a brittle run of blue notes, uninvolved.

"It's obviously a matter of mood," said Simpkins. "When poor Pavarotti was struck down, I recall Sister Clea as bein' in a snit, whereas today, makin' music with her heart's desire . . ."

"He's not!" squawked Clea; she leaped up and pointed at him, fuming. "Lessee what you can do with 'em! Nothin', I bet!"

Downey smiled, strummed a ripple of chords.

"If I begin to tweet," said Simpkins, "then indeed we have a proof positive of Sister Clea's talent. But frankly I'm more interested in seein' what Brother Harrison can achieve with our feathered friends."

Otille pursed her lips and tapped them with an ivory finger. She cocked an eye toward Donnell. "Would you mind?" she asked.

Donnell stretched out his legs and folded his arms in imitation of Simpkins, returning his bland smile. Simpkins was obviously a force to be reckoned with, despite his failed gift, and Donnell did not want to establish the precedent of following his orders by proxy. "I'll pass," he said. "I didn't come here to kill birds."

"You don't have to *kill* them," said Otille, as if that were the furthest thing from her mind. "I'm much more interested in the variety of psychic powers than their repetition. Why don't you just see what you can do. Experiment. I won't hold it against you if nothing happens."

But you will if I don't try, thought Donnell. "All right," he said. He took Clea's place in the midst of the cages, and she and Downey settled into chairs.

The birds appeared none the worse for wear, bright-eyed

and chirping, swinging on their perches. Their plumage was beautiful—pastel blues and pinks, snowy white, bottle greens—and their magnetic fields were hazy glimmers in the air, easy to influence at a distance like the fields of telephones and cameras. He found if he reached out his hand to a cage, the birds within it stilled, quieted, and their fields glowed. But he could produce no other effect. The two cages closest to him contained nine birds, and by spreading his fingers magician style he managed to still all nine, controlling each with one of his fingers, feeling the tug of the fields. He doubted, though, that this would satisfy Otille. Then, following Otille's advice—"Experiment"—and wondering why it had never occurred to him to try before, he maintained his hold on the fields and shifted his focus into the darkness of the *gros bon ange*.

Bits of whirling blackness and jeweled fire hung in the silver cages. Tentatively, he pushed a forefinger against one of the fields, stroking it, and a thread of iridescent light no thicker than a spiderweb shot from his fingertip. He withdrew the finger, startled; but since the bird displayed no ill effects, its fires undimmed, he tried it again. Eventually nine threads of light connected his fingertips with the nine birds, and the refractions inside their bodies flowed in orderly patterns. The pressure of their fields against his hands increased, and when he involuntarily crooked a finger, one of the birds hopped down off its perch. He repeated the process, and soon, feeling omnipotent, the ringmaster of the magical circus, he had gained enough control to send them marching about the cages. Tiny jewelbox creatures hopping onto silvery feeders and swings, twittering and parading around and around.

Clea gasped, someone knocked over a chair, and someone else contributed slow, ironic applause. "Thank you, Donnell," said Otille. "That's quite sufficient."

He relaxed his control, brought the ballroom back into view, and saw Otille smiling at him. "Well," he said, stung by the pride of ownership in her face, "was that out of the ordinary enough?" Then he glanced down at the cages.

He had not killed the birds. Not outright. That would have been merciful compared to what he had done. The delicate hues of their feathers were dappled with blood, and freed from his control, their cries had grown piercing, stirring echoes in the sunlit upper reaches of the room. Their beaks were shattered, crimson droplets welling from the cracks; their wings and legs were broken; and the membranes of their eyes had burst and were dripping fluid. All lay flapping on the floors of the cages except for a parakeet, its legs unbroken, which clung to its perch and screamed.

"Papa," said Otille. "Will you and Downey take the undamaged ones to my office?"

Downey was frozen, grim-faced; Clea buried her head in his shoulder. Papa hesitated, eyeing Donnell nervously.

Three, no, four of the birds had quit fluttering, and Donnell sat watching them die, stunned.

"Simpkins," said Otille. "Take the others out to my car."

"Yes, ma'am," said Simpkins. He came over to the cages, and as he bent down, he whispered, "Poor Dularde never knew what hit him, did he, brother?"

Sick of his snide comments, his contemptuous air, Donnell jumped up and swung, but Simpkins easily caught his wrist and with his other hand seized Donnell's throat, his fingers digging in back of the Adam's apple. "I ain't no goddamn parakeet, brother," he said. He tightened his grip, and Donnell's mouth sprang open.

"Simpkins!" Otille clapped her hands.

"Yes, ma'am." Simpkins released Donnell and hoisted the cages, once again bland and smiling.

Donnell headed for the door, holding his throat.

"Where are you going?" called Otille.

He didn't answer, intent on finding Jocundra, on washing away the scum of Otille and her pets. But he turned back at the door, waylaid by a thought. Why, while he was killing the birds, had their . . . their what? Make it their souls. Why not? Why had they showed no sign of injury? He stared at the bloody heaps of feathers, blinking and straining until the cages gleamed silver. They were empty. Then movement caught his eye. Up above Simpkins' head, rising and falling and jittering like jeweled sparks in a wind, the souls of the slain birds were flying.

* * *

Near the end of the second week, Jocundra ran into the Baron in the hall outside his room. He was adjusting his doorknob with a screwdriver, muttering, twisting the knob. He had never said a word to her, and she had intended to pass without greeting, but he called out to her and asked to borrow her for a few seconds.

"You just stand there," he commanded. "Give that doorknob a twist to the right when I tell you, then step inside quick."

He went into the room and began prying with the screwdriver at a narrow ceiling board. "Someone," he said, grunting, digging at the board, "someone been sneakin' round, so I'm riggin' myself a little security." He was wearing jeans and a ripped New Orleans Saints jersey, and his arm muscles bunched and rippled like snakes. His eyes, though, had a liverish tinge. She had presumed him to be in his forties, but now she reckoned him a well-preserved sixty.

He put down the screwdriver and held up his hands beneath the board. "Do it," he said.

She twisted the knob. The hallway door slammed shut, almost striking her as she stepped inside, and a second door dropped from the ceiling and would have sealed off the alcove if the Baron had not caught it. He staggered under the weight. "Sucker must weigh a hunnerd, hunnerd and fifty pounds," he said. He noticed Jocundra's bewilderment. "All the rooms like that. Ol' Valcours he liked to trap folks." He chuckled. "And then he give 'em a hard time." He pushed the door back into place until it clicked, then he stared at her in unfriendly fashion. "Don't you recognize me, woman?" She looked at him, puzzled, and he said, "Sheeit! Mama Zito's Temple down on Prideaux Street. I was the damn fool used to stand out front and drag folks in for the service."

"Foster," she said. "Is that right?" She remembered him as a hostile, arrogant man who had drunk too much; he had refused to be her informant.

"Yeah, Foster." He picked up his screwdriver. "'Cept make it Baron, now. That damn Foster name never done me no good." He stepped around her, opened the hallway door, and twisted the knob to the left until it clicked twice. "You ever get to Africa?" he asked.

"No," she said. "I quit school."

"Yeah, well, I figured you didn't make it, seein' how you hangin' with that green-eyed monkey." He registered her frown. "Hey, I got nothin' against the monkey. It's just that since he come the boy have put a charge into Otille, and that ain't good."

"What's your relationship with Otille?"

"You writin' another paper?"

"I'm just curious."

"That's good," he said. "You keep an edge on your curious, 'cause this one damn curious place. Huh! Curious." He walked over to his drawer and took out a shirt. "I'm Otille's friend. Not like one of them raggedy fuckers down at the cabins. I'm her *friend*. And she's mine. That's why she take to callin' me Baron after the death god, 'cause she say can't nobody but death be a friend to her. 'Course that's just the actress in her comin' out." He stripped off the jersey and shrugged into the shirt; a jagged scar crossed his right chest, and the muscles there were somewhat withered. "She don't make me do no evil, and I don't preach to her. We help each other out. Like right now." He brandished a fist. "I'm watchin' over you and the monkey."

"Why?"

"You think Otille's mean, don't you? Sheeit! She got her moods, ain't no doubt. But there's folks 'round here will cut you for a nickel, squeeze you for a dime. Take that smiley son of a bitch Simpkins..."

"Baron!" Otille stood in the door, her face convulsing.

The Baron calmly went on buttoning his shirt. "I be down in a minute."

"Have you seen Donnell?" asked Jocundra, hoping the question would explain her presence to Otille.

Otille ignored her. "Bring the car around," she said to the Baron.

"Nothin' to get excited 'bout, Otille," he said. "Woman's just helpin' me fix my door." When she remained mute, he sighed, slung his coat over his shoulder and strode out.

"I don't want you talking to him," said Otille in measured tones. "Is that clear?"

"Fine." Jocundra started for the door, but Otille blocked the way. Her temples throbbed, nerves jumped in her cheek, her coral mouth thinned. Only her eyes were unmoving, seeming to recede into black depths beneath her milky complexion, like holes cut in a bedsheet. It amazed Jocundra that when she next spoke, her voice was under control and not a scream.

"Would you like to leave Maravillosa?" she asked. "I can have you driven anywhere you wish."

"Yes," said Jocundra. "But if I left, Donnell would go with me; and even if he stayed, then I'd stay because I'd be afraid you'd hurt him."

"Bitch!" Otille lashed out at the wall with the side of her fist. "I'm not going to hurt him!" She glanced at the wall and saw that her fist had impacted the forehead of a screaming ebony face, and she laid her palm against it as if easing its pain. "I'm going to *have* him," she said mildly. "Do you like this room?"

"I don't think so," said Jocundra, enunciating the words with precision, implying a response to both Otille's remarks.

"It takes so much time and energy to keep the place up," said Otille, blithe and breezy. "I've let it run down, but I've tried to maintain islands of elegance within it. Would you care to see one?" And before Jocundra could answer, she swirled out the door, urging her to follow. "It's just down the hall," she said. "My father's old room."

It was, indeed, elegant. Gobelin tapestries of unicorns and hunts, dozens of original paintings. Klee, Kandinsky, Magritte, Braque, Miró. The black wood of the walls showed between them like veins of coal running through a surreal bedrock. Comfortable sofas and chairs, an antique globe, a magnificent Shiraz carpet. But opposed to this display of good taste, arranged in cabinets and on tables, was a collection of cheap bric-a-brac like that found in airport gift shops and tourist bazaars: mementos of exotic cultures bearing the acultural stamp of sterility most often approved by national chambers of commerce. There were ashtrays, enameled key rings, coin purses, models of famous landmarks, but the bulk of the collection was devoted to mechanical animals. Pandas, monkeys, an elephant which lifted tiny logs, a snake coiling up a plastic palm, on and on. A miniature invasion creeping over the bookshelves and end tables. The collection, said Otille, represented her father's travels on behalf of the Rigaud Foundation and his various charities, and reflected his pack rat's obsession with things bright and trivial.

The room appeared to have calmed Otille. She chatted away as if Jocundra were an old school friend, describing family evenings when her father and she would set all the toy animals in operation and send them bashing into one another. But Jocundra found this wholesale change in mood more alarming than her rage, and in addition, she was beginning to make an eerie connection between the generations of Rigauds. Valcours with his anthropomorphic toys, Otille's father's animals, Otille's pets and "friends." God only knew what Clothilde had collected. It was easy to see how one could think of the family as a single terrible creature stretching back through time, some genetic flaw or chemical magic binding the spirit to the blood.

"I'm afraid I have a luncheon in New Orleans," Otille said, ushering Jocundra out. "Foundation business. But we can talk more another time." She locked the door behind them and headed down the hall. "If I see Donnell on my way to the car," she called back, "I'll send him along."

It was said with such unaffected sincerity that for the moment Jocundra did not doubt her.

"An attic's the afterlife of a house," said Otille, opening the door. "Or so my mother used to say."

The air inside was sweetly scented and cool. She stepped aside to let him pass, and as he did, her hip brushed his hand, a silky pass like a cat fitting itself to your palm. She shut the door, and he heard the lock engage. The gable windows were shuttered, the room pitch dark, and when she walked off, he lost sight of her.

"Turn on the light!"

"Why don't you find me like you did Dularde?"

"You might fall."

She gave a frosty little laugh. Boards creaked.

"Damn it, Otille!"

"Take off your glasses, and I'll turn on the light."

Christ! He folded the glasses and put them in his pocket.

He imagined he could hear her breathing, but realized it was his own breath whining through clogged sinuses.

"What the hell do you want to show me?" he asked.

"You'll have to come to the window," she said softly.

A rattling to his left made him jump. Metal shutters lifted from the row of gables, strips of silver radiance widening to chutes of dust-hung moonlight spilling into a long, narrow room, so long its far reach was lost in shadow. It must, he thought, run the length of the rear wing. The rattling subsided, and seven windows ranged the darkness, portals opened onto a universe of frozen light. Bales, bundles, and sheet-draped mysteries lined the walls. And then Otille, who had slipped out of her clothing, stepped from the shadows and went to stand by the nearest window. Her reappearance had the quality of illusion, as if she were an image projected by the rays of moonlight. Her skin glowed palely, and the curls of black hair falling onto her shoulder, her pubic triangle, these seemed absent places in her flesh.

"Don't look so dumfounded," she said, beckoning.

From the window, Donnell saw white flickering lights beyond the conical hills. Welder's arcs, Otille explained. The copper had arrived, and the night shift had begun at once. The peak of the gable cramped them together, and in the course of talking and pointing, her breast nudged his arm. He couldn't help stealing glances at her, at the lapidary fineness of her muscles, the way the moonlight shaded her nipples to lavender, and whenever she looked at him, he felt that something was pouring out of her, that dampers had been withdrawn and her inner core exposed, irradiating him. Though he had steeled himself against her, his body reacted and his thoughts became confused. He wanted to turn and go back downstairs to Jocundra, but he also wanted to touch the curve of Otille's belly and feel the bubble of heat it held. Her black eyes swam with lights, her sulky mouth was drawing him toward her, and he lost track of what she was saying, something about his having validated her beliefs.

"Come along," she said, taking his hand. "I'll show you my room. It used to be Clothilde's, but I've had it repaneled and decorated after my own tastes."

At midpoint of the attic three doors were set into the wall, the central one leading along a short passage to yet another door, and beyond this lay a cavernous room hung with shafts of moonlight. The ceiling was carved to resemble a weave of black branches, leaf sprays, dripping moss; and the light penetrated through the glassed-over interstices. Trunks bulged from the walls, their bark patterns rendered precisely; ebony saplings and bushes—perfect to the detailing of the veins on the leaves—sprouted from the floor, and at the center of the room was a carpeted depression strewn with pillows and having the effect of a still, sable eye at the heart of a whirlpool. A control console was mounted in its side, switches and an intercom, and after pulling him down to sit beside her, Otille flicked one of the switches. Colored filters slid across the rents in the carved canopy, and the beams of moonlight empurpled. Donnell lay back against the pillows, watching her rapt face as she unbuttoned his shirt, and when she bent down to kiss his chest, he shivered. It was as if a pale beast the shape of Otille had dipped her muzzle into him and fed.

Her hips rolled beneath him in practiced shudders, her fingers traced the circuits of his nerves, yet her love-making was so adept, so athletic, passion reduced to ornate calisthenics, that the spell she had cast upon him was broken and his interest flagged. Still, like a good pet, he performed, pretending it was Jocundra touching him. And then, because he thought it would be appropriate to the mood, he took his first look at Otille's *gros bon ange*.

If one of her clever movements had not renewed his passionate reflex, he would have thrown himself off her in revulsion. The pile of the carpet resolved into a myriad of silver pinpricks against which her head was silhouetted like a coalsack; but instantly sparks of jeweled light rushed up from the area of her hips, defining the lines of her breasts and ribs as they flowed, and fitting a bestial mask to her face. It was a thing in a constant state of dissolution composed of emerald, azure, gold and ruby glints that coalesced into patches of mineral brilliance, decayed, and melted into new encrusted forms. Black rips for eyes, fangs of gemmy light. It roared silently at him, its mouth twisting open and gnashing shut. Yet each time their hips ground together, the mask wavered, loosing stray sparks downward, as if his thrusts were inducing its animating stuff to join in. He thrust harder, and the entire structure of the mask dissipated for a split second, fiery wax running from a mold. He felt a desolate glee in knowing he could overwhelm this monstrosity, and he turned all his energies to dismantling the mask, battering at Otille, who moaned beneath him. Whenever he let up, the mask's expression grew more feral, but at last it melted away, flowing back into her groin. Looking down to where their bellies merged, he saw an iridescent slick like a film of oil sliding between them.

Afterward he lay quietly, collecting himself, angry at his submission to her, still revolted by the aspect of her *gros bon ange*, her soul, whatever it had been. Finally he began putting on his clothes.

"Stay awhile," she said lazily.

"One bite is all you get, Otille. It won't happen again."

"It will if I want it to."

"You don't get the picture," he said. He started lacing his shoes. "Out there in the attic it was like the shuffling rube and the scarlet woman. But when it came down to strokes, your little tour of hardcore heaven bored the hell out of me."

"You bastard!"

"What did you expect?" He unfolded his sunglasses. "That one of your Blue Plate Special humdingers would make me profess undying love?"

"Love!" Otille spat on the carpet. "Keep your love for that dimwitted Bobbie Brooks doll you've got downstairs!"

The intercom buzzed, and she smashed down a switch. "What is it?" she snapped.

"Uh, Otille?" It was Papa.

"Yes."

"Uh, the hospital called. Dularde didn't make it. I thought I should tell you."

"Then make the arrangements! You don't need me for that."

"Well, all right. But I was wonderin' could I come up?" She cut him off.

"I want you to stay," she said firmly to Donnell.

"Listen, damn it! We have a deal, and I'll keep my end of it. But if you want hot fun, buy a waterbed and stake yourself out in a cheap motel. I'll write your name in all the men's rooms. For a good time, see Otille. She's mean, she's clean, she can do the Temple Hussy's Contraction!"

She tried to slap him, but he blocked her arm and pushed her away. He stood. The lavender beams of moonlight were as sharp as lasers, and for the first time he recognized the room's similarity to the setting of his stories.

"What is this place?" he asked, his anger eroded by a sudden apprehension. "I wrote a story about a place like this."

She appeared dazed, rubbing her forearm where he had blocked it. "Just a dream I had," she said. "Leave me alone." Her eyes were wide and empty.

"My pleasure," he said. "Thanks for the exercise."

The door at the end of the passage was stuck, no, locked, and the door into Otille's room, which had closed behind him, was also locked. He jiggled the knob. "Otille!" he shouted. A chill weight gathered in the pit of his stomach.

"Clothilde called this the Replaceable Room." Her voice came from a speaker over the door. "It's really more than twenty rooms. Most are stored beneath the house until they're shunted onto the elevator. Every one of them's full of Clothilde's guests."

The room was hot and stuffy. He wrenched at the doorknob. "Otille! Can you hear me?"

"Clothilde used to switch the rooms while her lovers slept and challenge them to find the right door. Back then the machinery was as quiet as silk running through your hand."

"Otille!" He pried at the door with his fingertips.

"But now it's old and creaky," she said brightly. A grating vibrated the walls, and a whining issued from ducts along the edge of the ceiling. The room was moving downward. "I'm not sure how long it takes for the pumps to empty the room of air, but it's not very long. I hope there's time."

"What do you want?" he yelled, kicking at the door. His chest was constricting, he was getting dizzy. The room stopped, jolting sideways.

"You're under the house now," sang Otille. "Push the

button beside the door. I want you to see something. Hurry!"

Donnell located the button, pushed it, and a section of the wall inched back, revealing a large window opening onto a metal wall set nearly flush with it. He pulled off his shoe and hammered at the glass, but it held and he collapsed, gasping. The metal wall slid back to reveal a window like his own, and behind it, their dessicated limbs posed in conversational attitudes, were a man and a woman. Black sticks of tongues protruding from their mouths, eyelashes like crude stitches sewing their lids fast to their cheeks. Rings hung loosely on their fingers, and they were much shrunken inside antiquated satin rags, the remnants of fancy dress. Donnell sucked at the thinning air, scrabbling back from the window. There was a metallic taste in his throat, his chest weighed a ton, and blackness frittered at the edges of his vision. Otille's voice was booming nonsense about "Clothilde" and "parties" and "guests," warping the words into mush. The thought of dying was a bubble slowly inflating in his brain, squeezing out the other thoughts, and soon it was going to pop. Very soon. Then he had a sharp sense of Jocundra standing beneath and to the right of him, looking around, walking away. He could feel her, could visualize her depressed walk, as if there were only a thin film between them. God, he thought, what'll happen to her. And that thought was almost as big and important as the one of death. But not quite. Otille's voice had become part of a general roaring, and it seemed the corpses were laughing and pointing at him. Bits of rotten lace flaked from the man's cuff as his hand shook with laughter. The woman's mummified chest heaved like the pulsing of a bat's throat, a thin membrane plumping full of air. The room vibrated with the exact rhythm of the laughter, and the air was glowing bright red.

Then he could breathe.

Sweet, musty air.

He gulped it in, gorging on it. The door to the attic had sprung open. His head spinning, he crawled toward the light of a gable window and slipped; a splinter drove deep into the heel of his palm. He rolled onto his back, applying pressure to the point of entry, almost grateful for the sensation. Blood and gray dust mired on his hand.

"I'm sorry, Donnell," said Otille's voice from the speaker. "I couldn't let you leave thinking you'd won. But don't worry. I still want you."

CHAPTER XVI

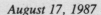

August 17, 1987

On the morning of Dularde's funeral, Donnell told Jocundra he had slept with Otille. He was contrite, he explained what had happened and why and said it had been awful, and swore there would be no repetition. Jocundra, who had tried to prepare for this turn of events, believed he was truly contrite, that it had been a matter of circumstance allied with Otille's charm, but despite her rational acceptance, she was hurt and angry.

"It's this place," she said mournfully, staring back at the angelic faces sinking into the black quicksand of their bedroom walls. "It twists everything."

"I can't leave . . ." he began.

"Why should you? You're the king of Maravillosa! Otille's prince consort!"

"You seem to think everything's fucking normal," he said. "That I'm a guy and you're a girl, and we're stuck in this little unpleasantness, but soon we'll be off to some paradisiacal subdivision. Three kids with sunglasses, a green-eyed dog, the *veve* in the back yard next to the barbecue. I'm walking a goddamn tightrope with Otille!"

"Is that what they're calling it now?" she sneered. "Walking a tightrope? Or is that Otille's erotic specialty?"

"Maybe Edman's right," he said. "Maybe you groomed me to be your soulmate. A sappy, morose cripple! Maybe you wanted someone to pity and control, and I'm not pitiable enough anymore."

"Oh, no?" She laughed. "Now that you've risen to the status of pet, I'm supposed to be in awe? I watch you swallow every treat she feeds you..." Tears were starting to come. "Oh, hell!" she said, and ran out the door, down the stairs and onto the grounds.

The sunlight leached the wild vegetation of color and acted to parch her tears. She found a flat stone beside the driveway and sat down, watching flies drone in a clump of weeds. The undersides of their leaves were coated with yellow dust. It hadn't rained in a couple of weeks, and everything was shriveling. She felt numb, guilty. He was in enough difficulty; he didn't deserve her insults. A butterfly settled on her knee. *If a butterfly lights on your shoulders, you'll be lucky for a year,* she remembered. Her father had been full of such bayou wisdoms. *Nine leaves on a sprig of lavender brings money luck. Catch a raindrop in your pocket and it'll turn to silver.* As he had grown older, he had stopped quoting the optimistic ones and taken to scribbling darker sayings on scraps of paper. During her last visit home she had seen them scattered about the house like spent fortunes, tucked between the pages of books, crumpled and flung on the floor, and a final one slipped under the door just before she had left. *Those who love laughter pay court to disaster,* it had read. *Prayers said in the dark are said to the Devil.*

Clouds swept overhead, obscuring the sun and passing off so that the light brightened and faded with the rhythm of labored breathing. Donnell came out of the house and headed toward the graveyard. Jocundra stood and was about to call his name, but a girl, one of the "friends," ran down the steps and fell in beside him. *Green eyes in a woman means passion, bitterness in a man,* Jocundra remembered, staring after Donnell's retreating figure. *One who has not seen his mother will be able to cure.*

There were six coffins in the crypt, walled off behind stone and mortar, all containing a portion of Valcours Rigaud's remains; there was space for a seventh, but Otille said it was buried elsewhere on the grounds. She lit a candle and set it into an iron wall mount. The yellow light turned her skin to old ivory, licked up the walls, and illuminated a carved device above each of the burial niches. Donnell recognized the design to be a *veve*, though he had only seen a crude version of it drawn on the back of Jack Richmond's guitar: a stylized three-horned man. The sight of it waked something inside him to a fury. His fists clenched; his mind was flocked with violent urges, shadowy recognitions, images and scenes that flashed past too quickly for recall. He had never had such a strong sense of being possessed, of being operated by some alienated fragment of his personality. For a long moment he could do nothing but stand and strain against the impulse to tear at the stones with his bare hands, smash the coffins, crush the rags and splinters of Valcours into an unreconstructable dust. At last the sensation left him, and he asked Otille what the design was.

"The *veve* of Mounanchou," she said. "Valcours' patron god. And Clothilde's. A nasty sort. The god of gangsters and secret societies."

"Then why not use *it* on your calling card?" he asked, still angry. "It seems more appropriate."

"I've rejected Mounanchou," said Otille, unflappable. "Just as I've rejected Clothilde and Valcours. Ogoun Badagris was the patron of. . . a family friend. A good man. So I adopted it." She brushed against him, and her touch had the feel of something roused from the dry air and darkness. "Why did you look so peculiar when you saw it?"

"I felt the bacteria moving around," he said. "It made me a little dizzy."

Otille went to the door. "Baron," she called. "Would you bring my parasol from my office. I don't want to burn."

Beyond the door, beyond rows of tombstones tilted at rustic angles, was the raw mound of earth covering Dularde's coffin. A group of "friends" was in line beside the grave, laughing and chattering; more were straggling toward the line along the path leading from the cabins. Simpkins stood atop the grave, a box of syringes and medicine bottles at his feet. As each of the "friends" joined him on the mounded earth, he would tie off their arms with a rubber tube and give them an injection. Then they would stagger away, weaving, and collapse among the weeds to vomit and twitch, their arms waving feebly, like poisoned ants crawling from their nest to die. It was, thought Donnell, an ideal representation of the overall process of Maravillosa: these healthy, attractive men and women bumping together in line, playfully smacking one another, being changed into derelicts by the cadaverous Simpkins and his magic fluid. He appeared to be enjoying his work, spanking the newly injected on the rumps to get them moving again, beaming at the next in line and saying, "This one's on Brother Dularde." Someone switched on a radio, and a blast of rock and roll static defiled the air.

Donnell stepped out of the crypt, squinting against the sun. Just above his head, surmounting the door, was a whitewashed angel with black tears painted on its cheeks, and he could relate to its languishing expression. Clea, Papa and Downey had not yet arrived, and their absence meant he had to put up with Otille nonstop. He peered down the path, hoping to see them. A man and a woman were walking toward the graveyard, dressed—he assumed at first—in gaudy uniforms of some sort. But as they neared, he realized the uniforms were a satin gown and a brocade jacket, and he saw that their faces were brown and mummified, the faces of corpses identical to those he had seen in the Replaceable Room. He wheeled about on Otille. She was smiling.

"Just a reminder," she said.

He looked back at the corpses; they were holding hands, now, skipping along the path, and he wondered if there really had been corpses in the Replaceable Room, or if there had only been these counterfeits. He turned back to Otille.

"I don't need a reminder of what a bitch you are," he said.

He had expected she would flare up at him, but she drew back in fright as if the sound of his voice had menaced her.

"What's the problem, Otille?" he asked, delighting in her reaction. "I thought you still wanted me."

At this, she whirled around and walked hurriedly off toward the house.

"Bitch!" he yelled, venting his rage. "I'd rather shack up with barnyard animals than make it with you again!"

The people by the grave were staring at him; some were

edging back. Still boiling with anger, he gestured at them in disgust and stormed off along one of the paths leading away from the house. He continued to fume as he walked, knocking branches aside, kicking beer cans and bottles out of his way. The thicket was festooned with litter. Charred mattresses, ripped underwear, food wrappers. Scraps of cellophane clung to the twigs, so profuse in places they seemed floral productions of the shrubs. His anger subsided, and he began to worry about his loss of control, not only its possible repercussions, but its relevance to his stability. He had been losing his temper more and more frequently since arriving at Maravillosa, and he did not think it was solely due to Otille's aggravation. Certainly she was not responsible for the feeling of possession. The path jogged to the right, widened, and he saw the sternwheeler between the last of the bushes. Against the glittering water and bright blue sky, it had the unreal look of a superimposed image, a black stage flat propped up from behind. Something snapped in back of him.

"Mornin', brother," said Simpkins.

Donnell looked around for an escape route, knowing himself in danger, but there was none.

"You just don't understand how to handle Otille," Simpkins said, advancing on him. "She's like a fisherman who's been havin' a good day, got herself a string of big cats coolin' in the stream. Every once in a while she hauls one up and thinks about fryin' him. And that's your situation, brother. Just floppin' on the dock."

Donnell started back up the path, but Simpkins put out a restraining hand.

"You gotta just hang there and let the water flow through your gills," said Simpkins. "You struggle too much and you bound to catch her eye."

"What do you want?" asked Donnell.

"A little talk," said Simpkins. "See, brother. Since you arrived, things been goin' downhill for the rest of us, and we'd like to know what it is you got. Maybe we can get some of it for ourselves. And then"—he chucked Donnell under the chin in good buddy fashion—"once that's done, the one and only Papa Salvatino is goin' to cure your ills."

* * *

Jocundra ran into the Baron on the path to the graveyard. He was standing lost in thought, twirling a yellow parasol. When he saw her, he spat.

"That monkey of yours put on some kind of show at the funeral," he said. "Used a trick voice or somethin'. Like to flip Otille out."

"Where's Donnell now?"

"You ain't seen him?"

"I saw him coming this way about a half hour ago."

"Ah, damn!" said the Baron. "Let's head on back up there."

Bodies were strewn among the tombstones, most unmoving, and most never stirred when the Baron prodded them. Others moaned or frowned groggily. The only person not lying down was a thin-armed, pot-bellied man wearing a bathing suit, who was sitting on top of a tombstone, his stringy brown hair blowing about his face. Static fizzed from a radio on his lap.

"Look like we gonna have to talk to ol' Captain Tomorrow," said the Baron. "Dude's been here so long he's fuckin' ossified. The light's on but nobody's home." He tapped his forehead. "Let me do the talkin'. He liable to think you an alien or somethin'."

He sauntered up casually to the tombstone and said, "Hey, what you know, Captain?"

"What I know," said the man, staring off at the roof of the main house emerging like a black pyramid above the treeline.

"I say, 'What you know, Captain?'" said the Baron, "and then you say back, 'What I know . . .' What you mean by that?"

"It's not ordered knowledge," said Captain Tomorrow. "It doesn't come in Aristotelian sequence. I'm trying to give it form, but I don't expect you to understand."

Despite the pomposity of his words, the man's manner was pathetic. His skin showed the effects of bad diet, his eyes were watery and blinking, and when he lifted his hand to scratch his neck, he did not complete the action and left his hand suspended in the air.

"I've been dreaming about flying lately," he said to Jocundra.

She remembered looking into Magnusson's eyes, feeling sucked in, but looking at this man produced a totally opposite phenomenon. Her gaze skidded away from his, as if his eyes contained polar contradictories to the human senses.

"Probably a result of my work," he informed her with solemnity. "I've been translating secret books of the ancient Hindus." He seemed to be waiting for Jocundra to respond.

"I have a friend who's compiling a Tibetan dictionary," she said. "She's working in Nepal."

"The Tibetan Book of the Dead." He stared at her with renewed intensity. "Is she translating that?"

"I think it's already been done," said Jocundra tactfully.

"Not correctly." He turned away. "Could you get me a copy of her dictionary?"

"I'll try," said Jocundra. "But it'll take a long time to mail it from Nepal. More than a month."

"Time," said Captain Tomorrow. He found the concept amusing. "It's very important I get the dictionary."

"That green-eyed fella..." the Baron began.

"No, not him." The Captain hugged himself and hunched his neck and shuddered.

"Naw," agreed the Baron. "Naw, he ain't worth a shit wherever he is. Good riddance to him. But whoever's with him is probably pretty scared."

The Captain smiled; it was a sick, secret-keeping smile.

"'Less he's with Simpkins. I don't reckon Simpkins would be scared."

The radio on the Captain's lap broke into faint song, then lapsed into frying noises.

"Where'd they go, man?"

"Going, going, gone," said the Captain.

"Jesus!" The Baron spun around and began trying to rouse others of the "friends," kicking them, shaking them, asking had they seen Donnell.

"Here," said Captain Tomorrow; he pulled a plastic baggie from the front of his bathing suit and withdrew a stack of Otille's business cards. He handed one to Jocundra. On the back was a neat, hand-lettered couplet:

Those who cannot cope with the reality of today
Will be literally crushed by the fantasy of tomorrow.

"It's my motto," he said, slowly reintegrating his gaze with the rooftop.

"Thank you." Jocundra pocketed the card and was on the verge of joining the Baron, when Captain Tomorrow reached out his hand toward the sun, then brought it back to his lips as if he were swallowing a mouthful of light, accepting communion.

"They're down at the riverboat," he said to his radio. "Down, down, down."

The hold of the sternwheeler had a resiny odor, and the wavelets slapping against the hull were edged with echoes, sounding like the ticking of a thousand clocks. Sunlight showed between the boards where caulking had worn away, and bars of light glowed beneath the hatch cover, dimming when Papa Salvatino lit a battery lamp and positioned it atop a crate. Clea and Downey stood beside him, their faces anxious. Simpkins threw a chokehold around Donnell's neck, wrenched his arm up behind his back, and Papa came toward him, rubbing his hands.

"What's ailin' you tonight, Brother Harrison?" he asked, and laughed.

He placed his hands above Donnell's head, and Donnell had a fuzzy, dislocated feeling. A high-pitched whine switched on inside his ears.

"I can't see what I'm doin' like you, brother," said Papa. "I got to work by touch, and sometimes . . . sometimes I slip up."

All the strength suddenly drained from Donnell's body; the weakness was so severe and shocking that his gorge rose, and he would have vomited if Simpkins had not been choking him. Then, as Simpkins released his hold, he sagged to the floor.

"I can make you bleed," said Papa. "You won't like it at all."

"Talk to us, brother," said Simpkins.

Donnell was silent a moment, and Simpkins kicked him; but Donnell's silence was not due to recalcitrance. He had had and continued to have an impression of Jocundra moving around above him, now standing somewhere near the prow.

The impression seemed to be compounded of the smell of her hair, the color of her eyes, her warmth, a thousand different impressions, yet its character was unified, an irreducible distillate of these things. He rubbed his throat and pretended to be straining for air.

"About what?" he gasped. "Talk about what?"

"Tell us what you did to them birds," Clea twanged; her voice trembled, and she stood half-hidden behind Downey, who was chewing on his thumbnail. Despite his masterful pose, belly out, thumbs couched behind his lapels, Papa was also exhibiting signs of unease. Even Simpkins' smile looked out of true. Donnell's sunglasses had slipped down onto his nose, and he let them fall, turning away from the lantern so his eyes would show to advantage in the dark.

"Remember, brother," said Papa. "You ain't hidin' out behind Otille's skirts no more. You down in dirt alley with the dogs howlin' for your bones." He drew forth a hunting knife and let light dazzle the blade.

"Just take it from the beginning," said Simpkins. "We got all kinds of time."

Maybe not, thought Donnell; Jocundra was moving again, stopping, moving, stopping, and there was a purposefulness to her actions.

"The beginning's not the place to start," he said, surprised to hear himself speak because he had been concentrating on Jocundra. Then he realized it had been his alter ego who had spoken, and this time he welcomed it. "I saw a man die once. He was shot, lying on a restaurant floor. His heart had quit, his blood was everywhere, and yet he still wasn't dead. That's the place to start."

He told them about the *gros bon ange,* about their specific incarnations of it, about his origins in the laboratories of Tulane, and was satisfied to see Downey and Clea exchange worried glances. The hunting knife hung loose in Papa Salvatino's hand, and his breath was ragged. Simpkins' Adam's apple bobbed. They were already nine-tenths convinced of the supernatural, and his account was serving to confirm their belief. He pitched his voice low and menacing to suit the mood created by the creaking timbers of the boat and began—again, to his surprise—to tell them of the world

of Moselantja and the purple sun, the world of the *gros bon
ange*. It was, he told them, a world whose every life had
its counterpart in this one, joined to each other the way
dreams are joined, winds merge and waters flow together;
and whose every action also had its counterpart, though
these did not always occur simultaneously due to the twisty
interface between the worlds. And there were many worlds
thus joined. In all of them the Yoalo had made inroads.

"To become Yoalo one must be gifted with the necessary
psychic ability to integrate with the suits of black energy,"
he said. "And all here rank high in the cadres, servitors to
one or another of the Invisible Ones, the rulers of Moselantja. Legba, Ogoun, Kalfu, Simbi, Damballa, Ghede or
Baron Samedi, Erzulie, Aziyan. Men and women grown
through much use of power to stand in relation to ordinary
men as stone is to clay."

The story he told did not come to him as invention, but
as the memory of a legend ingrained from childhood, and
in the manner of Yoalo balladeers—a manner he recalled
vividly—he gestured with his right hand to illustrate matters
of fact, with his left to embellish and indicate things beyond
his knowledge. It was with a left-handed delivery, then,
that he had begun to speak of his mission on behalf of the
cadre of Ogoun, when Clea broke for the stairs.

"Where you goin', sister?" Simpkins caught her by the
arm.

"I ain't havin' nothin' to do with this," she said, struggling.

"Me, either," said Downey, moving toward the hatch.

"What the hell's wrong with you?" said Papa. "You know
he ain't walkin' away from here."

"He'll come back," said Clea, her voice rising to a squeak.
"He's already done it once."

"In the cadre of Ogoun," said Donnell, wondering with
half his mind what Jocundra could be doing behind him,
"there is a song we call 'The Song of Returning.' Hear me,
for it bears upon this moment.

"The sad earth breaks and lets me enter.
My dust falls like the ashes of a song

Down the long gray road to heaven.
Yet as do the souls of the fallen gather
And take shape from the smoke of battle,
Casting their frail weights into the fray,
Influencing by a mortal inch
The thrust and parry of their ancient foes,
So will I return to those who wrong me
And bring grave justice as reward.
To those who with honor treat me,
I will return with measured justice,
No more than is their due.
And those who have loved me, a few,
To them as well will I return,
And all those matters that now lie between us
Will then be full renewed."

Cautiously, walking heel-and-toe so as not to be heard below decks, the Baron sneaked away from the hatch and back to Jocundra, who crouched in the prow.

"We need a *di*version," he said, wiping his brow. "All four of 'em's down there, and both Simpkins and Papa gon' be packin' knives. That's too much for me."

He looked around, and Jocundra followed suit. Something pink was sticking out from the door of the pilot house: a rag smeared with black paint. She peeked into the door. There was a box of rags against the wall, other rags scattered on the floor.

"Fire," she said. "We could start a fire."

"I don't know," said the Baron; he considered it. "Hell, we ain't got time to think of nothin' better. All right. See that far hatch? That goes down to the hold next to theirs. Here." He gave her his cigarette lighter. "You tippy-toe down there 'cause them walls is thin, and you pile them rags against the wall they behind. You be able to hear 'em talkin'. Soon as you get 'em goin', you gimme a wave and then yell like your butt was on fire." He shook his head, dismayed. "Damn! I don't wanna get killed 'bout no damn green-eyed monkey!"

He took off his jacket and wrapped it around his forearm and pulled a switchblade out of his trousers. "What you starin' at, woman?" He cast his eyes up to the heavens.

"They gon' stick him 'fore too long. Get your ass in gear!"

She gathered the rags, and carrying an armful of them, made her way to the hatch. The stairs creaked alarmingly. Voices sounded through the wall opposite the stair, some raised in anger, but the words were muffled. As she heaped the rags, something scurried off into the corner and she barely restrained an outcry. Holding her breath, not wanting to give herself away in case of another fright, she touched the lighter to the rags. The cloth smoldered, and some of the paint smears flared. She was about to bend down and fan them when, with a crisp, chuckling noise, a line of fire raced straight up the wall and outlined the design of a three-horned man in yellow-red tips of flame. It danced upon the black boards, exuding a foul chemical stink, seeming to taunt her from the spirit world. Terrified, she backed toward the stairs. Two lines of fire burst from the hands of the three-horned man and sped along the adjoining walls, laying a seam across their midpoints, encircling her, then scooted up the railings of the stairs. More fire spread from the central horn of the figure, washing over the ceiling, delineating a pattern of crosshatches and stickmen, weaving a constellation of flame and blackness over her head. Forgetting all about waving to the Baron, she ran up the stairs, shouting the alarm.

Clea brought her knee up into Simpkins' groin, and he went down squirming, clutching himself. She and Downey clattered up the stairs just as Jocundra shouted. Donnell saw smoke fuming between the boards behind him. He turned back. Papa Salvatino was coming toward him, swinging his knife in a lazy arc, his head swaying with the movement of the blade. Then the hatch cover was thrown aside, light and a thin boil of smoke poured in, and the huge shadow of the Baron hurtled down the stairs. He dropped into a crouch, his own knife at the ready.

"Get your ass away from him, Papa," he said.

Simpkins groaned, struggled to rise, and the Baron kicked him in the side.

Papa did not reply, circling, and in the midst of a step he made a clever lunge and sliced the Baron's chest with the tip of his knife, drawing a line of blood across his shirt front.

"Hurry!" shouted Jocundra from the hatch. "It's spreading!"

Simpkins rolled off the floor, still clutching his groin, and limped up the stairs. Jocundra cried out, but immediately after called again for them to hurry.

Flames began to crackle on the wall behind Donnell, and as he looked, they burst in all directions to trace the image of a woman very like Otille. It might have been a caricature of her, having her serpentine hair, her wry smile: a fiery face floating on the blackness. Donnell got to his feet, weak from Papa's manipulations; too weak, he thought, to engage Papa physically. He searched around for a stick, any sort of weapon, and finding none, he dug into his pocket and pulled out a handful of coins.

"Hey, Papa," he said, and sailed one of the coins at him. It missed, clinking against the wall. But even the miss caused Papa to lose concentration, and the Baron slashed and touched his hip.

Papa let out a yip and danced away, steadying himself; he cast a vengeful look at Donnell, and as Donnell sailed another coin, he snarled. The Baron nicked his wrist with a second pass and avoided a return swipe.

"You done lost the flow, Papa," chanted the Baron. "That iron gettin' heavy in your hand. Your balls is startin' to freeze up. You gon' die, motherfucker!"

Donnell kept throwing the coins, zinging them as hard as he could, and then—as he threw it, his fingers recognized the bulge of Mr. Brisbeau's lucky piece—the last coin struck Papa near his eye. He clapped his hand to the spot, and in doing so received a cut high on his knife arm. He backed up the stairs, ducking to keep the Baron in view; he half-turned to run, but something swung down from the open hatch and thunked against his head. He toppled into the hold face downward. A board fell across his legs.

"For God's sake!" Jocundra yelled. "Hurry!"

As the Baron hustled him up the stairs, Donnell had a final glimpse of the fiery smile floating eerily in the dark, the eyes already absorbed into a wash of flame. Then Jocundra, her face smoke-stained, hauled him toward the rail and onto the dock. The Baron slipped off the mooring line and heaved against the boat with his shoulder, trying to push it out into the current.

"Gimme a hand, damn it!" he said. "Else this whole place liable to go up!"

All heaving together, they managed to nudge the boat a couple of feet off the dock, and there it sat, too heavy for the sluggish current to move.

Donnell collapsed against a piling, and Jocundra buried her face in his shoulder, holding him, shaking. His mind whirled with remnant threads of the strange story he had told the pets, and he almost wished he had not been interrupted so he could have learned the ending himself. He had been near to death, he realized, yet he had not been afraid, and he was thankful to the possessive arrogance of his inner self for sparing him fear. But now he reacted to the fear and held to Jocundra, exulting in the jolt of her pulse against his arm.

"That goddamn Clothilde," said the Baron; he was peeling his shirt away from the cut on his chest. "Seem like she gon' have her funeral party after all."

The way the sternwheeler burned was equally beautiful and monstrous. Lines of flame crisscrossed the walls, touching off patterns buried in the paint, repeating the *veve* of Mounanchou and Clothilde's face over and over again, as well as *petro* designs: knives stuck into hearts, hanged men, beheaded goats. Little trains of fire scooted along the railings, illuminating the gingerbread work and support posts. Torches flared at the corners of the roof. Other flames chased each other in and out of passageways with merry abandon, sparking windowframes and hatch covers, until the entire boat was dressed in mystic configurations and fancywork of yellow-red flames, as though for a carnival. Amid a groaning of timbers, the smokestack cannonaded sparks and fell into the bayou, venting a great hiss, and thus lightened, the boat began to turn in a stately clockwise circle, its fiery designs eroding into the general conflagration. The paint of the hull blistered into black wartlike protuberances, the sky above the raging upper deck was distorted by a transparency of flame, and the sound of the fire was the sound of bones splintering in the mouth of a beast. A horrid reek drifted on the breeze.

The boat was about twenty feet off the dock, the prow pointing almost directly toward them, when Papa Salvatino stumbled out of the hatch, coughing, his trousers smoldering. He staggered along the deck, looked up, and they heard him scream as a blazing section of the upper railing fell away and dropped upon him, closing a burning fist around him and bearing him over the side. Charred boards floated off, and in a moment his head reappeared. He raised his arm. It seemed a carefree gesture, a wave to his friends on shore. The boat, continuing to turn, blocked their view of him, turning and turning, a magician's black castle spinning through fire to another dimension, and when it had passed over the spot where he had been, the water was empty of flotsam, undisturbed, reflecting a silken blue like a sheet from which all the wrinkles have been removed by the passage of a hand.

CHAPTER XVII

August 18–September 12, 1987

"Musta got caught up in the mangrove," said the Baron when Papa Salvatino's body could not be found. "Or else," he said, and grinned, not in the least distressed, "there's a gator driftin' out there somewhere's with a mean case of the shits."

Otille, however, was not amused. Screams and the noise of breakage were reported from the attic, and the "friends" slunk about the downstairs, fleeing to the cabins at the slightest suspicion of her presence. But to Jocundra's knowledge, Otille left her rooms only once between the day of

Papa's death and the completion of the *veve*—a period of more than two weeks—and then it was to oversee the punishment of Clea, Simpkins and Downey. She had them tied to the porch railing of the main house and beaten with bamboo canes, the beating applied by a fat, swarthy man apparently imported especially for the occasion. Clea screeched and sobbed, Downey whimpered and begged, Simpkins—to Jocundra's surprise—howled like a dog with every stroke. The "friends" huddled together in front of the porch, sullen and fearful, and in the manner of an evil plantation queen, Otille stood cold and aloof in the doorway. Her black mourning dress blended so absolutely with the boards that it seemed to Jocundra her porcelain face and hands were disembodied, inset, the antithesis of the ebony faces and limbs inside.

Without Otille's demands to contend with, Donnell relaxed and became less withdrawn, though he still would not talk about his thoughts or his days among the pets. But for a time it was as if they were back at Mr. Brisbeau's. They walked and made love and explored the crannies of the house. They were free of pets and "friends," of everyone except the Baron, who continued to exercise the role of bodyguard. Yet as the *veve*'s date of completion neared, Donnell grew edgy. "What if it doesn't work?" he would ask, and she would answer, "You believe it's going to, don't you?" He would nod, appear confident for a while, but the question always popped up again. "If it doesn't," she suggested, "there's always the project." He said he would have to think about that.

Jocundra had visited the construction site often, but because of the swarm of workmen and the *veve*'s unfinished state, she had gained no real impression of how it would look. And so, on the night Donnell first used it, when she climbed to the top of the last conical hill and gazed down into the depression where it lay, she was taken aback by its appearance. Three tons of copper, seventy feet long and fifty wide, composed of welded strips and mounted on supports a couple of feet high driven into the ground. Surrounding the clearing was a jungly thickness of oaks, many of them dead and vine-shrouded, towered over by a lone cypress; the spot from which Jocundra, Otille and the Baron were to observe was arched over by two epiphyte-laden branches. Floodlights were hung in the trees, angled downward and rippling up the copper surfaces. Bats, dazed by the lights, skimmed low above the *veve* and thumped into the oak trunks. The ground below it had been bulldozed into a circle of black dirt, and this made the great design seem like a glowing brand poised to sear the earth.

"I certainly hope this works," said Otille without emotion. She still wore her mourning dress for Papa, and Jocundra believed her grief was real. A cold, ritual grief, but deeply felt all the same. Beside her, the Baron settled a video camera on his shoulder.

"Good luck," Jocundra whispered, hugging Donnell.

"The worst that can happen is that I fall off," he said. He tried a smile but it didn't fit. Then he gave her another hug and went down the hill. He looked insignificant against the mass of copper, his jeans and shirt ridiculously modern in conjunction with its archaic pattern. She had the feeling it might suddenly uncoil, revealing itself to have been a copper serpent all along, and swallow him up, and she crossed her fingers behind her back, wishing she could come closer to a prayer than a child's charm, that like her mother she could find comfort at the feet of an idol, or that like Donnell she could shape her faith to the twists and turns of the *veve*.

If even *he* could.

What if it didn't work?

Shortly after he began walking atop the *veve*, a wind kicked up. Jocundra had been expecting it, but Otille became flustered. She darted her head from side to side as if hearing dread whispers, and she picked at the folds of her skirt. She started to say something to Jocundra, but instead took a deep breath and thinned her mouth. The Baron glued his eye to the viewfinder, unmindful of the wind, which now was circling the perimeter of the clearing, moving sluggishly, its passage evident by the lifting of branches and shivering leaves. Each circuit lasted for a slow count of ten. Strands of Otille's hair plastered against her cheek like whip marks every time the wind blew past; she stared open-mouthed, and Jocundra gave her a reassuring smile, then wondered how she could be so reassuring. A burst of static charges crackled along her neck, the hair of her forearms prickled. The air was chilling rapidly, and despite the humidity, her skin felt parched. With every few revolutions, the force of the wind increased appreciably. Hanks of gray moss were ripped from the branches, leaf storms whirled up, and the wind began to pour over the hilltop, its howl oscillating faster and faster, around and around.

Yet through all this Donnell's clothes hung limp, and he had done nothing more than walk.

The Baron staggered and nearly fell, overbalanced by the camera. Otille helped to brace him, but only for a moment. Then she screamed as the top branch of the largest oak tore loose and sailed away. Jocundra scrambled down into the lee of the hill and peered out over the edge. Donnell was standing on a central junction of the *veve*, swaying; his hands waved above his head in languid gestures, the gestures of a pagan priest entreating his god. And she remembered the films she had seen of possession rites, the celebrants' feet rooted, their arms waving in these same ecstatic gestures. Otille came crawling down, clutching at her. But Jocundra drew back in fright. Otille's hair was rising into Medusa coils over her head, twisting and snapping. Out of reflex, Jocundra touched her own hair. It eeled away from her fingers. Her blouse belled, as did her jeans, repelled by the charge accumulating on her skin. Otille pointed toward the *veve*, her face pleading some question. Jocundra followed her point, and this time, as her own scream shattered in her throat unheard, she had no thought of offering reassurance.

Movement, Donnell soon discovered, was the key to operating the *veve*. The magnetic fields of the copper were blurs of opaque white light, clouds of it, hovering, vanishing, fading into view; they drifted away from his hands whenever he tried to manipulate them. He walked along, trying this and that to no avail, and then realized he had been walking the course directed by the movements of the bacteria. He could feel them more discretely than ever, more strongly, a warm trickling inside his head. He continued to walk, following a trail inward, and from every junction of the *veve* but one—and that one, he saw, was to be his destination—a strand of white fire rose, forming into a webwork building up and up around him, a towerlike structure. High above, the milky specter of the geomagnetic field winked in and out across the sky, and he understood that the complicated flows of the web and his own path were in harmony with it, adapting to its changes. His customary weakness ebbed and he walked faster, causing the structure of the fields to rise higher and become more complex. His new strength acted as a drug, and his thoughts were subsumed by the play of his muscles, the rush of his blood. The fields were singing to him, a reedy insect chorus filling his ears, and he came to know his path as a shaman's dance, an emblem etched upon the floor of the universe by an act both of will and physicality. Then the movements of the bacteria ceased, and he stopped dead center of his predestined junction.

A tower of incendiary wires, intricate as lace, rose around him into the sky, and the geomagnetic field no longer flickered, but was a white road curving from horizon to horizon. Its cold gleam seemed to embody a unity of object and event, being both a destination and a road. Almost tearful, knowing himself unable to reach it yet reaching anyway, like a child trying to touch a star, he lifted his hands to it. The lowest strands of the tower shot toward him and grafted to his fingertips, and at the same time, the geomagnetic field bulged downward, its center fraying into strands that joined with the tower. A flash whitened the sky, and as the light decayed from the outer edges of the flash, it resolved into a latticework of fire, all of its strands flowing inward and pouring down into his outstretched hands.

He had not known his body could encompass such a feeling of power. It was like existing on the boiling edges of a cloud—a place where the borders between the material and immaterial were ceaselessly being redefined—and drawing energy from the transformations. A rapturous strength burned in him. For a moment his eyes were dazzled with whiteness, his consciousness drawn into an involvement of which love and joy, all human emotion, were but fractionated ideals.

Groggy, he blinked and shook his head and looked around.

He might have been standing inside a knot tied in a black rope, gazing up through the interstices at sections of a pale purple ceiling. But directly above him, perhaps a hundred feet distant and visible between coils of black wood, was a castle turret. He recognized it as the turret of Ghazes, the disciplinary post of the Yoalo high in the brambly growth of Moselantja. Characters testifying to the public desire for self-abnegation were carved in the teeth of the battlements.

The apparition of the turret was so unexpected, looming over him like a wave about to crash, that he flung out his right hand in a futile attempt to ward it off. His hand was a negative, featureless black; his fingers shimmered, and gouts of iridescent fire lanced from their tips, merging to a single beam and splashing against the turret, halating it with a rainbow brilliance. He tried to jerk back his hand, but it was locked in position; he wrenched and threw himself in all directions until he sagged from exhaustion, literally hanging by his arm. A few yards away, he made out a fanged door opening into one of the stems, the wall inside furred with lichen that shed a fishbelly phosphorescence. The air stank of ozone, and everything was motionless, soundless.

But then he heard a sound.

At first he thought it was speech of a sort, for it had the rhythm and sonority of words pronounced by a leathery tongue. He stared back over his shoulder and saw something bob up in silhouette against the sky, sink behind a stem and rise again. Something awkward and long-winged, with the bulbous body of a fly. Another creature appeared, another, and another yet. There were at least a dozen, all flapping lazily toward him through the maze of stems.

Once more, this time choking with fear, he tried to wrench himself free. Fire still lanced from his fingertips. The radiance about the turret was pulsing, and the turret itself rippled. Then, berating himself for stupidity, he remembered how to disengage the weapon capacity of the suit. He formed his hand into a claw so that the five beams splashed into each other and slowly brought his fingers together until they met.

The foremost of the beasts cleared the stem beyond his, its face a horror of white-rimmed eyes, an ape's flat nose, needle teeth, tendrils flapping from its lips. It beat its wings, gaining altitude for a dive, and he caught a whiff of fetor and a glimpse of its scabbed underbelly. He crouched down, but a wing buffeted the side of his head and sent him reeling to the edge of the stem. As he teetered, he saw below a puzzle of purple gleam and shadow and interlocking stems. Falling, he clawed at the air and felt a tension on his fingertips.

His fall should have been endless. He should have caromed off the infinity of stems beneath, being battered into shapelessness and blood. But he fell only a couple of feet through a burst of white glory and landed on his side. Dazed, he rolled onto his back. Overhead, slung like a sagging hammock, the crescent moon held sway amid the pinprick stars of a Louisiana night.

The wind shredded Jocundra's scream. From Donnell's fingers a stream of numinous energy, the ghost of a beam, lanced toward the top of the cypress tree. He was struggling as if his arm were gripped by a transparent vise, throwing himself backward, panicked. She started crawling down the hill, but the wind knocked her flat. Crumpled wrappers, tin cans, bottles and twigs skittered along the ground, all shining with coronas; the air was full of stinging grit. Something smacked against her cheek, clung for a second with sticky claws, dropped down into her blouse and walked across her breasts. She rolled over, beating at her chest until a half-crushed cricket fell out and flipped away in the wind, leaving a wet smear on her belly. She looked up just as Donnell toppled off the *veve*, and as the cypress top, surrounded by a halo of ghostly radiance, exploded.

At least it began as an explosion.

There was a blast, flames rayed out, a fireball grew. But when it had reached the limit of its expansion, the fireball did not shrink or dissipate into smoke. Instead, it held its shape; then the flames paled and condensed into a cloud of ruby sparks, which themselves settled into the outlines of a mechanism, one of enigmatic complexity. A piece of jeweled clockwork that folded in upon itself and receded into a previously unnoticed distance: a dark tunnel collapsed through the night sky. The last of the wind went with it, giving out a keening cry that set Jocundra's teeth on edge.

By the time she had crossed the *veve* to the spot where Donnell had fallen, he was sitting up and staring at the blasted cypress. Blood streamed from his nostrils. She jumped down beside him, held his head, and pinched his nostrils to staunch the flow. His eyes showed hardly any green. Thinking it might just be the brightness of the floodlights, she shaded them with her hand. A few flickers, vivid, but only a few.

"I feel good," he said. "My heart's not as erratic." He gazed up at her. "My eyes?"

She nodded, unable to speak, her own eyes brimming. She put her arms around him and rested her head on the back of his neck.

"You're smothering me," he mumbled, but held tightly to her waist.

A scream rang out from the hilltop. Jocundra looked back to see Otille struggling in the Baron's grasp. She swung her head back and forth, kicked his legs with her heels. He picked her up and started toward the house; but Otille managed a final scream, and this time it was intelligible. One word.

"Ogoun!"

Donnell stared at the hilltop long after they had gone, and though his features were calm, Jocundra thought she could detect a mixture of hatred and longing in his expression. "What's wrong with her?" he asked.

"The wind frightened her," she said. "And the tree. What did happen with the tree?"

"I don't know," he muttered. "An accident. Maybe you can figure it out." He turned to the cypress. A thin smoke curled from the ruin of its trunk, misting the stars. His voice became resonant, his tone sarcastic, as he said, "God knows what all this is going to do to Otille."

Within two days Donnell's eyes were as brilliant as ever, and he went back upon the *veve*, thereafter returning to it at least once a day. There was no danger of him overdoing it. While the treatment did serve to trim the size of the colony, it also appeared to have stimulated their rate of reproduction, and Jocundra doubted he could last much more than two weeks of abstinence. The Baron continued to film Donnell—he had dug a niche into the side of the hill for shelter against the wind—but Otille remained barricaded in her apartments. One experience with Donnell's newly augmented powers had apparently been enough. When asked about her, the Baron would grunt and make offhanded comments.

"Otille just need to sit and watch her forest grow," he said once. "She gon' get it back together." But he didn't seem to be convinced.

Terrified by the wind, which was shredding the jungles of Maravillosa as Donnell's power increased, growing in force and scope, some of the "friends" left the estate, and those who stayed hid out in the cabins. With the exception of Captain Tomorrow. He was delighted by the wind and had to be shooed away from the *veve*. Whenever he encountered Jocundra, he spoke to her in a scholarly fashion, informing her once that the physics of fantasy was "on the verge of actuation," and showing her his design for a thought-powered laser, inspired, he said, by Donnell's "wind trip."

As for Jocundra, since the Baron was present to watch over Donnell, she preferred to wait in their room during the treatments. Sometimes she worked on the principles underlying the operation of the *veve*, but she was not often successful in this. The wind unnerved her. Despite her rational understanding of it, charged ions, vacating air masses, she had the feeling it could carry the paper bearing her explanations off to a realm where explanations were no longer relevant. Mostly she thought about Donnell. He was hiding something from her, she believed, and she did not think it could be anything positive. His attitude toward the *veve* puzzled her. He had not been at all distressed to learn of his addiction to it; in fact, he had appeared relieved to learn he could use it frequently.

One evening, eleven days after the completion of the *veve*, while sitting at their window, listening to branches snap, leaves scuttering across the side of the house, Jocundra

noticed the corner of a notebook sticking out from beneath
their mattress. On first leafing through it, she thought it to
be notes for a new story because of the odd nomenclature
of towns and people, its references to the purple sun and
the Yoalo. But then she realized it was a journal of Donnell's
walks upon the *veve*. On the inside foreleaf was a sketch
of the *veve*, every junction numbered, and a list of what
seemed to be the ranks of the Yoalo. Inductee, Initiate,
Medium, Sub-aspect, Aspect, High Aspect. She had a twinge
of foreboding, and as she settled back to read the first entry,
she tried to tell herself it was only background for a story
written in diary form.

  Sept. 8. Ended up on Junction 14. The sun edging
down, a long pale bulge like a continental margin lifting
from the horizon, fringed by a corona of vivid purple.
Stars ablaze. No moon. Broken, barren hills to my left,
and I thought that Moselantja was somewhere behind
them. I was atop a cliff which fell away into a forested
valley. Massed empurpled trees locked in shadow, the
crooked track of a river cutting through, and two-thirds
of the way across the valley, at a forking of the river,
was a village laid out in a peculiar pattern, one I could
not quite discern because of my angle. I tried to shift
my field of focus forward; it was harder than usual.
Instead of snapping into place, it was as if I were pushing
through some barrier heavier than distance. Finally I
managed a perspective at eye level of the street. A door
opened in one of the houses; a man poked his head out,
gave a squeal of fright and ducked inside. How the hell
had he seen me? I looked down and saw that I was
sheathed in black. Shimmering, unfeatured black. Energy suit. I had been on a clifftop, and now was planted
smack in the midst of Rumelya (the name springing unbidden to mind). Memories flooded me, among them
information about the suit's capacity for nearly instantaneous travel along line-of-sight distances. The river—
the Quinza—was not safe for swimming, though I
couldn't recall why, and the name of the forest was the
Mothemelle.

  Bits of litter, black leaves, were drifting across the

dusty street. All the buildings were of weathered black wood, and most were of two stories, the topmost overhanging the lower and supported by carven posts. Every inch of the buildings was carved: lintels evolving into gargoyle's heads, roof peaks into ornate finials. The doorframes flowed with tiny faces intertwined with vines, and stranger faces yet—half flower, half beast—emerged from the walls. The similarity between these embellishments and those of Maravillosa was inescapable. Light issued from shutters pierced by scatters of star-shaped holes so that the appearance was of panels of night sky studded with orange stars. Though many of the details were not of my original invention—the names, for instance—it *was* the village of my story, complete down to the sign above the inn, an odd image I now recognized for a *petro* painting. The evilly tenanted forest looming over the roofs; the tense, secretive atmosphere; the cracked shells and litter blowing on the streets; it was all the same. Voices were raised inside the inn, and I had a strong intuition that some important event was soon to occur there.

As the sun's corona streamed higher above the forest, striking violet glints from the eddies in the river, I noticed an ideograph laid out in black dust centering the crossroads just ahead. The fitful breeze steadied, formed into a whirlwind over the ideograph, and dissipated it into a particulate haze. I had a memory of an old man wearing a dun-colored robe, bending over an orange glow, talking to me. His voice was hoarse and feeble, the creaking of a gate modulated into speech. "The stars are men's doubles," he said. "The wind is a soul without a body."

Shortly after this, I became afraid I would not be able to leave Rumelya. I had—hadn't I?—moved from my position on the *veve*. I walked back and forth, left and right, attempting to fall off as I had the first time. To no avail. Then, just as had happened beneath the turret of Ghazes, I recalled the necessary function of my suit, that it acted to orient me within the geomagnetic field. I reached up and felt the connections in the air. Again, the mystic experience of transition. It was losing its impact, and I remember thinking during transit that such depersonalized ecstasy might grow boring. I found myself back on Junction 14 waving my arms like a man drowning.

By the time she had finished half the entries, Jocundra's foreboding had matured into disastrous knowledge. Either the immense electromagnetic forces were unhinging him, fueling fantasies with which to form a surrogate past, or—and this she could not fully disbelieve—he was actually traveling somewhere. No matter what the case, and though she was certain he had not told her to protect her from worry, his secrecy was a barrier between them.

The last entry in the journal detailed his arrival in a great hall whose walls were ranked to the ceiling with mirrors. Translucent creatures—"crystalline imperfections in the air, as quick as hummingbirds"—flew between the mirrors. Images appeared in their wake. One mirror held a view of golden-edged green scales shifting back and forth, as though the coils of an enormous snake enwrapped the hall; a second showed a gem-studded game board, its counters swathed in cobweb; a third depicted a black-suited Yoalo standing atop one of the turrets of Moselantja, spinning around and around, his arms raised overhead, becoming more and more transparent until only a wind whirled in his place, bearing up dust from the turret floor. Each successive mirror image caused him to recall bits and details: the movements of military forces, names, a sequence of letters and numbers which reminded Jocundra of astronomical coordinates. A final mirror offered him the sight of a woman leaning forward, herself looking into a mirror, her face obscured by a fall of dark hair; she then bent her head and lifted her hair up behind her.

I was overcome with longing. The shade of her hair was identical to Jocundra's, dark brown wound through with gold, and her movements were Jocundra's, the way she held her back perfectly straight while bending. I envisioned the old man once again, his shoulders hunched, holding out something to me: an ivory sphere, one of those conceits carved and hollowed with smaller spheres within. It was cradled in his palm like a pearl in the meat of an oyster. "If you lose something," he said, "you will find it here. And if it truly is yours, it will return to you." I knew then that this woman, whether Jocundra by name or some other, was bound to me through worlds and time, and that all I had seen within the mirrors were the elements of days to come.

Jocundra set down the journal and went to the window. He was, it appeared, thinking about losing her, and now this same thought infected her. Though it was something she had once taken for granted, the prospect had become terrifying, impossible to accept. The house shuddered. Branches clawed and scuttered against the outer walls. She wished she had a word with which to shout down the wind, an incantation to still it, because it seemed to her a howling prophecy of loss. But growing stronger, it sang in the eaves and shaped groaning, inarticulate words from the open windows, mournful sounds, like sad monsters waking with questions on their minds.

The pale sun, its corona shrunk to a cyanotic rim, showed an arc above the forest of Mothemelle. Donnell stood with an ear pressed to the window of the inn at Rumelya, trying to assure himself that there were no patrons inside. At last, hearing only a tuneless singing, the clatter of crockery, he pushed in the door. A dumpy serving girl threw up an armload of dishes and ran through a curtained doorway, leaving him alone in the common room. Long gray benches and boards; whitewashed walls, one having a curtained niche; floors of packed sand littered with scraps of gristle, bones, and a striped lizard curled around a table leg; a high ceiling crossed by heavy beams and hung with ladles and pans of black iron. He took a seat near the door and waited. The most peculiar thing about the room was the orange light. It had no apparent source; the room was simply filled with it.

The innkeeper proved to be a chubby young man, his eyes set close together above a squidgy nose and a cherubic mouth. He wore a tunic of coarse cloth, an apron, and carried a tray holding a chipped ceramic mug. "Brew?" he asked hopefully, his lips aquiver. Donnell nodded, and the innkeeper set down the mug, jerking back his hand. "Sir," he said, "uh, Lord, uh..." Donnell looked up at him, and he stiffened.

Donnell indicated the curtained niche. "I will watch from there tonight," he said, toying with the handle of his mug. Black sparks from his fingers adhered to the ceramic, jittering a second and vanishing.

"Certainly, Lord." The innkeeper clasped his hands in an attitude of obeisance. "But, Lord, are you aware that the Aspect comes here of an evening?"

"Yes," said Donnell, not aware in the least. He picked up the mug—vile-smelling stuff, fermented tree bark—and carried it to the table behind the curtain. "Where does he usually sit?" he asked. The innkeeper pointed at a spot by the rear wall, and Donnell adjusted the curtain to provide an uninhibited view. He felt no need to urge the innkeeper to be close mouthed about his presence. The man's fear was excessive.

Over the next half hour, seven men filtered into the inn. They might have been cousins, all dark-haired and heavy-boned, ranging from youth to middle age, and all were dressed in fish-hide leggings and loose shirts. Their mood was weary and their talk unenthused, mostly concerned with certain tricky currents which had arisen of late in the river, due, one said, to "meddling." Their language, though Donnell had assumed it to be English, was harsh, many words having the sound of a horse munching an apple, and he realized he had been conversing in it quite handily.

Another half hour passed, two men left, three more arrived, and then a wind blew open the door, swirling the sand. A man wearing the black of the Yoalo entered and threw himself down on a bench by the far wall. His face made Donnell wish for a mirror. It was a bestial mask occupying an oval inset in the black stuff. Satiny-looking vermillion cheeks, an ivory forehead figured by stylized lines of rage, golden eyes with slit pupils, a fanged mouth which moved when he spoke. Every one of its features reacted to the musculature beneath. He proceeded to swallow mug after mug of the brew, tossing them off in silence, signaling the serving girl for more. Once he grabbed for

her, and as she skipped away, he laughed. "Trying to tame
these country sluts is like trying to cage the wind," he said
loudly. His voice was vibrationless and of startling resonance. All the men laughed and went back to their conversations. Though he was Yoalo, they accorded him only
a token respect, and Donnell thought that if he was Aspect
here, he would require of them a more rigorous courtesy.

The man drank heavily for a while, apparently depressed;
he stared at his feet, scuffing the sand. At length, he hailed
the innkeeper and invited him to sit. "Anyone I ought to
know about?" he asked.

"Well," said the innkeeper, studiously avoiding looking
at the niche, "there was a trickster by last week." And then,
becoming enthusiastic, he added, "He sent red flames shooting out of the wine bottles."

"Name?" inquired the Yoalo, then waved off the question. "Never mind. Probably one of those vagabonds who
was camped in the southern crevices. Must have stolen a
scrap of power with which to impress the bumpkins."

The innkeeper looked hurt and bumpkinish. "I wish I
could see Moselantja."

"Easy enough," said the Yoalo. "Volunteer." He laughed
a sneering laugh, and began a boastful account of the wonders of Moselantja, of his various campaigns, of the speeds
and distances attained by his "ourdha," a word Donnell
translated as "windy soul."

All at once the door banged open, and a ragged old man,
his clothes patched and holed, baskets of various sizes slung
about his shoulder, came into the inn. "Snakes!" he cried.
"Plump full of poison!" He plucked a large banded snake
from one of the baskets and held it up for all to see. The
village men gave forth with nods and murmurs of admira-
tion, but claimed to be already well supplied with snakes.
The old man put on a doleful face, wrinkling so deeply he
had the look of a woodcarving. Then he spied the Yoalo
and did a little caper toward him, flaunting the snake and
whistling.

Furious at this interruption, the Yoalo jumped up and
seized the snake. Blood spurted out the sides of his fist,
and the severed halves of the snake dropped to the sand,

writhing. He aimed a backhand at the old man, who dove onto the floor, and weaved toward the door and into the street. With the exception of the snake-seller—he was bemoaning the loss of his prize catch—the village men remained calm, shrugging, joking about the incident. But upon seeing Donnell emerge from the niche, they knocked over their benches and scrambled to the opposite end of the room.

"Lord!" cried the snake-seller, crawling into Donnell's path. "My eldest was a tenth-level recruit of your cadre. Hear me!"

"Tenth-level," said Donnell. "Then he died upon the turret."

"But well, Lord. He gave no outcry."

"I will listen." Donnell folded his arms, amused by his easy acceptance of rank, but quite prepared to exercise its duties.

"This," said the old man, picking up the snake's head, "this is nothing to the abuses we of Rumelya suffer. But to me this is much."

He began a lengthy tale of its capture, half a day spent among the rocks, tempting it with a gobbet of meat on a forked stick, breaking its teeth with a twist when it struck. He testified to its worth and listed the Yoalo's other abuses. Rape, robbery, assault. His complaint was not the nature of the offenses—they were his right—but that they were performed with such vicious erraticism they had the character of a madman's excesses rather than the strictures of a conqueror. He begged for surcease.

The old man's eyes watered; his skin was moley; his forearms were pitted with scarred puckers, places where he had been bitten and had cut away the flesh to prevent the spread of the poison. These imperfections grated on Donnell, but he did not let them affect his judgment.

"It will be considered," he said. "But consider this. I have witnessed great disrespect in Rumelya, and perhaps it is due. But had you honored the Aspect properly, he might well have served you better. Should another take his place, your laxity will be counted a factor in determining the measures of governance." As he left, he heard the village men haranguing the snake-seller for his lack of caution.

The Yoalo's trail—rayed depressions in the sand—turned left, left again, and Donnell saw the river at the end of the street. Above the treeline on the far bank, the sun's corona raised purple auroras into the night sky, and the stars were so large and bright they appeared to be dancing about into new alignments. The street gave out onto a grassy bank where several long canoes were overturned, and sitting upon one of these was the shadowy figure of the Yoalo. In order to get close, Donnell shifted his visual field forward as he had done on his first visit to the village. This time he noticed a shimmering, inconstant feeling in all his flesh as the suit bore him to the rear of a shed some twenty feet along the bank from the Yoalo's canoe. The man was rocking back and forth, chuckling, probably delighting in the incident of the snake. He touched his forehead, the mask wavered and disappeared. But before Donnell could see his face, the man flattened onto his stomach, leaned out above the river and splashed water over himself. Something *ki-yied* deep in the forest, a fierce and solitary cry that might have come from a metal throat. Sputtering, the Yoalo propped himself up on an elbow, staring off in Donnell's direction.

Except for the fact that his eyes were dark, betraying no hint of green, he was the spitting image of Jack Richmond. Skull-featured, thin to the point of emaciation.

All the man's behavior, his fits of violence and depression, his harassment of the serving girl, his obsession with speed, clicked into focus for Donnell. He was about to call to him when the man came up into a crouch, his right hand extended, alerted by something. With his left hand, he reached inside his suit and pulled forth a construction of—it seemed—wires and diamonds, and flicked it open. Its unfolding was a slow organic process, a constant evolution into new alignments like the agitated stars overhead. Drunkenly, the Yoalo stared at it, swaying, then fell on his back; he rolled over and up, and iridescent beams of fire spat from his hand toward a dark object on the bank. It burst into flames, showing itself to be a stack of bales, one of several such stacks dotting the shore.

The Yoalo shook his head at his own foolishness, chuckled, and folded the bright contraption; it shrank to a sparkle of sapphire light as he pocketed it, as if he had collapsed a small galaxy into a single sun. He touched his forehead, and the mask reappeared. Then he went staggering down the bank, his hand extended, firing at the stacked bales, setting every one of them ablaze. With each burst, he shouted, "Ogoun!" and laughed. His laughter grew in volume, becoming ear-splitting, obviously amplified; it ricocheted off the waterfront buildings. The fires sent dervish shadows leaping up the street, casting gleams over the carved faces on the walls, and illuminated the ebony flow of the river and the thick vegetation of the far bank.

Amid a welter of spear-shaped leaves, Donnell saw the movements of low-slung bodies. But, he thought, the truly dangerous animal wore a suit of negative black and roamed the streets of Rumelya without challenge. A vandal, a coarse outlaw. Yet though he despised the man's abuse of privilege, he was captivated by the drama of the scene. This maniacal warrior with the face of a beast howling his laughter, taunting the lie-abed burghers and fishermen; the rush of dark water; the auroral veils billowing over the deep forest; the slinking animals. It was like a nerve of existence laid bare, a glistening circuit with the impact of a one line poem. He filed the scene away, thinking he might compose the poem during his next period of meditation. Half in salute, honoring the vitality of what he had witnessed, half a warning, he sent a burst of his own fire to scorch the earth at the Yoalo's feet. And then he lifted his hands to engage the fields and returned to Maravillosa.

The sky was graying, coming up dawn. One of the bushes near the *veve* was a blackened skeleton, wisps of smoke curling from the twig ends. He sat down cross-legged on the ground. Within the fields, he thought, he was a far different person than the one who now doubted the validity of the experience. Not that he was capable of real doubt. The whole question was basically uninteresting.

"Hey, monkey!" The Baron waved from the hilltop.

The wind must have been bad. An avenue had been gouged through the undergrowth, and he could see a portion of the house between the hills. Gables, the top of his bed-

room window. Jocundra would be asleep, her long legs
drawn up, her hand trailing across his pillow.

"Man," said the Baron, coming toward him. "You got
to control this shit!" He gestured at the battered foliage.

Donnell shrugged. "What can I do?"

The Baron sat down on the *veve*. "I don't know, man,"
he said, sounding discouraged. "Maybe the best thing can
happen is for it to all blow away." He spat. "You got another
nosebleed, man."

Donnell wiped his upper lip. Blood smeared and settled
into the lines of his palm, seeming to form a character, one
which had much in common with a tangle of epiphytic stalks
and blooms blown beside the *veve:* fleshy leaves, violet
florets. More circuitry ripped up from beneath the skin of
the world. Every object, the old man had said, is but an
interpretation of every other object. There is no sure knowledge, only endless process.

"When you first come here, man," said the Baron, "I
thought you was sleaze like Papa and them other uglies.
But I got to admit you unusual." He coughed and spat again.
"Things is gettin' pretty loose up in the attic. You and me
should have a talk sometime 'bout what's happenin' 'round
here."

"Yeah," said Donnell, suddenly alert to his weariness,
to the fact that he was back in the world. "Not now, though.
I need some sleep."

But a few days later Otille sent the Baron away on business, and by the time he returned things had gone beyond
the talking stage.

CHAPTER XVIII

September 15–September 19, 1987

Ordinarily they would have been asleep at three o'clock in the morning, but for some reason Jocundra's adrenaline was flowing and she just tossed and turned.

"Let's get something to eat," she suggested, and since Donnell had also been having trouble sleeping, he was agreeable.

It was creepy poking around the house at night, though not seriously so: like sneaking into a funhouse after hours, when all the monsters have been tucked into their niches. These days it was rare to see anyone walking the corridors of Maravillosa. Clea and Downey had moved in together and were busy—said the Baron with a wink—"lickin' each other's wounds, you unnerstan'?" Simpkins, as always, kept aloof. Only two of the "friends" remained, a chubby man and, of course, Captain Tomorrow, whom Jocundra had come to think of as a ragged blackbird perched on a volume of Poe stories, pronouncing contemporary "Nevermores." And Otille never ventured downstairs. Jocundra imagined her wandering through her ebony shrubs, quoting Ophelia's speeches; and that set her to remembering how, during the early days of the project, Laura Petit had labeled certain of the patients "Opheliacs" because of their tendency to babble and cry. Jocundra had had one such patient, a thirtyish man with fine, pale red hair, fleshy, an academic suicide. He had licked the maroon stripe of the wallpaper, and at the end, unable to speak coherently, he had tried to proposition her by making woeful faces and exaggerated gestures, reminding her of Quasimodo entreating Esmerelda. She had nearly quit the project after his death.

Moonlight laid jagged patterns of light and shadow over the downstairs corridors, casting images of windows and blinds splintered by the wind. They had considered walking outside, but it started to drizzle and so they stood on the porch instead. The rain had a clean, fragrant smell, and its gentleness, the steady drip from the eaves, gave Jocundra the feeling of being a survivor, of emerging from a battered house to inspect the aftermath of a storm. As her eyes adjusted to the dark, she saw something gleaming out along the drive. A car. Long; some pale color; maybe gray.

"Company," she said, pointing it out to Donnell.

"No doubt Otille has found solace in a lover's arms," he said. "Or else they're delivering a fresh supply of bats to the attic."

"I wonder who it is, though."

"Let's go to the kitchen," he said. "I'm hungry."

But on the way to the kitchen, they heard voices from Otille's office.

"I don't want to get involved with her tonight," said Donnell, trying to steer her away.

"I want to see who it is," she whispered. "Come on."

They eased along the wall toward the office, avoiding shards of window glass.

". . . does seem that the hybrid ameliorates the tendency to violence," said a man's voice. "But after seeing him . . ."

"It's not his fault he's the way he is," said Otille. "It's probably mine."

"Be that as it may," said the man patiently. "We're not ready for live tests. Look. If your family's problems do result from a congenital factor in the DNA, and I'm not convinced they do . . ."

Jocundra recognized the voice, though she found it hard to believe that he would be here.

"I'm so sick of being like this," said Otille.

Jocundra pushed Donnell away, shaping the man's name with her lips, but he resisted.

"Have you been taking your medication?" asked the man.

"It makes me queasy."

"Evenin', folks," said Simpkins. He was standing behind Donnell, an apple in one hand, a kitchen knife in the other;

he gestured toward the office with the knife.

Donnell hardly reacted to him. "Ezawa!" he said, and brushed past Jocundra into the office. Simpkins urged her to follow.

Otille was standing against the wall, distraught, her hair in tangles, a black silk robe half open to her waist. Jocundra had not seen her since the night Donnell first used the *veve*, and she was startled by the changes in her. All the hollows of her face had deepened, and her eyes seemed larger, darker, gone black like old collapsed lights. Ezawa was behind the desk, his legs crossed, the image of control. He ran a hand through his shock of white hair and said to Otille, "This is unfortunate."

"It was inevitable," she said. "Don't worry, Yoshi. I'll take care of it." She leaned over the desk and pushed a button on the intercom. A man's cultivated voice answered, and Otille said, "Can you come meet my other guests?"

"Oh?" A rustling noise. "Certainly. I'll just be a few minutes."

"Do you need any help?"

"No, no. I'll be fine. I've been looking forward to this."

"The Rigaud Foundation," said Donnell suddenly; he had been staring at Ezawa. "They're funding the project."

"That's right," said Ezawa.

"And I've got the family disease. Christ!" He turned to Jocundra. "The new strain. They dug it out of her damn graveyard. Right?" he asked of Ezawa.

"Half right." Ezawa peered at Donnell, then settled back, building a church and steeple with his knitted fingers, tapping his thumbs together. The harsh lamplight paled his yellow complexion, making his moles seem as oddly shaped and black as flies, and despite his meticulous appearance, he looked soft, inflated with bad fluids.

"Actually," he said, "the entire project is a creation of the Foundation, of Valcours Rigaud specifically. He spent most of his later life trying to create zombies, and amazingly enough achieved a few short-lived reanimations. His method was clumsy, but there was a constant in his formulae—a spoonful of graveyard dirt placed in the corpse's mouth—and so I was led to my own researches." He sighed. "You,

Mr. Harrison, were injected with bacteria bred in Valcours' grave, as were Magnusson and Richmond. But . . ."

"That's impossible," blurted Jocundra. "Valcours is buried in the crypt. There's no dirt. The bacteria couldn't have bred."

"His head," said Otille; she was tying and untying the sash of her robe. "They buried it down by the pool."

"As I was saying," said Ezawa, frowning at Jocundra, then turning his attention back to Donnell. "You and Magnusson received a hybrid strain. One of the thrusts of the project, you see, has been to isolate a cure for Otille's hereditary disorder, and with that in mind, we interbred Valcours' bacteria with a strain taken from another grave located here on the grounds. The grave of Valcours' magus, his victim. Lucanor Aime."

"And Aime," said Donnell coldly, more calmly than Jocundra might have expected. "His patron deity, that would be Ogoun."

"Ogoun Badagris," murmured Otille.

"Astounding, isn't it?" said Ezawa. "The good magician and the evil apprentice still warring after over a century. Warring inside your head, Mr. Harrison. When Otille suggested the hybrid, I ridiculed the idea, but the results have been remarkable. It's enough to make me re-embrace the mysticism of my ancestors." He gave a snort of self-deprecating laughter. "The entire experience has been quasi-mystical, even the early days when the lab was full of caged rats and dogs and rabbits and monkeys, all with glowing, green eyes. Pagan science!"

"You're going to die, Ezawa," said Donnell angrily. "Just like in the movies, and pretty damn soon. One morning after this breaks, after the papers start howling for your blood, and they will, you can count on it, that old time religion of yours will stir you to wrap a white rag around your head and sit you down facing the sunrise with a fancy knife and a brain full of noble impulse. And the ironic part is that you're going to be swept away by the nobility of it all right up to the time you get a whiff of your bowels and see the tubes squirming out of your stomach."

He broke off and looked toward the door. Only Simpkins

was there, but Jocundra heard dragging footsteps in the hall.
"Who is it?" asked Donnell, whirling on Otille.

"He says he can feel you, too, but from much farther
away." Otille's voice was devoid of emotion.

"Our latest success with the new strain," said Ezawa.
"He's much stronger than you, Mr. Harrison. Or he will
be. I think we can credit that to his having been a full-
fledged psychic, not merely a latent one."

Donnell leaped toward Otille, furious, but Simpkins in-
tercepted him and threw him onto the floor. Otille never
blinked, never flinched.

"Fisticuffs," said a man at the door. "Marvelous! Wonderful!"

He wore a black silk bathrobe matching Otille's, carried
a cane, and the right side of his puffy face was swathed in
bandages; but both his eyes were visible. The irises flickered
green.

"Papa!" Jocundra gasped.

He regarded her distantly, puzzled, then inclined his head
to Donnell in a sardonic bow. "Valcours Rigaud at your
service, sir," he said. "I do hope you're not injured."

Jocundra took a step toward Ezawa. "You killed him!"
she said. "You must have!"

"It's questionable he would have lived," said Ezawa plac-
idly.

"Did you *kill* me, Otille?" Valcours affected a look of
hurt disillusionment. "You only told me I had died."

It was impossible to think of him as Papa anymore. He
was truly Valcours, thought Jocundra, if only a model conjured up by Otille. Death had remolded his face into a
sagging, pasty dumpling, reduced all his redneck vitality
into the dainty manners of a mouldering, middle-aged monster.

"I had to," said Otille; she walked over to him and took
up his hand. "Or else you wouldn't have come back."

Valcours drew her into a long, probing kiss, running his
free hand across her breasts. He cradled her head against
his chest. "Ah, well," he said. "The joys of life are worth
a spell of mindlessness and corruption. Don't you agree,
Mr. Harrison?"

Donnell sat up against the wall, his head lowered. "What have you got in mind, Otille?"

Valcours answered him. "There's a world of possibility to explore, Mr. Harrison. But as far as you're concerned, we'll keep you around until I learn about the *veve*, and as for your beautiful lady . . ." Before Jocundra could react, he prodded her breast with the tip of his cane. "I believe a fate worse than death would be in order." He laughed, a flighty laugh that tinkled higher and higher, traveling near the verge of hysteria. Tears of mirth streamed from his eyes, and he waved his hand, a foppish gesture that should have been accompanied by a lace handkerchief, signaling his helplessness at the humor of the situation.

"You had your chance," said Otille bitterly to Donnell. "I wanted you to help me."

"Help you rule the universe, like with the evil fairy there?" Donnell said. "I thought you wanted to be cured, Otille. How could I help you with that? But you don't want a cure. You want zombies and horrors and icky delights. And now"—he cast a disparaging glance at Valcours—"now your wish has come true."

"Be still!" said Valcours with a hiss of fury. He raised his cane to strike Donnell, and Jocundra recoiled, bumped against Simpkins, and jumped away from him. In his rage, Valcours possessed a malevolence previously muffled by his effete manner.

"You know, Ezawa," said Donnell, "you're in big trouble with all this. Maybe even bigger than you could expect. What if this fruit really is Valcours, what if you've really worked a miracle?"

"What if?" Valcours was once again the dandy, complaining of a gross indignity. "I'm the very soul of the man! Like the resin left in an opium pipe, the soul leaves its scrapings in the flesh. The essence, the pure narcotic of existence! Whether my dispersed shade has misted up anew, summoned forth by modern alchemies, or whether all is illusory, these are questions for philosophers and have no moment for men of action." He giggled, delighting in the flavor of his speech.

"See," said Donnell to Ezawa. "It's going to blow up in

your face. Fay Wray and the Mummy here will meet the Wolfman, have a group hallucination, and then comes the shitstorm. He's her puppet, and she's out of her fucking mind. Do you honestly believe they can keep it together?"

"Simpkins!" shouted Otille. "Get them out of here!"

Before Simpkins could cross the room, Valcours launched a feeble attack on Donnell, attempting to batter his legs with the cane. But Donnell rolled aside, pulled himself up by the desk and snatched the cane from Valcours. He spun Valcours around, levered the cane under his jaw and started to choke him.

"This bastard's weaker than I am," he said. "I bet I could crush his windpipe pretty damn quick."

Simpkins held his distance, looking to Otille for instruction; but she was again in thrall of the listlessness which had governed her during most of the encounter. Spit bubbled between Valcours' lips and he thrashed in Donnell's grasp.

"Look at her, Ezawa," said Donnell; he increased pressure on Valcours' throat until his eyes bulged and he hung limp, prying ineffectually at the cane. "Don't you see what they're hamming up between them? This is her big chance to make it in the Theater of the Real, to go public with her secret third act. A gala of obscenity. Otille and Valcours. Lord and Lady Monster together for the first time. Help us! Help yourself."

"I can't." Ezawa had risen and moved around to the side of the desk. "She'd ruin me."

"You're already ruined," said Donnell. "And it'll be worse if you let it go on. She's so far gone it won't stop until you're scraping dead virgins off the streets of New Orleans. This woman thinks evil's a nifty comic book and she's the villainous queen. Maybe she is! Whatever, she's going to do evil, and the word's going to get around. Help us! I'll finish this one, and we'll all jump Simpkins."

Ezawa's face worked, but his shoulders slumped. "No," he said.

"No, huh?" Donnell let Valcours sag to the floor. "Another time," he said, prodding him with his foot.

"Hit him," said Otille in a monotone. "Don't kill him, but hit him hard."

Jocundra draped herself around Simpkins' neck as he went for Donnell, but he threw her off and her head struck the desk. White lights seemed to shoot out of her eyes, pain wired through her skull, and someone was holding her wrist. Checking for a pulse, probably. She wanted to tell them she was all right, that she had a pulse, but her mouth wouldn't work. And just before she lost consciousness, she wondered if she did have a pulse after all.

On the fourth day of their confinement Jocundra remembered the trick door in the Baron's room, but for the first three days their position had appeared hopeless. Donnell's jaw was swollen, his eyes rapidly brightening, his skin paling, and he would scarcely say a word. He stared at the bedroom walls as if communicating with the peaceful ebony faces. The wind blew twice a day, not as strongly at first as it had for Donnell, but stronger each time, and they would watch out the window as Otille, invariably clad in her black silk robe, led Valcours back and forth between the *veve* and the house. Their meals were brought by Simpkins and the chubby "friend," an innocent-looking sort with close-set eyes and a Cupid's mouth, whose presence seemed to upset Donnell. Simpkins would wait in the hall, picking his teeth, commenting sarcastically, and on the evening of the third day he gave them some bad news.

"Brother Downey has gone the way of all flesh," he said. "We hog-tied him and put him on the *veve*, then the late Papa Salvatino started walking around and a pale glow came out of his fingers. Well, when that glow touched Brother Downey, you would have sworn he'd gotten religion. Quakin' and shakin' and yellin'. I was up on the hill and I could hear his bones snap. Looked like he'd been dropped off a skyscraper." He worried his gums with a toothpick. "Sister Clea ran off, or I reckon she was next. 'Bout the only reason you alive, brother, is Otille's scared of you. If it was up to me, I'd kill you quick."

It was then that Jocundra remembered the door. Two iron brads held it in place, but removing them was not the main problem.

"We've got to wire it so we can trip the release," said

Donnell. "Then we'll lure Simpkins in, try to trap him in the alcove, and hope we can take them one at a time."

They worked half the night at prying off the molding, both of them breaking fingernails in the process; they disconnected the release mechanism and undid the springs of their bed, straightening and knotting them together to attach to the mechanism; they jiggled loose two bed legs to use as clubs, shoring up the bed with books, and refined their plan.

"You'll be at the table," said Donnell, "and I'll be about here." He took a position halfway between the alcove and the table. "When the guy sets down the trays, I'll go for him. You drop the door as soon as Simpkins starts to move. Then you hit the other guy. The worst case will be two against two, and even if Simpkins does get through, maybe we can finish the other one off first."

"I don't know," she said. "When I hit Papa on the boat it was all reflexes. Fear. I don't know if I can plan to do it."

"I think you'll be sufficiently afraid," he said. "I know I will." He hefted his club. "Afterward, I'll head to the *veve* and see if I can get control of it."

While the wind was blowing the next morning, they ran a test of the door. Donnell stood on the table beneath it and caught it after it had fallen a couple of inches.

"Let's do it tonight," he said. "He's getting stronger all the time, but I still have a physical advantage. You keep away from the *veve* until it's over. Find some car keys, grab some of the videotapes. Maybe we can use them. But keep away from the *veve*."

Jocundra promised, and while he wound the bedsprings around the leg of the table beside her, she tried to prepare herself for swinging the club. It was carved into whorls on the bottom, but the business end was cut square and had an iron bolt sticking out from the side. The thought of what it could do to a face chilled her. She let it lie across her lap for a long time, because when she went to touch it her fingers felt nerveless, and she did not want to drop it and show her fear. Finally she set it against the wall and ran over the exact things she would have to do. Let go the wire, pick up the club, and swing it at the chubby man. The list acquired a singsong, lilting rhythm like a child's rhyme, drowning out her other thoughts, taunting her. *Let go the wire, pick up the club, and swing it at the chubby man.* She saw herself taking a swing, connecting, and him boinging away cartoon style, a goofy grin on his face, red stars and OUCHES and KAPOWS exploding above his head. Then she thought how it really would be, and she just didn't know if she could do it.

Donnell had never been more drawn to her than now, and though he was afraid, his fear was not as strong as his desire to be with her, to ease her fear. She was very nervous. She kept reaching down to check if her club was still leaning against the wall, rubbing her knuckles with the heel of her palm. Tension sharpened her features; her eyes were enormous and dark; she looked breakable. He couldn't think how to take her mind off things, but at last, near twilight, he brought a notebook out from his bureau drawer and handed it to her.

"What's this?" she asked.

"Pictures," he said; and then, choosing his tense carefully, because his tendency was to think of everything he had planned in the imperfect past, he added, "I might do something with them one of these days."

She turned the pages. "They're all about me!" she said; she smiled. "They're pretty, but they're so short."

He knelt down, reading along with her. "Most are meant to be fragments, short pieces—still they're not finished. Like this one." He pointed.

The gray rain hangs a curtain from the eaves
Behind her, as she tosses
The mildewed flowers to plop in the trash,
Tips the leaf-flocked vase water
Out the window, as she leans
Forward looking at the splash,
As she pours up from the ankle up to slim waist
And white breast and shawl of brown hair,
Every curve seems the process

Of an inexhaustible pouring,
Like the curves of a lotus.

"Just cleverness," he said. "I didn't do what I wanted to. But all together, and with some work, they might be something."

She turned another page. "They're not," she said, laughing.

"What?"

"My legs." She quoted: "'. . . the legs of a ghost woman, elongated by centuries of walking through the walls.' They're not that long." She spanked his hand playfully, then held up a folded piece of paper, one on which he had written down "The Song of Returning." He had forgotten about it. "What's this?" she asked.

"Just some old stuff," he said.

She read it, refolded the paper, but said nothing.

He rested his head on her forearm and was amazed by the peace that the warmth of her skin seemed to transmit, as if he had plunged his head into the arc of a prayer. He rubbed his cheek along her arm. Her fingers tangled in his hair, and he felt drifty. The lamplight shaded the skin of her arm from gold into pale olive, like delicate brushwork.

"Jocundra?"

"Yes?"

He wanted to tell her something, something that would serve as a goodbye in case things didn't go well; but everything he thought of sounded too final, too certain of disaster.

"Nothing," he said.

She bent her head close to his and let out a shuddery breath. "It'll be all right," she whispered.

Her reassurance reminded him of Shadows, how she had comforted him about the brightness of his eyes, his aches and pains; he felt a rush of anger. It had never been all right, and chances were it never would be. He did not know who to blame. Jocundra had made it bearable, and everyone else was either too weak or too riddled with sickness to be held responsible: it seemed that the whole world had *that* excuse for villainy.

There were footsteps and voices in the hall.

He fumbled with the wire, uncoiled it, thrust it into her hand, making sure she had the grip, and ran to his position near the alcove.

It almost didn't work. She almost waited too long. Simpkins yelled "Hey!" and came running in, and at first she thought the door had missed him. But then he pitched forward hard, as if someone had picked him up by the feet and slammed him down, and she saw that the door had pinned his ankle. The chubby man looked back at Simpkins just as Donnell swung, and the club glanced off the side of his head and sent him reeling against the wall. Simpkins screamed. The chubby man bounced off the wall and started walking dreamily toward Jocundra, his hands outstretched, a befuddled look on his face. Blood was trickling onto his ear. He heard Donnell behind him, turned, then—just as Jocundra swung—turned back, confused. She caught him flush on the mouth. He staggered away a step and dropped to his knees. He gave a weird, gurgling cry, and his hands fluttered about his mouth, afraid to touch it. A section of his lip was crushed and smeared up beneath his nose, and his gums were a mush of white fragments and blood. Donnell hit him on the neck, and he rolled under the table and lay still.

Simpkins' eyes were dilated, his face ashen, and he had begun to hyperventilate. The door had sunk a couple of inches into his leg above the ankle, and a crescent of his blood stained the wood. Just as they stooped to lift it, a pair of black hands slipped under from the other side and lifted it for them. Jocundra jumped back, Donnell readied his club. The door came up slowly, revealing a pair of brown trousers, a polo shirt, and then the sullen face of the Baron. Simpkins never noticed the door had been raised. His foot flopped at a ridiculous, straw-man angle, and he stared along the nap of the carpet with scrutinous intensity, as if he were reading a tricky green. His nostrils flared.

"You people don't need no damn help," said the Baron, surveying the carnage. Clea peeped out from behind him, depressed-looking and pale.

"Where's Otille?" asked Donnell.

"Seen her downstairs when we's headin' up," said the Baron; he kicked Simpkins' leg out of the way and motioned for them to pass on through; then he let the door bang down. "What the hell is gon' on 'round here? Clea say . . ."

"Stay away from the *veve*," said Donnell, taking Jocundra by the shoulders. "Understand? Find the tapes." And then, before she could respond, he said to the Baron, "Keep her here," and ran toward the stairs. Clea ran after him.

Despite the warning, Jocundra started to follow, but the Baron blocked her way. "Do what he say, woman," he said. "Way I hear it, ain't nothin' we can do down there 'cept die."

Dusk had settled over Maravillosa, and a silvery three-quarter moon had risen high above the shattered trees. Scraps of insulation and roofing blown from the cabins glittered among the debris of fronds and branches and vines. The only sound was of Donnell and Clea crunching through the denuded thickets. Because of Valcours' weakness, Otille would be leading him along a circuitous and relatively uncluttered path to the *veve*, so Donnell had made a beeline for it. Clea was breathing hard, squeaking whenever a twig scratched her.

"You should go back," he said. "You know what he did to Downey."

"I promise you," said Clea, hiccupping. "If you don't get him, then I'm gonna."

Donnell glanced back and saw that she was crying.

A dark man-shaped thing floated in the marble pool, and the shadowy forms of Valcours' other anthropomorphic toys were visible among the stripped branches of the shrubbery, leaning, arms outflung, like soldiers fallen in barbed wire while advancing across a no man's land. Towering above them, some twelve or fifteen feet high, was a metal devil's head, lean-skulled and long-eared. Its faceted, moonstruck eyes appeared to be tracking them, and its jaw had fallen open, giving it a dumfounded look. The rivets stitching the plates together resembled tribal tattoos.

As he climbed up the last conical hill, a drop of sweat slid along his ribs and his mouth went dry. There was a

terrifying aura of suppressed energy about the clearing. The
floodlights were off, but the copper paths of the *veve* rippled
with moonlight: a crazy river flowing in every direction at
once. He forced himself down the hill and climbed up on
it, feeling as though he had just strapped himself into an
electric chair. Clea climbed on behind him. He was through
warning her; she was her own agent, and he had no time
to waste.

He became lost in walking his pattern, in building his
fiery tower, so lost that he did not notice Valcours had
joined him on the *veve* until the fields began to evolve
beyond his control, rising at an incredible rate into the sky.
Valcours was walking alone on the opposite end of the *veve*,
and from the movements of the bacteria, the height and
complexity of the structure above them, from his understanding of the necessities of their patterns, Donnell judged
they would reach their terminal junctions simultaneously.
The knowledge that they were bound together wrapped him
in an exultant rage. No one was going to usurp his place,
his authority! He would write his victory poem in the bastard's blood, cage a serpent in his skull. He had a glimpse
of Clea trudging toward the man, her mouth opening and
closing, and though the whine of the fields drowned out her
voice, he knew she must be singing.

Then the white burst of transition, the perfunctory ho-
liness of a spark leaping the gap, and he was once again
standing in the purple night and dusty streets of Rumelya.

Somewhere a woman screamed, a guttering, bubbling
screech, and as he cast about for the direction of the scream,
he realized the town was not Rumelya. The streets were of
the same pale sand; the Mothemelle loomed above the
hunched rooftops; the buildings were constructed and carved
the same, but many were of three and four stories. Looking
to the east, he saw a black column. The splinter of Moselantja. This, then, was the high town of the river. Badagris.
Where he was Aspect. Normally the streets would be bus-
tling, filled with laughter-loving fools. Fishermen and farmers from upriver; rich men and their women stopping their
journey for an evening's festival; the *cultus* playing guitars
and singing and writhing as they were possessed by the

Invisible Ones. But not tonight. Not until the Election had been won. Then even he might relax his customary reserve, let the dull throng mill around and touch him, squealing at the tingle of his black spark.

He wondered who had been incautious enough to accept candidacy this year. It was no matter. His fires were strong, he was ready and confident.

Too confident.

If his suit had not reacted, urging him to spring into a back somersault, he might have died. As it was, a beam of fire seared his forehead. He came up running from the somersault, never having seen his assailant, half-blind with pain and cursing himself for his carelessness. He cut between buildings, remembering the layout of the town as he ran, its streets designed in accordance with the Aspect's seal. His strength confounded him. Even such a slight wound should have weakened him briefly, overloaded his suit, but he felt more fit than ever, more powerful. At last he slowed to a walk and went padding along, the sand hissing away from his feet. He was at one in stealth and caution with the crouched wooden demons on the roof slants, their vaned wings lifted against the starlight, and it seemed they were peering around the corners for him, scrying dangers. One day, when he finally lost an Election, his image would join theirs in some high place of the town. But he would not lose this Election.

Turning onto the Street of Beds, he saw a body lying in front of the East Wind Brothel, an evil place offering artificially bred exotics and children. The body was that of a girl. Probably some kitchen drudge who had wanted a glimpse of combat. It happened every year. Beneath the coarse dress, her bones poked in contrary directions. He rolled her over with his foot, and her arm followed her shoulder with a herky-jerky, many-jointed movement. Broken capillaries webbed her face and neck, and blood seeped from the orbits of her eyes. She had not died quickly, and he marked that against the candidate. He ripped down the bodice of her dress and saw the seal of the Aspect tattooed upon her right breast. She was of the *cultus*. Though she had been a fool, he could not withhold the grace of Ogoun. He touched her lips with his forefinger, loosing a black spark to jitter and crawl inside her mouth, and he sang the Psalm of Dissolution.

"I am Ogoun, I am the haze on the south wind,
The eddy in the river, the cadence at the heart of light,
The shadow in the mirror and the silence barely
    broken.
Though you may kill me, I will crawl inside of death
And dwell in the dark next-to-nothingness,
Listening to the tongues of dust tell legends
Until my day of vengeance breaks."

Since she was a mere kitchen drudge, he chanted only the one verse.

Lagoon-shaped shadows from the forest crowns spilled onto the street. He shifted forward, streaming from darkness to darkness, materializing beside walls carved into the faces of forest animals and spirits. What had the old man said? Sorry past and grim future pressing their snouts against the ebony grain of the present. The Aspect poured through the streets, a shadow himself, until finally, near Pointcario's Inn, his favorite spot in the town because of the carved figure of a slender woman emerging from the door, her face half-turned back to someone within, there he found the candidate: a big man with a face half spider, half toad set into his suit. Without hesitation the Aspect attacked, and soon they were locked in combat.

Their beams crossed and deflected, their misfires started blazes on the roofs, and sections of nearby walls were lit by vivid flashes into rows of fanged smiles. The candidate was incredibly strong but clumsy; his patterns of attack and parry were simple, depending on their force to overwhelm the more skillful play of the Aspect's beams. Gradually, their fires intertwined, weaving above and around them into an iridescent rune, a cage of furious energy whose bars flowed back and forth. After having fully tested the candidate's strengths and weaknesses, the Aspect disengaged and shifted toward another district of the town to consider his strategy and rest, though truly he felt no need for rest.

Never before had he been so battle ready, his suit so attuned to his reactions, his rage so pure and burning.

He sat down on the porch of Manyanal's Apothecary and stroked the head of the ebony hound rising from the floorboards. The beauty of the night was a vestment to his strength and his rage, fitting to him as sleekly as did his suit. It seemed to move when he moved, the stars dancing to the firings of his nerves. Talons of the purple aurora clawed up half the sky, holding the world in their clutch and shedding violet gleams on the finials and roofpeaks, coursing like violet blood along the wing vanes of a roof demon. The stillness was deep and magical, broken now and then by the hunting cry of an iron-throated lizard prowling the Mothemelle.

A door creaked behind him.

He somersaulted forward, shifting as he did, and landed in the shadows across the street, playing his fires over the front of the doorway. A scream, something slumped on the porch, flames crackling around a dark shape. He shifted back. Beneath the web of broken capillaries was the face of Manyanal, his eyes distended, smoke curling from his stringy brown hair. Had everyone gone mad? One fool was to be expected, but two . . . Manyanal was a respected citizen, accorded the reputation of wisdom, a dealer of narcotic herbs who had settled in Badagris years before his own Election. What could have driven him to be so foolhardy? The Aspect had a notion something was wrong, but he pushed it aside. It was time to end the combat before more fools could be exposed. He would harrow the candidate, engage and disengage, diminish his fires and lead him slowly by the nerve-ends down to death. Still vaguely puzzled by the constancy of his strength, he started off along the street, then stopped, thinking to bestow the grace upon Manyanal. But he remembered that the apothecary was not of the *cultus*, and so left him to smoulder on his porch.

Otille came pelting into the house just as Jocundra and the Baron came out of her office, each carrying cans of videotape; she flattened against the wall, staring at them, horrified. Her black silk robe hung open and there was dirt smeared across her stomach and thighs. The wind drove something against the side of the house, and she shrieked, her shriek a grace note to the howling outside. She ran past them, head down and clawing at the air as if fighting off a swarm of bees.

The Baron shouted something that was lost in the wind.

Jocundra signaled that she hadn't heard, and he shook his head to say never mind, gazing after Otille.

Wind battered the house, a gale, perhaps even hurricane force. The walls shuddered, windows exploded, and the wind gushed inside, ripping down blinds, overturning lamps, flipping a coffee table, all with the malevolent energy of a spirit who had waited centuries for the opportunity. A maelstrom of papers swirled out of Otille's office like white birds fluttering down the hall.

"I'm going out!" shouted Jocundra.

The Baron shook his head and tried to grab her. But she eluded him and ran out the door and down the steps. The night thrashed with tormented shadows, the air was filled with debris. Branches and shingles sailed across the ridiculously calm and unclouded moon. Shielding her head, she made for the cover of the underbrush, stumbling, being blown off course. She crouched behind a leafless bush that offered no protection and pricked her with its thorns, but there was no greater protection elsewhere. The fury of the wind blew through her, choking off her thoughts, even her fears, absorbing her into its chaos. The Baron threw himself down beside her. Blood trickled along his jaw, and he was gasping. Then, behind them, a tortured groan split the roar of the wind. She looked back. Slowly, a hinged flap of the roof lifted like a great prehistoric bird hovering over its nest, beat its black wing once and exploded, disintegrating into fragments that showered the bushes around them. In the sharp moonlight, she saw boxes, bundles, and furniture go spiraling up from the attic, and she had the giddy idea that they were being transported to new apartments in the spirit world. The Baron pulled her head down, covering her as a sofa crashed nearby and split in two.

It took forever to reach the *veve*.

A forever of scuttling, crouching, of vines flying out of

the night and coiling around them. Once a rotten oak toppled across their path, and as she crawled through its upturned roots, the wind knocked her sideways into its hollow bottom. The moon looked in on her, shining up the filaments of the root hairs. She was groped by claustrophobia, an old man with oaken fingers who wanted to swallow her whole. By the time the Baron hauled her out, she was sobbing with terror, beating at the invisible things crawling beneath her clothes. They went on all fours, cutting their hands on pieces of glass, ducking at shadows. But at last they wriggled up the hill overlooking the *veve*.

Valcours and Donnell stood about a dozen feet apart, and from their fingers flowed streams of the same numinous glow that had destroyed the cypress; the streams twisted and intertwined, joining into a complex design around them, one which constantly changed as they moved their hands in slow, evocative gestures, like Kabuki dancers interpreting a ritual battle. Suddenly Valcours broke off the engagement and limped away along one of the copper paths. The weave of energy dissolved; the pale light bursting from Donnell's hands merged into a single beam and torched a bush below the hill. Maybe, she thought, maybe she could sneak through the wind, get beneath the *veve* and pull Valcours down. She wriggled forward but the Baron dragged her back.

"Look, goddamn it!" he shouted in her ear, pointing to a part of the *veve* far from Valcours and Donnell.

Two bodies lay athwart the struts. One, her dress torn, was Clea, and the other—Jocundra recognized him by the radio clutched in his hand—was Captain Tomorrow. Even at this distance, the deformity of their limbs was apparent. She turned back to see Donnell racing after Valcours. With incredible grace—she could hardly believe he was capable of such—he turned a forward flip, came out of a shoulder roll, and landed on the junction behind Valcours. The bush he had set afire whirled up in a tornado of sparks into the darkness and was gone.

Weakened beyond the possibility of further battle, cornered, the candidate appealed for mercy. He dissolved his mask; his puffy features were strained and anxious. The

Aspect was surprised by his age. Usually they sent the youngest, the angriest, but no doubt this man's exceptional strength had qualified him.

"Brother," said the candidate. "My soul is not ripe. Grant me two years of meditation, and I will present myself at Ghazes."

"Your soul will ripen in my fires," said the Aspect. "Should it not, then it would never have borne with ripeness."

"How will it be, brother? I would prepare."

"Slowly," said the Aspect. "Two of my children have died this night."

He savored the moment of victory. The clarity accessible at these times merited contemplation. He noticed that the glitter of the stars had grown agitated, eager for the death, and in the distance the river chuckled approvingly against the pilings of the wharf. The shadows of the roof demons stretched long across the sand, centering upon the spot where the candidate stood. Everything was stretching toward the moment, adding its strength to his.

"Ogoun will judge me," said the candidate.

"I am his judgment here in Badagris," said the Aspect, irked by the man's gross impiety, his needless disruption of the silence. "And like his mercies, his judgments hold no comfort for the weak."

He drew his left hand back behind his ear, extended his right, and set an iridescent halo glowing about the candidate. The man began to quiver, and with a series of cracks like a roll of castanets, his fingers fused into crooked knots. A foam of blood fringed his nostrils; the web of capillaries— his new mask of death—faded into view. Another crack, much louder, and the pyramid of a fracture rose at the midpoint of his shoulder. Oh, how he wanted to scream, to retreat into meditation, but he endured. The Aspect silently applauded his endurance and tested it more severely, causing his eyes to pop millimeter by millimeter until the irises were bull's-eyes in the midst of veined white globes rimmed with blood. Loud as tree trunks snapping, his thighbones shattered and he fell, his suit changing shape with every subsequent crack. His chest breeched, and something the size of a grapefruit was pushed forward; it dimpled and bulged against the coating of black energy; before long, before the candidate's skull caved inward, it had become still.

After victory, diminution.

The old cadre wisdom was right. He derived no real pleasure from the aftermath of battle. It simply meant he must now live until the next one, and despite his poetry, his meditation, that was never easy. Soon the townspeople would pour out the doors, throw open the shutters and debase the purity of night with their outcries and orange lanterns. Full of praise, they would gather around and ogle the corpse who, having met his death with courage, deserved better. Perhaps he would go to Pointcario's Inn, touch the waist of the ebony girl lost forever in the doorway, pretend some other woman was she. But first there was something to do. The business of the aberrant High Aspect of Mounanchou. He reached up for the circuits of his *ourdha,* concentrated his thoughts into a point of sapphire light, and spun round and round until he arrived at Maravillosa.

The inside of his head was warm, unpleasantly so, as he jumped down, but his muscles were supple, his strength undiminished. He started toward the house, but was brought up short by the sight of the two corpses lying apart from the candidate. From Valcours. Disoriented, he looked around at the moonlit devastation, the gaping roof of the house, and a part of him which had been dormant raised an inner voice to remind him of certain verities. He understood now the meaning of the warmth, the nature of his newfound strength, and as another voice—a more familiar one of late—whispered to him, he also understood how that strength must be put to use.

CHAPTER XIX

September 19, 1987

Donnell was standing beside the *veve* when Jocundra and the Baron came down from the hill. Hearing their footsteps, he glanced up. His skin was pale and his eyes were terminal, the pupils gone inside radiant green flares. She ran toward him, but he thrust out his hand and boomed *"No!"* with such force that she held up a dozen feet away.

"They're all over," he said dully. "All goddamn over!" He slammed his fist against the *veve*, and the copper bulged downward half a foot. He lifted the fist to his eyes, as if inspecting a peculiar root; then, with an inarticulate yell, he struck again and again at the strut, battering the welded strips apart. His hand was bleeding, already swelling.

"Please, Donnell," she said. "Get back on it. Maybe..."

"Too late," he said, and pointed to a spray of broken blood vessels on his forehead. "I was dead the second he hit me. It changed them, it..."

She started toward him again.

"Stay the hell away," he said. "I'm not going to end up twitching at your gates, mauling you like some damned animal!" He looked at her, nodding. "Now I know what all those other poor freaks saw."

"He ain't got no way to come to you," said the Baron, pulling at Jocundra's arm. "Get away from him."

But everything was balling up inside her chest, and her legs felt weak and watery, as if the beginning of grief was also the beginning of an awful incompetence. She couldn't move.

"They wanted to wallow in life right until the moment their hearts were snatched," said Donnell. "And, oh Jesus, it's a temptation to me now!" He turned away.

"God, Donnell!" she said, clapping her hands to her head in frustration. "Please try!" The Baron put his arm around her, and its weight increased her weakness, dissolved the tightness in her chest into tears.

"Where's Otille?" asked Donnell casually, seeming to notice the Baron for the first time.

The Baron stiffened. "What you want with her? She crazy gone to hell. She past hurtin' anyone, past takin' care of herself."

"They can do wonders nowadays," said Donnell. "I better make sure."

The Baron kept silent.

"Where else," said Donnell. "She's upstairs."

"Yeah man!" said the Baron defiantly. "She upstairs. So what you wanna mess with her for?"

"It needs to be done," said Donnell, thoughtful.

"What you talkin' 'bout?" The Baron strode forward and swung his fist, but Donnell caught it—as easily as a man catching a rubber ball—and squeezed until it cracked, bringing the Baron to his knees, groaning; he flung out his hand at the Baron, fingers spread. When nothing happened, he appeared surprised.

"What you want to hurt her for?" said the Baron, cradling his hand. "Hurtin' her ain't 'bout nothin'."

Donnell ignored him. He opened his mouth to speak to Jocundra, but only jerked his head to the side and laughed.

It was such a corroded laugh, so dead of hope, it twisted into her. She moved close and put her arms around him; and at a distance, curtained off from her voice by numbness, despair, she heard herself asking him to try again. He just stood there, his hands on her waist.

"Maybe," he said. "Maybe I . . ."

"What?" She had a flicker of hope. Nothing concrete; it was unreasonable, all-purpose hope.

His fingers had worked up under her blouse, and he rubbed the ball of his thumb across her stomach. He said something. It started with a peculiar gasp and ended with a noise deep in his throat and it sounded like words in a guttural language: a curse or a fierce blessing. Then he pushed her away. The push spun her around, and by the time she had regained her balance, he was gone. She could hear him crashing through the thickets; but dazedly staring at the place where he had stood, she kept expecting him to reappear.

The dark shell of the house was empty. Splinters of glass glinted on the stairs between the shadows of the shredded blinds. Climbing up to the attic took all his self-control, his training; he wanted to go running back to her, to breathe her in again, to let his life bleed away into hers. Even the knowledge that the way was closed did not diminish his desire to return to the *veve*, to try once more, and only his compulsion to duty drove him onward. He hesitated on the top step; then, angry at his weakmindedness, he rattled the knob of the attic door. It was locked, but the wood split and the lock came half-out in his hand. He kicked the door open and stepped inside.

Part of the roof was missing, and the moonlight shone on a shambles of burst crates and broken furniture and unrolled bolts of cloth. All Otille's treasures looted and vandalized, their musty perfumes dissipated by the humid smell of the night. It was strange, he thought as he walked toward the three doors, that killing Otille was to be the summary act of his existence, the resolution of his days at Shadows, his life with Jocundra, healing. It seemed inappropriate. Yet it was essential. These aberrations had caused enough trouble in the worlds, and it had been past due that someone be elected to befriend the cadre and eliminate the seam of weakness, disperse the recruits, punish the High Aspect and her officers. He had been an obvious choice; after all, twice before the Aspects at Badagris had dealt with the cadre of Mounanchou. Such purges were becoming a tradition. It might well be time for a restructuring of the cadre's valence, for bringing forth an entirely new aspect from the fires of Ogoun. He was nagged by a moral compunction against the killing, and the frailty of the thought served to remind him how badly he needed a period of meditation. Disdainful of her guessing games, he ripped the central door of the Replaceable Room off its hinges, lowered his shoulder, and charged along the passage. He shattered the second door with ease, but as he came to his feet, he experienced a wave of weakness and dislocation.

The roof of the apartment had been torn off, and the light of moon and stars gave the walls and bushes the look of a real forest. A clearing in a forest. Hanks of moss had been blown into the room and were draped over the branches. An oak had caved in part of the far wall, and through the branch-enlaced gap he could see a tiny orange glow. Probably somebody nightfishing, somebody who didn't know better than to venture near Maravillosa. Otille was standing behind a shrub about twenty feet away; a branch divided her face, a crack forking across her ivory skin. She sprinted for the door, but he cut her off. She caught herself up, flattened against the wall, and began to edge back.

"Come here," he said.

"Please, Donnell," she said, groping her way. "Let me go." The O sound became a shrinking wail, and then a word. "Ogoun." She shivered, blinked, as if waking from a dream. Her silk robe, which hung open, was speckled with leaves and mold, and a large bruise darkened her hip. Her eyes flicked back and forth between Donnell and the door, but her face was frozen in a terrified expression. Black curls matted her cheeks, making it appear her head was gripped within the scrollwork cage of a torturer's restraint. "Let me go!" she screamed, demanding it.

"Is that what you really want?" He kept his voice insistent and even. "Do you want to go on hurting yourself, hurting everyone, screwing your sting into people's lives until they curl up in your web and waste?" He eased a step nearer. "It's time to end this, Otille."

She edged further away, but not too far. "I'm afraid," she said.

"Better to die than go on hurting yourself," he said, inching forward, trying to minister her madness, seduce her with the sorry truth. "Think about the suffering you've caused. You should have seen Valcours die, bleeding from the eyes, his bones crunching like candy. Downey, Clea, Dularde, Simpkins, all your supporters. Gone, dead, vanished. You're alone now. What's there to look forward to but madness and brief periods of clarity when you can see the trail of corpses numbering your days, and feel sorrow and revulsion. Better to die, Otille."

She raised her hand to her cheek, and the gesture transformed her face into that of a young girl, still frightened but hopeful. "Ogoun?" she asked.

"I am his judgment," he said, wondering at the archaic sound of his words, gauging the distance between them.

Otille blinked, alert again, tipped her head to one side and said, "No, Donnell." Her left hand, which had been shielded behind her, flashed up and down so quickly that he did not realize she held a knife until he saw the hilt standing out from his chest. A gold hand was carved gripping it. The blade had struck his collarbone dead on, deflected upward, and stuck; she tried to pull it out and stab once more, but her fingers slipped off the hilt as he staggered back.

Angry at his carelessness, he plucked it out and threw it into a far corner. The wound was shallow, seeping blood. "That was your last chance," he said. "And I don't even think you wanted to take it."

She pressed against the wall, her head drooping onto her shoulder in a half swoon, her eyelids fluttering, helpless; but he could not lift his hand to strike. For the moment she seemed fragile, lovely, a creature deserving a merciful judgment, involved in this tortuous nightmare through no fault of her own. Seeing his hesitation, she hurled herself toward the door; he dove after her, clutching an ankle and dragging her down. He scrambled to his feet, still hesitant. His cold and calculating mood had fled, and he was not sure he could do it. One second she was a monster or a pitiful madwoman, the next a lady frail as alabaster or a little girl, as if she were inhabited by a legion of lost souls not all of whom merited death. And now she stared at him, another soul duly incarnated, this one displaying the sulky pout of adolescence, ignorant and sexual: a black-eyed child with pretty breasts and a dirt-smeared belly. A trickle of sweat crawled into the tuck of skin between her thigh and abdomen. He was bizarrely attracted, then disgusted; he stepped around her and opened the first door of the Replaceable Room.

"Go on in," he said. "This is the way out."

Stupefied, she pushed herself up onto an elbow, gazing into the dimly lit passage, her head wobbling.

"You can't hush up what's happened, Otille. Not this time. You're too far gone to deal with it. And you know what they'll do? They'll lock you up somewhere a thousand miles from Maravillosa, in a room with iron bars on the windows and a bed with leather cuffs and leg straps, and a mirror that won't break no matter how hard you hit it, and a blazing light bulb hung so high you can't reach it even if you stand on a chair and jump. And all you'll hear at night will be muffled screams and scurrying footsteps."

There was no indication that she heard him. She continued to gaze into the room, her head swaying back and forth, lids drooping, as if the sight were making her very, very sleepy.

"And in the day, maybe, if you don't mess the floor or scream too much or spit out your medication, they'll let you into a big sunlit room, the sun shafting down from high windows so bright the light seems to be buzzing inside your ears and melting the glass and glowing in the cracks. And there'll be other women wearing the same starched gray shift as you, and their faces will be the same as yours, dulled and lined and depressed about something they just can't get straight, gnawing their fingers, talking to the cockroaches, shrieking and having to be restrained. Sometimes they'll wander silent as dust around the room, the loony housewives and the mad nuns and the witchy crone who eats cigarette butts and dribbles ash. And there you'll be forever, Otille, because they'll never turn you loose."

Otille got to her feet, shrinking from the room but unable to tear her eyes off it.

"They'll stuff you with pills that turn the air to shadowy water, put larvae in your food that uncurl and breed in your guts, give you shots to make you crazier. Electroshock. Maybe they'll cut out part of your brain. Why not? No one will be using it, and nobody will care. The doctors and lawyers will grow gray-haired and fat spending your fortune, and you'll just sit there under your light bulb trying to remember what you were thinking. And in the end, Otille, you'll be old. Old and dim and sexless with one sodden black thought flapping around inside your skull like a sick bat."

Without any fuss Otille took a stroll into the room. She ran her eye along the walls, her attention held briefly by something near the ceiling. The calmness of her inspection was horrifying, as if she were checking a gas chamber for leaks prior to consigning her mortality to it. Then she turned, her slack features firming to a look of fearful comprehension, and darted at him.

The attack caught him off guard. He tripped and landed on his back, and she was all over him. Kneeing, biting, scratching. She had the strength of madness, and he was hard put to throw her off and climb to his feet. As she circled, looking for an opening, it seemed to him a wild animal had become tangled in her robe. Her eyes were holes punched through onto a starless night; her breath was hoarse and creaky. Every nerve in her face was jumping, making it look as though she were shedding her skin. She rushed him again. Wary of her strength, he sidestepped and hit her in the ribs. The bones gave, and she reeled against the wall. He aimed a blow at her head, but she ducked; his fist impacted a carved trunk, and ebony splinters flew. Panting, she backed away. She stroked her broken ribs and hissed, appearing to derive pleasure from the wound. Then she let out a feral scream and threw herself at him. This time he drew her into a bear hug, and she accepted the embrace. Her hands locked in his hair, her legs wrapped around his thigh, and she sank her teeth into his shoulder, tearing at his tendon strings. He yanked her head back by the hair. Blood was smeared over her mouth, and she spat something—something that oozed down his cheek, something he realized was a scrap of his flesh—and tried to shake free. He took a couple of turns of her hair around his wrist, pried a leg loose, walked over to the door of the Replaceable Room and slammed her against the wall. She lay stunned and moaning, her hair splayed out beneath her head like a crushed spider.

"Oh, God. Donnell," she said weakly. She reached out to him, and he squatted beside her, taking her hand.

He should finish her, he thought; it would be the kindest

thing. But she had regained her humanity, her beauty, and he could not. From the angle of her hips, he judged her back was broken; she did not appear to be in pain, though—only disoriented. She whispered, and he bent close. Her lips grazed his ear. He couldn't make out the words; they were a dust of sound, yet they had the ring of a term of endearment, a lover's exhalation. He drew back, not far, and considered her face a few inches below. So delicate, all the ugly tensions withdrawn. He felt at a strange distance from her, as if he were a tiny bird soaring above the face of the universe, a floor of bone and ivory centered by a red plush mouth which lured him down, whirling him in a transparent column of breath. Half-formed phrases flittered through his thoughts, memories of sexual ritual, formal exchanges of energy and grace, and he found himself kissing her. Her lips were salty with his blood, and as if in reflex, her tongue probed feebly. He scrambled to his feet, repelled.

"Donnell," she said, her voice rough-edged and full of hatred. And then she pushed up onto her arms and began dragging her broken lower half toward him. Dark blood brimmed between her lips.

He stepped back quickly and closed the door.

He went to the carpeted depression at the center of the room, knelt beside the control panel and began flicking the switches two and three at a time. As he engaged a switch on the middle row, her voice burst from the speaker, incoherent. A harsh babble with the rhythm and intensity of an incantation. He switched her off, continuing down the rows, and at last heard the grumble of machinery, the whine of the pumps. He waited beside the panel until the whine had ceased, until whatever was going to die had managed it.

It was very quiet, the sort of blanketing stillness that pours in between the final echo of an explosion and the first cries of its victims. The quietness confused him, lending an air of normalcy to the room, and he was puzzled by his sudden lack of emotion, as if now that he had completed his task, he had been reduced to fundamentals. He stood and almost fell, overwhelmed by the bad news his senses were giving him about death: dizziness, white rips across his vision, his chest thudding with erratic heartbeat.

Done.

Stamp the seal of fate, tie a black cord round the coffin and make a knot only angels can undo.

Both life and duty, done.

Filled with bitterness, he smashed his heel into the control panel, crumpling the metal facing. Smoke fumed from the speaker grille. Then he spun around, sensing Jocundra behind him. No. She was elsewhere, coming toward the house, and she seemed to surround him, every sector of the air holding some intimation. He could taste her, feel her on his skin. He started to the door, thinking there might be time to go back downstairs.

No, not really.

Not according to the twinges at the base of his skull or the dissolute feeling in his chest.

The leaves on the ebony bushes seemed to be stirring, and the dark loom of the forested walls held lifelike gleams of color, a depth of light and foliage showing between the trunks. To the south a road of pale sand plunged off through the trees, and at the bend of the road was a tiny orange glow. He laughed, recalling the light he had seen earlier in the gap made by the toppled oak; but he walked toward it anyway. The place where the road left the clearing was choked with branches, and they scratched him when he crouched to gain an unimpeded view. He must be very near the edge, three floors up, yet all he saw beneath was the starlit dust of the road. He shifted his field of focus toward the glow. The orange light rose from a metal ring, and beside it, sitting with his back against a stump, was a lean, wolfish man. Heavy eyebrows, dark hair flowing over his shoulders. He appeared to be gazing intently at Donnell, and he waved; his mouth opened and closed as if he were calling out.

Someone did call to him, but it was Jocundra, her voice faint and issuing from a different quarter. He forced all thought of her aside. Without access to his *ourdha*, it would be essential to concentrate, to synchronize thought with vision, or else the winds would take him and there would be no hope of return. He pressed forward into the gap, ducking under the branches. Right on the edge, he figured. He shifted his field of focus beyond the wolfish man, who

was now waving excitedly, and out to the bend in the road.
The forest plummeted into a valley, and below, nestled in
a crook of the river, were the scattered orange lights of
Badagris. Above the town and forest, the aurora billowed,
and higher yet were icy stars thick as gems on a jewel
merchant's cloth.

Pain lanced through his chest, an iron spike of it drove
up the column of his neck. His vision blurred, and to clear
his head he fixed his eyes on the hard glitter of the stars.
Something about their pattern was familiar. What was it?
Then he remembered. The Short War against Akadja, the
Plain of Kadja Bossu. There had been a night skirmish with
a company of *dyobolos,* a difficult victory, and afterward
he had stood watch on a hummock, the only high ground
for miles. The myriad fires of the cadre burning about him,
the sable grass hissing with a continental pour of wind. It
had seemed to him he was suspended in the night overlooking a plain of stars, its guardian, its ruler, and he had
thought of it as a vision of his destiny. Solitary, rigorous,
lordly. Yet he had been much younger, barely past induction, and despite the elegance of the vision, the clarity, it
had been a comfort to know the war was over for a little
while, that the shadows in the grass were friends, and the
hours until dawn could be a time of peaceful meditation.
The memory was so poignant, so vivid in its emotional
detail, that when a branch scraped at the corner of his eye,
aggravated by the distraction, he knocked it away with his
hand—a black, featureless hand—and thinking to avoid
further aggravation, he took another step and shifted forward
along the road.

Epilogue

July 15, 1988

The outcry surrounding the public disclosure of the project had taken only three months to die, this—thought Jocundra—a telling commentary upon the spongelike capacity of the American consciousness to absorb miracles, digest them along with the ordinary whey provided by the media, and reduce them to half-remembered trivia. Coil by coil, the various security agencies encircled the remnants of Ezawa's project and drew them down into some mysterious sub-basement of the bureaucracy. Several people disappeared, evidence was mislaid, an investigative committee foundered in the dull summer heat of the Congress. Ezawa's suicide caused a brief reawakening of interest, but by then the topic had lost vitality for even the off-color jokes of talk show comedians. After her interrogation and release by the CIA, Jocundra submitted a copy of one of the videotapes to a network newswoman and suffered debunking by a professional debunker, a pompous tub of a man, a beard and a belly and a five hundred dollar suit, who claimed any of Donnell's feats could be duplicated by a competent magician. Throughout the winter she was besieged by obscene phone calls and letters, offers from publishers, badgered by the illegitimate press, and when someone painted a pair of devilish green eyes on her apartment door, she packed and moved back to a rented cottage on Bayou Teche.

She used the cottage as a base from which to send out her applications to graduate schools, the idea being—as her psychiatrist had put it—to "get on with life, find a new direction." She had agreed to try, though she did not think there was any direction leading away from all that had

271

happened. Not being able to feel the things she had felt with Donnell was intolerable; it was as if she had been given a strength she never knew existed, and once it had been taken from her, her original strength seemed inadequate. And whenever she sought comfort in memory, she was brought up against Otille's conjuration of her fantasy, of Valcours, and the sickly light this shed on her own relationship with Donnell.

"You're underestimating yourself," the psychiatrist had said. "You've handled this surprisingly well. Look at some of the others. Petit, for instance. Her incidence of trauma was much less than yours, and I doubt they'll ever put her together. You'll be just fine in a while."

His pious smile, and everything he said, had come across as an indictment, an unspoken comment that she was an unfeeling bitch and should quit wasting his time. She had flared up, offered an angry apology for not having crumbled into schizophrenia, and walked out. But she had followed his advice. She had been accepted at Berkeley, and if everything went as planned, within a year she would be doing fieldwork in Africa. She had goals, much work to do, yet nothing had changed.

It was all empty without him.

The people of Bayou Teche, those Donnell had cured and others, had raised a stone to him at Mr. Brisbeau's. For a month she had avoided visiting it, but then, thinking this avoidance itself might be unhealthy, she drove to the cabin early one morning and—hoping not to rouse Mr. Brisbeau—sneaked through the palmettos to the boathouse. It was there the stone had been erected facing the bayou. Her first sight of it appalled her. The stone was ordinary, gray-white marble shot with black veins, TO THE MEMORY OF DONNELL HARRISON incised in neat capitals. But fronting it was a litter of candle stubs, gilt paper angels, satin ribbons, mirrors, rosary beads, and plate after plate of rotting food. Ants and flies crawled everywhere; mites and gnats swarmed the air. Greenish mounds of potato salad, iridescent hunks of meat. The stench made her gag. Dizzy, she sat down on a rickety chair, one of several crowding the boathouse. After a moment she regained her composure. She should have expected it considering how his legend had grown over the year, considering also the cultish nature of religion on the bayous. The chairs, no doubt, had been used in some rite or vigil.

When she looked up again, she paid no attention to the horrid feast and saw only the stone. It glowed under the morning sun, and the glow seemed to be increasing, dazzling her, as if her eyes had suddenly become oversensitized to light. She noticed with peculiar clarity the way the black veins of the marble twisted up through the letters of his name. She had to rest her head on her knees, overcome by emotion. Everything was bright and familiar, yet at the same time it was vacant-feeling, haunted; not by him, but by old husks of moments that flocked to her like ghosts to a newly abandoned castle, wisping up, informing of their sad persistence. God, she never should have come. There was nothing of him here. His body was potions and powders in some government laboratory, and all the stone served to do was punish her.

Someone whistled on the path.

She sat up and wiped her eyes just as Mr. Brisbeau appeared around the corner, an empty burlap sack slung over his shoulder.

"Hello," she said, trying to smile.

"Well," he said, hunkering by the stone, "it didn't take you *twelve* years, anyhow. How you doin', girl?"

"I don't know," she said, incapable of affecting happiness. "All right, I guess."

He nodded. "I jus' come here to pick up the garbage." He showed her the burlap sack. "I takes 'em to ol' man Bivalaqua's hogs. Better'n leavin' 'em set." He opened the sack and dumped one of the plates into it. "You can't let go," he said after a bit. "Ain't that right, girl? It's a hard thing, lettin' go, but there it is."

"It was so strange at the end," she said, eager to explain it to someone, someone who would not analyze it. "So many strange things were happening, and there were things he said and wrote...I'm just not sure. It sounds foolish, but I can't accept..." She shook her head, unable to explain it. "I don't know."

"You ain't thinkin' he's still alive?"

"No," she said. "I saw him fall. I've seen it for a year. I could see his face peering out a break in the wall. It was the only pale spot in all that blackness. And then he jumped. But not down. Forward. As if he were in a hurry to get somewhere. I'm sure he didn't think he was falling, but I don't understand what that means."

"Girl, you know I believe in the mysteries," said Mr. Brisbeau, continuing to empty plates into the sack. "In the now and forever, the here and hereafter. I'd be a damn fool, me, if I didn't. Ain't no point in not believin'." He held up a moldy orange. "See this here. That Robichaux boy he come 'bout ever' week and leave an orange, and the way that family is, so damn mean to each other and poor, this orange stands for somethin'! Somethin' special. The boy here"—he patted the stone—"who knows what he could do if he can bring out the soul in Herve Robichaux's boy. Maybe you got reason to hope." He tossed the orange into the sack.

"It's not hope," said Jocundra. "It's just confusion. I know he's dead."

"Sure it's hope," said Mr. Brisbeau. "Me, I ain't no genius, but I can tell you 'bout hope. When my boy he's missin' in action, I live wit hope for ten damn years. It's the cruelest thing in the world. If it get a hook in you, maybe it never let you go no matter how hopeless things really is." He closed up the sack and laughed. "I remember what my *grand-mère* use to say 'round breakfas' time. My brother John he's always after her to fix pancakes. Firs' ting ever' mornin' he say, 'Well, I hope we goin' to have pancakes.' And my *grand-mère* she tell him jus' be glad his belly's full, him, and then she say, 'You keep your hope for tomorrow, boy, 'cause we got grits for today.'" He stood and shouldered the sack. "Maybe that's all there is to some kinds of hopin'. It makes them grits go down easier."

He worried the ants with his toe for a few seconds, weighing something, then said, "You come 'long wit me while I slop ol' man Bivalaqua's hogs, and after that I buy you breakfas' in town. What you say, girl?"

"All right," she said, thankful for the company. "I'll be up in a minute."

As soon as he was out of sight, she opened her purse and took out the folded piece of paper on which Donnell had written "The Song of Returning." She went over to the stone and laid the paper on the ground. It fluttered and unfolded in the breeze. An ant ran along the central crease, using it as a bridge between scraps of food, and a stronger breeze sailed it toward the bayou. She started to chase it down, but held back. Even though she remembered the words, she had an idea that if she let it go she would finally be able to let go of Donnell. The paper caught on a myrtle twig beside the boathouse, tattered madly, and then, obeying a shift in the wind, it skittered to rest under the chair where she had been sitting. She waited to see where it would blow next, but the wind had swirled off into the swamp and the paper just lay there. After a while, she picked it up.

AWARD-WINNING
Science Fiction!

The following titles are winners of the prestigious Nebula or Hugo Award for excellence in Science Fiction. A must for lovers of good science fiction everywhere!

☐ 47809-3	**THE LEFT HAND OF DARKNESS,** Ursula K. LeGuin	$2.95
☐ 79179-4	**SWORDS AND DEVILTRY,** Fritz Leiber	$2.75
☐ 06223-7	**THE BIG TIME,** Fritz Leiber	$2.50
☐ 16651-2	**THE DRAGON MASTERS,** Jack Vance	$1.95
☐ 16706-3	**THE DREAM MASTER,** Roger Zelazny	$2.25
☐ 24905-1	**FOUR FOR TOMORROW,** Roger Zelazny	$2.25
☐ 80697-X	**THIS IMMORTAL,** Roger Zelazny	$2.50

Prices may be slightly higher in Canada.

Available at your local bookstore or return this form to:

ACE SCIENCE FICTION
Book Mailing Service
P.O. Box 690, Rockville Centre, NY 11571

Please send me the titles checked above. I enclose _____. Include 75¢ for postage and handling if one book is ordered; 25¢ per book for two or more not to exceed $1.75. California, Illinois, New York and Tennessee residents please add sales tax.

NAME_____

ADDRESS_____

CITY_____STATE/ZIP_____

(allow six weeks for delivery)   SF-3